Tides

Of

Emora

Victoria Nance

First edition

ISBN: 979-8-9937229-0-0

Editing by Stephanie Taylor

Cover art by Kelly Carter

This book is dedicated to my supportive and loving
husband. Thanks for being my rock.

Preface

It's hard to contain adult-sized excitement in a seven-year-old body. I can't help but bounce in anticipation. My curly pigtails bouncing along with me.

Mama squeezes my hand. "Careful, Constance, or you're going to bounce right off the dock and into the ocean." She gestures toward my belly with her fingers curled inward like a set of teeth, ready to take a bite out of me. "We wouldn't want the sharks to get you!"

The sun has barely begun to rise on the horizon, but this is our routine. We wake up before the sun and stand on the dock, watching. Waiting to see the white sails of the ship glide into view. It's tradition.

"I'll just punch them in the nose and swim faster than them!" My fist punches through the air, the momentum almost sending me over the edge of the dock.

Mama pulls me back with her hand still clasped in my own. She gives me a knowing look.

"Sorry, Mama, I can't help it. I'm just too excited!" I exclaim, although the word *excited* is difficult for me. I lost both of my front teeth last week and can't wait to show Papa.

Mama fidgets with her long, flowing hair. She adjusts the layers of her dress.

"Mama, you look so pretty," I say, tugging on the long, baby-blue fabric of her dress.

She smiles warmly at me. "Thank you, my sweet, but I think *you* look very pretty." Her delicate hand adjusts the collar of my pale-pink, lacy dress.

I don't like fancy dresses, but Mama insisted I look nice for Papa's return. He's a merchant and goes on long journeys so Mama and I are well fed and can pay our household help. Mama says it's respectful to look nice for someone who's been away for a long time.

I'm not sure I believe her. I think she just prefers I look like a lady. Hopefully Papa can convince her to let me put on pants when he reaches the dock.

"What do you think he brought us this time?" I ask.

The sun turns the sky into a hazy orange that meets a soft purple.

Then I see it. On the horizon comes the best view I've ever seen: white sails.

I point with my free hand. "Mama, look. Look!"

Mama smiles brighter than the sun's reflection on the ocean's surface. She places a hand on her chest and exhales a breath of relief.

It feels like forever before the ship lays anchor. Crewmen come tromping down the gangway carrying loads of crates. Probably items from other islands to be sold here. That's what it usually is.

I pull up on my tiptoes, searching the dock when a man with curly blond hair and sun-kissed skin skips the gangway entirely. He chooses to leap over the side of the boat, landing right in front of Mama and me.

"Ah!" I squeal with delight. "Papa, you scared me," I giggle.

Papa hooks his hands under my armpits and swings me through the sky. I feel like a seagull in full flight.

"Aww I missed you so much! How's my Little Guppy doing today?" Papa asks before squeezing me close to his chest so tight it makes it hard to breathe, but I don't care. Papa is home, safe and sound.

I wrap my arms around his neck in a suffocating hold.

After one more tight squeeze his arms loosen, and he tries to put me down, but I tuck my legs up, refusing to be let go.

"I must greet the most beautiful Mama in the world, too. We can't leave her out!"

Mama chimes in, "That's right, Constance. Mama deserves some love too!"

I look at her before burying my face in Papa's shoulder one more time and sliding down his torso to stand on my own two feet.

Papa looks to Mama and embraces her. He cradles her head against him with one hand. His other hand splays over the small of her back before his head tilts away at an angle to better look at her face.

She looks happier than ever. Her green eyes sparkle against the morning light. Her freckles fold in on themselves as her nose crinkles with glee.

They stare at each other for a long time, lost in some intangible world, before she speaks. "I have missed you, my love. My heart's home." Then she leans close and plants a firm, endearing kiss onto his mouth.

Their lips stay interlocked for far too long.

"Eww…" I giggle. "Papa, look. Papa, look!" I tug on the side of my father's pants to regain his attention.

They disconnect. Mama's cheeks turn a light shade of pink.

"I lost my two front teeth!" I point with both hands at the large gap in my mouth.

Papa bends down to my eye level. "That's great!" he exclaims. "Did you get any coins under your pillow for them?"

"Uh-huh. Two coins each time! Papa, what did you bring me?" My head tilts to the side.

"Constance, it's rude to ask if someone brought you a gift," Mama scolds, "even if it is your father," she adds, looking to Papa, an upturned smirk on her lips.

"Sorry, Papa," I say, folding my hands over my belly.

"That's okay, Little Guppy. It just so happens that I did bring something for you." He shuffles through his pockets before pulling out the most prettiest necklace I have ever seen.

It's a flat, green and brown shell held together by a thin strip of leather.

Papa takes the ends and leans over me to tie it at the back of my neck.

I stare at the shiny piece of jewelry in awe. "It looks like a mermaid scale." The colors shift when I rotate it against the morning sun. "Where did you get it, Papa?"

He looks at Mama and back to me before responding, a knowing gleam in his eyes. "That's because it *is* a mermaid scale." He moves to my side and points to the open expanse of ocean. "Far, far away there's the most beautiful land you can ever imagine called the Island of Waterfalls. I took a special trip there just for you." He pokes my belly, causing a giggle to escape.

"Waterfalls?" I look out at the giant body of water hoping to see it from the dock.

"Yes, Little Guppy. Waterfalls cover the island. Big ones, small ones, and everything in between. And if you're lucky you can see mermaids sunbathing on the rocks just underneath them."

"My love, don't fill her head with wild stories." Mama rolls her eyes before scooping me up into her arms and placing a peck on my cheek. "She already wants to go on adventures with you as it is!"

Still in Mama's clutches, I turn to face Papa. "Can I, Papa? Can I go with you one day to the Island of Waterfalls and look for mermaids?"

He closes the gap between us and embraces Mama and me in a bear hug before responding. "Maybe one day.

But for now," he looks at Mama and makes his eyes large and pleading, "can we go deep sea fishing together, Mama? Please?"

I perk up immediately. "Mama, can we? Can we go?"

Her eyebrows pull close as she shakes her head. "You have your nice dress on…" she argues.

"Oh, come now, Helena, she can go put pants on before we set sail," Papa suggests. He takes a piece of mom's long flowing hair and tucks it behind her ear. His eyes grow soft as he gazes into her disapproving face.

My excitement returns and I can't help but bounce in Mama's arms with anticipation.

She darts her eyes between Papa and me. A defeated sigh escapes her. "I suppose I'm outvoted, aren't I? Yes, we can go," she says. "You're lucky I love you so much," Mama directs toward Papa who plants another firm kiss on her lips in thanks. She lets out a laugh lighter than air before motioning for me to run back to the house to change clothes.

I run up the sandy hill toward our house overlooking the beach and look back at my parents.

They are molded together in an embrace, pure joy radiating off them. They talk to each other with their eyes closed, like no one else is in the world but them.

Mama says I want adventure, which is true. But what I really, really want is a love like theirs.

Chapter 1

14 Years Later

Life is worth living for one reason and one reason only: to love and be loved most ardently. Mama has found me a suitor. I ponder over what kind of love this suitor will bring me as delicate hands fuss over my hair. Will his love be shown with gifts or words of affection? Will it feel like a warm summer breeze or all-consuming like an ocean storm?

"Ouch!" I gripe as Mama yanks a hefty bit of curl from my scalp.

"Sorry, Constance," she murmurs over my shoulder. Our eyes meet for an instant in the vanity mirror. Her gaze is hopeful, reassuring.

"You look lovely," she says with a smile. "I was blessed with a beautiful daughter. Now, all we need to do is tame this lion's mane of yours and then we shall go down together and greet your gentleman caller."

"Won't you please tell me something of the man I am to be courted by?" For weeks, Mama has left me in the dark. "It could be his hair color or how tall he is. I'd even take just the first letter of his name!"

Through the mirror, she meets my pleading gaze. "You will know soon enough, dear. They will arrive any minute." She taps pieces of my hair to test their security before bringing her hands down on my shoulders.

"Oh, there's one more thing," I say. I pull on my vanity drawer and lift an emerald and umber colored piece of shiny jewelry up in the air. "I think it's only fitting to wear this today since Papa is away on business. At least he can be with us in spirit."

Mama looks to the necklace Papa gave to me when I was seven years old. "I think that's a great idea, my sweet. But I doubt it fits around your neck anymore," she says apologetically.

"That's alright," I say and come up quickly with a solution. "I'll just wear it on my wrist like a bracelet." I pass the shell and leather to Mama and show my wrist to her.

She takes the small necklace and wraps it around my wrist in two loops before tying it in a secure knot. "If he were here now, he would say you are the most beautiful thing in the world." Her bottom lip trembles before she takes a giant inhale of breath to regain her composure.

I roll my eyes. "Mama, are you okay? It's not like he's gone forever."

She doesn't have time to answer because a faint knock has us turning in unison to the door.

A small blonde head peeks through. It's my maid, Ally. "'Cuse me, madam, your guests have arrived."

I look to my mom while she puts the finishing touches on my hair, excitement crinkling my face, but what I see in return is not what I expect. Her lips turn slightly downward and her eyes fill with thin lines of liquid before she blinks them away.

"Mama?" I question.

In an instant that solemn look is replaced with a grin; the epitome of poise. "Oh, my darling," her hands take a break from pulling and re-pinning my hair to pull on some silk gloves. She squeezes my shoulders. "I want more than anything for you to be happy." Gently as she can, she places the last of my curls securely on top of my head and leans down to kiss me. "We will get through this. There is nothing to fear."

Her choice of words sits uneasy in my stomach. What was there to fear when love was waiting downstairs?

Excitement quickly turns to nerves. My gloved hand slides over the wooden railing leaving behind a streak of sweat. Only a few steps ahead of me is Mama, walking with the grace of a queen. Her head is high, her back is straight, and even though I cannot see her face, I can tell from the side that she is showcasing her perfect pearly whites.

At the last step, a couple and a young man wait impatiently. Not a smile to be seen among the pristine cluster of bodies.

Breathe. Just smile and breathe.

When she reaches the bottom, mother bows deeply, "Duke Braxton and Duchess Gretta, how lovely it is to be in your presence this late morning." Neither one shows any sign of a warm greeting in return, but nod once as I descend from the last step. My mother continues, "You remember from our previous discussions my accomplished daughter, Constance."

As my name is spoken, I drop my face to the floor then slowly rise back up to meet the scowls of our guests. The Duchess takes me in piece by piece, eyes lingering on my hair. I can tell she disapproves by the purse of her paper-thin lips.

"Constance," Mama continues like she doesn't notice the cold judgment oozing off of our company, "The Brownings are from Weatherington all the way up north. They are in the process of building a summer home on Ohani this season."

Word travels quickly around the islands. From what I know, Weatherington is cascaded in winter weather for half the year but is said to be beautiful with a lot of wildlife in the short spring and fleeting summer. And word on the street is that the Browning family is one of the wealthiest families in the eastern hemisphere. I know because my maidservant,

Ally, has been talking about it for the past week nonstop. All the servants have been gossiping about the new wealthy family building a home on Ohani.

"A pleasure," the duke responds. "This is our son, Oliver Browning, the Earl of Browning." The duke gestures behind himself to his son.

The earl takes a clear step forward and bows from the waist in pleasantries. His hair is blond and slicked back from his face. His eyes are a heavy brown, and his jaw is strong and defined. I would consider him handsome if not for the sneer plastered on his face. He takes my gloved hand in his, never breaking eye contact, while he places a tight-lipped kiss atop the silk. "Lady Constance."

"The pleasure is all mine," I reply. I wonder if he thought I'd look different somehow and is as displeased with my appearance as his mother. I know I'm not considered ideally beautiful according to the standards on Ohani Island but looks aren't everything. Right? I try not to linger on the thought while he takes my arm and leads me to the parlor without another word.

Our parlor is painted a pale yellow. The windows look out to the ocean, letting in plenty of natural sunlight.

Silence. Awkward silence. I sit on the green embroidered sofa glancing about the room to the others lingering near. Oliver stands with his hands clasped behind his back looking out the window toward the ocean waves lapping against the sand.

My mother sits with the Duke and Duchess on the opposite side of the room. Each pair of eyes are looking at different spots in the room, like they are trying to give the Earl and me privacy, but I know better. There is no privacy here. Everyone's ears strain to hear every syllable, every sound uttered between my gentleman caller and me. There is no room for error. No room in this cramped space to even breathe too loudly.

"So, Oliver…" I pause thinking of something to say. "What's it like in Weatherington? I hear the winter snows are absolutely breathtaking."

Without breaking his outward gaze he replies, "Dreary is a more accurate description. Whoever told you that is a fool."

My mouth starts to gape open before I remember to keep my composure.

Mother almost spits out her tea.

The Duchess' eyes dart in my direction with a pointed glare like I am the one to blame for her son's unruly comment.

"Well, it may be cold I imagine, but at least it is accompanied by beauty and change. The ocean here brings chilly winds, but that is the only distinguishable difference we get in the winter months. I'd love a change of scenery now and then."

Still, he stares out the window.

I continue, "I can only assume it makes spring and warm weather more enjoyable, more worthy of admiration. Do you not agree?"

The only sound in the room is my pumping heart, flooding my eardrums with each beat. I swear everyone in this cramped space can hear it beating, trying to break free of my chest.

Finally, he looks in my direction and utters, "I suppose some may believe that."

It goes on like this for the longest hour I have ever endured. I make light conversation. He responds in short. By the end, I am exhausted. How can someone who says so little be so emotionally draining? One hour of conversation feels more like an entire evening. Thankfully lunch time arrives and our guests leave for the day.

* * *

A week of awkward conversations went by. I'd wake up. Mama would dress me up like a bride for auction. The Brownings would arrive late morning. I would attempt to converse with Oliver, but it was as though he wanted nothing to do with me at all.

Don't touch. Don't smile. Don't joke. Don't compliment.

It was like talking to a snapping turtle; any attempt to reach out in affection was met with a cold, sharp snap.

The Duchess would glare at me and my untamed hair, and then we would depart for lunch.

Each day was like holding my breath under water; the longer our courtship lasted, the more I felt like letting the water consume me.

* * *

One afternoon when the Brownings leave for the day, Mama and I eat our lunch in the dining hall. Herbed chicken and greens.

A row of three staff members waits patiently against the wall to fill our goblets or serve us more food, if need be.

Either my mood has soured the feel of our home, or something is amiss. Our table is normally decorated with five candles and a centerpiece. Only one candle stands alone.

There used to be a painting of a ship in a storm on the wall behind Mama's chair, but there's only a slight discoloration of wall paint reminding me of its absence. What is happening to all our belongings?

I opt to look outside at the ocean instead, a view that never ceases to amaze me. The waves are calm and lazy, but in my heart a storm is brewing.

I look to my mother. Surely, I'm missing something. *Surely*, she is not serious about chaining me to the earl.

I swallow a piece of my herbed chicken and murmur, "Mama?" She looks up from her plate of food. "Do you hate me so much?"

"Whatever do you mean, my sweet?" Her eyes look puzzled. Concerned. Maybe even hurt.

The chicken lodges in my throat and my body starts to heat. "I just…" I tread carefully on my words, "…I don't understand why, out of all of the prospects you could have chosen for me, that Oliver Browning is best suited to become my betrothed." I turn my gaze to the vegetables on my plate, pushing them around with my fork. "I fear he has no love for me at all."

Silence echoes in the room, so I look up from my plate to see Mama. She's spending more time than necessary chewing her most recent bite. Her delicate hands dab at the corners of her mouth with a napkin before letting out a long sigh. "You may not like the match, Constance, but it is the best we can do in such short notice. There are far worse fates."

"But if you would just—"

"Enough!" mother interrupts. The table rumbles as she slaps her silverware down hitting her palms flat on the table. "My word is final."

I twitch away at her tone.

The staff in the room freeze. Everyone holds their breath.

Mama looks around the room and notices everyone's reaction. She softens her voice, but her words remain clipped. "Look around, Constance. Look at what we have already given up."

I turn my eyes to the lonely candle, the vacant spot on the wall. Has she—has she been selling items from our estate? Why would she do such a thing?

"You do not understand the predicament we are in. Your father has been gone for months and there is no sign or word that he will ever return to us. You and I are left vulnerable." With one exasperated breath, she continues to cut her chicken into dainty pieces, refusing to make eye contact.

I can't believe what I am hearing. "I don't understand. I thought you said father had been writing to you." It felt odd these last few months when I asked to read the letters Papa always sent home during his voyages and Mama refused. There was always an excuse. He sent a special love note solely for her eyes or the servants accidentally threw them out before I could get to them.

Knowing the truth now is a punch to my gut. I sit in silence for Mama to continue. Unable to breathe from the blow.

Her eyes become bleary. "I'm so sorry. I wanted to tell you about him, but I couldn't face the fact that he may be lost to the sea forever." Her lips pinch tightly together, refusing to let a sob escape before she continues. "The wealth he provided us is dwindling fast, and if we don't do something soon, we will lose *everything* he built for us. We will lose the house help, our home, our place in society. There will be no balls, no social events. You and I will be outcasts. But most importantly, you will be labeled unfit to wed anyone of rank. You're already past the age most girls marry in the first place."

It was true. The sudden realization of a future without a happily ever after closes in around me. I *am* older than most girls still on the market for a husband. Not only that, I am not the ideal standard of beauty with my curly hair and tan, freckled face. Nor am I part of a family with great wealth.

Papa was a successful merchant, but we have no long lineage or titles on our family tree like many of the families we socialize with on the island.

When Papa was home, he always assured me he would find someone worthy of loving me just as he has loved Mama. He never worried about balls or social events. He never taught me how to be a proper suitress or fight for the affections of a high-ranking suitor.

He focused on teaching me skills like tying an arbor knot to fish or changing the direction of the sails to speed up a boat or helping me find my way home with my hand and the stars and a compass.

I must be silent for quite some time because Mama clears her throat before she says my name once more. "I am sorry I could not have done better for you. But the Brownings are wealthy and of good name in society. It may not be love at first, but it is a relationship where love can grow in time."

I'm not sure what to say. It doesn't feel like Oliver will ever love me. He doesn't give compliments; he doesn't joke or laugh or do anything resembling the relationship that my parents have. Could he and I truly turn what little relationship we have into love?

The heated atmosphere in the room remains, circling the air around us while we finish our lunch in silence. At my last bite, I quickly excuse myself to my room and remain there for the rest of the day. Alone.

* * *

I sit on the light green alcove and read with the window open. Salty sea air rustles the light cream curtains.

As I look out, I notice orange, purple, and pink have encompassed the sky. Seagulls in the distance begin to settle down for the night. The sound of their croons mixes with the crashing waves, filling the air like a sweet lullaby.

Gone forever. My papa is gone forever. It cannot be true. Wouldn't I sense it in my heart if he was truly lost to the depths of the ocean?

A deep sigh escapes me. My fingers continue to flip through page after page. Reading is its own kind of adventure, and this book is particularly enticing. It has all I've ever wanted. Adventure, enchantments, witches, heroes, and above all, love. A nice distraction to my current predicament.

Mama mentioned growing in love with time, but the more I thought about it, the more I came to realize it won't happen. I am to be trapped in a loveless future with a man who doesn't love me in the slightest. To be fair though, I find it hard to believe Oliver is apt to love anyone really. Always so serious and uptight like his knickers are caught too far up his bum. It would be very difficult to be happy if that were, in fact, the case.

I continue reading my book until there's barely any sunlight left to light the pages. Lost in another world entirely, my reading is interrupted by a faint knock at the door followed by elegant fingers and lavender fabric.

Back to reality.

"Come in." Two stoic words that are the exact opposite of what I want to say.

My mother's head peers into the room. Her eyes are no longer angry, and her voice is calm when she speaks. "My darling," she begins before stepping farther into the room.

I busy myself with looking at the light green vanity, the floral-patterned walls, the wooden floor. Anything but my mother.

But she is not so easily deterred from coming toward me and taking my hands in hers. She kneels on the floor beckoning me to look at her. "Constance," she whispers tenderly.

I force myself to drag my eyes down at her. She has a faint smile on her lips; the familiar warmth I am used to seeing. One of her fingers traces my cheek, catching a tear. I hadn't even realized I was crying.

"My sweet darling, I am sorry for not telling you sooner about our circumstances." Snot runs down my nostrils before I sniffle them back. "With your father gone and you being—" she hesitates.

"Old? Unfit to wed?" I finish for her. Not that twenty-one is really all that old. But when you are a woman seeking a husband, the younger you find one the better. In a few years, what little beauty I have will start to fade and then no man in this world will want me.

"He should have represented you better when he was alive." Mother too develops wet blobs in the corners of her eyes. "But he was so stubborn. No one was good enough for you." A small laugh escapes her as a tear trails down her cheek. "Of course he was right… Oliver does not deserve you."

"Then why are we even bothering with him?" I retort.

At this, she looks back at me with a vague resemblance of the intensity at lunch. "Because without your father, we won't have enough money to keep what we have. We wouldn't have staff or money for food. Without him, you and I both would have to find jobs." The words pitch an octave higher. "Do you realize the hardships all of us will face if you do not marry into that wretched family?"

I did know about the hardships. I knew we would have to get rid of our staff and find other ways to make a living no matter how demeaning it may be.

And I did not care.

I did not care, because that alternative is much more desirable than marrying someone I cannot love. I would rather scrub kitchen floors or chase off rodents or even cut up chum for a living than be shackled to Oliver.

However, the look on my mother's face, the fear, holds me back from saying any of my true feelings out loud.

"Okay. I guess I can try to soften Oliver up a bit. Maybe tomorrow night at the ball he will be able to open up more. Perhaps he will even ask me to dance if he's not too busy sneering at everyone there." I imitate Oliver's narrowed eyes and slightly flared nostrils.

Mama wipes a few tears from her cheeks with her knuckles and chuckles. "Yes, well with a face like that, he has to." She kisses my cheek before continuing. "Get some rest darling. Tomorrow is a new day."

Yes. Perhaps at the ball I can find some connection with him. I must find a way to make it work, if not for myself, for my family and the servants we must take care of, as well. Where would they go if they couldn't work for us? I decided then that I may not love Oliver, but he and I can still be civil.

We can become friends. We will find a way to make a happily ever after for ourselves and for everyone who's counting on me. I hope.

Chapter 2

I look in the mirror as my maidservant, Ally, finishes the last few buttons on my ballgown. It is a light rose color with bold floral patterns stitched near the hem. The look ties together nicely by the white ribbon accentuating my cinched waist. Curse whoever invented the corset. The color isn't the best complement to my sea green eyes, but it does go well with my skin tone.

When the last button of my dress is secured, Ally starts to brush through my hair, pulling my scalp with each stroke. An exasperated noise slips from her mouth when a particularly stubborn knot refuses to be untangled.

I wince. My head feels like it's bleeding.

Ally must notice because she immediately mutters an apology and eases up on the brushing. "Are you excited for tonight, my lady?"

I roll my eyes. *Why does everyone have to be so proper?* "Ally, call me Constance. I am not lady of the house, and my mother isn't here to hear you anyways."

Her only response is a grin as she continues to work on my hair.

"And no, I'm not particularly excited about the ball," I whisper admittedly.

A puzzled look crosses her face.

"But you're being courted by an earl. His family is one of the richest in the eastern hemisphere. With a match like that we can all keep our jobs and this house for the rest of our lives and our children's lives!" Ally's eyes travel off into some distant fantasy of hers as she clutches my hairbrush in both hands. At least one of us is giddy about the idea.

With Mama busy getting ready in her own room, I take the chance to expose my thoughts. Just enough to ease the growing roar within me and possibly find someone who understands—even empathizes with— my worries.

Through the mirror, I meet Ally's eyes. "And what if I don't love him?"

Her hands pause for a moment in the cluster of hair ready to be pinned. "Marriage is not always about love." She takes the cluster of hair and wraps my locks into an elegant, tight up-do as she continues, "Besides, I am sure wherever you live there will be plenty of space to avoid him if you wished. I'm sure there will be other means to entertain yourself." Ally gives a knowing wink like we share some secret even though I do not know what it could be.

She finishes my hair with one final pin to secure the last unruly curl. I'd go so far as to call myself pretty now that it's all secured and flat against my head.

I give her a close-lipped grin. It's the only thing I can manage as my heart sinks further into the deep abyss.

Perhaps she is right. Maybe I do not even have to love him to be happy, I think. No matter what I think, it appears I have no choice but to grin and bear it. Not just for my own sake but for those of this household as well. *Grin and bear it.*

* * *

The sun sets as my mother and I make our way up the long pathway to the party. It's paved, with palm trees covered in lanterns, lighting our way to the front.

The hosts are the Hayward's: friendly and well-established residents of Ohani Island. Mr. and Mrs. Hayward greet each guest with a warm smile. Next to them, lined up like little ducklings, are their six daughters all dressed in different shades of yellow, greeting the guests as they enter as well. At the end of the row is their one and only son, Conner. How unlucky for him to be the middle child in a sea of sisters; and not one of them is married yet.

I gaze at his familiar face while he greets the guests with his family, completely unaware that he has an admirer watching from a distance. He is my age and a dear friend. Surely, he can make this night more bearable.

Music becomes clearer the closer we get to the entrance. Our eyes meet, and he shoots me a grin that could light up a room.

"Well, well, well… who let the likes of you join in on the fun?" Conner teases as we approach.

I bow deeply and smirk with mischief. I raise one eyebrow before scanning his attire for the evening. He has chosen a light blue suit and tan shoes and an orange bow tie that is in stark contrast to the rest of his ensemble.

His hair is shorter than most, hanging a little above his ears in a very boyish way. But he has become anything but boyish over the last few years. Truthfully, he has become very handsome. Not that I would ever admit it to his face.

"Whoever it was at least has better taste in company than you have in bow ties." I reach out to pull the bright orange fabric before mother clears her throat in protest. My hand falls to my side.

A line forms behind us, and I know I cannot stand in the way. It would be rude to hog the attention of the hosts at the entrance.

Mama and I continue our journey into the open ballroom, but I say one last thing to Conner. "Save me a dance, will you?" I wink before Mama presses her hand against my back and ushers me away.

Conner bows. His grin grows into a full toothed smile. "I wouldn't miss it."

The ballroom is already swarming with lords and ladies pairing up to start the festivities. The first dance is folksy. An interesting choice to start a ball, but then again, I would not expect anything other than something different from the Hayward family.

People find partners and lose themselves to the song, bouncing to the staccato rhythm.

I make my way to the food table. Chocolate covered strawberries ornately decorated with sugar buttons on top have caught my eye. I pop one, two, three into my mouth and already feel my stomach expanding against my corset.

Curse this dress for being too tight. Just as I decide to eat one more, a tap on my shoulder halts me.

Behind me, Oliver stands poised. He is wearing a typical black suit with a bow tie to match. I might have died from shock if he had worn anything else. Heaven forbid he shows favoritism to any color. *No, Constance, be friendly. Become friends with this man. Do it for your household.*

"Miss Constance." He bows slightly and extends a hand. "May I have this dance?"

The folksy song shifts into a more traditional waltz; slow and serious. Typically, the type of song I would avoid.

"Miss Constance?" Oliver continues to wait for an answer. My head says yes, but my heart says no. Did he ask me to dance? Yes. Could he have picked a more boring song to dance to? No.

His eyes become expectant, daring me to deny him.

"Of course, Oliver. It would be my pleasure." I take his extended hand, his fingers firmly securing my palm as he leads me to the dance floor.

"Call me, my lord," is his only response.

Two lines form. Ladies on one side and lords on the other facing one another. Oliver releases my hand to stand opposite of me. In sync, the men bow at the waist first and the women sink low to the ground in return.

I glance along the line of men and notice Conner is about to dance as well. He's looking at me before he averts his attention back to his dance partner.

Heat flushes my cheeks and the dance begins.

The rhythm is slow and graceful so in turn the steps are as well. One, two, step to the right. One, two step to the left. Circle around your partner. Don't touch. Don't talk. Don't feel. The rhythm breathes death on my skin. It crawls all over me and makes my hairs stand on end. I hate it.

"This song is invigorating, is it not?" Oliver whispers as he passes.

Wait. Did he really just initiate conversation?

"I must admit," One, two, step. Circle. "I usually prefer dances with faster tempos."

The dance changes choreography as each pair takes turns walking together between the river of people.

"I can't imagine why," he speaks but his eyes remain facing forward when we take lead, trotting down the middle of the dance couples. My hand hovers his, but we do not touch. The faint hint of a smile tugs at his lips. "I hate to break a sweat. Just the thought is sickening."

A smile cracks over my face. We reach our original dancing positions before I reply, "Oliver, I had no idea you had a sense of humor." *However little it may be*, I restrain from adding.

In an instant, that small hint of amusement vanishes from his face. His eyes dart around the room; scanning to see who overheard.

I have a strong sense to keep my mouth shut for the remainder of the dance.

As soon as the final note sounds, Oliver's bulging eyes narrow and beam in my direction.

My palms begin to sweat.

"Might I have a moment, Miss Constance," he hisses into my ear. A surprisingly firm hand grips my forearm inconspicuously, as to make sure no one else notices. He hastily leads me toward the Hayward's study. My arm aches underneath his hand's smothering hold.

Oliver shuffles me into the room, letting go of my arm. A pulsating throb lingers.

The study is small and full of books that line the walls all the way up to the ceiling. It smells of musk and paper; probably the room where Mr. Howard keeps track of his transactions and hosts meetings with trademark companies.

My heart hammers and sweat continues to pour from my hands. If we were caught in here together, we would be even more trapped in the marriage I didn't want. It would be the scandal of the ball, and everyone would hear about it.

"Oliver," I whisper, rubbing at my throbbing arm, "we shouldn't be in here alone."

Oliver closes the doors and barrels toward me. "Were you raised in a barn?"

I flinch. "I beg your pardon?"

"It is my lord to you," he hisses. Rage fills his eyes as he berates me. "Do you have any idea how important it is to keep up appearances in my family? The utter disgrace of being so openly informal…" his voice trails off.

I do my best to put some distance between us, back pedaling until my back hits one of the bookshelves on the wall. Oliver closes the gap easily. He traps me between his outstretched arms. His fingers clutching the shelf by my head.

The rug suddenly looks like the most interesting thing in the room. I can no longer look him straight in the eye. One, for fear of enraging him further by not looking the least bit ashamed. Two, to hide the rage kindling inside me.

"My deepest apologies Ol-" slowly I lift my eyes to meet his, "my lord."

Our eyes lock. I can feel his rage simmer, a hint of triumph radiating off him. He pulls back and takes his hands on each side of his jacket, straightening it before targeting my face with his glare. "Wait five minutes before leaving this room. I will not be a part of some scandal," he says before turning and leaving me alone in the study.

* * *

Going back into the ballroom would have been the smarter choice, but thinking of putting on an air of placidity is unthinkable at the moment. Instead, when I leave the study, I head straight to the balcony that oversees the massive front lawn. From up here, I can see the trees aligning the paved road up to the front of the house, as well as the flowers and hedges that scatter throughout the thick grass. Two fountains trickling with water are placed on each side.

Jolly music fills the background, but its sounds are muddied by my own thoughts.

A slight summer breeze ruffles my sleeves as I inhale the sweet salty air.

"You know the party is inside, correct?" a familiar voice asks behind me.

"Ah, but I thought the party was wherever you are," I jab.

"Touché, Cons," Conner chuckles as he glides into a position next to me. "What's wrong? The song the musicians are playing is one of your favorites. Yet here you are looking like your favorite pet just kicked the bucket." He smiles warmly, inviting me to tell him what's on my mind. Somehow, he always knows when I am upset.

Idly, I rub my arm, still sore from earlier. "I guess I am just not in the mood for dancing." I nudge him playfully. "Some of us have a deeper capacity for thinking about more important things than girls and dancing." I focus my attention on a palm tree in the lawn. Its large leaves sway and swirl in the breeze.

Conner knows me too well to know my teasing is a facade.

"Cons," he speaks softly. He looks around casually before his hand gently rests upon mine. Warmth runs up my arm and my cheeks tint pink. "What's really the matter?"

The palm tree continues to swish and swirl. My eyes don't dare leave it. "Did you know I am being courted by the Earl of Browning?" Even though I can only see him out of the corner of my eye, I can tell this news makes him uncomfortable. But he only waits for me to say more. "But he is insufferable."

A loud roar of laughter escapes Conner. At this I break my trance to fully look at him. He smiles so wide his dimples have made an appearance. "Oh, come now. He can't be all that bad. He's rich and," he takes his hands to brush an imaginary comb through his hair, "he's got a nice blond mane."

"A nice blond mane?" I ask incredulously. "Well, if blond hair is the deciding factor on who someone should marry, your prospects are drastically reduced." My hand reaches out to ruffle his short dark red hair. "You might want to grow that out like a normal lord if you want more ladies to choose from. Honestly, I'm surprised your mother lets you walk out of the house like that."

A look of false shock crosses his features. One hand spreads over his chest. He acts like my words have hurt his pride, but the small gleam in his eye gives him away.

A real smile spreads across my lips. I make a move to shove him playfully. Instead, Conner snatches my hand mid-motion and holds it in his own. Our eyes lock. Silence fills the air around us.

"Is that so?" His eyes search my face and linger on my lips. An unusual intensity fills his eyes. They continue to simmer, glancing between my lips and my eyes. A silent question lingers in the air.

"Yes," I breathe.

Conner begins to lean in. Inch by inch his breath becomes warmer. Heavier. Closer. His Adam's apple bobs ever so slightly before his lips part.

I dare not even blink. One of his hands come up to cup my face as his lips tentatively brush against mine.

"Miss Constance?" The Earl of Browning calls out into the dark.

That was it. My first kiss ever, and it's interrupted by my least favorite person.

Whatever little space Conner and I had between us has increased threefold.

Conner continues to look at me. Hunger sizzles in his eyes.

Oliver strides over. "Ah. There you are. Come." He extends an arm for me to take. "I have arranged a waltz for us. Best to keep up appearances for mother and father." Only then does he acknowledge Conner's presence and nods in his direction with a keep-your-hands-off-my-property kind of sneer.

Conner barely glances his way, before they focus back on me. "Oliver." He grits out.

I break my gaze with Conner and reluctantly lace my arm with the earl's. We rejoin the party arm in arm without another word spoken to each other.

The rest of the night, Oliver keeps an annoyingly close proximity to me. All I can do is catch stolen glances within this crowded ballroom of the man I wish I was arm and arm with instead. Conner keeps his distance, but I feel his attention on me even from across the room. Each time our eyes meet, I feel the sparks between us, the promise that there is something more. But that is all we will ever be: sparks. Sparks that will never turn to flame.

Chapter 3

"I cannot believe Conner kissed you last night!" Ally squeals. Her hands work quickly through my lion's mane, separating it into three sections.

"It was unbelievable, Ally. Just like from a fairy tale."

These are the mornings I enjoy the most. Sunshine filters through the cream curtains. Gossip with Ally. Giggles. Not a care in the world.

"How was it? Did he seem…" she struggles with the words, "…good at it?"

Pink paints my cheeks. "It's not like it was very long. The *Earl of Browning* interrupted the kiss before it truly began." I turn around to face my maidservant. "But…" I recall the way his eyes were blazing into me. His hand covering mine. "His lips were warm and soft. No doubt it was not his first."

She giggles. "Well, he is quite handsome. I know the servants in the Hayward's estate talk of him often. How kind he is. How smart and attractive he has become these last few years." Her eyebrows wiggle with mischief.

"He is what any woman would want to marry. It's unfortunate that he has six sisters to provide for after he inherits his father's estate." I look out my window, picturing what it would be like to marry him. If he was my betrothed, I think Papa would be proud, joyous even. But that fate will never come to pass. Even though Conner showed interest in me, I would have to wait years for him to be ready. And even then, his sisters would all have to marry off quickly. The Hayward family isn't rich enough to take care of six daughters and a household that isn't theirs.

"I cannot believe he kissed you last night of all nights! Of all the times he could have tried and now you are engaged to someone else."

Wait.

"Engaged?" My brows furrow in confusion. "Ally, I'm not sure where you heard that, but Oliver has not proposed to me yet."

She stops doing my hair. Her lips pull sheepishly inward.

"I beg your pardon, my lady. It was not my place to say anything."

"What do you know, Ally?" I pin her with a demanding glare.

"I just," she hesitates, "I overheard your mother talking this morning that there was to be a wedding. She said he planned to have you as his bride within the next month."

The next month? The words echo in my mind. *It's too soon. Everything is happening too fast.*

Immediately, I shoot to my feet. "This isn't happening." The sleeve of my gown breaks open exposing the five dark marks plastered on my arm from the night before. I begin to feel the panic rising in my throat.

Ally notices my panic but not the bruises. I hide the marks by pulling my sleeve back over them.

"My lady, this is a good thing." Her hands rake over my upper arms in a soothing motion. "It is for the best. This household needs you to be strong. Perhaps it is not so bad."

I can tell she truly believes in her words, but my thoughts keep going to the bruises left on my arm and the emptiness in my heart.

"Please do not fret, my lady. Everything seems to have a way of working itself out in the end. You'll see." Ally plasters on a reassuring smile.

For her sake, and all the others involved, I swallow down my fears and my wants. This marriage. This I can do for our house. This I can do for my family.

But first, I need some stress relief.

* * *

The sun hangs at its peak, blazing down on my exposed skin.

Papa's personal sailboat rocks gently on the passive waters of the ocean; my refuge.

On deck, I lay on my back, sun hat resting over my face to protect my eyes from the scorching sun. One hand I keep splayed over my belly. The other grips the fishing pole that's been sitting idly in the water for far too long.

What a few weeks it has been. A whirlwind of emotions and nowhere to put them.

Papa is gone. *Gone*. Mama claims he is never coming back.

Mama has been selling our belongings behind my back to make up the difference in funds to keep our estate running.

Conner has finally shown interest in me. He kissed me. But it's too little too late.

The earl is planning to propose.

So many things to wrap my head around when all I really want to do is go fishing. Except it seems the fish have abandoned me too. It's been hours and not a single bite.

I groan and sit up. My hat falls to the boat's deck before I pull the fishing line out of the water. My line is bare.

Apparently, they are biting, just not taking the hook with the bait. Real clever of them today.

My hands put the rod down and I trod over to the extra bait and pick some up before hooking it back on and tossing the line into the water.

Engaged. More like enslaved.

The bruises on my arm are angry and tender. If I received these for being informal about Oliver's title, then what will happen to me if the offense is worse than that?

He knew what he was doing in Mr. Hayward's study when he backed me into the bookshelf. He knew how to intimidate me. I shiver at what his next steps would be if I stepped out of line again.

A snag on my line practically rips the rod right out of my hands. Finally!

I stand up, fighting whatever sea creature has been hooked on tight. It tries to swim free, but I wrangle it in with expert precision.

The fish is almost completely in my clutches until a dot in the distance catches my eye.

A woman waves her arms frantically to get my attention. It's Mama.

Suddenly my line snaps and sinks into the ocean. The fish has escaped.

I let out an exasperated sigh before dropping the rod onto the deck and preparing to return to shore.

"Constance," Mama says. Urgency spreads in her tone. "The Browning family is having dinner with us and," she *tsks* waving her hand to address my attire, "you look filthy and sweaty."

"Of course, I do," I retort. "What am I supposed to look like on a ninety-degree kind of day?"

She puts her hands on her hips. "My sweet, you are meant to look like a proper lady before our guests arrive in a few short hours. Now please," she points back to our house above the sandy hill, "go wash up and get dressed. Be presentable before dinner tonight."

I throw my head back in annoyance. "I thought dinners were still just a family thing. Now we have the entertain the Boringtons during then too?"

"Constance," Mama warns. "The Brownings have made a very generous offer for you. One that no other family can match. It's enough to keep our own household help for quite some time. It may not seem like it on the surface, but based on the offer alone, they really like you. You'll be taken care of."

I scoff. Taken care of? A husband intimidating his future wife into submission isn't being taken care of. I am about to pull up my sleeve to show her the bruises when she takes a step closer to run her hands up and down my arms. Her eyes light up with a familiar look I thought was lost on her: hope. She has hope in her eyes. It glistens against the morning light, showing me exactly how she feels about this arrangement: hopeful, excited, relieved. That look stops me from saying anything. How can I throw her mind back into desperation and despair when she is looking at me like I am a savior?

She speaks. "Oh, my darling, I am just... so proud of all you've accomplished with such little time you've been given. You make your mother proud. Maybe they're just...maybe their behavior is stress from building their new home and meeting new people. It takes a great deal of patience to build a home away from home. So can you please, please give them the benefit of the doubt and be on your best behavior today?"

I swallow up my feelings and nod before walking up the hill to our house.

Mama follows close behind. "I would like you to wear your white blouse with the matching skirt. You always look lovely in it."

Without turning to look at her, I raise my hand and give her a thumbs up to show I heard her.

* * *

Later that evening, after an awkward dinner with the Brownings, I find myself gliding on the white sandy beaches, holding an umbrella over my head to escape the brunt of the sun's rays. It is uncommonly hot for this time of day.

I've opted for flat, white slippers hidden mostly by my skirts. Sand seeps its way into them, rubbing against my feet. But I don't mind the feel of the tiny pebbles. In fact, I quite prefer it. If I wasn't among company, I'd have opted to go barefoot.

Oliver trudges next to me, not so pleased to be out on the beach in the heat of the day. He keeps rubbing sand from his face that the wind has carried off the ground and occasionally I catch him falter slightly in the ever-shifting ground or rub sweat from his brow. Despite all of these clues, the look on his face is all anyone would need to understand he takes no enjoyment in our *leisurely* walk.

"Would you like to head back to the house, my lord?" I inquire. A slight smirk creeps up the side of my lips.

"Nonsense," he barks. "We must keep up appearances for my parents. We can't walk back, or they will think I do not enjoy your company."

"And do you enjoy my company?" A bold question to ask considering last night's events.

Oliver continues to look forward. "You are tolerable. That is enough for me." A small part of me pities his genuine response, and my hopes of any facsimile to love sink even further.

"Tolerable?" I question. "A hot summer day in a corset is tolerable, but it doesn't mean I wouldn't rather be wearing slacks," I counter.

He has no response; only to continue our walk in yet another awkward silence. *Keep trying, Constance. There must be something you can find common ground on.*

We almost reach the dock where my father's personal sailboat remains tethered to a post. An idea flickers in my mind. "How about this? It's a windy day, and I am sure your feet could use a break from the shifting sand. I'll have you know I am quite the accomplished sailor. How about we sail on the ocean for a bit?"

The idea of sailing brings thoughts of my papa. The first time he tried teaching me how to sail, I accidentally flipped us over. We poked our heads out of the water, and he just shook his hair and laughed. "Well, that's one way not to sail," he chuckled as we did our best to push the boat upright.

"Miss Constance!" the earl's voice cuts sharp into my memory. "Did you hear a word I said?"

Truth be told, I hadn't heard a single word he said. Thoughts of Papa had a way of pulling me out of reality. "I apologize, my lord, I was just in my own head space. What do you say to a quick sail?"

"I said we will do no such thing. It's not right for a lady to dirty her hands with the work of a servant's job."

My eyes desperately fight the urge to roll to the back of my head.

We reach the dock, and the earl takes my arm and veers me to stand on the wooden beams. He does so with an all-too-tight grip that makes those bruises ache underneath my long and flowy sleeves. "When we wed, you will act your rank."

"But my lord, you haven't even proposed yet." I look over to where Mama and the duke and duchess stand.

In that small moment, the earl gets on one knee and pulls out a small circle of silver metal clasping a giant yellow stone.

The yellow stone is an ugly old thing, the color of urine. It stares at me with the same kind of judgment Oliver does.

"That is about to change. Miss Constance Price, will you marry me and one day become the Duchess of Browning?" Although he phrased it as a question, it came out a command.

I look to Mama for support. But she stands there next to the duke and duchess. Her hands clasped together, hiding her smile. She will be no help to me now.

I've always thought that drowning would be a terrible way to die. Your lungs burn. Your muscles ache. Your body screams for the one thing it needs until eventually water breaks through and there's nothing left to do but give in to the imminent arms of death. That is what this moment feels like.

I dare one more glance at my mother whose expectant eyes and encouraging nod lead me to the only answer I can give.

"I suppose tolerable will have to suffice for me too," I say as Oliver wedges the yellow shackle onto my finger.

Chapter 4

I look out the window at the orange, pink, and purple sky. The colors have never looked so dull before.

My thumb idly rotates the ring on my finger. It has been only a few hours that I sold my life away for a stupid, hideous rock. *No, I sold my life away for the protection of my family, for my mother, for the servants in our household, for Ally.*

She delicately pulls pins out of my hair so she can brush it before bedtime.

"It could be worse, you know?" she chimes as her fingers attempt to separate the knots I've accumulated throughout the day.

"How?"

"At least he's rich, and I'm sure his home in Weatherington is plenty big enough for you to roam on your own."

I have no answer but to cast my eyes down from the sky to the lapping waves below.

"You're doing a great service for everyone here, Constance. That must mean something. I know it does to me." Ally grabs my shoulders for a brief moment, and I turn to look up at her.

"You're right. This isn't just about me. It's about everyone here. Not everyone gets their happily ever after anyways," I return her smile, "but at least I can make it better for the Price household; Mama and you, especially."

That makes her smile. She continues working on my hair.

By the time Ally is finished detangling every strand of hair, the sun has set completely. I swear she pulled out a quarter of my curls in the process. She bids me goodnight before gliding out the door to sleep in the servants' quarters.

The company of my own thoughts are at war with each other and the feeling of drowning pulls me into dangerous depths.

* * *

Sleep is what I am supposed to be doing. Sleep is what I need. Sleep is the last thing I am capable of. I toss and turn in my suffocating sheets as the night peaks to its darkest hour. It must be around two in the morning by now.

My thoughts are a raging fire, consuming any rest I could ever hope to get. One second, I think of this ring on my finger, the weight it carries on us all.

The next moment, I think of Conner and his fun-loving demeanor. And then I think I could easily fall in love with him.

It's hard not to compare him to my betrothed. *Betrothed.* What a sickening word when I think of who I am to wed: Oliver, oh— I mean *my lord.*

Then I think of my father. The one man who could stop all of this from happening in the first place. My father who loves my mother. My father who taught me everything about love and relationships. Where is he now? Mama thinks he's dead, but I just know it can't be true. I would feel a hole in my heart right where I keep him. There's no hole, only hope that one day he'll return. He *has* to return.

I throw my sheets off and walk barefoot to the window. I swiftly unlock the clasp, and it swings open sending a warm, salty breeze into the bedroom.

I glance down at the dock where the earl proposed no less than twelve hours ago. Papa's sailboat rocks back and forth on the surface of the water.

What would Papa say when he found out I am to be shackled to someone I do not love? If he were here, even if our family was still strapped for funds, he would never offer me up to the Brownings.

He would find another way.

I continue to gaze at the empty sailboat when an idea comes to mind. Not just an idea. A way out of this whole mess. An idea that can save us all.

* * *

I change into more appropriate sailing gear and rummage through my vanity drawer for the emerald and umber necklace Papa gave me. With my teeth and my other hand, I wrap the necklace around my wrist and tie the thin piece of leather into a secure knot before tiptoeing out of my room.

The house is completely silent as I sneak around gathering a week's worth of provisions into a cloth sack. I try to take minimal supplies to save the rest for Mama and the help.

The most important equipment I gather from a drawer in Papa's workroom. A map and a compass. I heave the sack of supplies over my shoulder and tip toe to Mama's room with a note in hand.

Her door is closed. Faint snores can be heard coming from the other end.

I love you, Mama, and I will make things right, I think. My hand takes the neatly folded paper and glides it under the door along with the ring the earl gave me. I blow a silent kiss in her direction and head outside toward the dock. To freedom.

The moon is on full display in the early hours of the morning. The water is peaceful. It's high tide which is in my favor because it'll be easier to navigate the waters and set out to open sea.

Crouching low, I sidle up to the sailboat, glancing side to side to make sure no one has seen my traitorous behavior, not that any neighbors take a stroll on the beach at this early hour. But it never hurts to be cautious.

The sailboat bumps the dock with every lap of water, inviting me to jump aboard. My arms easily toss the sack over the side, and I crawl in feet first. I dare to raise my head just high enough that my nose sits atop the side of the boat as my hands work quickly to untie the rope that tethers my escape. Heartbeats later and the boat is set free of its bonds.

Using an oar, I gently push off the dock before the ocean embraces us, drawing us closer to its center like a hug from mother nature herself.

Soon enough, the shore is nothing but a speck in the distance. Gingerly I raise to full height and pull out the compass. *I'm coming for you, Papa.*

* * *

It's hard to navigate when you aren't exactly sure what your destination is, but I've narrowed it down to a few possibilities.

Morning light's blush begins to peek above the horizon, so I decide it's a good time to pull out the map of the islands Papa has told countless stories about. It's a raggedy old thing with small holes here and there like the map has gotten too close to a candlestick a time or two.

Papa always has specific routes he takes and certain islands he favors when doing business across the ocean. There's the main merchant's route that begins at Ohaku Island, our sister island, and trails through the winding Kiwani Pass to the Culooko Islands.

There's also Anne's Isle. It's comprised of multiple smaller islands that form a well-organized and extensive community. They make the most beautiful colored fabrics.

Papa also makes special trips just for me, like sailing to The Island of Waterfalls. I fiddle with the shell on my wrist, thinking about the stories he told me about the mystical island. The most beautiful seashells ever brought back to me have been from there.

I remember the countless times I had asked him to take me there, but he had always refused.

"We tread near dangerous waters to get there. It's not safe for a Little Guppy," he always warned.

The map warns me too.

My eyes continue to scan it, trying to ignore the black ink tainting a piece of the parchment. Just between Anne's Isle and The Island of Waterfalls awaits a different kind of threat. A place few dare to venture, and none have ever come out of. The only reason there is even a spot on the map for it is because of the families that have suffered its wrath; losing loved ones and never knowing what truly happened to them.

A menacing thought taps the borders of my mind, that for some reason, somehow, Papa is stuck there with no way out. I stare at the splotch of black, my mind falling into thoughts I'd rather never have.

Maybe his ship got caught in a storm and they've needed months to repair it. I try to convince myself that's the most likely scenario. Although I can't help but question why it has taken so long to repair, or why he hasn't been able to find paper and ink to write to us if it were true. Negative thoughts of his death lurk in my mind.

No. I reassure myself. *Papa is alive. I just need to find him, and everything will be as it should be.*

With my index finger I trace around my first destination: Ohaku Island. It's considered my home island's twin and only a day and a half journey from what Papa has described.

A seagull squawks above me, breaking my concentration, and it's a good thing too.

Somehow, in just a few moments the boat has shifted directions. I open the compass and notice I am no longer heading north, but southeast. In one exaggerated movement, I heave up to my feet and wobble to the wheel. It always did take me a bit to put my sea legs on. I yank at the wheel until the boat travels east. Now that I am on the right track again, I open the sails and let the wind keep me on target to my first destination.

Complete daylight is still a few hours away and my eyes grow heavy. It might be a good time to take a quick nap considering I didn't sleep at all last night and instead busied myself with an escape-slash-rescue plan.

The sailboat doesn't have a below deck, but there's plenty of room for me sprawl out on the deck with a thin blanket Papa always keeps stored on the boat for our chilly morning fishing trips.

It will be good to close my eyes just for a moment. My head barely hits the deck before sleep embraces me.

Chapter 5

A tremor from beneath jostles me awake. The sailboat rolls onto its side, dipping into the ocean before rolling back on its belly. My hands shoot out from under me just quick enough to catch myself from toppling over the side. I scan my surroundings.

Before I fell asleep the sky was clear and promising, but now it's blanketed with angry clouds. A drop of water splashes my cheek, and I wipe it away. But the gesture is pointless because one sprinkle quickly turns into a torrential downpour. The rain is so heavy I have to squint my eyes to see anything.

One day into my journey, and I'm met with a thunderstorm? *Maybe it's my punishment for leaving Mama*, I think as thunderous claps echo in the sky followed by giant bolts of lightning. My hands immediately cup over my ears. It's one thing to be indoors tucked under warm covers when thunder booms, but out on the water there is nothing to dull the temper of a vengeful storm.

The sailboat is jostled once more. I fear a whale or shark has come hunting for its next meal when something much worse catches my attention. A sight that's sure to be the end of me and my boat.

Not fifty feet from where I stand is a menacing, massive wave, ready to crush everything it chooses to topple over.

I have only a moment to tighten my grip on the side of the sailboat and inhale oxygen before the wave punches me into oblivion.

The wave is too powerful. My sailboat doesn't stand a chance. It leans, the wood cracking, protesting as the water smashes into it. My hands are no match for the force of the wave as it pries my fingers from the side, sending me flying into the dark waters.

Water surrounds me in every direction. My eyes burn from the salt water, but I have to keep them open. I have to find the surface.

I'm not sure how long I've been holding my breath as water continues crashing down, but the need to breathe grows stronger. I kick off my shoes and throw my arms out of my jacket; anything to make myself lighter.

My efforts are futile as wave after wave pushes me farther down into the ocean. My lungs scream for air. I thrash and kick and do everything I can, but it's no use.

I can't take it any longer. With one huge gasp, saltwater fills my lungs. At first it burns, but then I get this peculiar feeling. I never thought dying would be peaceful, but an unusual calm spreads throughout me as I think *this is the end.*

That's when I see him. My papa is here swimming toward me with open arms, welcoming me home. I was supposed to find him, but here he is rescuing me instead. That's the last thing I remember before everything goes black.

* * *

If this is what heaven's like, I don't want to imagine the alternative. My eyes are still closed, but I'm shivering on what feels to be a cold, hard, stone floor. I'm soaked to the bone, and my head throbs as if someone whacked it with a hammer.

Papa. I thought I saw him in the water. Did he save me? Where is he now?

Then I hear it, an argument.

My eyes fling open. Reality hits me. This is definitely not heaven.

No. It wasn't Papa that pulled me from my death. Papa would never leave me in a place like this.

I'm lying in a cage made of wet stone. It's the size of a storage closet, just big enough for me to walk a few steps from one end to the other. The only light comes from a small lantern casting shadows on the wall.

I look down at my feet. Both are bare and bluish. My body struggles to get warm. If I were to shiver any harder my teeth would break. In spite of my desperate need for some warm clothes and a blanket, I try to be as silent as possible as the two voices continue to bicker at one another. Without moving from my position on the floor, I strain my ears to overhear.

"Do you not understand the predicament you have put us in?" an angry male voice hisses.

Another male voice responds in a much calmer, more authoritative tone. "My prince, it was not I who put us in our situation, but you."

The angry male, a prince, scoffs. "And how is it my fault that you brought that creature into our home?"

"I did what was right and honorable. You put her here when you decided not to control your temper," the even-tempered male stated. By the way he speaks, I picture him as the older one of the two. If the angry male is a prince, perhaps this other male is the king. Who else would be bold enough to argue with royalty?

"You should have let her drown. And I didn't lose—" the prince began.

"Regardless," the older male interrupts, "she is here because of the storm you created. She is now your responsibility." The prince does not respond, which leads the older male to continue, "We do not take lives unnecessarily. We protect life. We protect the innocent whether they are like us or not. I taught you this and you would be wise to remember it. Now, what do you propose we do?"

The prince makes a disgruntled sound. Boots scuff the wet stone as if he is pacing back and forth.

A few heartbeats go by, but I can't tell if they had lowered their voices so I could not hear, or rather they were not speaking at all. The moments of silence lead my mind to worry even more so.

I pick at my thumbnail, considering all of what they might do to me. What did the older man mean when he said the prince was responsible for the storm? Would this prince really have let me drown? What kind of person would choose to let someone die even when he had the ability to save said person?

If he finds out I've been listening, will he hurt me like Oliver did? Will he do something worse? I stop picking at my nails to lightly trace the bruises left on my arm.

"It is decided." The prince interrupts my thoughts. "When she wakes, we will interrogate her. Figure out what she knows and why she was sailing in our waters. Then we will determine her fate."

"A wise choice, my prince."

Those are the last words I hear before two sets of boots shuffle away from the cell, opening and closing what sounds like a very heavy door.

Only until the door has long been closed do I finally feel safe enough to sit up and tuck my legs in to my chest. I wrap my arms around my wet clothes and rub vigorously.

I am to be interrogated by a mad prince. A prince who can somehow conjure a storm… and for some reason doesn't like me.

Would drowning have been better?

If my teeth chatter any harder, I fear they will break. My arms close around my sides tightly, doing their best to create any semblance of warmth.

A heavy door creaks open in the distance.

I pretend to be asleep, even though my body refuses to be still, as a pair of large boots scuffle straight up to the bars near my head.

"Miss," the older male voice whispers. "Miss, are you awake? I have something for you."

My initial instinct is to ignore him. Pretend he is not there and I am not awake, but the kindness in his voice catches me off guard. I assumed from the conversation I eaves dropped on earlier was a strong indication I am not welcome here and will receive no kindness. Well, the conversation and the fact I am trapped behind bars.

"Miss?" The male voice is lower this time. Closer. As if he crouched down to the floor next to me.

I give in to his gentile inquiry and look up. The first glimpse I get is giant black boots. My eyes work their way up to fully take in the features of my captor. He is a strong man, no doubt. Although he wears armor across his chest, his ebony arms are bare and rippling with muscle. A dagger rests on his hip. I figure he's in his mid-thirties or early forties by the slight crease in his forehead. What's most shocking about his appearance is a long scar slashed through his eyebrow.

He looks upon me with intrigue. "You must be freezing, miss. Here." His arms push something through the bars toward me.

It looks like a set of clothes; more importantly, dry clothes. Wordlessly I grasp them in my hand, not breaking eye contact with the stranger before me.

He also continues to look at me, as if his mind is working something out but hasn't figured out what yet.

"Thank you," I manage to spit out between shivers.

He offers a closed-lipped smile and turns around, waiting for me to peel out of the soaking fabric, so I can put on the new ones he brought.

My fingers are numb as I fumble out of the slacks and shirt that cling to every inch of my skin. It feels odd, undressing in front of a man I've never seen before, even if he is turned the other way.

I can tell by the sheer size of the long sleeve blouse I pull over my head—as it runs down past my knees—that these clothes aren't made for women. The pants are no better. I have to hike up the waist far above my belly button for them to stay on at all and the socks fit more like stockings, running up my thighs, but I don't care. All I know is they are much warmer and softer than anything I could have hoped for being a prisoner and all.

I clear my throat loud enough for the man to hear. He slowly turns around. Another closed-lipped grin spreads from ear to ear as he surveys the new look. "I am sorry miss. Hopefully we will be able to get you fitted for more appropriate clothing later. Ah," he reaches down for one more thing, a wool blanket. "I know it isn't much, but the dungeon can get quite chilly, especially for your kind."

My kind?

"I must go. Try to get some sleep." He turns to go away.

"Wait!" I reach my hand out of the cage as if it would stop him from leaving. "Please. Why am I here? What happened? The last thing I remember is drowning and seeing my father swim toward me, and now I'm here. Where is here? What are you going to do with me?" All the questions come tumbling out in one long breath. I had to find answers. This man has me caged but brings me clothes and gives me genuine smiles. None of this adds up.

He halts like he wants to explain. Then he lets out a short huff. "In time, you will know. For now, get some sleep." Without another word, the man leaves.

The cell feels so cold, so hollow, so empty of life. It makes me wish for the sun on my skin and the ocean breeze caressing my face. But I find no solace in unfulfilled wishes.

Chapter 6

I tried to sleep. I really did. With the over-sized but dry clothes and the wool blanket, my shivers finally settled down. It was difficult at first to find a comfortable position on the stony floor. I tossed to one side, then I'd roll to the other. Eventually I rolled up a part of the blanket to make a tiny cushion for my head.

Hours must've passed of tossing and turning before sleep finally found me. For a brief moment. When I finally felt comfortable and began to drift off, a most horrid screech reverberated in the dungeon. A sound I'd never heard before from a creature I'd no intention of ever crossing paths with. That screech kept me up the rest of the night.

Was it nighttime? I could only assume the time of day. There are no windows down here, just that one lantern that continues to flicker.

I gaze at that dancing light, twirling my necklace against my wrist over and over again until a door some distance away creaks open. My body shoots to an upright position, waiting for the man from last night. Who comes into view isn't who I expect.

A man around my age comes waltzing up to the bars. A mischievous smirk spreads across his face as he munches on some kind of apple. "Well, well, well," he speaks between bites, "I guess the rumors ring true!" He takes another chomp out of his apple and sits right in front of my cell, legs crisscrossed. I'm not sure what to make of him as he continues to look at me in awe with every bite of that apple in his hand.

Seeing the fruit juice trickle down his chin reminds me I haven't eaten since before I left my home. My stomach gurgles at the thought.

The young man is handsome, if I'm being honest. Dark wavy hair sits on his head and covers the tips of his ears. His skin is fair and smooth, but it's his eyes I can't look away from. Staring at me are cool blue eyes like that of a spring storm cloud. Yes, he's quite striking to be sure.

"What do they call you?" he asks through bits of apple in his mouth.

I hesitate. This is a stranger after all, and I'm in a strange place. Who knows what he wants. But then I realize, what's the harm? I'm already in a cage.

"Constance," I reply.

"Constance," he says out loud, testing it out. "I like it." He grins.

"And you are?"

"Me? Oh, I'm sorry where are my manners? It's not every day a human enters our borders. I'm Sebastian." He slides his open hand through the bars.

I take it hesitantly and give a firm shake before releasing him.

His hands feel like sandpaper. Rough and callused. Maybe he's a carpenter or a sailor? Perhaps an apprentice of some sort considering his age.

My arms cross over my chest, as if that would somehow put a protective barrier between me and this strange man. "You say *human* like it's foreign on your tongue," I say.

"Well, yes," Sebastian tosses the core of the apple over his shoulder and continues, "Technically I'm not supposed to say anything to you, but why not?" He raises just a bit so he's sitting on his knees. "I may look a lot like you, but I'm not. I'm what humans typically call a *merman*." His fingers raise to make air quotes around the word.

Despite being locked up I can't help but chuckle at him. "No, I'm being serious."

"As am I." Sebastian takes his hands and raises his shirt to reveal his torso. I've never seen anyone shirtless besides myself before. It would be considered improper. A scandal. But seeing him now, I can't help but stare. Abs line the middle of his stomach. On the outside of those abs are three long open slits of skin on each side.

My mouth falls open slightly. It's like nothing I've ever seen before.

"What?" My fingers reach for those slits and instead halt before they pass the bars. "What are those?"

"They're gills. For breathing underwater." Sebastian lowers his shirt and tucks his knuckles under his chin. Contemplative. "I'll tell you what. You can ask me three questions, and I will answer truthfully. In return, I get to ask you three questions. Any questions I want at any time, and you must answer."

His proposition sounds like some sort of trap, but I've way more than three questions and need answers now. The longer I stay here, the less time I have to find Papa and save our household. I need to make these three questions worth it.

I narrow my eyes at him. "As long as you don't count my first two questions I already asked. I know your name and what you are, but those aren't the first two of my three. Then we have an accord."

"Deal." He grins.

What questions will get me out of here? What do I need to know now in order to escape wherever this place is? After showing me his gills, my mind races with questions that don't even matter but they pop up in my head regardless. *If he has gills, how can he breathe air? Does he live underwater? How many mermen are there? How do humans not know of their existence?*

I shove those thoughts down and try to focus. *Make the questions count, Constance.*

I raise my index finger in the air. "First question, I overheard two men talking about rescuing me from that storm. Why would I be rescued just to be locked up in here?"

"Good question, Constance," Sebastian prolongs the "s" sound at the end of my name. "The merman who rescued you is Darius. I like to think he has a hero complex. All life is precious to him. He saw you as innocent and decided it was his duty to rescue you. I can't say I blame him." He looks me up and down in my oversized clothes making my cheeks warm. "As far as this ever-so-cozy room you've been locked up in, it's for your protection. And ours. My brother's idea in fact. Humans aren't supposed to know we exist, and if anyone else found you down here there's no telling what they would do to you."

That horrible shrieking sound from earlier comes to mind. Can a merman make that noise? Is that some kind of battle cry or warning they'll attack? I shiver at the thought.

"Come now, next question. This is fun, do you agree?" His stormy blue eyes sparkle. Perhaps I am the only human he has come across. Maybe he's as intrigued about my life as I am about his, and I can use that to my advantage.

"Okay… question number two," I begin. "How do I escape out of my cell and out of this dungeon?" My eyes narrow, expecting him to refuse to answer truthfully. Daring him to tell me how.

His first response is to laugh out loud. A big belly laugh that bounces off the dungeon walls. "You're quite spirited. I can tell." he says as his laugh slowly dies down. "The only way to escape out of the cell is to get the key. And the only one with a key is the captain of the guard, Darius. I'm sure if you played damsel in distress well enough you could convince him to get close enough to the bars, snag the keys off his belt, wait until he leaves, and try to unlock the cell door yourself."

I fold my arms across my chest. His response somehow feels like mockery.

He continues, "And if, which is a big if by the way, you manage to walk up the dungeon steps and out into the open without being noticed by anyone, you'd need to get to the city's back entrance clear across from where we are at this moment in time. But that's as far as you'll ever get on your own."

"And why is that?" I challenge.

"Because we're hundreds of feet below the surface."

Chapter 7

Hundreds of feet below the surface. *Hundreds of feet below the surface?* It couldn't be possible. It's *impossible.*

The walls of my cell suddenly feel closer. Tighter. Suffocating. I look at Sebastian with disbelief stricken across my face. My eyes are wide, and my jaw clamps shut. I start wringing the ill-fitting shirt between my hands which have become slick with sweat. I pace back and forth, my over-sized socks getting damp from the small puddles of water scattered on the cell floor.

Hundreds of feet. I consider myself a good swimmer. Great in fact, compared to anyone else I know. My father taught me from a young age and made it a point that I keep my swimming skills sharp since we lived on the ocean's border.

Papa. How was I going to save him now? I think of him, of Mama. I abandoned her for nothing if I don't find a way to escape. There has to be a way.

"Please," I say with urgency now. My hands unravel from the shirt fabric and grip the bars. My gaze bores into Sebastian's eyes. He jumps up to his feet with his hands raised. "Please let me out. Help me escape. I must get out of here, now!"

Sebastian keeps his hands raised. They remind me of a white flag being swung in the air. He takes a few small, hesitant steps forward as he says soothingly, "Listen, Constance. I want to help you. I do. But I'm not the one in charge here. It may take some time, but I'm sure you'll be set free—"

"Time is what I don't have! You don't understand!" my voice cracks. I shake the bars testing their durability.

He gingerly reaches out toward my hands as if to comfort me, but the door to the dungeon opens with a loud bang.

Strong and angry steps come barreling through what I can only assume is a hall as Sebastian and I gaze upon the new company.

"What are you doing down here? I forbade you to come down here and you insist on undermining me," the angry voice booms. I recognize that voice from the first moment I woke up in this cell. The same voice that said I should've drowned.

Sebastian tucks his hands into his pockets nonchalantly. "Oh, come on. Nothing this exciting has ever happened. I had to see it for myself. And to be fair, you should really be blaming yourself for telling me in the first place." He shrugs to emphasize his innocence.

The angry man—no, merman— looks as if he's going to strangle Sebastian. His face is red with rage. Even with the distance he has kept between us, I can see a vein bulging from his neck. "You know how dangerous she is to us. To our kingdom." His hands open and close into fists. Clearly this male is the one in charge. He's slightly shorter than Sebastian but much broader. Built like a soldier with brawny biceps and forceps. His black hair is the exact shade as Sebastian's but shorter, clean cut. And unlike Sebastian's baby skin face, this merman has a full, close-trimmed beard that defines a strong, clenched jaw.

The two males stare each other down, leaving heated silence in their wake.

"Please," I beg, looking up at the furious male.

He forfeits his staring match with Sebastian and draws his attention toward me. Mercy! He is uncommonly strong. Just by looking at him, I can tell he would win any fight against the men on my island. Every single one of them.

"I have to get out of here and find my father. Do you know what it's like not knowing what happened to someone you love? Not knowing whether you'll ever see them again? If you could change your fate by finding the one person who could change it all for the better… would you?"

Both males are now focused on me. Eyes boring into me. From this angle, the color of their hair isn't the only similarity I notice between them. Both have strong jawlines and a straight nose. Both have full lower lips and larger than average ears. They must be related somehow. They must be brothers.

Neither one speaks, so I continue, "I promise, I won't utter a word about this place or what I saw or how I got here. You can even blindfold me all the way back to the surface and leave me on an island. Any island of your choosing. I'll count to a hundred before I even take the blindfold off so I can't trace back where you and your kind are at all." I push my face between the bars as far as I can without getting stuck. Pleading. Looking as innocent and desperate as possible. "I beg of you. Have mercy on me."

The two brothers continue to study me.

Sebastian breaks his gaze first and glances sideways at his brother. Trying to see what his reaction will be to my plea.

His brother narrows his eyes and crosses his arms over his chest. Muscle ripples under his shirt. He takes one step closer to the parallel bars and holds my gaze with slitted eyes. If Sebastian's eyes are a blue storm cloud, then his brother's are tropical waters. Warm, with a greenish tint. The color is so far from the cold look he manages to give while he decides my fate.

"No." It comes out a guttural growl. "I can't let you free. You're a danger to our kind."

"Soren," Sebastian begins, "I think she's telling the truth. Why don't we—"

"Enough!" Soren, the one who wishes I'd drowned, the one who refuses to let me leave, turns to his brother and glares. "Come now, Sebastian. There are things we need to do." He walks off without so much as another glance in my direction.

Sebastian takes one apologetic look at me and gives a sympathetic crooked smile before following his brother's lead out of the dungeon.

My ears feel red hot. Water pools in my eyes as I yell after them. "Fine! It's obvious you have no compassion! Just let me starve to death and rot down here when apparently you were the one that got me into this mess in the first place!" I remember what Darius, the kind merman who gave me dry clothes had said when I eavesdropped on their conversation. It was Soren's fault I was even here. I'm not sure how it was his fault exactly, but I threw the accusation at him anyway.

The only reply I receive is a hard slam to the dungeon doors, leaving me alone and hungry. How long had it been since I last ate? By now I had to have been held against my will for over a day at the very least. Tears stream down my cheeks followed by violent sobs. I rest my back against the cell wall and slowly descend into a crouching position, curled up like a snail in its shell.

I should never have run away. I should never have tried to find Papa. It's bad enough that he went missing, but now? Now I'm missing too and will never be found. I sought to be a savior for my family. Instead, I doomed us all. Who knows how long Mama will have before she must get rid of the staff. How long will the money last? Who will be the first to make her a social pariah when they find out about our family? About what I did and how I left?

I can't bear the thought. My violent sobs turn ragged. I desperately gasp for air between each weep.

Eventually, I have no more tears to give, and exhaustion overcomes me. I fall asleep curled up against the wall.

* * *

A clatter near my legs startles me. I jolt up and look around to find a metal tray has been dropped near my feet. I can't see whoever dropped it for me, but I am grateful. It has a small, cooked fish, a loaf of bread, and an apple like the one Sebastian was eating earlier. Next to the plate is a large pitcher of water. Suddenly I'm all too aware of how dry and cracked my lips feel. I reach for the water first. It's a little piece of heaven as the smooth liquid glides down my throat. It may be because I've gone too long without any, but in this moment, it's the best water I have ever tasted. Small streams of it roll down the corners of my lips as I guzzle it down.

Next, I rip off large chunks of bread with my teeth and follow it with small bites of the apple. I save the fish for last, using my nails to pick away all the flesh and meat off the bone, sucking my fingers when there's nothing left to pick off. If anyone were to see me devour this food, they would think I'd gone feral. But I can't help myself. Everything is so good, and I am ravenous.

It takes no time at all to finish off the food and water. I sit there in my cell rubbing my belly. If I touch it just right, I can hear water sloshing inside. *Well, I may be a prisoner, but at least they didn't let me starve to death. Yet.*

With some food in my belly, I have a newfound energy. I pick myself up off the floor and pace back and forth, boggling my mind for a way to escape.

If Soren, who apparently has the final say about what to do with me around here, won't let me out, then I need an alternative outlet.

Maybe the kind and noble Darius will let me out. He hasn't heard my case yet. Sebastian said he has a thing about damsels. I just need to play on his weakness.

Or there's Sebastian. He's curious and sweet and younger than the other two. He tried to get his brother to let me go. Maybe I just need to talk to him more. Get him to steal the keys for me and sneak me away. If his brother will ever let him back here.

As I try to figure out plan B, the dungeon door swings open with a loud grate.

Mid-step, I stop and look at who the guest will be this time. I hope it's Sebastian.

My hope sinks into my stomach as fair skin, short black hair, and warm blue-green eyes come striding in. Following Soren is Darius armed to the teeth. I wonder if he's decided to finally kill me and the meal I had consumed was to be my last before Soren orders Darius to end my life.

Soren comes right up to the bars, one finger pointing at me, and opens his mouth. Nothing comes out. He glares with those narrowed eyes before closing his lips and pacing the stone floor.

My head follows him side to side with each heel turn he makes. I refuse to break the silence first.

Darius waits patiently against the stone wall opposite of the cells. Hand on his sword, at the ready.

Minutes go by and I start to feel awkward. My fingers have found the hem of my shirt, and I rub the seam in anticipation.

Finally, Soren stops pacing and faces me. He clasps his hands behind his back before speaking. "It appears…" he begins to say through clenched teeth, like it's painful even to talk to me. He takes a slight glance over his shoulder where Darius continues to wait like the perfect soldier. Darius gives the smallest inkling of a nod before Soren draws his stare back to my eyes. "…I'm in need of a human."

Chapter 8

I furrow my brows. "What do you mean?"

"I mean, you have some…" he struggles to find the next words, "…value to me."

Value could mean many things. I stare at him, unsure what to say.

He continues, "It would seem you and I are in a special circumstance. You have something I cannot get from anywhere else, and I hold your freedom in my hands."

This is it. Plan B. Something I have been hoping for. A bargain. I didn't expect negotiations to be with him, but I'll take whatever I can get. Whatever he needs from me I'll give as long as I can get out of here in one piece. However, I've absolutely no idea what I could give him in return for my freedom. Everything I had was on my sailboat or at home. Not even the clothes on my back are mine.

"And what is it you want from me?" I question.

Soren looks back at Darius and pulls off an invisible speck of dust from his shirt before responding. He takes a long stride forward, close enough I can feel his hot breath against my nose as he says, "I need you to be my thief."

My eyes widen. "A thief?" I've never stolen anything a day in my life…apart from Papa's boat and Oliver's engagement ring, but those are of special circumstance. "I'm sorry, what exactly am I stealing? Aren't you some sort of person in charge here with this great authority? What could you possibly need me to steal that you can't obtain yourself?"

He huffs impatiently at my evasion. "There's something of great value to me that'll be in the city in less than a week. You'll get it for me. It will give me answers I've been looking for, for a long time. Once I have it and the answers I need, I'll set you free." His warm blue eyes bore into me, daring me to take the deal.

I swallow a large chunk of saliva caught in my throat and cast my eyes downward. "I'm no thief. Why can't you get someone else to steal for you like Darius over there?" I want to get out of here. I do. My gut tells me there's something off about this bargain. Or maybe the growing knot in my stomach is due to the realization I'll be here way too long. I'm on a time crunch as it is and being in this cell has already taken a chunk out of the small time I do have.

Soren huffs impatiently. "Keep in mind, human, this is the only chance you have of getting out of here. I offer it to you now. I'll not offer it again."

I glance over Soren's shoulder to Darius. Although his eyes remain forward, his head gives the slightest nod of assurance before my eyes slide back to Soren.

"Fine." If making a deal with this hot head is my only ticket out of here, then so be it. I'll be his thief and help him find whatever answers he's looking for. "Then we have an accord." I slide my hand through the bars like men do when coming to an agreement.

Soren glances at my open palm. "Captain," he calls over his shoulder, "let the human out."

* * *

Without another word, the three of us take a right toward a long set of seemingly endless stone stairs leading up and out of the dungeon. Darius leads the way. I travel behind him with both hands clasped around the pants I'd been given. They're so large, any movement I make threatens the possibility of them falling off completely. I end up doing a kick-walk as we trudge up the stairs just to keep from tripping over the train of fabric.

Soren sulks closely behind me. He obviously doesn't trust me. The feeling's mutual.

After what feels like an endless spiral of cold stone beneath my sodden socks, I finally see a sliver of light just ahead. Darius pulls out that large ring of keys, picks out one with a rusty handle and slides it into the lock before he opens the door.

I inhale fresh, spring air. It's so much warmer than the dungeon below.

What lays before my eyes is a display of beauty unlike anything I've ever witnessed before. It's a city made of crafted rock. Stone pillars are decorated with full vines in bloom. Walkways are lined with exotic flowers, their petals enclosed for the night. I wonder what colors they are in the light of day.

Homes must be carved into stone along the edges as well, because I see doors of all different colors to my left, sticking out like sore thumbs against the brown and grey terrain. Water seemingly flows through an endless maze of streams running through the city streets below. However, the most impressive thing in view is a giant waterfall on the farthest end of the land.

In the middle of it all is an impressive castle surrounded by a moat. And above that is the most peculiar looking light I've ever seen. It looks like the moon, casting dim rays of light over the city, but it can't be if we truly are under water. I gaze at the beauty before me.

"No time to gawk, human," Soren says from behind as he nudges my back with the hilt of his sword. "Keep moving and keep quiet." He nods to Darius to continue walking down the stone path toward the city. I turn my head slightly to give him a sneer before following.

We keep to the shadows even though no one is out on the walkways. It takes us a solid hour to get to our destination across the city. Right to the giant waterfall. The waterfall under the sea. It all feels surreal. I have but a moment to admire its beauty before Soren nudges the hilt of a weapon into my back again. I roll my eyes at his impatience. The sooner we get this deal done, the better.

The three of us find a narrow stone path hidden by the edge of the waterfall and walk in. Sounds of the falls crashing into the water below drown out every other noise. Spritz of it splatter my face with each step.

Behind the waterfall, the pleasant and fresh air is now freezing. A cave is hidden behind the waterfall. I lean as far as I dare over a pool of water; black, depthless water. It's the only thing in here. No sun, no fish, no life. Just endless black. The thought of being in that pool sends chills down my spine. I take a moment to rub my hands over my arms.

Darius stops and turns around. At the ready to do his master's bidding.

Soren steps in front of me. One finger points at the water. The other remains on the hilt of his sword. "You see this? It's the only way in and the only way out of this place. Below is a long cave of numerous tunnels full of wrong turns. You would lose your way almost instantly. Not that it matters since you're," he hesitates, "human. Escape for you would mean certain death. It's too cold and too deep. You would have to swim a hundred feet through the underground caves and then hundreds more to reach the surface. So don't even think of trying anything stupid." He takes a step closer. "Oh, and if you so much as think of betraying our bargain or harming a single hair on anyone's head while you're here, I'll take it upon myself to throw you in and the let the undertow drag you to your death."

I shiver at the thought. Soren's eyes rage like the waves of a hurricane. It's all the confirmation I need to know he's being serious. We continue to lock eyes before I nod my head to show him I understand the seriousness of his threat.

"Good. Darius will show you to your room. I have other matters of business," Soren says. And with that, he walks away through the falls without a single glance back.

* * *

Darius is much kinder than Soren. As he leads me away from the entrance to whatever this place is, I have more time to gawk and gaze at my surroundings. However, we still keep to the shadows and remain silent in case anyone is out. We reach one side of the giant castle that stands in the very center of the city.

Darius takes a few looks around before creeping behind some bushes and pushes one of the stones on the side of the castle. As he does so, the ground beneath us rumbles slightly to reveal a hidden entrance. He walks down into it then halts. A hand reaches out to me before he goes any further.

"Miss, it's a bit slick through here, and the way is quite dark. I'll make sure you don't slip or get lost."

I take his calloused hand and cautiously step into the secret entrance with him. He's right. It's extremely dark in here. How on Earth can he see where he's going? Darius lets me put my hand on his back as he leads me through the dark abyss.

It's eerily silent in the tunnels. The only sounds are our scuffling feet and my numerous apologies every time I step on his heels.

My gut becomes knotted in this place. It feels like being in the ocean at night surrounded by sharks. I can't see them, but I know they are there, lurking about, waiting for an opportunity to strike.

A whisper of warm breath creeps up my neck. Abruptly, I turn around, causing a collision between Darius and myself.

He lets out a small grunt. "Are you alright, miss?"

"I'm sorry," I whisper. "I thought someone was behind me."

He remains silent. Hesitant on what to say. "It's okay, nothing will get you in here. We're almost to our destination. Just stay close."

Even though he can't see me behind him, I nod and return my hand to his back, and we continue.

Minutes went by. An apology here. A grunt there. And then Darius stops.

"We are here. Give me a moment to open the door."

Although I can't see what Darius is doing, I can hear him running his hands along the stone wall until a *click* echoes. The stone moves revealing what I can only assume is my room.

My mouth gapes. This isn't just a room. It's more like five of my rooms put together. To my left is a set of intricately carved double doors that must be fifteen feet tall. That's the way we would've entered, if my presence here wasn't such a scandal.

In the middle is a bed fit for a queen. Four posts man the corners with the same wood as the entry doors. Fitted pale pink sheets drape from end to end and pillows pile up against the headboard. The bed reminds me of just how little sleep I got in the dungeon. It calls to me to lay down and close my eyes, even if it's just for a moment.

"Oh, you poor child," a voice I don't recognize comes from the far corner of the room. It's a woman—a mermaid. Her skin is brown and dewy like grass in the early morning. Black curls are pulled halfway up her head. I've never seen curls as soft and bouncy as hers. A hint of jealousy bubbles up my insides. Her eyebrows rise ever so slightly as she gives Darius a knowing glare and crosses her arms in disapproval. "Now what kind of tom foolery have you gotten yourself mixed up in? And why didn't you bring her to me sooner?"

"I'm sorry, my love," Darius responds. "I was under strict orders not to say anything to you until Prince Soren knew what had to be done." He crosses the room and lays a gentle kiss on the woman's head. Her arms ease just a little, but she continues to keep that one eyebrow popped up accusingly. Then she turns her attention back to me.

She scoffs. "Now where are my manners?" With haste, she unfolds her arms and expands them as she walks toward me, like a friend ready to embrace after not seeing each other for quite some time.

I don't know what to do as she approaches, so I remain still. Fingers clasped to my all-too-big pants. She reaches me in an instant and firmly grips my arms, taking in each part of me in equal measure.

"My name's Addeah Bricker, and I'm here to serve you however I can." Without letting me go, she turns her head in the direction of Darius. "And this fool of a soldier is my husband, Darius. Hopefully he introduced himself by now, but I can imagine a certain someone might not have wanted him to." She looks back at me and scoffs. "Loyal to a fault that one."

"Excuse me, my love, but loyalty can never be faulted. If you were discussing our marriage, you'd say anything less than a hundred percent loyalty is abominable." Darius retorts with a smirk creeping up his lips.

"That it is, and best not forget it." She grins in return.

I can't help but remain silent through their exchange. This woman isn't disgusted by me or afraid to touch me the way Soren was. She seems warm and friendly. She brought out a side of Darius I hadn't seen in the time I was in the dungeons. He seems calmer, more at ease. However, that could also be due to the fact Soren isn't around.

"Dear child," Addeah directs at me, "tell me your name."

I swallow and clear my throat. "It's Constance. Constance Price."

"Well, Constance, you're soaked through the bone and wearing clothes four times your size. Come this way." She looks me up and down again *tsk-tsking* in disapproval as she maneuvers herself behind me and shoves me toward a large door opposite of the entry way. "Honey, we have a lot of work to do."

I turn my head to see her better and ask, "What do you mean?"

"I mean we're going to make you royalty."

Chapter 9

One minute, Addeah's telling me I'm going to be royal, and the next Darius is excused from this colossal sized room, and I'm ushered into a connecting room used solely for bathing.

The room by itself is still larger than my room back home. A bathtub the size of a pond sits in the middle. Water runs down from a slit in the ceiling; my very own waterfall.

I stick a toe in the bath. It's warm. I've never seen anything so extraordinary before.

The entire room is exquisite. One wall is made entirely of glass, giving me a bird's eye view of the city.

Light casts morning shadows on the trees and pillars, probably thanks to that strange light in the sky.

At first, I refuse to get naked and climb into the water, but Addeah assures me the glass that makes up the entire far wall is somehow created so on the inside you can see out, but nothing on the outside can see in. Reluctantly, I decide to trust her and strip off the dingy, over-sized man clothes and walk toes first into the bubbly, blue pool.

Instantly, my muscles relax.

Addeah excuses herself to the other room and tells me to take all the time I need to wash.

Alone for "however long I need", I decide to take a long look at my surroundings, even though it's just the bathroom. A walkway of cemented stones surrounds the water. One edge of the path, closest to the door, has an array of soaps and scrubs, likely put there by Addeah to give me some choices. She seems thoughtful like that. The ceiling is dome shaped and decorated in rows of pearly dots marching up to a large chandelier illuminating the room.

The water smells divine; like coconut and papaya.

Some species of bird I've never seen before with bright head feathers and a needle-thin beak comes fluttering in front of the window. A much larger bird of the same kind flies right next to it, flapping its wings away from the window toward a tree off in the distance. The larger bird acts motherly as it chirps at the little bird to move.

It reminds me of Mama. It's only been a couple days by my guess that I'd run away from my engagement, from home…from her. A single tear escapes my eye, causing a ripple in the bath. I draw my knees up, clutching them with my hands and lay my chin down on the top of one. I miss Mama. I miss Papa too. Thoughts slither in my mind, that maybe I shouldn't have run away at all. Maybe I should've married Oliver. Maybe I should've forgotten about Papa and taken whatever money I could from the Browning's proposal and given it to Mama. Maybe all of our lives would be better off if I hadn't been so reckless.

I wipe a second tear that threatens to trickle down my cheek and notice the bruises on my arm. The bruises Oliver gave me. They're no longer deep purple but a wash of purples and greens and yellows. They're fading. Seeing them brings new determination to my mind. No. I will *not* regret the choices I made, because I will find Papa. I'll bring him back to our home and we'll live happily as a family again. Together. Whole. It may just take a little longer than I thought.

I decide to wait in the bath until the water gets cold, but it never does. Just one more strange thing about this strange place. My fingers and toes become shriveled and pruney. Only then do I grab one of the shampoo bottles Addeah left me. It smells like the water; coconut and Papaya. I scrub every inch of my scalp with my fingernails until suds cover each curl. Then I hold my breath and take a plunge.

* * *

"Oh, sweet child, there you are. You look and *smell* tons better which I hope makes you feel better too," Addeah says when she sees me exit the bathroom. She has a long sleeve night gown in one hand and a strange bottle in the other. "I hate to hurry you along, but you have visitors." She walks toward me and helps me put the night gown on. It's soft and comforting and to my surprise fits quite well. If she saw the bruises on my arm she doesn't say a word about them.

Then she grabs my wrist with the necklace still attached.

"Is this what I think it is?" she asks, rotating my arm to get a look at the smooth shell.

"My papa gave it to me many years ago," I say.

She looks at it, brows furrowed. "We'll have to take it off for now, child. But I promise I'll keep it in the vanity safe and sound for another occasion. Just… don't tell anyone you have it, okay? It could lead to trouble."

I have no idea what she's talking about, but something in my gut tells me to trust her. Reluctantly, I let her undo the knot and place it far back in the vanity drawer, out of sight.

Hastily, she ushers me to sit in front of the vanity in the room. It's covered in pearls with gold handles for the drawers and a gold rim that encircles the mirror. I take a good look at my face after Addeah drops me into the velvet chair and starts fiddling with the bottle in her hands.

I'm positive I look cleaner than I had been in that cell, but the lack of sunlight has begun to show on my skin.

Although my hair is clean, it still looks as if a bird had been nesting in it with all its tangles and knots. The presence of dark spots threatens beneath my eyes. Overall, it isn't my best look.

Addeah squeezes out some kind of liquid from the bottle and combs it through my wet, tangled curls. "I use this after every bath in my own hair," she says with a grin, "It's the best investment I ever made. Your curls will look and feel soft and bouncy, just like royal hair *should* look and feel."

Like magic, the strands of hair began to separate and form perfect curly cues with each run through of her fingers. It's the best thing that's happened to me since finding out about my rotten engagement to Oliver. Addeah's fingers feel great running through my hair. She wraps each individual curl at the end with her pointer finger. I'm seconds away from closing my eyes and purring with contentment.

Addeah hums a tune softly while she works her magic. I figure now is as good a time as any to ask some questions. Surely, she would answer.

"Miss Addeah…"

"Hmm?" her lips hum as she continues to work.

"What is this place?"

She looks at me puzzled. "Honey, this is your room while you visit with us."

"No, no. I mean, what is this entire place? The city?"

Her fingers pause their work as she looks me in the eye through the mirror in front of us. "Well child, you're in the most splendid city on Earth of course. The Kingdom of Emora. A land of beauty and peace. Has been that way for quite some time with our ruler, King Cyrus."

The way Addeah talks about her city, her home, is with pride. But her eyes speak a slightly different story. Sadness lurks underneath her words.

"Are you troubled?" I ask.

My question seems to snap her out of her sadness.

She replaces it with a false smile portraying happiness. "Oh yes, child. I guarantee you will love it here…

even under your unique circumstances. There." She finishes running that liquid through my hair and gives my mane one final fluff, cupping her hands and lifting the bottom of my curls. "You're looking like royalty already. These curls are stunning, if I do say so myself."

It's magic. Never had I been able to run my fingers through my hair without snagging a knot or getting my fingers caught in a minefield of tangles. I can now put my whole hand in and run it through as easily as if it were water itself. The curls immediately spring back into place. I give Addeah the first real smile I've had since being here.

"Thank you," I offer my gratitude.

"Don't thank me just yet, child. There's a lot more work to be done."

As if on cue, we hear a loud rap coming from the wall.

"Is she ready yet?" a muffled angry voice hisses against the stone. My small moment of happiness shrivels up.

Addeah walks in haste to the secret entrance, pushes in a single stone, and opens the door. "Come in your highness, but a word of advice. A secret like the one you're trying to pull off is a whole lot easier to keep as a secret when you learn to keep your voice down."

Soren, Darius, and Sebastian come walking through the open wall each with a different expression on their face. Soren is glaring at Addeah for her comment. Darius is stoic, the ever-faithful soldier, and Sebastian comes waltzing in last with a bowl of pineapple in his hands and a cheesy grin spread across his face when our eyes meet.

"It took you two long enough," Soren growls.

Addeah's not threatened. "Have you seen the before and after images of this girl? You brought her to me dingy, cold, and starved. Speaking of..." Addeah grabs the pineapple from Sebastian's hand and gives it to me. "Eat up, child. When's the last time you ate anything?" Addeah puts the bowl of pineapple in my hand and gestures for me eat. I do so hesitantly, feeling slightly awkward that I'm the only one eating anything at the moment. But the sweet smell alone makes my stomach rumble, so I dutifully nibble on the fruit. With a grin of approval, she turns her attention to the three mermen standing in the room. "Don't any of you understand common courtesy?"

"She's our prisoner—" Soren snaps.

"She's our guest," Addeah retorts. "And one willing to help you out with your little plan you dragged us all into. I suggest you be nice to her."

Soren glares at Addeah before turning his attention toward me. He takes in my hair and my nightgown. That rage in his eyes turns to something else, just for a moment before he blinks it away, turns his heel toward the bedpost, and lays a shoulder on it for support. "So," he looks between Darius and Addeah, "did you fill her in?"

"I figured it'd be best to let you do it since it's your bargain," Addeah speaks.

"Can I just interject here and say how excited I am for this opportunity to be working with each of you on this little scheme you hatched up," Sebastian says enthusiastically. "I haven't had this much excitement since…well never, really."

"I'm sorry, but I would really like to know what's going on here, especially when my freedom's at stake. I don't want to stay here any longer than you want me here," I interject to the four merpeople in front of me. "What did Addeah mean when she said I was going to be royalty? And what am I supposed to steal for you?"

Soren stays leaning against the bedpost, arms crossed over his broad chest. He takes in a deep breath before responding. "You can't be a human down here. If anyone outside this room found out, our entire kingdom could suffer. You would be tried and found guilty and sentenced to your death… or worse. For this…deal to work, we must give you a cover story. You're going to be a princess."

Immediately, Sebastian starts howling hunched over his knees in laughter. "You can't be serious, brother!" He gestures to my face. "Look at her freckles. No one will believe she's a princess. Merpeople don't get freckles. Not that I mind them." Sebastian looks at me with those storm cloud eyes and winks. "I think they're quite attractive."

I can feel my face heat again. The younger brother has no qualms being forward. I quite enjoy it.

Darius chimes in. He's been so silent, and still, I almost forgot he was here. "We've thought of that. King Greyson of the Eastern Seas has many children. Some of which take to land to do his bidding and trading under the guise of being human. No one knows how many children he really has considering he has so many wives. Even with the face markings, the girl can be sold as one of them with proper training and etiquette."

A princess. I'm to pretend to be a princess. That'll go over well. I wasn't even raised to be a proper lady, let alone a lady of noble blood. Papa always said there were more important things than etiquette. I swallow a growing lump in my throat.

"Exactly," Soren speaks. "Being underwater already will help strengthen your cover story. No one will suspect a human could reach the borders of Emora on their own. You'll be able to keep your first name this way and since you're already human, pretending to trade with them will be easiest for you to lie about." Soren pushes off his post and strides toward me. The others look at him with each step he takes. I don't even dare to breathe when he reaches his destination; inches away from my face. He towers over me easily and bores those tropical eyes into my very soul when he says, "As for what you need to steal, I'll tell you when the time comes. For now, you just focus on being the most authentic princess you can be."

He's so close I can feel the warmth of his breath on my nose. Each word sends a puff of spearmint up my nostrils.

"Mercy, brother, intimidate much?" Sebastian chimes in with a cough.

Soren stays right in front of me. "You need to start your training now."

"Oh no, no, no," Addeah butts in. "This girl needs a proper meal and some rest before you run her into the ground. Otherwise, she'll be useless to you."

Soren turns to glare at Addeah again, but she holds her ground.

"It would be wise to have her rest up a bit before we do anything else, prince," Darius speaks. I wonder whose loyalty he puts above all others, his wife or Soren?

Soren's jaw puckers, like his teeth are grinding together. Without so much as a sound, he surrenders and puts some distance between us but continues to radiate anger toward me.

I take a long exhale of air, not realizing until now I'd been holding my breath the entire time.

"Fine," he speaks. "You can rest for a while. Sebastian," Soren barks at his brother, "go fetch her a hot meal. And then tomorrow, *princess*, you hold up your end of the bargain."

Chapter 10

Without another word, Soren exits through the same way they came in followed by Darius and then Sebastian who gives two thumbs up. Then the wall closes, leaving Addeah and me by ourselves in this spacious bedroom.

"I swear Soren can be such a hot head when he doesn't get his way," Addeah mutters. She shakes her head in disapproval. "I promise you, he's not always like that."

"Really?" I ask. "Are you sure he's not a hot head all the time? Because that's the only way I've seen him. It's like he has seaweed up his bum, and it's been itching his crevice all day."

Addeah chortles at my comment. "Oh, child, trust me. If that were truly the case, he'd be in a much fouler mood than you saw him. He's just..." she hesitates, "...he's got a lot on his mind lately. He's next in line for the throne, after all, and with that comes a heavy load to bear and a lot of responsibilities."

So, he isn't just a prince, but he is *the* prince: next-in-line royalty. It also means Sebastian is a prince as well and most likely the younger of the two. How can those two be brothers and have completely different personalities?

Soren told me I'll be disguised as a princess for his plan. He said something will be here in a week's time. Something he doesn't think he can steal on his own. I wonder what I'll have to steal. Is it a creature? Can it move on its own? Is it some other merperson? If Soren stole him or her, would he be the main suspect? Once again, I'm left with more questions than answers.

"You okay?" Addeah asks, concern on her face. "I reckon being in a strange place against your will, finding out whole worlds have existed without your knowing, can be quite a shock to your system."

I look at her, not really knowing what to say. Because this whole thing has been a shock. It's been shocking and terrifying and completely against what I planned out for my life. So, for the moment I don't say anything. I just look at her and nod.

Addeah comes closer to me. Her palms find my back as she leads me to the bed. She sits me down and strokes my hair the way Mama would after a bad dream. "It'll all be okay, dear. Things have a way of working out the way they're supposed to when you have faith they will. And I have faith you were sent here for a reason even though we don't know the why of it all." She takes my shoulders and urges me to rest and close my eyes. "This is a trying time for all, but you need to know I'm on your side and when you're ready to ask questions about me or our people or this place, all you have to do is ask. But for now, get some rest." Gingerly, her fingers pull the sheets from under me before she tucks me into the bed.

Exhaustion washes over me like a tidal wave, and before I know it, I'm drifting off into a deep sleep.

* * *

I'm not sure how long I sleep, but I awake with my heart pounding. It thumps two times harder than it should. It's not until I see a man with storm blue eyes and wavy black hair staring at me from a chair near the entrance of the room, that I realize where I am.

Sebastian is holding a bowl of something warm and steaming. He looks nice sitting there with his black pants tucked into leather boots and a loose shirt to match his eyes. When he notices me staring, he runs a hand through his waves. "Hey, Constance! I was wondering when you would wake up. Been eleven hours straight. You missed breakfast and lunch, but dinner's just around the corner." He gets up from his seated position and walks over, offering me the bowl of food.

I sit up and fold the sheets over my lap. Then I consciously mess with my hair. Do I have bed head? I've never had a man—or merman— in my room alone before. Especially one who acts so casually, like we're old friends ready to laugh about the latest town gossip.

I stare at the bowl and slowly take it from his hands. It smells okay, but I'm not sure what kind of food merpeople eat.

"Don't worry, Freckles, it's clam chowder. Something I'm sure you humans eat a lot of considering it's a human main dish. We aren't as different as you might think." He sits on the end of the bed with his hands folded over his lap, waiting for me to dig in.

I take one more whiff of the soup in front of me before dunking my spoon in and taking a bite. That one bite is all the confirmation I need to devour every last drop of the clam chowder. I even use my tongue to lick out the remnants. Hunger can make you forget your manners.

"Freckles has an appetite!" Sebastian exclaims, looking at me with awe. "Is that how humans eat all the time?"

I look at him sheepishly. "They do when they've been starved for a couple days."

"Awe gee, I'm sorry about that. If it were up to me, I would've never put you in the dungeons in the first place. That place sends chills up my spine." His whole body quivers as though a cold draft were in the room. "Anyways, I'll make sure to bring more before bed." His eyes look away from me right before a knowing smirk creeps up his cheeks. "You know, Constance, we still have our bargain to finish."

I think for a few ticks before remembering we do have a bargain. Three questions for three questions. "Oh right," I say, "I still get one more question."

"What do you mean you have one more question? You already used all three of them. One, you asked why you were rescued just to be locked up. Two, you asked how to escape. And three, you asked why you weren't going to be able to get out of here all on your own." He raised a finger with each question he repeated back to me. He's right. I'd wasted my last question, too focused on trying to figure out how to get out of here.

I narrow my eyes at him, putting my hands up in defeat. "Okay," I begin, "then ask away."

A look of triumph spreads across his face. He falls backward onto the bed arms splayed behind his head, looking up at the ceiling. "Just so we're clear, asking if all humans eat the way you do was a conversational piece, not one of my three questions."

I smirk at his response and oblige before I set the cleanly licked food bowl on the nightstand next to me and tuck my legs up to hug them as I watch Sebastian's unusual behavior. Even Conner back home had more sense of personal space than this and we had been friends since before either of us were walking.

I miss how easy it was to be with Conner. I'd thought that maybe if I had found Papa and righted everything with our family perhaps Conner could be my betrothed. He may not have made my knees weak, and I certainly didn't daydream about him, but he was one of my best friends. Conner clearly loved me. To what extent I'm not sure. But he was kind and caring and loved my family almost as much as I do. He would've been a smart match.

"You know Constance, if I only get three questions, I must make them good. Make them count." Sebastian says, pulling my thoughts away from Conner. He sits up on his elbows and looks at me. "Okay first question, how did you end up here?"

I roll my eyes. "You know how I got here. Darius saved me from the water."

"No, I mean, what got you to board a boat all on your own and sail the ocean blue?"

"I feel like that should count as your second question." Truthfully, I didn't want him to know how much of a coward I was. How selfish I was to leave my mother and our household all because I didn't want to marry a boorish, abusive man. How I was desperately trying to find my father to stop my mother and me from becoming penniless and outcasts of our society.

Sebastian puts his hands together and pushes out a large pouty lip. "Please let it be just one. You're the only human I've ever come across! I need to know!"

I let out a deep sigh as I think of a response. "I set out to look for my father. He's been missing for a few months now, and my mama and I miss him terribly." I decide not to tell him anything else. It's still pieces of the truth, and he doesn't push for more.

"Hmm…" he ponders, "…a woman of action. I like that quite a bit."

I give him a small smile. "What's question number two?"

Before he has a chance to respond, the double entry doors swing wide open. Soren enters in with a plate of food in one hand and the other rests on his hilt. He still looks angry, but his eyebrows furrow in a way that makes me think he's uncertain what he's doing here.

"Hey, brother! Good thing you brought Constance here some more food. She devoured the meal I brought her, but in a very lady-like fashion." Sebastian looks over at me and gives me a wink.

Soren mumbles, "I just figured she'd want more since she missed the first two meals today." He puts the plate of food next to the empty bowl on my nightstand. It looks like fish, bread, and fruit. He also silently pulls a tin of liquid from his belt and places it next to my food.

"Thank you," I direct toward him.

He doesn't respond to me at all. Instead, he barks more orders at his brother. "Sebastian, let's leave the human to her food. You and I have duties to attend to before dinner." Without another word, he walks out just as abruptly as he came in followed by Sebastian.

"I still have two more. Remember that, Freckles," he jokes before closing the door behind him.

Chapter 11

The rest of the night is uneventful. I eat the food Soren had brought and fall asleep tucked under the light pink covers, exhaustion consuming me. It isn't until the following morning that I'm awoken by Addeah. She gently shakes my shoulder.

My eyes are still closed, but something heavenly floats up my nostrils. I blink open my eyes and take a good long stretch.

Addeah stands next to the bedside with breakfast and some kind of fruit juice. I take the drink with both hands, nodding my thanks before washing it down in one gulp. *Note to self, drink more water.*

"Good morning, Constance." She holds out her hand to take the empty glass.

"Good morning, Addeah."

She smiles at me and hands me a heaping plate of breakfast food. It all looks so…normal. Eggs, bacon, toast, and some kind of biscuits with jam. It makes me wonder. "Addeah? Are there chickens and pigs under the sea?"

She chuckles a little. "Heavens no, child. We have special merfolk that go to the surface and do some undercover trading with your people." I take small bites of food and listen attentively as she continues. "And for your knowledge, not all the eggs we serve will be from chickens, but it looks like someone went out of their way this morning to make you feel at home." She gives me a knowing look, winking at me before walking toward the closet.

I wonder who would have gone to the trouble to make me feel at ease with the food here. My options are limited. Addeah didn't do it or else she would have said so. Certainly it wasn't Soren, that was a laughable thought. There's either Darius or Sebastian, both of whom have tried to be at least friendly with me. I have the smallest hope in the pit of my stomach that it was Sebastian.

I stab at the eggs and am pleasantly surprised. They taste as though they've been mixed in with cinnamon and honey, a comforting and warm experience for my taste buds. They are the sweetest, most delightful eggs I've ever had the pleasure of eating. It takes no time at all to devour the rest.

After swallowing my last bite of breakfast, Addeah sends me to the vanity to get ready for the morning. She tells me Soren has instructed her to make me "princess presentable" every morning until our deal is complete.

I sit crossing my legs at the ankles, facing the vanity mirror while Addeah runs her fingers through my hair and recreates some of the curls on the ends.

"The key is to never use a brush unless it's right after your bath. Otherwise your curls become frizzy puff balls."

It baffles me how easy it is for her to run her fingers through my mane even after a long night of deep sleep. Less than two minutes and my hair looks just as good as it did last night. Only today, instead of wearing it completely down, Addeah picks out a pearl barrette and gathers half of my hair, securing it at the back of my head. She then pulls out just a few baby curls to frame my face.

Next Addeah moves on to my face. She mentions something about forgoing foundation and opts for some creamy blush. "The color is made from our very own berries we grow in the castle gardens." She places two fingertips in the berry-colored cream and dabs it across my cheeks, looking from side to side to make sure one cheek looks proportional to the other. She finishes off the look with a small smudge of kohl on each eyelid, making the color of my sea-foam green eyes pop.

We move on to dressing me for the day. The fabric is teal blue, like the ocean near a coral reef. It's just as soft and flowy as my night gown, but hugs at the right places, showing off my figure without showing too much. The biggest advantage to this dress? I can easily breathe in it. No corsets here!

Addeah wordlessly laces up the back and my mind begins to whirl with all the questions I still have about her and this place. "Addeah?" I ask hesitantly.

"Hmm?"

"How come, you, I mean, merpeople, don't live in the water? I always thought you had, well, fishtails and searched for shiny things in the ocean. At least those were the sort of stories my papa told me." I stare straight ahead.

She laughs. "Well, some of our kind in other regions of the world *do* grow tails when they dive into the water, but for our kind here in Emora, we prefer to stay dry and not grow slimy with algae." Her shoulders shake at the thought as if a spider had just crawled on her back. "Think of us more like amphibians and less like fish. We have gills, but we also have lungs. It depends on what our body needs at the time. Does that answer suffice?"

"More than enough," I smile.

She finishes my princess transformation with a set of rose-colored heels, which are surprisingly comfortable.

"My, my, my," Addeah begins, "I believe we found ourselves a bona fide princess."

Just then, three knocks sound at the door. In walks Darius in full uniform. He strides up to me and bows, giving me a smile that reaches his eyes. Then he turns to his wife, and they share a whisper of a kiss.

"Hello, my darling," he speaks.

"Doesn't Constance look divine? I would say I'm a miracle worker, but she requires very little work to look royal," Addeah comments, giving me a side wink.

Darius turns his attention back to me. "You look regal, Miss Constance. Today we will stay in here and work on your back story before presenting you tonight."

I dart my eyes between the two of them. "Present me?" I ask.

"Yes, Miss Constance. At dinner, you will be presented to the Royal Court."

Chapter 12

I take a deep breath and exhale as slowly as I can. Then I do it again. Darius offers me an arm before we exit through my bedroom's double door entrance.

I am Princess Constance of the Eastern Seas, daughter of King Greyson of the Eastern Seas. I repeat this introduction in my head over and over as the double doors swing open inviting more waves of anxiety to crash over me. *I am Princess Constance of the Eastern Seas, daughter of King Greyson of the Eastern Seas.*

Darius must feel my hand tighten around his bicep because he looks down at me and gives me a single reassuring nod before leading me out into the hallway toward our destination.

The hall is splendid. The ceiling must be thirty feet high. The floor is an exquisite shade of shimmering ivory laced with lines of ebony. The walls have lanterns nestled in simple white sconces every twenty paces. Pillars, like the ones outside the castle, line the hallways with greenery coiling up each one in a warm embrace.

Darius and I take a few right turns and end up at another set of double doors. These ones are even larger than my bedroom's. We stop. He glances side to side, making sure no one else is around. He turns his attention forward at the doors while he speaks. "Remember your title, princess. The hardest part of this whole thing is convincing other royalty who you are. This is a test run. It's only family for dinner tonight. Prince Soren and Prince Sebastian will be in there, but Princess Lamia will also be joining them for dinner. She's who you'll have to convince." He takes a moment to ponder how to word what he tells me next. "Don't…don't let her intimidate you." And without another word, the doors open for my first test.

Soren and Sebastian are already sitting at the giant dinner table. It must fit at least fifty people. Both look pristine in their dinner attire. Soren's wearing a navy blue blouse with gold embroidery accentuating his broad chest and matching gold cuff links. Sebastian opted for something simpler. A black shirt with buttons trailing down the middle and a small ruffle of fabric running down each side.

They sit on the far end talking quietly with each other until they see Darius and me come in. Each prince notices my entrance simultaneously, their reactions practically opposite of each other's. Sebastian's eyes widen, looking at me from head to toe in my teal dress. He smiles and waves us over. Soren on the other hand never takes his eyes off my face, one hand tensing into a fist, the other lying flat on the table. *How could he hate me so much? Just because I'm human? It wouldn't kill him to at least* pretend *he's grateful for the help I'm giving him.*

Darius walks me all the way to the two awaiting princes.

Sebastian's the first to stand up. He quickly walks around the head of the table to the opposite side of them and pulls out a chair for me. I nod in thanks and give him a small smile before I gradually lower myself into the seat. He pushes me closer to the table before running back to the other side and sitting down next to his brother.

Soren is still tense as he opens his mouth, but before he can say anything the doors to the dining hall fly open. A mermaid struts in, hips swaying with each step. I let my mouth drop slightly before remembering I'm supposed to be a princess. I'm pretty sure princesses aren't supposed to gawk at others, so I quickly gain my composure as I take in this confident female.

Her dress is a champagne color that cuts into a deep v below her neckline. She's gorgeous to be sure. Probably one of the most beautiful creatures I've ever seen. Thick and straight teal blue hair cascades well below her belly button. Her large lips are tinted red, a stark contrast to her porcelain skin. Unsettling bright blue eyes pin me with a fleeting look before she turns her attention to her seat. If this is how a princess should look, I'm certain I don't I fit the criteria.

I almost stand up out of respect for this princess but then remember royalty doesn't stand for royalty unless it's a king or queen, one of the tidbits Darius and Addeah had taught me before coming here tonight.

This time Soren gets up and strides over to the beautiful female. He bows and gives a swift kiss to her hand. She in turn gives Soren a peck on his cheek before he leads her to the seat next to mine and sits her down.

When Darius told me this person, Lamia, was joining us for dinner, I had assumed it was a sister. But she looks nothing like the princes, and I don't believe brothers and sisters kiss. So, how's she family?

Once seated, Lamia turns her head to look at me with those pale blue eyes; judging the mediocrity of my attire in comparison to her own. One eyebrow rises in confusion. "And you are?" she questions.

I plaster on my most pleasant smile. "Good evening," I nod. "My name is Princess Constance of the Eastern Seas, daughter of King Greyson of the Eastern Seas." I repeat it out loud just as I had practiced.

Lamia doesn't look impressed. She turns her attention to the princes. "Soren?" she questions. "Who is this, and why is she here?"

Soren looks at her with an expressionless face. "This is Princess Constance, like she said. She's here for the festivities in a few days."

"Very well, but why is she here? At dinner?" Lamia accuses.

My leg bounces rapidly, trying to contain my nerves. Has she already seen through our ruse? Does she already know I'm not a princess but an impostor just by the single sentence I exchanged? *Oh, good acting, Constance, very good indeed.*

"Be nice, Lamia," Sebastian interjects. "It's fine to have a guest at dinner every now and then." He puts his feet on the table and lounges with his hands woven behind his head. "Besides, it will be refreshing to have someone with an entire brain to talk to instead of your half-wit one."

She isn't deterred. "I wasn't addressing you," Lamia spits, "Soren, why is she having dinner when it's family only?"

Soren rubs his temple before answering. "She's our guest. She arrived early because of the way her trade routes lined up, and we are obliged to be excellent hosts." He stares at Lamia with those expressionless eyes, daring her to question him again.

She looks at him. Then looks at me before plastering a fake smile on her crimson lips.

"I'm Princess Lamia of Andwera, Soren's betrothed." Lamia says *betrothed* like she owns Soren.

So *that's* why she's here. She's supposed to marry Soren.

Just then, a kitchen door swings open from the side of the room and out comes a line of servants with silver serving platters in hand. Like a dance, they walk in sync to each of our empty place mats and set the platters down to reveal our meal.

It looks like some kind of fish on a bed of seaweed sided with some kind of weird gelatin. The others pick up their fork and knife and begin eating. I try to follow suit by slicing through the fish first. Luckily it tastes okay, and I continue eating with the rest.

"I picked out flowers today for our royal wedding," Lamia says between bites, trying to address Soren. "They're mostly blue with blush accents. I think it'll really complement our eyes."

Sebastian answers instead. He splays his hand across his heart in mock feeling. "That's so lovely you thought of me when you picked out your wedding flowers."

Lamia rolls her eyes in return, clearly unamused by his joke.

I pretend to be interested in my mystery gelatin next taking a small bite and instantly regretting it. The mystery gelatin is salty and bitter. It's one of the grossest things I've ever tasted in my life. I cough as I try to choke it down with much effort. Then I take my glass of water and gulp it down as elegantly as I can knowing full well that all eyes are on me as I nearly choke on this disgusting food.

Once my humiliating near death experience is over, I mumble a small apology.

"I'm glad you found flowers to suite you, Lamia," Soren speaks taking the attention away from me. He then continues to gobble down his food.

"Yes!" She beams forgetting all about me again. "And I was hoping you would join me some time before the ball next week to look at rings."

Soren is more enthusiastic about finishing his meal than conversing with Lamia. I wonder if it was his choice to marry her or some kind of business arrangement like Mama tried with me. "We shall see," he says before finishing his last bite of food and standing up from the table. "There's much work to do before the ball. I must assign the guards their duties during the event, finalize the menu with the head chef, work with the housekeeper to ensure every guest will be roomed appropriately for the event, and that's just the surface."

Lamia puts down her silverware. "I understand, but we also get married in less than three months."

Soren works his way over to a pouty Lamia and grabs her hand. "We'll see, princess. If you'll excuse me, I have important matters to attend to tonight." The prince gives his princess a swift kiss on top of her hand and strides toward the kitchen doors.

I wonder why he didn't go out the double doors like Lamia and I did. Maybe he didn't like the food and was going in to complain. I know for certain I'll never be eating that nasty gelatin again.

Sebastian continues eating.

Lamia stares longingly after Soren, before she turns to me.

"So, Cadence, why have I not heard about you before?"

Sebastian looks up mid-bite at the exchange.

"First off, it's Constance. And I do a lot of traveling." That was part of my cover story, the reason I'm a mermaid with freckles. I travel and trade for my father, King Greyson, under the guise of being human. Apparently, King Greyson has many children, many of whom he doesn't even announce to the public because he wants his children to live the lives they choose without the pressures that royalty brings. He sounds like a fair king from what Darius and Addeah taught me. So here I am, an unannounced princess who chose to trade with humans unbeknownst to them. Merpeople "like me" are the reason certain foods and plants exist under the ocean, making life for merpeople more pleasant and varied. At least that's the story I must convince others to believe.

"What kind of traveling do you do?" She gives me an accusatory glare before taking a long sip of her drink. "I know almost every princess in the five oceans, and yet here you are, days early to an event, where I don't even recall your name being on the guest list."

Don't be intimated by her. That's what Darius said. So I look at Lamia, trying to mimic her demeanor. "Like I said, I do a lot of traveling. I wasn't sure I was going to make it until yesterday. I'm sure if you checked that invitation list again, my name would be on it."

"Hmm…" she speaks, thinking about my answer, trying to solve me like a puzzle that is missing pieces. Then she plasters on that big fake smile again. "Well, *Cadence*, I'm sure you and I will become the best of friends in the next few days."

Lucky me.

Chapter 13

After dinner, I excuse myself from Sebastian and Lamia's company and decide to do a little exploring of the castle. Or at least, all the places I'm allowed to explore. Apparently, Soren ordered Darius and Addeah to be explicitly detailed on the halls I'm allowed to walk in by myself. But I don't mind too much. After all, how many humans can say they've wandered around a mermaid castle? I take a left from the dining hall doors and pass a few guards walking by, probably making their rounds and checking for anything suspicious.

I do my best to not look suspicious and give them a slight nod and curtsy before walking past them. One guard turns around to look after me before resuming his walk with the other guard. Perhaps curtsying to guards is not princess-like? I'll have to ask Addeah about that later. Oh well. Being courteous to others is never a bad thing, so I think nothing else of it and continue my stroll, looking around at every painting and piece of decor displayed on the walls. I turn another corner.

That's when I see it. A stunning painting of a family. A king, with tropical eyes, smiles, showing off perfect white teeth. Under his crown is a splatter of peppered hair that goes down to his shoulders. He's holding a young boy with a matching set of eyes. The boy couldn't be much older than five or six. He too looks happy in his royal blue shirt and tan vest. The boy's arms wrap around the king's neck lovingly.

Next to them is a woman holding an even smaller boy, no more than three. The woman is striking. She's wearing a lavender dress with a gold and pearl necklace that accentuates her long, elegant neck. Her hair's dark brown and wavy, cascading down to her hips. But her eyes are what captures my attention. They're light brown and warm. So warm I feel as though I should reach out and hug her myself.

Sharp stilettos smack the ground and echo down the hall, so I peer back the way I came to see who is strutting toward me. It's Lamia. She's asking the guards I just passed a question. I hear my name spoken before she continues in my direction.

Please not now. I don't want to be cornered by her and have any resemblance of a conversation. Who knows what kind of questions she'll ask me if it's just the two of us without the princes to act as a buffer. I've only had one day of training to be a princess, and she's had her whole life. One wrong move, and I'll be found out and ruin everything.

I want to run, but I also know my own heels will make noise as well, and she'll know I'm trying to avoid her if she hears me running in the other direction.

I search around the hallway to see if there is any door I can get to or something to shuffle my body behind until she passes me. That's when I notice some golden drapes near the painting and hide behind it. I try to quiet my breathing so she can't hear me. My back is as close to the wall as it possibly can be, and I decide to raise myself as far on my tip toes as I can to keep my heels from poking out of the bottom of the drape.

Lamia's sharp heels grow louder and louder the closer she gets, until I can hear them stomping right in front of my hiding place. Suddenly they stop and the hall is silent.

Breathe quietly. Breathe quietly, and she will go away. Seconds feel like minutes while Lamia has stopped. I wonder if she knows I'm here or perhaps she too is admiring the painting. I hope for the latter.

Then, as quickly as she'd appeared, she's gone. The *click clack* of stilettos grows quieter and quieter with each step she takes.

I let out a deep breath and try to push off the wall. That's when I hear a strange click. Instead of moving forward my body's thrown back onto dirty ground. The hiding place I was in moments ago is now gone, behind a closed door. I stand up and rake my hands over the stone wall, searching for a trigger to open the secret entry I accidentally fell through.

After minutes of searching for a way back into the hall, I huff. There isn't any clear way to get back to the other side. At least not one I can find. I can't believe I fell through a door. I turn around and look at the dimly lit passageway. Only a few candles are lit every fifty yards or so. *At least there's some sort of light this time*, I think. Chills run up my arms, and I must rub them away with my hands.

There are two ways to go. But which one will be easier to find my way out? The dining hall is probably to the right. I was walking to the left before I hid from Lamia. Eenie-meenie… left it is.

I'll admit, it's not ideal walking in a creepy secret passage by yourself, not knowing how to get out and only being able to see a few feet in front of you. No. It isn't ideal at all. But I try to remain calm. Eventually, someone will know I'm missing if I can't find a way out myself. Besides, how many halls can a secret passageway have anyway?

A lot, apparently. Secret passageways have a lot of halls and turns to choose from. I must be walking for thirty minutes before I see a light in front of me. It's not a light coming from the lanterns, but some kind of small hole in the stone wall. I race up to it trying to see if there's anyone or anything I can see that will help me. The hole is partially covered by a piece of metal. I reach up and rotate the rest of the metal to get a clearer view of the hole.

Even with heels on, I have to get on my tip toes to look through it. What I see is startling. My body instinctively hides away from the hole, drawing back against the stone wall. I clasp my hand over my mouth to keep my gasp of shock from echoing off the walls.

It's not what I ever thought I would see. It couldn't be. Ever so slowly, I creep back up to the hole and take a second look.

It's Soren. But it's not just Soren. He's seated on the edge of a bed covered in purple and gold sheets with drapes to match on each bed post. In his hand is a bowl of some kind of soup and a spoon.

Laying in the bed's an old man. His hair's almost completely gray, with just a few strands of black sprinkled here and there. His fingers tremble as he tries to take the spoon from Soren, but Soren refuses to let go and offers to feed him instead. Eventually the old man accepts Soren is going to feed him and lets him ease the spoon into his mouth before giving him a loving smile. Those frail fingers come up to cup Soren's cheek.

"So," the old man croaks. "What's this I hear of an unannounced guest?"

Unannounced guest? Is the old man talking about me?

I strain to hear Soren's response, but he speaks so low I can only make out a few syllables.

"Well, my dear boy, don't be too hasty. All things happen for a reason. Let time unfold your questions and troubles."

Soren stops feeding the old man for a moment and smiles at him. He actually smiles, a brilliant, toothy smile. I wouldn't have believed it if I hadn't seen it for myself.

Suddenly the hairs on my neck prick up in warning. Someone, or something, is watching me.

"You're not supposed to be here."

Chapter 14

I whirl around ready to throw a punch when Sebastian grabs my wrist with one hand, putting the other hand up in surrender.

He keels over in silent laughter.

"That's *not* funny," I hiss, smacking his shoulder.

"I know, I know, I'm sorry," he whispers between those silent snickers. His hands raise up as if he knows I want to smack him again. "You know, you kind of deserve it, for spying and all."

He had me there. In my defense, I didn't intend to spy on Soren. It just sort of happened.

"Hey, how did you know I was in here?" I ask, careful to keep my voice low enough to not be heard through the walls.

"I didn't, as a matter of fact. My real purpose for being here is the simple fact I'm hiding from her royal pain in my rump." Sebastian runs his fingers through his hair. "I swear she thinks she runs this kingdom already. They're not married yet, for crying out loud."

So, both of us are inside the walls because we were trying to hide from Lamia. I smile at the thought.

"Well, in my defense," I start, "I didn't actually mean to be here in the first place. I too was hiding from Lamia when I stumbled across the hidden passageways and literally fell on my back side on the way in. I've been trying to find my way out for over thirty minutes."

Sebastian stifles another laugh. "No wonder your back side is covered in dirt, not that I was admiring too long." He winks at me, making me blush yet again. This prince has no restraint on his tongue.

I turn to look at the back side of my dress and true enough, there's dirt tainting the teal blue fabric from my shoulder blades all the way down to the hem. "Just wonderful; very royal of me," I say in irritation.

"Don't fret. It's okay. I actually thought you did great at dinner tonight," he pauses thinking for a moment, "except when you almost choked on the eel gelatin. That was just hilarious."

So that's what it was. If I never have to eat eel gelatin again, it still won't be long enough to get that nasty taste out of my mouth.

"But in all seriousness," Sebastian speaks, "Lamia's not easy to fool, and you didn't back down from her. The way you looked her straight in the eyes all calm and composed— that was exactly how a princess would act."

"Thanks," I say. At least he thinks I did a good job of convincing her. Who knows what anyone else will think if they see me all dirty like this though. "Do you think we can we get out of here now? Maybe a way that's right back to my room so no one sees how dirty I got in here?"

Sebastian looks at the hole I was peeping through before taking that metal piece and completely covering the light coming from the room. "I would, but these specific passages don't connect with the ones to your room." He thinks for a second before taking my hand in his, leaving my cheeks burning. I think he just likes seeing me flustered. "Come on," he says, "I know a way out where we can almost certainly not run into anyone."

He walks me through the dark passages taking multiple turns. I try to memorize them but eventually give up. These passages are confusing.

Next thing I know, Sebastian stops at one of the walls. It looks exactly the same as every other wall in here, so I'm not sure how he came to this one. But then, he pushes in a single stone and poof. Like magic, we are no longer in darkness, but standing between two shelves lined from end to end and top to bottom with books.

"Welcome to the library, Princess Constance." Sebastian lets go of my hand and closes the door to the secret passageway.

The library's already my favorite part of the castle so far. It smells like a warm, rainy day mixed with ink. I feel the sudden urge to snuggle up under a blanket, pick out one of these books, and read all day in a cozy nook.

We walk out of the stack of books to reveal a dome shaped ceiling and more books than I could ever have imagined. Rows of books cover the walls. There are two stories worth. To my left I notice a double staircase in the shape of a U leading to a second level.

Scattered across the floor are couches and chairs. Some are by themselves. Others are set in small groups. Not a single space is occupied. No one's in here, it seems. The library's just as deserted as the secret passageways.

"It's marvelous, isn't it?" Sebastian says when he notices me taking it all in. "A lifetime of knowledge right at our fingertips. All the knowledge you could ever want… or most of it anyways." His hands go into his pockets as he too looks around the library.

"It really is beautiful," I respond. "I've always loved books."

He looks back down at me, contemplative. Then his eyes grow serious and his smile fades to a frown. "Constance, you have to promise me you won't tell anyone what you saw back there."

"Do you mean your brother and the older gentleman in bed?"

"Yes."

It was hard to imagine Soren being so kind to anyone. It makes me wonder who the old man was. Curiosity gets the best of me, so I ask, "Do you mind if I ask you who that man was and why your brother was feeding him?" Sebastian looks as though he may not answer me, so I add, "It's just easier to keep a secret when I know why it's important to keep."

He looks at me, contemplative, before he answers. "That merman," he begins, "isn't just any merman. He's the king. King Cyrus of Emora. Soren's and my father."

"Oh." I think back to the painting of the family. The king with salt and pepper hair.

"He's sick. He isn't doing very well. If anyone, I mean anyone found out that he's not fit to rule before Soren's coronation... well let's just say it would be devastating for our entire kingdom."

"That's why he wasn't at family dinner?" I inquire.

"Yes. Occasionally, he can get out of his room, but more and more often he's bedridden." His eyes search mine before he says what he wants to say next. "I just don't how much longer he's going to last in his condition."

I nod in understanding. The information regarding their father is private. I can keep it secret which I convey to Sebastian before he wordlessly offers me an arm and we sneak out of the library.

He walks me to my room. We only have to dodge a single set of guards on the way there. Not that we are doing anything wrong. I just don't want anyone to see how filthy I have become. It could ruin my cover story.

"Well, my sweet Constance," he begins, "It was an unforgettable adventure tonight with you."

I tuck my hair behind my ear. "Likewise."

Sebastian takes my hand and gives it the slightest kiss before opening the door for me and turning to leave. I look after him as he walks away from my bedroom. He turns once and gives me a grin from ear to ear. My cheeks brighten before waltzing into the room for the night.

Chapter 15

That night, Addeah was waiting for me. Her eyes bulged when she saw how dirty I was and immediately threw me into a bath before putting me to bed.

It's been a couple days since then, but each morning, I wake up with a new sort of energy. I touch my hand where Sebastian pressed his lips and grin. I may be here against my will, but at least the company's good. Well, most of the company.

Practically every waking moment, Addeah teaches me how to properly carry myself for the upcoming ball. She taught me how to enter the ballroom, who I should know to be friendly with and who I should avoid, and what topics of conversation are appropriate.

It's been a bit overwhelming if I'm being honest; particularly trying to remember all the names and faces of the other guests.

Today's lesson is dancing. Darius is with us today and has agreed to be my partner. Maybe it's his military training, but he's surprisingly light on his feet.

We go through dance after dance all morning. I count the steps and feel the rhythm of the music as Darius twirls me around. Some are slow and intimate. I can't help but imagine dancing to these songs with Sebastian.

Apparently, he and Soren have been desperately preparing to host the hundreds of guests from the different kingdoms for this ball.

According to my studies, there are five ocean kingdoms in total. One is the Eastern Sea Kingdom where my alias originates from. It's west of Ohani Island and probably has the largest expanse of territory.

Then there's Andwera, Lamia's home up north. Apart from Emora, Andwera has the strongest battalion.

Third is Meridwen. Addeah warned it's a rotten kingdom full of thugs and crooks. Most of the merfolk I'm to avoid hail from Meridwen.

Indolia's on the opposite side of the Earth and for the most part, governs itself.

Then there's Emora. The head of the oceans, where the one true king always resides. At the moment, the one true king is King Cyrus; Soren and Sebastian's father. One day, it'll become Soren's responsibility to lead the five oceans.

Addeah informed me this particular ball only happens once a year. It's to celebrate the upcoming summer harvest as well as strengthen the bonds between kingdoms. Many rulers bring their children that have come of age to this event in hopes of finding an alliance with another kingdom for future peace.

I had asked her if my "father" was going to attend. She told me no. He was the type of ruler who allowed his children to do what they want. Some of his children may come, but it should be easy to avoid them in such a large crowd. I have their names and faces memorized; at least the ones known to the public.

Once my feet ache and sweat drips down the bridge of my nose, I ask Addeah if I can have a break and take a walk around the castle.

She gives me a look like I'd lost my mind. "Last time you were left to wander the castle you ended up looking like a scullery maid with dirt from your nose to your toes."

I put my hands together in a promise. "I admit that was not my best moment, but I promise you I will not sully myself or my dress like that again."

She side-eyes her husband who also has broken a sweat. "I'll take her around myself. There are some things I need to oversee. She can join me on my rounds." He waves in my direction as he takes a seat near the door.

I look at Darius, then at her, giving my best innocent smile.

"Fine, but we need to get you cleaned up and changed again before you head out of this room. No princess walks out all sweaty and smelly."

"I'm not smelly," I contradict.

"But you will be soon if you leave that sweaty dress on," Addeah retorts. "Get back in the bathroom and wash off. I'll pick out a dress for you to stroll the halls."

I do as Addeah says. She strides to the closet to pick out an afternoon dress for me while I close the bathroom door, strip off my sticky clothes, pull my hair up into a messy bun on the top of my head, and hop into the giant bath.

The warmth feels so good on my aching feet. Since being here, I've looked forward to getting into this bath every time I'm asked to do so, which is a lot because "princesses are supposed to be the epitome of clean," as Addeah puts it.

Today I've chosen guava and water lilies to scrub with as I look out into the city. It seems so peaceful out there. I wish I could explore the outdoors too, but Darius told me he was under strict orders to keep me in the castle. I'm not sure why. It's not like I'm dangerous or planning to escape. Like I could escape by myself anyway.

My thoughts go back to that cave under the waterfall. It was so cold in there if I'd stayed long enough, I probably could've caught hypothermia. Just the thought of going in that water raises goosebumps on my neck.

I think of Papa and Mama and I long to get out of here, to see them both again. I'm just not sure how it's going to happen yet.

While I'm busy thinking of what I need to do to get out of here, Addeah raps on the door. She mentions that Darius is on a schedule and must leave soon. There's no way she'll let me out of this room without him, so I hurry up, scrubbing every nook and cranny and jump out so Addeah can dress me.

She's opted for a dark rose colored dress with tiny gold trim dancing along the side seams. It's simple enough for a stroll around the castle but looks very royal. Then she chooses to braid my hair and let it hang over my shoulder before pinning a couple small rose pins near my ear.

The shoes are matching flats designed for long walks. She puts each one on before shooing me out the door where Darius awaits.

"Honey, don't you dare let her get dirty before dinner tonight," Addeah warns.

Darius looks at her amused before placing a delicate kiss on his wife's lips. "I wouldn't dream of it, my dear." He offers up his arm before we stroll toward whatever duties await him.

Our first stop is in the armory. As captain of the guard, Darius informs me he's responsible for checking on everyone else's duties.

An older soldier sits in front of the armory. One of his legs is missing and is replaced with a peg. Scruffy white facial hair covers the lower half of his face. In his hands appears to be a long list. When he notices Darius and me approaching, he straightens up in his chair and puts four fingers over his heart in salute to the captain.

"At ease, Jed. How do you find yourself today?" Darius asks, reaching his free hand out to the older gentleman.

"As good as any other day, Captain," Jed responds while handing over the list. I can't tell if the rasp of his voice is from his clearly ripened age or from smoking too many cigars as pineapple and smoke hits me, invading my nose the moment we get too close to the fellow. "Who do you have here? I know your wife, and this isn't her." The old soldier looks at me with furrowed brows, his white scruffy beard shifting into a frown.

Darius gestures to me with one hand as he reads through the first page. "This is the lovely Princess Constance of the Eastern Seas. She's here for the festivities in two nights time."

Jed gives me a wide grin showing off a set of chompers with one front tooth missing. "Pleasure to meet you, princess. Must be a real treasure for the heir to have his most trusted soldier looking after you."

"Thank you," I say to Jed's supposed compliment, but in my head, I think I'm quite the opposite. Soren doesn't see me as a treasure, but as a threat. No wonder he has Darius and his wife keep me close to them the majority of the day.

Darius finishes checking the list and then moves on to counting items in their arsenal. Writing down numbers as he goes further and further into the inventory room.

I choose to take a seat next to Jed and his eyes perk up.

"Never have I had the honor of having the company of a princess during my duties." Jed says, gawking at me like he can't believe I would just sit down next to a commoner.

Little does he know we are both commoners, me probably more so in the eyes of the merfolk here, but I don't want to spoil the moment for him— or blow my cover. So instead, I grin back and reply, "No, Jed, the pleasure is all mine. Tell me, what's it like working for King Cyrus?"

I can tell from the corner of my eye that Darius is listening intently, if not pretending to continue his counting of shields. I think my question is innocent enough, but maybe Darius thinks I'm prying.

Jed can't believe I asked him either. At first, he doesn't respond. He just looks at me in awe. Seconds tick by before he answers. "Well, Princess Constance, working for King Cyrus is the best thing I ever did."

Darius must feel that his answer is good enough to leave us alone because he turns his head and walks away from us to count some spear-like weapons.

Jed recounts tales to me of when he went to war for the Kingdom of Emora. How he fought with brothers in arms for the merfolk, how he lost his tooth and his leg, and another time when he almost lost an arm.

I listen actively and diligently to him as he goes from story to story until Darius is finished counting.

"Alright, soldier, that's enough. I'm sure the princess can only take so much story time in one sitting." Darius hands Jed the papers he was jotting notes on and crosses his arms. "Everything appears to be in order apart from one stiletto dagger. Know anything about that, soldier?"

Jed takes the papers and looks through the numbers again. "Huh, not that I can recall. No one's signed for any stilettos that I can remember." His brows furrow, confused by the missing weaponry. "I'll be on the lookout for it, Captain," he says, scratching his white, scruffy beard.

"Do so with haste, soldier. We need to keep everything accounted for," Darius replies, offering me his hand to stand up.

Before I take it, I stand up and look at Jed. "Thank you for entertaining me with your stories. I should like to hear more adventures in the future." I mean what I tell him, even though I'm not sure if I will ever see him again. Then I loop my arm through Darius' and we walk off to the next task at hand.

Within the next couple of hours, Darius and I talk to all the soldiers who will be on patrol during the ball the next couple of days, check each exit of the castle to ensure its security, and have lunch together in the servants' quarters.

It feels nice to be so active even when the bottoms of my feet begin to ache. No doubt they'd grown used to being lazy down in the dungeons and then again in my room. But this day is good for them and good for me too. It's nice seeing all the different parts of the castle. There are a multitude of turns and twists that lead to different wings in the castle. It would be so easy to get turned around in here. It's interesting watching so many soldiers diligently patrol the halls. Servants of every shape and size scatter about, attentively cleaning every nook and cranny in the castle.

I receive some strange looks from some of the servants as we enter their domain. Probably wondering what a princess is doing in the servants' quarters I imagine, but Darius acts as though none of their stares concern him, so I try to as well.

A princess would probably act like they weren't here at all from what Darius and Addeah have been teaching me about proper princess mannerisms, but there's no way I can do that completely. So I opt for something in between; passing smiles and light nods to anyone who dares to look too long at the misplaced princess. Friendly, but not overly friendly. That's the key, I believe.

Darius is polite to everyone we come across. The soldiers and guards clearly respect him. He knows each one by name and rank. The kitchen staff give him an extra bowl of soup and bread, thanking him for his service. He knows most of them by name as well when he told them how delicious lunch was. Overall, Darius seems like the nicest, most loyal captain a prince could hope for.

The last piece of our agenda Darius tells me is to oversee the royal training. He leads me into a hall and up some narrow stairs. What lay before us is something I do not expect.

Twenty yards below us an arena is displayed in a grandeur fashion. The middle is a grid made up of bobbing sparring platforms surrounded by what looks to be very deep and very cold water.

My eyes focus on the mats. Soaring above them is a giant stream of water, like a wave from the ocean jumping out of nowhere before crashing down. Wave after wave pounces on the platform and rolls back into the water grid until suddenly it stops like a rain shower pouring down without a cloud in sight. It doesn't make sense.

Without the continuous crashing of water, I see two mermen standing on the soaked platforms.

Dead center in the arena is Soren and Sebastian sparring…shirtless. Sebastian is dripping from head to toe in water as he tries to catch his breath. One knee is down on the mat. One hand is bracing his leg while he struggles to stand straight up. He's heavily panting like he's just finished a sprinting match. Water and no doubt sweat trickle down the tips of his curls and onto his nicely shaped, lean torso.

My cheeks burn at the awareness. Here I am standing next to the captain of the guard who is responsible for serving these two princes, and I am ogling over the younger brother as he dances and dodges his brother's advances. *Think of anything else, Constance. Look at anything else.* I pry my eyes away from Sebastian. Surely, the human-hating, solemn Soren won't have the same effect on me as Sebastian does.

I look at Soren and instantly regret it. *Wrong move. Clearly and most notedly the wrong move.* If Sebastian was a lean, trim fox, then Soren was… well I didn't even know. It's like his body is solid rock chiseled from the strongest waters. It's unfortunate his exterior resembles chiseled perfection, yet his disposition is as cantankerous as they come. He isn't nearly as drenched as his leaner, smaller brother, but sweat still slides down his muscular biceps with each liquid movement. Suddenly I'm looking around trying to find anything more interesting to look at than the two princes. But I can't help it. No matter how hard I try, my eyes refuse to look away from the undeniably attractive mermen before me.

"Ahem," Darius coughs slightly, relieving me from my trance. He puts his hands over the railing and looks down at the two mermen. "I'm sure you're curious about how they do that, since I am certain no human can move water in such a manner. Correct?"

My first instinct is to reply *"what"* until I look closer at the scene before me. Darius is right. The water isn't being moved by some hose or bucket. It is being summoned by the princes. When they are going head-to-head with fists and kicks, the water remains calm, like a pond with nowhere to go.

It isn't until Soren plants his feet firmly on the wobbly platform and presses his palms flat into the air that the water erupts from its slumber, towering over Sebastian. Soren moves one hand down in a forceful motion, sending water collapsing onto his crouching brother. *How did he do that?*

When the water subsides and Sebastian is back on his feet, he repeats a similar motion. Water yet again rises from the streams around them and flies straight toward Soren. This wave of water isn't nearly as large or fast as the one Soren conjured. Soren easily dodges the attack by jumping onto one of the adjacent platforms.

"How do they do that?" I turn to face Darius who looks at me with a small glimmer in his eye.

"They are royal heirs. Their father is not only King of Emora but King of the Seas and with it comes the power to control the seemingly uncontrollable. The blood of royalty has the power to move the waters of the sea to do their will."

"Oh." Dread dawns on me. "Does that mean I have to figure out how to move water? Because let's be plain-spoken and agree it will be impossible for me. I can't convince anyone I'm royalty if that is the standard." Panic begins to inch its way up my belly and into my throat until Darius' firm hand lands on my shoulder.

"Princess, you will never be asked to do such a thing. Besides, my heir and my prince are exceptionally talented because of who their father is. Other royals have merely an inkling of what they possess. Many don't have the capability at all. Don't fret."

Darius is so kind. I don't feel I've ever met someone with such a fatherly presence like that of my own Papa's. I place my measurably smaller hand on his and give him a thankful grin, before we both turn our attention back to the match.

Sebastian is on his back, hands in the air in surrender. Soren towers over him with a fist in the air and water dangling at his side, ready for the finishing blow. He stares down at his pleading brother before taking an exasperated sigh and lowering his fist. Next, he reaches down to grab Sebastian's hand to help him back on his feet. Only Sebastian has other plans up his sleeve. As soon as Soren lets his guard down, Sebastian snatches his brother's arm simultaneously winding up his legs, kicking Soren in the stomach and sending him sailing over Sebastian's head, splashing into the water.

A wicked grin spreads across Sebastian's face; laughing at his brother's defeat. Soren's head bobs out of the water. If eyes could kill, Soren would have torn his brother to shreds. His eyes look different somehow. Brighter. Bigger.

Sebastian pays no heed. He continues laughing as he offers his brother a hand back onto the platform which Soren takes with reluctance.

The two brothers jump from platform to platform until they are at the arena's edge. Each grab what looks to be their shirts and shoes before walking up the steps to the second floor. Right where Darius and I await them.

Darius comes to attention in his loyal soldier stance while I stupidly stand by him. Fidgeting with invisible specks on my dark rose-colored dress. Neither has put their shirt on yet as they walk in our direction, deep in conversation, blissfully unaware Darius and I stand twenty feet away.

Our eyes meet. Soren stops dead in his tracks but refuses to break eye contact with me. Oh, the humility and shame I feel from gawking at them while they trained creeps into my mind and shows on my cheeks. I put a tentative hand up in an effort to greet them. Soren hastily throws on his shirt covering the rock-solid canvas below. Good. Less for me to accidentally gawk at.

Sebastian on the other hand gives the toothiest grin he can muster before strutting over. His shirt lazily drapes over one shoulder. "Freckles," he greets the closer they get. "Were you peeping on our glorious daily sparring match? Did you find it agreeable?" Sebastian proceeds to wiggle his eyebrows at me. Was he flexing his biceps too? I strain to keep my eyes on his face.

Soren turns to his brother and gives him a death glare. Probably because he doesn't want Sebastian anywhere near me more than he needs to be considering I'm a "threat."

"Prince," Darius speaks next to me, addressing Soren. "The auxiliary is in order. The soldiers who'll be working the night of the ball are aware of their assignments and stations. The soldiers on duty today are hard at work patrolling the grounds. Other soldiers off duty from the castle grounds were told to tend to our elderly in the city, just as you ordered."

"Thank you, Captain." Soren's face is flushed. Likely from the extensive workout he just endured. His hands cuff behind his back which is straighter than a plank. "And the other… matters of today have been taken care of as well?" He glances at me almost imperceptibly before drawing his attention back to Darius. The two continue their conversation on whatever *matters* Soren so clearly doesn't want to identify in front of me; talking in code so I do not understand.

Sebastian continues to gaze in my direction. He rakes his eyes over me from head to toe, lingering on my lips before shaking more water from his hair, swooping it back casually with one hand away from his face. "So, princess…" he elongates the -s sound, "…have you had a splendid day with the finest soldier in all of Emora? More importantly how would you like to spend the evening with Emora's most dashing and eligible prince?"

Before I can even answer Soren interjects, "The princess cannot do anything tonight. We have plans." He won't even acknowledge I am here as he bores that accusatory look at his brother for even implying he spend extra time with me.

"Oh," Sebastian nods, apparently remembering something they had discussed about my plans without actually letting me in on my plans for the night. "Right, right, right," he continues to nod as if figuring out a puzzle. "Well then, I guess I will just walk you back to your room until supper time." Without another word, his hands fly up to his shirt, and he gracefully lets each arm glide into the sleeves and fall onto his torso like a curtain closing on a show. Clearly, he is enjoying taking his sweet time doing it.

I must constantly remind myself not to ogle. My goal is not to fall in love with a merman. My goal is to get out of here as quickly as possible and find Papa.

Sebastian offers me an arm I gratefully take, now that everyone is dressed and modest again.

"Thank you, Prince Sebastian. That sounds lovely." We make our way out of the arena leaving Soren glaring after us, and Darius doing his best to douse the growing ire within the prince.

Neither of us say a word to each other till we are far away from Soren's ears.

The walk is pleasant, my mind rather empty except for the enjoyment of being arm in arm with the sweeter of the two royals.

"So," Sebastian begins, sliding his eyes in my direction, "you never answered my question. Which is my second question of our bargain by the way. So you are obligated to answer truthfully."

We continue to leisurely walk toward my room. The halls are quiet except for the guard rotations and occasional servant bustling around likely getting something ready for the ball coming up. "Pray, what was your inquiry?"

"Did you enjoy the spectacle? In the arena?" The question sounds tentative, lingering on his tongue like he isn't sure he really wants to know the answer. Afraid it isn't what he wants to hear.

I halt him in his tracks and look straight into his stormy blue eyes before answering. "I think what you and your brother can do is incredible." And I mean it. The power they each possess to move water, an element so liquid and free, to do their bidding, is awe worthy.

His face beams at my response. He bows low at the waist. "Why thank you, Princess Constance." A pair of guards walks past, and we each keep our eyes on them before I offer my arm to his, and we continue our walk. "But really, my brother is incredibly strong and agile. I was getting my rump handed to me time and time again today."

"Yes," I agree. "But you won the match in the end, did you not?"

"Absolutely, I did! But in a real fight," he begins, "well, in a real fight, Soren would drub me nine times out of ten."

"According to those odds, you win some of the time at least," I counter, trying to keep his spirits up. It's clear by the slightly quicker pace he's given us and the way his back becomes stiffer, that his brother being the stronger of the two bothers him. But if I were being completely honest, I'd tell him that his brother is no match to his character therefore, more gallant and worthy of being called a winner than Soren ever will be. Sheer strength doesn't win everything. But I don't say it out loud. I listen intently to his next words instead.

"My brother may have the size and strength, but I've inherited the mind. If I am to ever best him, I must use his weaknesses against him. Outsmart him, as it were." He taps a finger to his temple. Sebastian sighs and takes a deep breath before responding. "My brother is next in line for the throne, as you know. But what you probably didn't know is that the majority of our father's birthright goes to him because of it."

"How so? Like the title of king?"

"Well, yes, but much more than that. The heir who holds the birthright, is the one who controls the oceans. It's why Emora has had so many years of peace. My father is an excellent ruler who's ruled by peace through strength. We've lived blissfully for so long because he's been fair and just in his decisions. He shows power when he needs to and mercy. But there were also times where he needed to show strength against enemies." Sebastian's gaze goes to a place I can't follow as he thinks of his father.

"Your father sounds like a wise leader." I place my free hand over his firm bicep.

"He was—is." I can tell by that vacant stare that Sebastian drifted back into his thoughts. I don't want to push any questions on him that he may not want to share. So instead, we walk the rest of the way arm in arm in blissful silence.

Chapter 16

That evening, I walk to the dining room alone. I am the last to arrive tonight. Soren and Sebastian sit in their usual chairs across from Lamia.

She's chosen to wear crimson red tonight. The all too revealing slit dress rides up her mid-thigh. The front is modest enough but her back lay bare except for two strings that ride up her sides and rest on each of her shoulders. The lipstick she has chosen perfectly matches the bloody red of the dress.

If this was a power play on her part to make me feel inferior and completely under dressed, it's working. No one should look quite so resplendent just for dinner. *Do not let Lamia intimidate you.* Those were Darius' words before my first encounter with her some nights ago. I hadn't seen much of her since then. Typically, only at dinnertime, but each meeting is as awkward as the last. Lamia is the type of female to belittle others. No doubt her entitlement comes from her royal upbringing and the fact she is betrothed to what will become the most powerful merman in all the ocean—according to Sebastian.

I take a deep breath before walking closer to the small group sitting at the massive dinner table. Sebastian pulls out my chair for me before striding over to sit next to his brother.

It appears dinner has already been served. Tonight is some kind of soup with bread. As long as there's no eel gelatin, I think it will be safe to eat. I pray there's nothing like that in this soup. There is no way I can pretend to eat something so disgusting ever again. Even if it is considered an underwater delicacy.

Soren is sitting in a more relaxed position tonight. His posture is slightly hunkered down with his head resting on a propped fist. He looks at me with those tropical storm eyes and refuses to break eye contact.

An image of a shirtless, sweaty Soren pops into my mind unannounced. *Stop it, Constance. That is highly inappropriate to think about at the dinner table. Especially about a merman who hates you.* Long, awkward moments go by with us just staring at each other. I want to look away. I really do, but his eyes are magnetic.

"Ahem." Sebastian breaks me from my trance. Him and Lamia are staring at me. One quizzically. The other with the intent to kill in her eyes.

"I apologize for my tardiness," I address to the table. "What were you discussing before I arrived?" I take the intricately folded napkin that lay before me and drape it over the same dark rose dress I have worn all day.

Lamia is the first to respond. "Well, *Cadence*, our discussion wouldn't have been of any significance to you. They were highly important royal matters. Is that not so, Soren?"

Do not be intimated by Lamia. "I don't think what length your wedding veil will be is really considered highly important, but please continue." I offer a wry smile. I don't know what she was talking about but considering all she ever talks about at the dinner table is the wedding to Soren, my guess was probably close to a bullseye.

Sebastian about spits out a spoonful of soup. Even Soren's mouth twitches at the edge.

Lamia offers her own smile and decides to ignore my comment before addressing Soren. Like she always does. "I picked out a suit for you to wear. Blue like your eyes. Would you be a dear and try it on for me later?"

"Isn't that bad luck to see the groom before the wedding?" Sebastian laughs.

Lamia clangs her spoon onto the table sending sprinkles of soup flying over the greenery in the middle of the table. A small splatter bounces off my cheek. "It's the bride, you moron. It's bad luck to see the bride in her dress before the wedding. I swear if I have to——"

"I can't tonight, Lamia," Soren interjects. He takes his time eating a few more spoonfuls of soup before continuing. Lamia hangs on every silent moment. "The three of us have other matters to attend to tonight."

She perks up at the mention of the three of them. "What are we doing tonight? Is it firelight gazing? Or diving into the hot springs up the mountain?"

Between mouthfuls of bread, Sebastian answers, "No, Lamia. He means me, him, and Constance. That way you can keep working on the wedding."

If looks could burn holes right through my face, then I would have two huge gaping cinders of ash in mine right now. Lamia stops eating all together to turn to me. Her nostrils flare. For someone who is supposed to be the epitome of grace and poise, Lamia falls short of that.

Why did Sebastian and Soren have to bring me into this? Why did they tell her I was going to be around them tonight when she was not allowed? It was like they were trying to get her to hate me even more. Like putting a target on my back.

I hold my gaze with Lamia. Eventually, she blinks the look off her face and opts for a big red pouty lip. "Soren, can't I come too? We haven't done anything together in weeks, and if she is going to help you with something…" Lamia points her thin, perfectly polished finger in my direction, accusingly, "…then let me help also."

"No, Lamia." Soren is firm but apologetic. "Sebastian is right. There's so much to be done for the wedding. Focus on that. Princess Constance is merely helping with the organization of imports and exports from different regions of human territory. That's what she does for a living."

She puckers her lower lip in response.

"You would find it wearisome if you joined us," Soren adds to his argument. He finishes his last sip of soup before calmly placing his spoon down and meeting Lamia's gaze, giving her a rare, sympathetic smile.

"Seriously Lamia, you would be bored to tears. Plus, I'll be there and would only distract you from our task by my dazzling wits." Sebastian teases before tearing off a large chunk of bread, loudly smacking his lips with each chew.

Her only response to Sebastian is a snarky look, like she's just smelled rotten fish. For the rest of dinner, she continues to pout. If I were a betting lady, I would say Lamia kept far, far away from anything involving business matters.

Wisely, I continue to eat my soup in silence.

* * *

Lamia did not give up as easily as I thought she would. The moment we had all finished our soup, dessert was brought out. Then as we all stood to exit, she begged Soren yet again to join us. Her lips puckered and her lashes drooped while she grazed her hand over his bicep. Soren had to go as far as to walk her all the way to her room and promise her he would spend all of the next day working on the wedding with her before she stopped prying in on our business.

While Soren was dealing with her, Sebastian led me to a room he called "the strategy room." The room is enclosed by four deep-red walls. It is cluttered with books lining the shelves and smells of ink and mold. The ceiling is lower in here too, with one orbital light in the middle, shining down on a large table that sits in the center. The table is round and can easily station ten men around it. The farthest end of the room sits a desk piled high with scrolls and yet more books with a well-worn red leather chair resting idly by it. The leather is warped in the shape of a person. Clearly, it is used often.

"You know I still have my third question." Sebastian traces circles on the round table in front of us.

I walk farther from him in the direction of one of the shelves on the bookcase. It reads *The Art of Peace in Times of War.* "Yes, I suppose you do. But I feel like you should really think on it. Your first two questions were…" I think of a way to tease him, "…not very enlightening." I turn from the bookshelf and give him a simple shrug.

He scoffs. "What do you mean they weren't enlightening? One, I found out you have a heart for roguish antics sailing out into the ocean blue, all by yourself no less, and two, which this one was very enlightening by the way, you enjoy seeing me fight with my shirt off." He then proceeds to run his hands over his chest and belly, giving me an all-knowing kind of look.

I can't help but laugh at the gesture. "You have no shame, do you?"

"Only when I am trying to impress a girl." He says as he closes the space between us and looks into my eyes.

My face heats as he searches my features, taking his time scanning my eyes, my nose, my freckles.

"Oh, stay still," he whispers before lifting his thumb up to his lips, taking a quick lick before rubbing that same thumb along my jawline. "You had some soup on your jaw."

Right, that stupid splatter of soup Lamia sent flying my way. The heat in my face increases, and I can't help but look down at my shoes that have become the most interesting thing in this stuffy room.

Sebastian uses his thumb that still lingers on my face to raise my chin. I look up in response and see those storm blues orbs go from gazing into my eyes to slowly tracking down my lips. He leans in closer.

Then the door swings open and in stomps Soren. We fly apart from each other quicker than a pod of fish making way for a tiger shark swimming through the middle.

Soren bypasses us and goes straight for the desk, using some weird hand gestures before pounding his elbow on the top to reveal a hidden drawer that pops open. He rummages through some papers and pulls out an unmarked manila colored file and walks back to us.

Sebastian and I are statues, afraid Soren caught his younger brother trying to kiss me. Was he trying to kiss me? It certainly felt as though that was his intention.

I am not sure yet what the laws are in Emora about mermen and women in rooms alone together. But I do know I don't want to give Soren another reason to despise me. I'm pretty sure kissing his brother would put me even higher on his hate list; if that's even possible.

"How did the queen of self-centered-ness react when you left her? Wanting more Soren sweetness before you left her pining at her bedroom door?" Sebastian says jokingly, puckering his lips.

Soren opens the file for the three of us to see, revealing a detailed black and white drawing of a middle-aged man. "Leave her be, Sebastian, and focus on the task at hand." He points to the drawing. "This is Count Pesilfer Veridum of Meridwen. He resides in the southeastern regions of the ocean. More importantly he is our target tomorrow night."

I take a closer look at the picture. Pesilfer's features remind me of a rat. The portrait shows a pointy nose and beady black eyes accompanied by large protruding ears. His hair is nothing to be desired either. Thinning at the top and slicked back.

"Pesilfer Veridum is a collector. He uses his wealth to acquire anything and everything rare, exotic, or valuable." Then Soren turns his head away from the pictures briefly and scans my face. Was he looking at my nose? "As a *human*, you will easily catch his eye at the ball." He says human like it tastes disgusting in his mouth.

"Wait a moment, I thought we weren't supposed to let anyone know Constance was human?" Sebastian chimes in. "Isn't that why she has this whole alias thing?"

And then it dawns on me. "He means my freckles. Most merpeople don't look a thing like me. Tan and freckled. It will pique his interest, will it not?"

Soren's lips tug slightly upward. "Exactly. He won't know you're not a mermaid, but your looks will intrigue him enough that he will try to collect you."

My throat bobs a little at his choice of words. "Collect me?"

Sebastian shivers like a cold draft blew through the room. "Jeez, brother, we can't put Constance out as chum for that creep to devour."

Soren isn't deterred by his brother's words. He merely states the facts. "Yes, Pesilfer Veridum collects merfolk as well as artifacts. Usually, he keeps them locked up like pets. The lucky ones get to be servants. Or perhaps those are the unlucky ones depending on who you're asking."

"So…" I look down at the picture of the collector, "…you want him to collect me? Is that how you get rid of me, Soren? Was this whole bargain with you a sham to lead me to the enslavement of some other merman just so you didn't have to deal with me? Or was it that you want me to suffer in the worst way possible while clearing your conscience of me? Is that it?" I can feel my blood start to boil. How dare this prince insinuate I could be collected like some inanimate object. That my life wasn't even worth saving, and worse, it's going to end in enslavement to this rat of a merman.

"You dare question my honor?" Soren asks with deathly calm. The room heats as he straightens to his full height towering over me.

I puff up my chest in response. I am utterly sick of his attitude toward me. "Is it honorable to admit to a lady you would have her drown merely because she wasn't part of your world? To keep her locked in a dungeon, barely feeding her for days even when she is at no fault in this situation? When apparently it was your fault to begin with! Where is the honor in that, *prince*?"

My words strike a chord. Soren's rage seems to simmer for a moment, showing something else emerge in those bright tropical eyes of his. Was it remorse? Whatever it was, is quickly blinked away, rage winning out. Even if it was slightly dampened. "For your information, *princess*, first, I would never betray a bargain. Second, the bargain was for you to steal something, not be collected."

He proceeds to slap another image on the table in front of me. It's a large orange pearl. Something I have never come across before in all my years of finding washed up clams on the beach. I found white pearls, silver pearls, even the occasional pink pearl, but never this. The pearl gleams like the beginnings of the setting sun. Rare and exotic indeed. "Your duty at the ball is to make yourself known to Pesilfer, lure him in, and figure out where this pearl's being hidden. Then steal it when his guard's down."

I look up from the photo. Soren still towers over me, waiting for my reply. A challenge is in his eyes. I can feel my heart racing, ready to fight him. "And why is this object so important? Why can't you get close to him yourself?" *And just let me go free?* I want to add.

"Pesilfer and I don't get along. He knows I don't agree with his way of life, so any interest I inquire about his hobby is bound to leave him suspicious. I'll be the first suspect on his list once he finds out the pearl's missing. As for its importance, well that's on a need-to-know basis. Which in your case, you don't need to know." He crosses his arms.

Sebastian on the other side of him gawks at the two of us, for once silent.

Even though Soren is at least a head taller than me, I do my best to look down my nose at him, show him he doesn't scare me in the slightest. Why does he feel he can treat me this way?

I glance around the room to all the supplies at his disposal. He has an entire kingdom's worth of assets to aid in his endeavor... and yet he needs me for this task. The realization strikes me. If I don't help him, his plan falls apart.

I purse my lips. "Upon further consideration, perhaps I won't help you at all."

"What?" Soren's nostrils flare.

"It would appear I'm not in the mood to help someone so pompous." I step back to cross my arms over my chest in defiance.

From the corner of my eye, I notice Sebastian snickering.

Soren, however, is not amused. "We had a deal," he growls.

"Yes, we did," I unfold my arms and stroll around the table, lazily running a finger over its surface. "However, now that I think on it, the deal seems rather one-sided, is it not? My boat becomes wrecked from a storm you created. In return you hold me captive and force me to do your bidding to earn back my freedom; something that shouldn't have been taken away from me to begin with!" I pause for dramatic effect, let the meaning of my words sink in.

The room's filled with quiet anticipation. Both princes stare at me, dumbfounded.

Soren follows the path around the table and steps in front of me. A condescending leer stamps on his face. "Then perhaps, *human*, you shouldn't have agreed to our bargain."

I don't back down. I know he needs me, and he knows that I know. "I believe a renegotiation is in order. I believe you owe me that."

Soren looks like a teapot ready to boil over.

"Brother," Sebastian chimes in, using a calm tone, "let's listen to her offer. I'm sure it's worth at least hearing out." He sits in one of the chairs and kicks his feet up on the table.

Soren remains in my face. His hot breath caressing my nose. "Come now, speak your mind. You haven't kept your thoughts to yourself yet."

"Supplies," I speak into his face. "Everything I lost from the storm returned in full. Food, funds...a boat. All of it."

The prince is silent. It feels like ages have passed before he responds. "Deal." He crosses his arms over his chest, revealing veins that course through his biceps. "But after this, I *won't* yield to renegotiations."

A sense of triumph jolts through me. I step back enough to put out my hand to confirm our altered accord.

Just like the first time, Soren stares at my hand but refuses to take it.

His demeanor may never change toward me, but at least I got what I yearned for; a better chance at finding Papa once this is all said and done. I drop my hand and gesture to the file still splayed open next to Sebastian's feet. "Well then, let's get ready for the ball."

Chapter 17

Sebastian offered to walk me back to my room, but I don't feel like having company at the moment. Soren just gets under my skin so easily, I am still broiling with anger long after he excused himself to attend to "other matters." Whatever that means. He is always excusing himself.

I had asked if I could take the count's file with me to study it before tomorrow night, but he swore if I took them out of the strategy room, he'd lock me back up in the dungeon and serve me eel gelatin for breakfast, lunch, and dinner. Apparently, it was quite obvious the first time I tried that horrendous food that I loathed it.

I huffed in his direction before asking Sebastian to leave me alone in the strategy room to learn more about my target. He reluctantly left with a quick bow before closing the door.

I must have been in there for longer than I thought. The halls of the castle are now lit with only the lanterns to keep the night's darkness at bay. Every now and then a pair of soldiers would walk by on their security routes guarding the castles sleepy residents from unwanted guests. I do my best to look as princess-like as possible, giving each a royal smile and slight nod before passing them.

I'm a few turns away before I reach my double-doored bedroom when something catches my eye in the shadows of an unlit hallway to my right. The hairs on the back of my neck prickle. Even though I look in that direction, scanning every inch of the dark dim hall, my eyes can't detect anything or anyone. Still, I have the sudden urge to turn and make a run for it.

"Hello?" I call out into the emptiness despite my uneasy feeling. "Is anyone there?"

I wait for a few long moments. Water wells in the corners of my eyes as I continue to stare refusing to close them even for a millisecond. Afraid I'll miss something or someone moving in the shadows. For a while, nothing. I'm frozen in place searching this gloomy, lifeless hallway.

Then it moves. A figure. Dark and foreboding. Creeping closer to me.

"Who's there? Who are you?" I demand.

The dark figure glides closer and closer to me until the shadows of the hallway end. Clearly whatever it is doesn't like the light or doesn't want me to see it. I am perfectly fine if it wants to stick to the shadows. If that's the case, I'll stay in the light thank you very much.

The creature is mostly hidden under a black, raggedy cloak. The only features I can make out are a few spindly, deathly pale fingers and a pair of black soulless eyes. Those eyes are a nightmare incarnate. Like they can see through my flesh and bone, only promising death and destruction.

The creature cackles before pointing one of those long spindly fingers at me. "It is not I she should be worried about but thee. Yes, I know what she is. She is a key." Another cackle escapes behind that black curtain.

I look around keeping one eye on this black covered thing, the other searching for anyone else. Surely a pair of guards will pass by any minute, right? My heart quickens in response.

"A key? What key? Do you mean me?" I point to myself and scan the halls again. Where were the guards?

The creature, I think a female, glides in an unnatural predatory movement before clawing the edge of the wall, daring to get even closer to the light. "Yes, human. A key. A key to not one, but three." She ticks off three of those fingers as she continues talking. "Be careful pretty human. Keys unlock all sorts of things. Some that you may not want to see."

"I don't know what you're—"

"One to treasure, one to power, and one to be free."

Wait, free? "Are you saying you know something about my freedom?" This creature clearly has knowledge of me. How did it know I was a human? What does it mean I am a key? Most importantly, can it tell me how to get free from this place?

Those soulless black eyes don't respond. It stands there motionless, lifeless, sending yet another wave of chills down my neck.

Off in the distance, boots thud on the marble floors. I take a single moment to notice two soldiers finally walking this way before looking back at the creature. It's gone. Like it had never been there in the first place.

When the soldiers get closer to my spot, I ask if one of them can escort me the rest of the way to my room. One of them kindly obliges, offering an arm the entire way. Needless to say, I will not be sleeping well tonight.

Chapter 18

The time has come.

Addeah helps me into my ball gown for the evening. It's a shade of shimmering green to match my eyes. The sleeves fall off my shoulder. The bodice hugs my curves and my hips. From there the skirt drapes down like a bell made of flowing water. The illusion of roses snakes up from the hem of the dress, drawing attention to the narrowest part of my waist. It's truly an eye-catching dress. Unfortunately, my bust is also eye catching. It makes me uncomfortable showing this much cleavage.

I poke a finger at my exposed breasts. "Addeah?"

"Yes, child?" She is down on her knees making sure every layer of my skirt lays the way it is supposed to.

"Is there any way we can, um, adjust the chest line?" Truth be told, it was gorgeous and really accentuated all my good features. My mama always said I was blessed with all the right kind of curves that would make any husband happy, but it still didn't mean I wanted just anyone ogling them. I took my hand and tried to pull up the neckline a little to cover up a least a fraction of the exposed flesh.

Addeah stands up and surveys my neckline puckering her lips slightly. "We are most certainly able." She proceeds to pull out a tin from one of the drawers on the vanity, revealing a small sewing kit and begins working her magic. It takes no time at all to adjust the neckline, now leaving just the slightest peek of cleavage showing. Now, the dress is perfect. "Do you remember everything for tonight?"

I thought of all the things Addeah and Darius have been teaching me. The dances, the etiquette, when dinner is served, what kind of talk is normal at a ball like this one, how many times I can dance with the same merman before it becomes improper. Most importantly, who's who. I repeat as much of the information as I can recall about Count Pesilfer Veridum in my mind. His occupation: collector. His likes: rare and beautiful things other merfolk want. His dislikes: being denied anything he desires. The file Soren had on the count even mentioned which songs he was more likely to dance to, what his food allergies are; clams apparently. It even included his favorite hobbies like fish watching and reciting boring texts of plays I've never heard of.

Soren came by this morning to debrief exactly how I am to grab the count's attention. Step one, look like a lonely vision of beauty; someone easily approachable. That will be a piece of cake considering I won't know anyone there. Step two, wait until his favorite song starts to play and see if he asks me to dance. If he doesn't, ask him—which isn't considered proper etiquette, but apparently, he will be so flattered, Soren highly doubts he'll refuse. Step three, get him talking about his collections and figure out where he keeps the pearl. Step four, steal it from his personals or his room without him noticing.

Easier than catching a shark with chum; except in this instance, I think I am the chum.

"Hon… it's gonna be alright. You're going to do just fine." Addeah must see the worry on my face in the vanity mirror. She steps behind me and places her head on my shoulder, giving each arm a reassuring brush with her delicate hands. Through our reflection, I see myself take one of her hands in mine and give her a tentative smile. "Besides," she continues, "it would take some pretty hefty magic to resist you in this dress if I do say so. I think I've outdone myself.

Now…" She lets go of me and pulls out a key from her white apron pocket and unlocks one of the drawers at the top of the pearly vanity to reveal a set of jewelry: a headdress and matching earrings. They contain sparkling white diamonds and pink pearls, all held together with gold.

She takes the prongs from the headdress and tucks them into the side of my hair so it emphasizes the beauty of Addeah's chosen hairstyle for me tonight. Then she proceeds to clip the earrings onto my ears before taking a large step back admiring her work.

The key she pulled out of her pocket gives me flashbacks. The creepy creature, her spindly fingers, and soulless eyes. Her words. *A key of three. Treasure, power, and freedom.* What could she possibly mean that I am a key? Goosebumps rise up my neck at the thought.

"I know the shoulders are a little drafty, but you'll be plenty comfortable when you start dancing in that crowded ballroom." Addeah gives me one more look over before leading me to the double doors of my bedroom.

I suck in one deep breath and slowly exhale before walking out.

* * *

I thought the dining room was large, but the ballroom could swallow up at least four dining rooms. All the servants scurrying around the last week definitely paid off. Brightly colored flower arrangements stand on marble pillars stationed every ten feet on the perimeter. The half-circle staircase is also adorned in vines and flowers of blues, and pinks, and oranges. A gold, intricately painted mandala covers the dance floor. Above me, the high dome ceiling holds a giant crystal chandelier that casts tiny shimmers of light on the ground with each subtle movement. However, my favorite part of the entire ballroom must be the floor to ceiling windows that show the center of the castle grounds where the castle's royal garden rests in all its glory. *Note to self, walk out on the balcony later to see the gardens.*

As I stroll into the crowd, I use the momentum of my legs to push my skirt in front of me, creating a gentle swish of the fabric, and preventing me from stepping on the front by accident and falling flat on my face. I am met with numerous stares and gawks of merfolk every shape, size, and color. Each pair of eyes I meet, I cast out a pleasant smile as I pass by. No doubt they are looking at my face. The freckles that are splattered all over my nose and cheeks. Although some have blue or green or even purple hair, I notice not a single merman or merwoman has even a mole to speak of on their blank canvases.

There is an orchestra at the top of the curved staircase playing an introductory tune while merfolk flock in from the entry way. Underneath the curved staircase, I see a smaller set of steps that lead to four thrones. The two in the middle are slightly higher than the two on the sides, and three of them are occupied by pristine merpeople. Soren and Lamia are in matching deep blue fabric. Like the beginnings of night in a clear starry sky. Soren has cut his beard close to his skin, accentuating his strong jawline. A crown sits atop his head. Lamia is less revealing than normal, apart from the deep slit in her skintight dress that shows off her never-ending legs. She too wears jewelry on her silky-straight teal hair; a tiny sparkling tiara. In some ways, her outfit makes me feel young and girlish in comparison.

Then there's Sebastian. He's in a deep green velvet tux with a clean white shirt underneath. His curls are perfectly in place. Probably with the same gel that Addeah uses on me and herself.

I notice a semblance of a line of merfolk, readying themselves to greet the hosts. Soren and Lamia greet each guest with a hospitable smile. Her fingers loop around Soren's forearm, displaying their betrothed status and a giant blue diamond sitting atop her ring finger.

Sebastian also greets the guests but with less enthusiasm, before scanning the crowd. For what or whom, I don't know.

I join the small line to greet the hosts just like any civilized princess would. Each guest is greeted with quick pleasantries before rejoining the party. One by one the line moves up.

One merman, with a pork belly and a single strip of purple hair in his white mane, remains in front of me. He waddles up the five steps to where the royals stand. I wonder if he is also some kind of king to claim that right and get so close. He is the only one I have seen do this so far. Soren recognizes him at once and offers his free hand to the plump bellied merman before he begins talking about something I cannot hear. Soren remains respectful of the merman, listening intently to whatever it is he is babbling about.

Lamia quickly loses interest. She looks over the crowd. Her warm eyes immediately freeze over when she spots me. Her fingers grip Soren's arm tight enough to create deep creases in his night blue jacket.

Tight enough that Soren looks down at his arm, glancing at Lamia's face, and follows her line of sight straight to me. His jaw tightens as well, his back becomes taut the moment he lays his eyes on me. It's enough of a reaction that the big-bellied merman stops his chitchat and turns around to see what all the fuss is about.

"Well, miss, you are a sight for sore eyes," the merman bellows.

I curtsy and grin in thanks before the merman looks back at Soren, Lamia, back to me, and decides to make his way down the steps.

"I'll discuss the logistics with you in the near future, Soren. Enjoy the night!" He waves before joining the rest of the party, shaking his head in dismay at what he just witnessed.

I gingerly walk toward the stairs and curtsy deeply, pretending like their disapproving glares don't bother me.

"Prince Soren, Princess Lamia, the decorations are exquisite tonight, as I'm sure the rest of the occasion will be."

"Constance, how nice to see you," Lamia pauses, "again." Her eyes rake over my dress. "And the dress you wear suits you. It's very… quaint." Her lips form a slight sneer as she possessively runs her free hand over Soren's chest.

I've a powerful urge to retort at her snide comment. My ears burn at her quip. Before I can say something I will regret, Sebastian turns and notices me for the first time. His eyes light up at my appearance before he springs down the steps nearly landing on my skirt.

He looks even more handsome tonight than usual. Perhaps it's the charged atmosphere surrounding us, but I have the sudden urge to rise on my tip toes and plant a firm kiss on his supple lower lip. It protrudes just slightly, secretly taunting me.

"Milady." He bows deep at the waist before offering an arm. "Might I say you are the most beautiful, freckled princess in the castle tonight."

I scoff instantly forgetting Lamia's remark. "I'm certain I am the only freckled *princess* in attendance."

Seriousness touches his eyes. "Then maybe I should have said you are the most beautiful living creature in this room." With his words, the atmosphere around shifts. Every move I make I am hyper aware of; not sure whether to gaze into those serious stormy eyes or smile at him or walk in the completely opposite direction as I feel the heat creep up my neck. "Apart from me, of course," he adds blinking away whatever was in his eyes and replacing it with that typical playful mischief I am growing accustomed to. "Please grant me the honor of accompanying you on this fine evening."

I gratefully take his arm as we take a turn about the room leaving Soren and Lamia to greet the guests alone.

Sebastian talks low to my ear so I can hear about all the people he is refreshing my memory on. Who is from which region, what's their title, who owes him money from last month's card game. It's enjoyable listening to him rattle on about everyone in here. This is not our only goal walking around together though. The true goal is to find our target: Pesilfer Veridum. As Sebastian continues talking, I nod and smile at appropriate times to make sure it looks like we are in deep conversation, while my eyes every so often scan the room for the rat-featured collector.

We decide to walk up the u-shaped stairs, closer to the music, to get a better vantage point. Sebastian continues talking and pointing out mermen he plays cards with while I look at each face in the bustling crowd. It takes me two full room scans before I see a balding clump of black hair and giant rat-like ears protruding from an undersized head.

I look to Sebastian talking with closed teeth like a ventriloquist. "I see him, near the food spread." Pesilfer is holding a glass of clear liquid, fingering through some freshly cut fruit.

Sebastian whispers so low even I can barely hear him, "Give me the signal when you've got the information." He turns his head to look before placing a hand on the small of my back and saying good luck before becoming suddenly interested in talking to one of the violinists playing a slow and romantic tune.

I turn my sights back to the target and kick-walk my way down the steps, my hand grazing the railing the whole way down. I weave my way to the impressive spread of finger foods, pretending like I can't decide what to eat first and place myself right in front of the count's eyeline. Almost immediately, I feel those beady black eyes rake over me, but I refuse to look until he loudly clears his throat.

I flutter my lashes in his direction and make shy eye contact. "It's difficult to decide what to try first when everything looks so delectable, wouldn't you agree?"

"Yes," Pesilfer says, revealing a bottom row of slightly crooked teeth, "everything before my eyes is quite…delicious." Those beady eyes scan me head to toe again. "However, I find that this, a froya berry is a great place to start." He picks up the foreign berry and pops it into his mouth, leaving a small droplet of crimson red juice pooling at the corner of his lip.

I give him a brilliant grin. "Thank you for the sage advice, sir—"

"—Count Pesilfer Veridum," he offers with a bow.

"Princess Constance, daughter of King Greyson of the Eastern Seas," I recite just as I did in my room a hundred times over.

"Pleasure." He gestures to take my hand before placing a cold, dry kiss on the top. It takes everything in me not to cringe away. "I wasn't aware King Greyson beheld such a beautiful daughter. He's been keeping secrets."

"I'm sure we all are, but I am no secret. I just work outside the castle walls, but I would hate to bore you with such details," I say, picking up a froya berry and pressing it to my lips before sucking it into my mouth and popping it with my teeth, leaving juice to spray all over my tongue. He was right. This berry is the sweetest thing I have ever tasted.

Pesilfer's eyes continue gaping at my lips long after he says, "My dear, I don't think that's possible." His gaze makes the hairs on the back of my neck rise like a warning call yelling danger, but I continue to look intrigued and innocent, playing the part.

Just then, the romantic music ends and a staccato, serious song begins. In Pesilfer's file, it said his favorite song was called March of the 500. If this song didn't sound like a serious march off to some war, I didn't know what would, so I say, "Is this not March of the 500?" gesturing to the orchestra playing above and looking at the group of people gathering on the dance floor with partners in hand, ready to dance to the beat.

"It is indeed, my dear."

I clap my hands together in delight. "Oh, I do love dancing to this song. It is my favorite after all," I say in response, giving him an opening to ask me to dance.

One of his wiry eyebrows raises. "Well then, Princess Constance, shall we?" He turns his palm upward, beckoning me to take it, before leading me to the dance floor.

Let the games begin.

Chapter 19

Pesilfer leads me to the ladies' side of this particular dance before joining the mermen across from us. Addeah, Darius, and I have practiced these steps numerous times, especially this morning, since I had learned it was the count's favorite song. It has a lot of stomps and twirls that one does facing their partner. It also has many opportunities to get close enough to talk while dancing. To my relief, this song has a lot less touching than some of the others.

"So," I start between a twirl in front of the count, our hands held up to each other's without actually touching, "tell me about yourself. What do—" another twirl before I finish my question, "—you do?" Like I didn't already know everything I needed to know about him. Collector. Cruel. Creep.

"I collect rare and valuable artifacts. Many to preserve our water's history. Other items are collected merely for their beauty." We trot along the line like everyone else before each set of partners stops at a new stomping ground on the dance floor.

"Anything I may be interested in seeing? I do love pretty things." One, two, stomp. Two, two, stomp.

That possessive look in his eyes grows larger in his pupils. The song is wrapping up, just a few more measures of dance before the mermen are meant to dip the mermaids into the final beat of the song.

The count presses his clammy hand on the small of my back and dips me low to the ground at the final note of the song. I linger there for a second just like the other mermaids before he brings me back up to my full height, and we clap for the musicians. They soon begin another song leading some to leave the dance floor and others to join.

I quickly scurry off the dance floor, the count at my heels. "Princess," he calls, "'It would be my honor to show you my home and all its wonders."

Going to see this man's home feels more like trading one cage for another. Except I am certain his cage is much worse.

In contradiction to my actual feelings, I clap my hands together in delight. "Oh, would you? I would be delighted! Anything exceptionally pretty I could look at? I do love jewels, particularly orange ones. They complement my eyes, you see? Anything to make a princess like me feel like the prettiest girl in the room." I motion to my headpiece and earrings Addeah put on me. The jewelry that accented my green, flowery ballgown. *Please take the bait. Believe I am some naive, vain princess.*

Pesilfer's face lights up at the mention and offers me his arm. I take it with a toothy smile as he leads me to a corner of the room. He looks around as if not wanting anyone to listen. "Actually, my dear," he leans in closer. He's so close I can smell the rot on his teeth and do everything I can to not cringe. "I brought something very suiting to your tastes. Something of astronomical worth. I could uh… show you later, if you'd like?"

I mimic his secrecy, looking around before replying. "Astronomical worth, you say? My, that's very brave of you to bring to a celebration like this. How can you ensure it's safe?"

He smiles to reveal that crooked row of bottom teeth again, as if laughing at my silly question. "Oh, I assure you, it's safely tucked away in my quarters, in a black box that can only be opened with this key and my own personal code." He proceeds to pull out a rusted old key from his tux and puts his fingers to his lips, asking me not to tell anyone.

I roll my eyes and shake my head playfully. "Silly me, someone like you would of course take necessary precautions to guard something so beautiful. But I must inquire, what's in the box you so clearly believe I would like?"

He takes another look around, bending down closer to me. "The rarest pearl in the world. And seeing as you enjoy adorning yourself in pearls, perhaps I can show you after everyone leaves the ballroom. You can try it out for size. What do you think?"

I playfully swipe at his forearm. "You flatter me, Count Pesilfer. I'm not sure I can possibly thank you enough for your generous offer."

He straightens and bores those beady eyes into mine. "Come back with me to my home." His eyes linger over my face, my cheeks, my lips. "Has anyone ever told you that you are the most exotic mermaid to grace this ball tonight? I have never seen one with such pleasing beauty marks across her face. I could have my artists craft a painting of you so superbly that all the kings of the sea would weep at your beauty."

I give his arm a flirty nudge. However, this conversation grows increasingly uncomfortable. What he doesn't add is the fact that he'll lock me away forever. Especially when he finds out I am not a mermaid at all but a human. In his file, it said he keeps slaves for all sorts of evil purposes. I shiver at the thought of being caught and held captive by this merman.

"My dear, are you cold?" The count begins to take off his jacket.

I dramatically roll my hands over my exposed arms. The signal Sebastian and I had come up with to tell him I had got what I needed. I don't know what kind of code I'll have to decipher, but I know what to look for and know I need to get that key from his tux. It was enough. I was done having this disgusting rodent look at me like some prize to collect. "Oh, thank you but—"

Within heartbeats, Sebastian and Soren are at my sides. Sebastian looks pleased. Soren has rage in his eyes. His hands ball into white knuckled fists.

"Count Pesilfer Veridum," Sebastian takes his hands and shakes it enthusiastically. The count's other arm is still outstretched toward me, his tux jacket draped over it. "You are just the merman I wanted to see."

The count, clearly displeased by their interruption begins to protest, "Prince Sebastian," he nods and looks to Soren. "Prince Soren, I was just about to—"

Soren doesn't let him finish. "Princess Constance, I would be honored to have your hand for this next dance." He opens up one of those tight closed fists and offers it to me. The other one still white knuckled at his side. No wonder he looks so angry. Ever since I've been here, Soren has refused to touch me. Because I'm human. Because in his eyes, *I'm* the rat. Dirty and diseased. And now he has to dance with me in order for our plan to unfold.

I tentatively put my hand in his. It's warm, if not slightly sweaty, and swallows up my own. I curtsy deeply before responding, "Of course, Prince." Over my shoulder, I call out to Pesilfer. "'Twas a pleasure meeting you, Count."

Then Sebastian drags the count away from me, talking his ear off about something I can't hear.

Soren leads me through the crowd. If I thought all eyes were on me before, I was wrong. This moment, with the heir to the throne, leading me, an unknown princess, to the dance floor, is clearly going to be the tittle-tattle of the night.

I dare take a look at the thrones below the orchestra to see if Lamia's there. She's standing a few steps below the throne. Her face pale white, until it begins glowing increasingly red with malice. All of it directed toward me. The nobody who eats with her and her betrothed. The fake princess who's stolen what clearly was meant to be her limelight.

My hands shake. The room starts to spin, and all I hear is an unnatural ringing in my ears. I can't hear anything or anyone except the deafening ring until a solid hand squeezes my own, the other wrapping around the small of my back. Comforting. "Focus, princess. Focus on me," Soren says sternly but quietly. Just loud enough for me to hear and no one else. He's right. I need to focus. This is part of the plan. Make it obvious that I am a part of the party, where everyone can see. When the pearl goes missing, I should be the last on the suspect list, seemingly in this ballroom the entire time.

I take a deep steadying breath, focusing my energy on the merman in front of me. Become the focal point, to blind the eyes of the observers from everything else that moves.

When we had originally come up with the strategy, I had asked why Sebastian couldn't be the one to take me away. "*Because Sebastian is far better at deceiving than I am. He can take what we need off anyone without them ever realizing it. Plus, we need you to look as desirable as possible. Dancing with the future king will make Pesilfer want you even more the more valuable you seem,*" Soren had explained. Even during his explanation his fingers curled inward, and his voice became taut. No doubt at the thought of having to touch me. I couldn't help hiding my slight disappointment, casting my eyes downward at his plan but nodded once firmly.

The song hums through the hushed crowd and the lights to the ballroom dim to a soft glow.

Soren's hand splays across my back and draws me closer, his face merely inches from mine. Our warm breath intertwines as the music continues to build. He smells of coconut and musk.

I recall the name of the song, *Lover's Journey*, the most intimate of the songs I had practiced.

I kept laughing in Darius' face, just from the sheer embarrassment I felt at our closeness while his very own wife instructed us.

At our balls, men and women were never allowed to be so close for so long. It was considered improper.

But here, it's considered to be an honorable form of dance. A dance to show your love and affection to the world.

In this moment, I don't feel like laughing at all. Something warms inside my chest, my heart quickening at Soren's lips so close to mine.

He keeps our bodies close as he leads us through the steps. "What did you find out?" he whispers in my face, so close our lips almost touch.

This is why he chose this song for us. It was the only song he could keep close enough to talk to me without anyone else hearing or noticing we were even conversing at all, even when I could feel all eyes boring into my back.

"Sebastian needs to get the key inside Pesilfer's tux. He also told me where it's hidden."

I dare a look up into Soren's eyes through my lashes and notice he's looking in the direction of his brother and Pesilfer. He blinks rapidly three times before spinning me out and back into his broad chest.

"Does Sebastian know—"

"He does now. When you get a chance, find Darius at one of the exits. He will have what you need." Soren then dips me low to the ground before bringing me back up into his warmth. For a prince so burly, he moves like a dove's wings; graceful and flowing.

"Soren…" I begin, not sure if I even want to tell him I didn't get all the details I really needed to steal the pearl, "…there's something I didn't find out."

Only his eyes show a slight change, intently listening to what I am about to say.

"There's also a code. To get into the box. And I have no idea what kind."

Soren takes a deep pondering breath before replying, "If it's numbers try his birthday. He never was very creative and has always been egotistical. That's probably what it is."

I look up through my lashes and nod once. Not sure what to say next, I stay silent until he continues speaking. Surprisingly.

"Pesilfer can't take his eyes off you. He's clearly bewitched by you."

I scoff. "I'm sure he'd be bewitched by any mermaid that showed interest in him."

Another spin followed by a dip. Soren's eyes pry away from the count's whereabouts to gaze at me. His hands close almost imperceptibly tighter around my waist and hand before he speaks his next words. "No, it's more than that, princess. You look," he hesitates, "nice."

My heart sinks a little. Was I really expecting a full-blown compliment from the merman who wishes I had drowned a week ago? Still, at least he attempted cordiality.

Soren's eyes dart between my eyes and my mouth. I can feel the song is about to end in just a few more measures. Perhaps I am of unsound mind, but I get the strangest feeling he's going to close the last inch between us and plant a kiss on me, for everyone to see.

Then the song is over, and he jumps back a good three feet, bowing deeply before striding off to a pouting Lamia.

I take a moment to let out a breath, unaware I had been holding it in.

That's when a swarm of suitors surround me from every angle asking for the next dance.

* * *

I accepted the next eight suitors that asked me to dance, trying to ignore the growing envy in the mermaids' glares piercing my back. On the ninth one, I respectfully declined, fanning myself with my hand and declaring I needed to rest. I make my way to the drink table and pick up a glass of iced water, sipping gingerly as I scan the room.

Sebastian still keeps Pesilfer occupied with incessant chatter, Pesilfer growing ever so bored, his hand resting under his chin, as he slumps in one of the chairs on the outer skirt of the ballroom.

With Pesilfer still occupied, not knowing where I am because of Sebastian's talent of endless conversation, I discreetly weave my way to the nearest exit.

Darius waits at the ready, pretending he doesn't see me or know me at all. I walk near him and pretend to trip over my skirt, sending my water flying into Darius' face.

"Oh my, Captain, I am so sorry." I fan at his face and look for a napkin.

Darius' pulls out a handkerchief, and I motion to dab the water off his face.

"I'll go fetch a towel." I say, tucking that heavy handkerchief in my hands on the way out.

Chapter 20

Finding the count's room is easy enough. There are no guards stationed outside of it. Darius made sure his soldiers followed a strict rotation of the halls, then proceeded to tell me the exact times where I could elude all of them.

I open up the handkerchief to reveal the black, rusty key that once hung from the rat's neck. Next to it sits a master key to all the guest rooms in the castle. Compliments of Captain Darius.

I slide the key into the lock and turn until a faint *click* releases the door. I look left. Right. The coast is clear still, so I slide into the door and shut it silently behind me.

Count Pesilfer Veridum's room is set up similar to my own but on a smaller scale. There's one bed. The sheets are already crumpled and used even though all the guests arrived just this morning.

The room has a moldy smell to it, like water sitting too long in a bucket.

Bags and suitcases and duffels are strewn across the floor creating a messy maze. How much luggage does one man need for a night? It is like a hurricane has gone through and washed up all this junk. More importantly, how am I ever going to find the pearl in this mess?

Near the window, a small cage of strange shimmering, gray iron imprisons a pale pink, almost translucent, creature I have never seen before. I would say it's some sort of salamander, but the sides of its head have pronged fins and its tail ends with a leathery, darker pink fin. Its small beady eyes are pleading. Petite, bubbly, webbed hands grasp at the bars, exposing the creatures tiny little belly.

My heart skips a beat when I see three puncture wounds there.

The creature chirps at me and sniffs the air with its slated nostrils. I wish I had something to give it, understanding that it's probably hungry. Starved even by the look of the protruding set of ribs.

"I'm sorry, little one. I wish I had something to give to you," I whisper.

Disappointment falls on its face, like it understands what I am saying. Which gives me an idea.

"Say," I begin. Bending down at eye level of the creature. "You wouldn't happen to know where I can find a small black box, do you?"

The pink fella slumps onto its bottom and gives a low chirp. His head slumps too. I'll consider that a no.

I look around the room, careful not to move anything out of place. Even though I'm sure the count wouldn't notice. It doesn't seem like there's any order with which he threw his stuff in here.

I start on the wall farthest away from the door. Carefully opening every suitcase and bag. I find shoes, soiled handkerchiefs, endless jewelry sets of rubies and sapphires, books with languages I have never seen scribbled all over them. Even one bag contains a few small paintings. But not one little black box.

I blow out enough air that my lips sputter and vibrate. If that little box isn't in any of the bags, then where would an egotistical, clammy, rat hide it?

I look toward the bed. Surely he wasn't naive enough to hide the box under it. I clamber around the maze of junk until I reach the side of the bed and lay belly down.

Nothing. The only space clear of anything at all.

I put my hands on the top of the bed and begin to haul myself to my feet. But I don't feel the soft plush of the mattress. Instead, I feel something cold and bumpy under the thin sheet of fabric.

It seems impossible. But it isn't. Because as I peel back that tousled sheet, an old, black box appears before my eyes. The box is small enough to hold in one hand. Rusted at the edges. Two locks keep the box shut tight.

I take the handkerchief Darius gave me and unravel its contents, but this time I take out the black, rusted key that goes with it and begin to insert, when the hinges on the door creak open.

The creature begins chirping wildly in its cage. An alarm going off.

I freeze. My body too afraid to do anything as a clammy hand that's connected to a merman with greasy, balding, black hair begins to walk in, his face looking behind his shoulder.

"Hmm, I could have sworn I locked this door before heading to the ball," the count speaks, talking to someone I cannot see. "Did you not lock the door before we headed out, Felonious?"

"Sire, I apologize—" Felonious begins before being interrupted.

"Don't apologize! Just do your job. What else am I paying you for?" the count counters. "Stand guard, Felonious. I'll be but a minute."

I take action, quicker than I ever thought my body was capable of moving, pulling the key out of the lock and ducking under the bed, stuffing my ballgown in with me. It's like being stuffed into a gift box with all the wrappings. Suffocating. But I remain as silent as night, while I watch the heavy footsteps of the count walk around his room.

My heart thunders against my chest, pulsating in my ears. My entire body fully aware of every creak and breath and sound that occurs in the room.

The creature starts chirping loudly again.

"Oh, quiet you! Or you'll be punished," Pesilfer threatens, "again."

The creature obeys. I can hear it slumping back down in its cage.

Black dress boots trot between the maze of junk toward the vanity. I can hear a drawer opening and something gel-like being squeezed out of a bottle. Then something is sprayed in the air like perfume before Pesilfer turns back to the door.

Except he doesn't make it to the door. Something halts him in his tracks.

"Hello lovely, what are you doing here?" He croons.

That's it. I've been spotted. This whole deal is ruined because I couldn't get in and out of this room fast enough. Some burglar I am, getting caught within five minutes of my heist.

I shut my eyes and send up my prayers, begging for my punishment to be swift and painless.

The count walks to the edge of the bed, his feet mere inches away from my face. Only, he doesn't drag me out of my hiding place. His feet don't move from their position as he picks up something heavy from the bed.

The box.

"Now what is my most precious artifact doing out in the open like this? Huh?"

The pink creature chirps in response as if saying, "I don't know."

I move my hand to cover my heart in an effort to silence its thunderous beating.

"Shall we take a quick peek? Make sure our lovely is still in its proper place? Hmm?" The count's feet shift slightly to accommodate the movement of his arms. Is he searching for the key? The key in my sweaty clenched hand?

Like a prayer answered, the count's bedroom door opens. "Sire, the prince, Sebastian says there is a merlady looking for you in the ballroom."

"Ha! I knew she would come back to me. There may be princes and heirs in the ballroom, but there is only one Count Pesilfer." He trots away after covering the box with the sheet once more and heads out of his room with a loud thud.

I count to sixty before I dare squirm my way out of my hiding spot.

The box is nestled back under the sheets. I pull it out again and quickly make work of the key lock. It loosens easily.

The second lock is a four-digit code. Soren said if its numbers try his birthday. From his file, he was born July sixth. I scroll the numbers 0-7-0-6. Nothing. Maybe he reversed the numbers? 0-6-0-7. Still nothing. The lock won't budge.

Chirp, chirp, chirp.

I whirl around. Two beady little eyes are staring at me knowingly. The creature's paws grip the bars firmly.

"What? Do you know the code to this thing?"

Chirp! A nod.

"Okay. I'll trust you since you warned me before the rat entered." I carry the black box to where the creature's imprisoned and sit next his cage. "What's the first number?"

Chirp, chirp, chirp.

"Three?"

Another nod.

I scroll the first number until the three faces up. "What's the next?"

Chirp.

One. "Next?"

The creature chirps seven times in a row.

"And what's the last number?"

Chirp, chirp, chirp.

Three again. I roll my thumb over the numbers. The final code says 3-1-7-3. Then it clicks setting the lock free of its hinges.

I open the box. There it is shimmering in all its glory. The rare and beautiful orange pearl. The size is more impressive than any pearl I have ever come across. It would swallow up three of the pearls that decorate my hair.

I lift the pearl off its cushion and carefully wrap it in the handkerchief with the keys. Then I put the locks back on the box and hide it under the covers as if it had never been moved before heading to the wall near the vanity. Soren said one of these bricks will lead me to the secret passages and from there I can find the library near my room before hiding the pearl until morning.

The fifth stone I press gives a little, telling me I found the correct one. I have found the lever that opens the secret door in the wall and begin to leave the moldy, cluttered room.

I pause with my hand on the bricks and turn back, looking at the pale creature. Its eyes are fixed on me, sad and pleading.

"Thank you for helping me tonight. You have no idea what you did for me," I say.

It purrs in response.

And then I do something I'll most likely regret. I stride over to the creature's cage and set it free.

Pearl in tow. Keys in tow. And a new squishy companion in tow, I set off to find the secret door to the library, careful to get as little dirt as possible on my ballgown.

The little creature drapes over my neck, its sticky paws clinging to my skin as it places tiny wet kisses on my cheek with its tongue. Clearly, it's grateful for the idiotic decision I made to set it free.

We find the library in no time at all. Thanks to the directions Soren had me memorize last night. Soon enough I and the creature are surrounded by stacks of books.

"Okay little one, I can't take you to the ballroom with me or else the rat is going to see you and know what I did." I offer up my hand for the creature to crawl on before placing him on top of a row of books. "You stay here, okay? I promise to come get you when it's safe. And I'll bring you some food to eat."

It licks its lips in response before circling the books and plopping down, curled up, paws tucked under his belly.

I turn on my heels before pausing and turning around. "Actually," I reach into the handkerchief and pull out the pearl. "It might be safer if you held onto this too. In here. Can you promise me you'll keep it safe until morning?"

The creature blinks in response, tucking the pearl under its belly like a hen warming her egg.

"Good." I use my nails and scratch under his chin causing purrs to rupture from his vocal cords. "I'll see you in the morning. Stay here."

I turn away and head out of the stacks of books, almost making it to the entrance of the library when an aged, gruff voice speaks behind me. "I know you. You don't belong here."

Chapter 21

I stop with a hand splayed on the door. So close to freedom only to get caught.

I turn around to find a withered old man in long purple drapes, a giant crown resting on his thick, peppered, black and white hair. His beard is a matching white and trimmed close to the jaw. If the crown and royal colors didn't give him away, the tropical blue eyes would have.

This is the King of Emora, Soren and Sebastian's father.

"My King," I drop low enough for my face to hit the ground.

"Oh, nonsense child, stand up. Stand up." The king waddles over to me. He runs his arms in small circles, beckoning me to get back up. "A beautiful dress like that shouldn't get all dirtied up from the library floor of all places." He chuckles before it turns into a hacking cough. It takes him a moment of clearing his throat to speak again. "Now what is Miss Constance doing here anyways when there's a ball to be enjoyed?"

Shock crosses my face. He didn't address me as princess. He said *miss*. Does he know I am a human? Did one of his sons reveal this to him? He is the king after all. "You know who I am?" is all I can whisper.

He puts his hands together. Fingers playing with his numerous rings. "Oh yes. My son fancies you, you know? Can't stop talking about the infamous Constance. He hasn't confessed his feelings outright yet, but a father always knows. Your freckles were a dead giveaway."

Sebastian. He's been talking to his father about me. I blush at the thought. "I guess it's hard to blend in with freckles, isn't it?" I touch my cheek with my fingertips.

"Oh deary, to stand out is a blessing… when used properly, of course." The king finds one of the cozy reading nooks in the room and sits, patting the seat next to him.

Surely this isn't proper to sit next to a king. However, who would punish me for being improper? He is the king.

I gracefully kick-walk my way next to him and sit down, crossing my legs at the ankles, running my fingers over my skirt to smooth out any wrinkles.

"So, Miss Constance, what is a beautiful merlady like yourself doing in the dark library?"

Merlady. So, he doesn't know. Good. "Well…" I pause giving myself a moment to think of some excuse. "…Many mermen asked for my hand to dance. It was breathtaking. Literally."

He laughs.

"So here I am, trying to find some peace before I head back out to the swarms of suitors."

"This is a fine place to run off to," the king says thoughtfully, nodding his head toward the books that surround us. "I too am here for a breather. This was my wife's favorite room in the entire castle."

His wife, the queen. The beautiful woman in the picture I had seen earlier in the week with the kind light brown eyes holding her son.

He continues, "She loved the smell of the leather and ink and glue that binds the books together. Said it reminded her of simplicity and peace." He inhales deeply before letting out another cough. "I come here when I'm able, to remind myself of her. To feel close to her once again."

"That's beautiful, My King." Against my inner voice telling me I shouldn't, I take my hand, place it on his warm wrinkly one, and give it a comforting pat. "It sounds like you really miss her."

"Oh, yes. But I've never truly lost her. No. Not when I hold her here." He points to his chest. "My Selina died too young. But one day, we will be reunited, and it will be the best day of my existence."

I smile. Clearly the king's love for his queen has surpassed time. I pray he's right and one day they can be rejoined.

"Well, I better get back to the ball. Someone may worry if I'm gone too long. I would hate to cause unnecessary panic." I stand up and fluff out my skirt. "Will you be alright, My King?"

"Actually, I would love for you to bring me with you. It has been a long while since my people have seen me. I think I'm quite ready for some merriment." The king grasps his knees as he groans up to a full stand. "As long as the lovely Miss Constance doesn't mind escorting me there?" The king puts out an arm and smiles. Judging by the way he coughs and wobbles, I doubt he can get there without my help.

Cheerfully, I oblige. "Of course, My King, it would be an honor to take you to the celebration."

* * *

Rage. Pure, undiluted rage clouds Soren's face when he sees me walking in with his father.

The room came to a halt as well. Everyone gawks at the old king. Even the musicians stop to stare at him. He waves and smiles fully as I help him wobble to his throne; the throne Soren was sitting on next to Lamia. Her face is flabbergasted at the sight. Full mouth gaping open.

I am not sure where Sebastian is. Most likely still trying to keep the count occupied until I returned.

Soren practically runs down the steps of the throne and takes his father's free side. Helping him up the stairs. "My King, it's a surprise to see you tonight." He whispers so that only the three of us can hear. "Are you sure you're well enough?"

The king sits down on his throne and waits a moment before responding, "You mean to say am I well enough to sit on my royal behind and watch the merriment of our peoples on this fine night?" He gives Soren a knowing look before addressing the stunned crowd. His voice becomes louder than I thought possible. It echoes off the ballroom walls. "Welcome everyone. Apologies for my late arrival, but here I am! I want to wish you all merriment and joy as you indulge in tonight's festivities!" He looks up to the orchestra. "Continue!" he commands and without another word the entire ballroom is dancing to music and laughing and conversing as if he had been here the whole time.

"Can I talk to you for a moment? In private?" Soren says through clenched teeth. "Lamia, please keep my father company. I will be back in a brief moment."

Lamia opens her mouth to complain, her brow furrowing and mouth opening, but before she can utter a single syllable, Soren already has his fingertips at my elbow and is leading me down the steps, out the giant glass doors, and into the castles royal garden.

He didn't care that people looked and whispered as we passed by. His steps were quick and sure as he led us to the center of the garden where scattered couples sit and converse intimately close.

Right in the middle of it all is an intricately carved fountain in the shape of some kind of serpent with wings. Its serpentine features coil and loop. Water sprays from its open mouth, cascading down onto its scaly splayed wings. It is both beautiful and menacing.

I would have looked longer at it, had Soren not interrupted my gawking. One growl from him had all but one couple fleeing for the light coming from the ballroom.

The last couple is hesitant to leave until Soren lifts his finger, sending a stream of water to spray the couple, causing them to run in the same direction as the rest. Trying to get off the water from their formal clothes on the way out.

"Was this really necessary?" I hiss. What a temper he had. Over nothing.

"Do you realize what you've done?" He hisses back, spewing spit balls in my direction. "You could jeopardize everything by what you've done tonight."

"What I've done tonight? Your father, your *king* asked me to bring him here. What's wrong with him being here? Does it make little Soren feel powerless? Oh, Daddy isn't here, so I can have all the authority to brood and intimidate whoever I want."

"He's sick!" Soren yells before looking around and lowering his voice. "He's sick, and he shouldn't be out of bed. Let alone surrounded by people who will take one look at him and decide to try and overthrow him as king. Your actions," he points a finger at me angrily, "could cause a war among our people—across the oceans."

I scoff softly. "Did you not see your father's smile as he greeted those merpeople? I think an old king who enjoys being around his subjects, if only for a night, is worth it to him. What was I supposed to say to him? No?" I cross my arms in defiance. "The only thing dangerous that's happened tonight is the fact that I almost got caught because you and your brother couldn't stick to the plan."

"What do you—"

"He went back to his room. Even though you promised to keep him busy, occupied." I step closer, pointing *my* finger at him. "If I had been caught, this whole deal would have blown up in my face. And I don't intend on staying here any longer than necessary."

He doesn't back down, closing the gap between us, towering over me, his muscled chest puffed up.

But I don't back down either.

The two of us face off. Head-to-head. Anger rises in my chest with every heartbeat.

"Ahem," a voice from the walkway startles both of us. Sebastian is there, looking sheepishly innocent as he gradually steps toward us, hands raised. "Constance, I'm so sorry about earlier. I truly tried to get him to stay but he insisted on freshening up before he pursued you again tonight."

I take a giant step back from Soren, now fully aware just how close we actually were. "And where is the count now?"

"Went back to his room to clean up. I may or may not have spilled my drink on him when I noticed you two running for the gardens."

My hands take a grip full of my skirt and hoist up the fabric, ready to run out of here. "Well, I believe I'm going to call it a night. I'll have breakfast in my room tomorrow morning as well. Goodnight." I quickly curtsy and pull out the handkerchief, with the count's key, still stuffed in one of the folds of my dress before pressing it against Soren's chest and strutting out of the gardens, into the ballroom.

The party is the same way we had left it. Merfolk dancing, eating, conversing. Oh yes and then stopping to gawk at me as I walk out of the gardens alone. I doubt any of them could hear our conversation. Soren wasn't stupid enough to take me to a place and yell at me just so everyone could hear him. But no doubt they were curious at the prince's sudden exit with the mysterious princess.

I plaster on my most pleasant smile and offer it to anyone who stares at me too long. Eventually I am mostly forgotten as I stroll toward the exit.

A scream halts me in my tracks. I search for the source when I spot a merman armed to the teeth, running toward the throne. Running toward the king.

His arm is outstretched, a sharp blade in hand as he roars.

It happens all so fast I don't even have time to scream.

The king spots the perpetrator just quick enough to throw up a shield of water. Only it's not strong enough to stop the blade from breaking through.

This is it. What Soren was afraid of. The king is going to die, and it will be all my fault for bringing him here.

But he doesn't die. Out of nowhere a tidal wave of water soars through the air and crashes into the merman, sending him colliding into the ballroom wall along with the dagger. He's knocked out cold before a group of guards gather around him, cuffing his limp body in chains.

Sebastian comes running from the edge of the ballroom and up the stairs. He scans his father's face, his hands, his chest; looking for any sign of harm before he turns his attention to the perpetrator and the guards that hold up his limp body. "Guards, take the traitor to the dungeon."

Without hesitation, the guards carry the traitor away, leaving the rest of the ballroom stunned into silence.

No one knows what to think as the prince hovers protectively over his father.

"Does anyone else want to try anything?" Sebastian calls over the gawking crowd. His eyes promise death to anyone else that attempts something against his father.

No one says anything. A room full of merfolk so quiet one could hear a pin drop.

Only then do I spot Soren walking back in from the gardens, hands in his pockets. He looks up to notice the quiet crowd. His brother hovered over his father. A flick of his eyes tells me that the events that occurred have registered in his mind; a dreadful turn of events has happened.

Too casually he looks around the sea of merfolk and spots me. His eyes narrow before he gives me a slow and disappointed head shake. He knows whatever happened while he was in the gardens is my fault.

And I can't say I disagree.

No one knows what to do. Does the party end for all of us? Will we be directed back to our rooms because of the violent turn of events?

The king speaks up. "What's a summer ball without a little assassination attempt? Everyone please, enjoy the rest of the festivities!" He calls out laughing, acting like he wasn't about to be murdered moments ago.

But his words ease the rest of the guests. Little by little, merfolk begin to converse and scatter. The music continues to play. The dancing begins anew, and I take this moment to sneak away to my room.

* * *

Addeah wouldn't be in to help tonight. Apparently, she was also allowed to enjoy the ball after a certain hour had passed, leaving me to undress, bath, and tuck myself in for the night. Which was all fine by me. I hadn't particularly wanted to talk about the events that unraveled tonight.

I couldn't wrap my head around anything that happened this evening. I stole something. I danced with a prince. I met a king. That king was almost assassinated, and it would have been my fault. It was overwhelming to process.

It took me a bit to get out of my dress, but I managed before dipping into the steamy hot bath, looking out at the city.

The strange light at the top of the city glows a moon-like orange tonight, casting dancing shadows on the greenery below. Even the streets are filled with the common folk dancing and laughing—celebrating the upcoming summer.

I take a deep breath and try to refocus on the most important thing.

One step closer to you, Papa. Just hang on a little longer wherever you are.

Chapter 22

Knock. Knock. Knock. "Let me in now, or I will personally see to it that this door is broken down!"

I startle awake at the angry knocking on my door. Judging by the shy morning light still creeping up through my window, I'd say it was too early for this.

Another angry knock.

I jump out of bed, find a robe to cover myself and throw on my heels from last night. A quick look at myself in the mirror reveals major bed head. Hopefully Addeah can use some more of that amazing gel to tame my mane later.

Three more angry knocks.

"I'm coming," I call through the doors. I tie the robe on my way to unlock the door and open it.

Standing there, ears steaming red, beady eyes bulging out of their sockets stands Count Pesilfer Veridum.

His hands are in strained fists at his sides, and his black receding hair is slicked back with even more product than it was last night, like he hasn't yet bathed from the evening's festivities.

I plaster a shocked and confused face before curtsying. "Count Pesilfer. What an honor to see you this morning. Are you alright?"

"Don't play games with me, you harlot," he bellows before taking his hand and slamming the door shut on his way into my room. "Where is it?" he barks.

"Where is what?"

"Where is it?!" His hand comes up as if to slap me before my door bolts open. I hear a clatter in the hall. Sebastian comes barreling in and grabs the count by his collar and shoves him to his backside.

Soren isn't far behind, placing a foot on the count's chest forcing the rat to lay belly up.

"What is going on in here?" Soren demands.

"She stole it. I know she did," the count spits.

"Stole what?" Sebastian seethes. He turns his body in a way that acts as a barrier between me and the count. Protective.

"My pearl. She was the only one I told about it to last night and now it's gone missing. My prized creature's missing as well." Pesilfer tries to get up, but Soren puts more pressure on his chest causing him to boil in his anger even more.

I must act fast. This doesn't look good for any of us if word gets out I stole something and that the two princes of Emora came to my rescue, placing blame on them as well.

I cross my arms and give him my best mock impression of hurt. "My dear, Count, how could you think I would ever steal from you? I thought we were on good terms. I had even planned to come visit your home as you had requested." A lie, all of it, but hopefully something he could believe was true.

"You did it. I know you did." He does his best to wriggle out of Soren's foothold to no avail.

I sigh wearily. "I'm sorry you lost something precious to you, but I can assure you it wasn't me. Please, have your men check." I wave to Soren to let him off the floor. He hesitates at first, reluctantly releasing Pesilfer from the crushing weight of his boot.

Pesilfer stands up and straightens out his jacket. "It would be my pleasure. Guards!" He snaps and three mermen in matching black armor come clomping in. "Search every inch of this room. The mattress, the curtains, the vanity, the bathroom, even the princess herself." With that last command, Pesilfer's beady eyes rake over my body, eyeing my bare legs.

I desperately try to cover up as much as possible.

Simultaneously, both princes protest.

"Never," Sebastian states.

"No," Soren snarls. "If you lay a finger on her, I will end you."

I gulp down the growing angst in my throat. "Prince Soren… Prince Sebastian," I direct to my two protectors, "if that's what will prove my innocence then I insist one of his guards search me." I make sure to add in that little bit about the guard, hoping it isn't Pesilfer who pats me down.

Sebastian and Soren both have their jaws clamped and their fists clenched tight but make way for one Pesilfer's guards to get to me.

Pesilfer smiles in triumph. "Very well. Felonious, search the princess."

Felonious, younger than I thought based on the voice I heard last night, comes up hesitantly to me. "I'm sorry, princess," he mutters, "I'll make haste."

I nod and raise my arms out for easier access to my sides. Sebastian and Soren both stand with arms at their sides, hands clenched, revealing white knuckles.

The count smirks in satisfaction as Felonious pats me down. I cast my eyes down, humiliated by the spectacle even though the guard is being gentle, careful not to touch me in specific places. The other guards are destroying every inch of my room.

Long dreadful minutes tick by before one guard exclaims, "Sire, the room is cleared. The pearl nor the creature are in here."

The count scoffs in disbelief.

"You heard them. From the mouths of your very own guards. My room doesn't hold what you seek." I say, wrapping my arms around my chest. "Neither do I."

"Apologize for your behavior," Soren says still as night.

The count looks as if he's about to charge me again, but Soren and Sebastian step in front. "I don't know how you did it or where you put it, but I know it was you." He points an accusatory finger at me.

"Count," Sebastian interjects, "Is it possible if you were talking to Princess Constance last night at the ball that someone may have overheard you? You converse quite loudly," he adds.

Good thinking, Sebastian.

The count thinks on it for a moment before passing those beady little eyes of his back and forth between Soren, Sebastian, and me. Next, he's turning to leave to my room. "I have my eyes on you, you little tramp. Don't let your guard down."

Before I can even blink, Soren is barreling him into the wall causing the brick to chip. "You are not welcome here. Leave!" he yells, with his fists still clinging to the front of the count's jacket.

The count ever so slowly raises his hands in defeat. "Felonious," he trembles before looking at his guard, "pack my bags. We're leaving."

Without another word, the guards file out of the room along with the count, limping and clutching his neck from the impact of Soren's force.

The three of us watch the mermen walk out of sight before we each let out a breath.

"That could have gone better," Sebastian states.

"It also could have gone a whole lot worse," I retort. "Thank you," I say, "to both of you for coming to my aid."

Sebastian grins and bows dramatically, "Of course, my lady."

Soren just mutters something under his breath I can't comprehend.

I look around my room. It is like a hurricane has swept through. Nothing is where it is meant to be. Wall frames lay broken on the ground, pillows are strewn apart, all the makeup in the vanity ruined. My seashell necklace lays under some makeup strewn on the floor.

"Well, this is a mess."

"I'll have some maids come clean it up for you," Soren says. "We have more important things."

Right. The pearl. "We should wait until the guests leave Emora. Then I can take you to where our target has been stashed."

"That's… that's actually a good idea," Sebastian says pointing to me. "In case someone wanted to follow us, do you agree?"

"Fine," is all Soren responds with.

"In the meantime, I need Darius or Addeah to send some breakfast to the library." The princes both give quizzical looks. "Probably some fruit or bread would do. Meanwhile, I'll be putting this room back together and getting dressed."

* * *

Soren sent Addeah to the library with food after she dropped off some breakfast for me.

A few hours. That's all it took for the entire ballroom of guests the night before to have breakfast, pack up their things and leave. I watch from my window while I clean up the mess as the count and his men exit the castle and head toward their transportation. I wonder how such a large group could get out of those tiny holes under the water. Unless there was another entrance I wasn't allowed to know about.

Now is the time to retrieve the pearl. Soren and Sebastian had come back to my room after Addeah had helped me with my hair and dressed me for the day. I had opted for a simple lavender and cream dress.

"So?" Soren asks impatiently.

"Follow me," is my reply.

Sebastian walks step by step next to me on the way to the library. Soren is at least five yards behind us, his typical broody self. Most likely still mad at me for letting his father walk into the ballroom last night. I won't blame him for that. I would be angry too.

The library is lighter with the energy of Emora radiating through the windows. The smell of ink and paper caress my nose as I inhale its familiar scent.

"Well?" Soren presses. Crossing his muscular arms.

I reply by turning around to face him with a raised eyebrow and then show him my backside while walking to the correct row of books.

"Come on out, little one," I croon, putting my hands on my thighs and bending down slightly to peer at the pale pink creature crawling out of his hiding place. He sits on the top of the books, belly side up. Clearly filled by whatever breakfast Addeah had brought him. He smiles at me and chirps. "You good boy. I told you I would return." I scratch his belly with my nails, causing him to purr in response.

Sebastian and Soren are speechless. If I didn't know any better, I would say Sebastian's eyes are about to roll out of his eye sockets and onto the floor.

Soren shows less emotion on his face but clearly is at a loss for words.

"Can you get me what I asked you to keep safe now?"

The creature chirps and flaps its head fins before crawling behind the books, orange pearl in its paw. It reaches out to me and drops the pearl into my open palm.

"Good work! That means an extra special lunch will come your way. Thank you!" I proceed to pet the creature's back, causing him to roll back over, exposing his squishy belly.

"Do you realize what that is?" Soren asks.

"Um… my new favorite friend?" I retort, continuing to scratch the creature.

"Constance, that's an axmor." Sebastian has reeled in his bug eyes and points to the creature. "It's one of the rarest and most magical creatures in the world. There's barely anything known about it. It could be dangerous."

I furrow my brows. "Dangerous? You aren't dangerous, are you? You are just the best-est little buddy ever, aren't you?"

The creature chirps again, happy to get the compliment.

"Constance," Soren demands, "take your hands off it. We can't trust it."

"For your edification, he is the only reason we have what we need in the first place," I retort.

Soren folds his arms, eyeing the creature warily.

I continue, "Your tidbit about the birthday code was wrong. If this little creature didn't help, we wouldn't have obtained the pearl. He saved me by warning me to hide before the count came barreling through the door. I owed him to set him free. And besides," I point to the markings on his belly, "he was stuck in this weird, shimmering cage and clearly being mistreated. I couldn't leave him there."

Sebastian, trying to mediate, chimes in, "I mean, Soren, if this creature did help Constance like she said it did, maybe—"

"I will not take care of that beast," Soren interjects.

"Of course *you* won't. *I* will." I counter, steeling myself for another argument with the prince. The pearl, I realize, is still in my hand. I grab Soren's wrist—even though he flinches at my touch—rotate his palm upward and drop it in before I pick up the creature in my hands, cradling it like an egg. "I owe it."

Sebastian looks between the two of us.

Soren and I stare each other down. This time he gives in first, sighing heavily and throwing his free hand in the air. "Fine, but don't let it out of your room until we know more about it. I'll add it to my list of things to research," he mumbles before stalking off with the pearl clutched in his fist leaving the creature, Sebastian, and me alone.

Once the prince is far gone from the library, Sebastian looks at me and grins. "You are incredible, you know that?"

I bite my inner lip to keep from smiling too big. My muscles relax at the compliment.

"Really, you are," he continues as he tentatively strokes the creature's head. "First you steal a pearl we've been looking to have for years now within one night. Then you rescue this little guy. You get my father to come out in public. Plus, you are the only living thing here that willingly goes head-to-head with my brother, not batting a single eyelash in the process." He chuckles to himself lightly. "Are all humans like you? No wait, don't answer that. I want my last question to be special." He proceeds to gently entangle one of my loose curls between his thumb and pointer finger.

Heat colors my cheeks. This wonderful, beautiful merman, a prince no less, thinks I am incredible. And to think I wouldn't be here if I hadn't been so reckless. Maybe being trapped here isn't so bad after all.

Then I think about Mama. Is she faring well enough? Did she do as I had asked and sell the engagement ring? Is she using the money sparingly until I have time to find Papa? Oh Papa, is he even alive still? Where could he possibly be and why? I feel it in my gut he is out there. Waiting. But how can I be certain until I see his face?

The creature chirps in my hands bringing me back to the conversation with the merman in front of me. Concern etched on his face. "Oh um," I try to shake off, the guilt weaving its way into my soul. "I guess you'll just have to find out some other day." I smile but it doesn't reach my eyes.

Sebastian looks at me—contemplative. He chooses to not ask about my sudden change in demeanor which I am thankful for and instead asks, "So what is the little guy's name?"

"Well, I haven't named him yet," I say as I pull the pink blob up to my eye level. "What do you think you should be called, hmm?"

The creature's beady black eyes blink at me. His head turning sideways.

"How about… Squish?" I suggest.

The creature chirps in delight.

"Squish, it is!"

Chapter 23

I carry Squish back to my room and stay with him there through lunch, feeding him some of my pineapple.

Addeah comes in before dinner time and adjusts my hair. She puts it in an intricate five plaited braid.

Then I'm off to dinner, even though I really don't want to be around Soren, even more so than Lamia which is saying a lot.

The air feels different as I walk into the dining hall. It's not just three seats that are occupied, but four.

Sitting at the head of the table is an old merman, with a clean-shaven white beard, purple robes, and a crown atop his head: the king. "There she is! The precious Princess Constance," he announces as I take my seat next to Lamia.

I could have sworn I heard Lamia choke on her drink at the king's proclamation.

"Good evening, My King. It is so good to see you again."

"Likewise, my dear, likewise." The king gestures for us to eat.

Sebastian gives me a thumbs up and a wink. I feel my heart flutter at the gesture. It's a shame he and I never received the opportunity to dance last night. It was the one thing I was truly looking forward to.

Soren sends daggers at me with his eyes briefly, before turning his attention to the food in front of him. Clearly, he is still mad about the king being brought to the ball. Or maybe he's mad because I ignored his warning and kept Squish. Perhaps both. Both seems most likely.

I look at the plate before me. Grilled salmon, tropical fruit, and some kind of seaweed roll. Everything looks safe enough, so I cut tiny pieces of fish with my knife.

The sound of silverware scrapes against our plates, filling the silence in the room. The king chews on one bite for quite a while before swallowing. "So, Constance, I didn't find the opportunity to see you dance at the ball last night. What happened to all the suitors you mentioned?" He lifts his cup to his mouth, giving each of his sons a knowing look.

"My King, I was so tired from all the dancing, I retired to my room earlier than anticipated."

Lamia chimes in. "Or was it that the suitors came to find out about your lack of interest in them? Rumor is you had your eyes on a special someone?" Lamia doesn't look at me, but I can see a smirk creeping up the corner of her mouth. "The Count Pesilfer Veridum was under the impression you would be going home with him."

I stop mid-chew and face Lamia as she continues cutting her food with those delicate princess hands. "What do you mean, Lamia?"

"Oh, nothing. Just that you were with him for a good portion of the night and that this morning he apparently came bursting into your room claiming you had stolen something." Her smirk turns feral.

It was foolish of me to think the little incident this morning wasn't heard or witnessed by anyone other than Sebastian, Soren, and myself.

The brothers stiffen at the mention of the altercation. Sebastian looks to his father to see his expression.

"What is she talking about, Soren?" the king asks.

Soren looks at his father for a moment, before digging back into his food. "Nothing to concern you with, father. The count did accuse Miss Constance of stealing, but he was sorely mistaken. Sebastian and I took care of it."

The king frowns a little, trying to puzzle out what to say. "Well, I'm glad the misunderstanding was settled. And my dear," he directs toward me, "perhaps next ball you can take me to the dance floor." He chuckles, revealing a straight set of slightly yellowing teeth. I suppose in his younger years the king would be considered quite handsome. Just like his sons.

"Don't get too excited about the prospect, Father," Soren interjects.

"Oh phooey, my boy. I haven't felt so wonderful in years as I did last night, and it's all thanks to Miss Constance. Thank you deary for such a wonderful memory." The king smiles and starts digging into his fruit.

"Father, you were almost killed because she brought you there last night," Soren retorts. "I've had to double the guards on border patrol and at your personal quarters because others are now made aware of your... condition."

The king stops eating to look at his oldest son. "My dear boy, people have tried to kill me for many years. It only made the ball all the more memorable. And of course, you and your brother threatening the entire ocean on my behalf helped the situation. It was all under control. Speaking of such matters though," the king takes a pause to drink from his goblet, "Have you set a date for your coronation yet?"

Soren shifts uncomfortably in his seat. "No, father. But I will soon," he replies.

"Yes, my boy, I think that would be wise," the king says giving Soren a wide smile before skewering a slice of banana.

Soren's steely expression softens as he studies his father eating with us. I have grown accustomed to his glares and his indifference, but this look is unknown to me. I've but seen it one other time cross Soren's features. The look he gives his father is one that portrays wholly reverent love.

This is the first time since I've been here that the king has eaten with us. Then I remember that first night after dinner with the royal family. Getting trapped in the secret passages. Seeing a smiling Soren feeding an old stranger, except it wasn't a stranger. It was the king. His father. All those times he had said he had other matters to attend to, was he taking care of his father the entire time? Maybe there's more to Soren than I gave him credit for.

My heart aches for that bond. It makes me miss all those moments I had with my papa that I took for granted. The fishing trips, sneaking into the kitchen at night to eat leftover biscuits, sunrise walks on the beach, teasing Mama endlessly together.

It all feels surreal, like it had happened only in my dreams.

Suddenly I don't feel like finishing my food. I push my plate away.

"Are you okay, Constance?" a concerned Sebastian asks causing the room to look at me.

"If you aren't feeling well, maybe you should go home. Your own home. Away from here," Lamia chimes.

"Lamia," Soren hisses at her.

Lamia puts her hands up innocently, silverware still connected. "I'm just saying maybe she would feel better in her own bed instead of in one of our guestrooms. She's been here quite a while, and I'm sure she's ready to go home."

"I'm fine," I begin, "I just need some air, I think. If you will please excuse me." I dab the corners of my mouth with my silk napkin and stand up abruptly, practically running through the door.

* * *

I'm not sure how I got here, but here I am. In the middle of the royal gardens hyperventilating. I can't seem to breathe. My chest tightens with every struggling breath. I try to breathe deeper, heavier but it isn't working.

Panic rises up my throat.

Firm hands rest on my shoulders and turn me around to face concerned storm cloud eyes and curly black hair.

I stare at those stormy eyes as he takes his hand and applies pressure to one of my nostrils, then the other, alternating between the two until my breathing has slowed. My body feels like jelly. Luckily Sebastian's strong arms hold me upright. His eyes don't leave me once.

I get lost in those storm-cloud eyes. They're mesmerizing, reassuring.

Eventually, I have the breath to say, "Thank you."

"Think nothing of it." He grins softly. "Are you okay? What happened back there? Was it Lamia's comments? Because if so, I'd gladly—"

"No, no… it wasn't that. I just…" I can't tell him why I became so anxious. Was it the fact I am entirely in over my head being a thief and a princess and a *mermaid* in a world I had no idea existed until a week ago? Or the fact I left my mama to find Papa because I didn't have the guts to go through with an abusive engagement that would lead to an abusive marriage? Not even knowing for a fact that it would save our staff or our household. For all I know, I could be chasing shadows.

Seeing Soren look so lovingly at his father, the way he yelled at me for bringing him into the ballroom, keeping him locked away from the public eye, hand feeding him his meals. In that look I could tell Soren would do anything for his father to protect him. The selflessness of his actions punched me right in the face. And it made me realize I wasn't going to find my papa just for him, but mostly for me. It made me selfish. And I couldn't bear to look at my motives, my heart, and not despise what lay within me.

But I can't bring myself to let Sebastian know any of this. Instead, I deflect the question with another question. "The heist, the scheming, the deal you made with me, it all has to do with your father, doesn't it?"

Shock crosses Sebastian's face briefly before he blinks it away. He motions for me to take a seat on the rock surrounding the water with the serpentine fountain.

So, I sit.

"Yes," he begins, taking my hands in his, examining them instead of my eyes as he continues. "Our father is very…sick, which you knew. But…he's practically on his death bed according to the healers in the castle."

That explains the lack of his presence, the coughing, and the fact he needed me to help him to the ballroom. I thought maybe it was just age, but it's worse than I thought.

"And this pearl will cure him?" I guess, encouraging Sebastian to explain more.

"No. The pearl is rare and beautiful, but it has no magical qualities. Only magic can save him now, but we don't have the resources to find that kind of magic yet. It's forbidden to save someone from their fate." His eyes slowly rise up from our hands to my face. A look of sadness glazing over his eyes.

"So the pearl…"

"The pearl is a means to the magic. Or at least that's what Soren hopes will happen." He exhales a heavy breath. "This kingdom is put in jeopardy by my father's sickness. And if Soren doesn't agree to a coronation date to be declared king soon…well let's just say anyone could take the throne by any means necessary." Sebastian shakes his locks and looks up at the sky, or whatever they called the top part of their city. "You saw what happened in the ballroom, right?" He looks to me for an answer.

I nod.

"That's just the beginning of what could be a long war between oceans. Soren's risking everything to save our father. I just hope he knows what he's getting himself into."

"What does the coronation have to do with your father's health?" I had heard the king mention that in the dining hall, but I do not understand.

Sebastian shifts his gaze upon the serpentine fountain. "The coronation's a ritual to solidify the heir's birthright. Soren already will receive our father's abilities to control the water. But the coronation is a legal proclamation to the five oceans that Soren is the new one true king. After his coronation, no one is allowed to try and overthrow him without the rest of the kingdoms to contend with too.

"But without it…if the king, our father, dies before he proclaims Soren king, anyone can challenge him for the throne. Anyone can bring their battalion right up to our doorstep and seize control. No one will be obligated to stop them. And that's what Soren is dangling in front of our enemies. I just hope he's making the right choice."

I nod in understanding. Addeah mentioned how peaceful King Cyrus' reign has been. I imagine what it would be like if Soren doesn't save him or doesn't take his place. Would someone like Count Pesilfer usurp him? Would war break out like Sebastian said? I shudder at the thought of this beautiful place turning to rubble.

"Oh, you must be freezing. Here." Sebastian takes off his jacket and wraps it over my shoulders. His eyes drift to my mouth in the process. "I know what my third question is, Miss Constance."

He has a look in his eyes. A pining look like that of a child having to wait for their dessert sitting just inches in front of him.

"And what is that?" I squeak out, chest swelling with warmth.

"If I were to kiss you right now, what would you do?"

My heartbeat quickens, and I lick my lips. "I guess you'll have to try and find out," I say, breathless.

Then his lips are on mine, warm and soft like velvet.

It isn't my first kiss, but it feels like it. Conner's kiss that night at his family's ball was quick and fleeting and interrupted by my would-be husband. But Sebastian's kiss? It lingers like dew on a bright spring morning, warming with the rising sun the longer it lasts.

Briefly I think of the consequences of a human kissing a mer-prince, but Sebastian's lips soon have me forgetting everything. All my worries and guilt recede to the back of my mind.

The kiss lasts a lifetime and yet feels too short the moment he pulls away, grinning from ear to ear and placing his forehead against mine. He chuckles breathlessly. "Constance, have I ever mentioned how incredible you are?"

"I think I've heard that before, yes." I giggle in response.

"We better get you to your room. As far as I know, you have a big day tomorrow."

"That's probably true, but—"

"Don't ask me how. Soren will explain everything in the morning. For now, let me bask in the moment. But, uh, Constance?" he asks.

"Yes?"

"Can we step out of the fountain yet?"

I look down and notice now that my feet and shoes are entirely immersed in the fountain water. The bottom of my dress soaks up the lapping water.

"Oh… well I am quite mortified," I laugh as Sebastian steps out of the fountain and offers me a hand as I raise my leg over the rock.

He holds me close all the way back to my room.

This may very well be the best moment of my life, soaking feet and all.

Chapter 24

I know Sebastian told me Soren would explain the next part of our deal in the morning, but I didn't know it was going to be this early.

He barely knocked before barreling in and tossing me black clothing and demanding I get dressed before hauling me out to the entrance behind the giant waterfall.

I gape at the black lifeless water. A river of goosebumps over my arms, not necessarily because I'm cold. No. The black uniform Soren gave me is what he calls a body suit. It's tight fitting but stretchy. The black fabric covers my arms, even my fingers, and runs down to tightly constrict my legs and feet which are also completely covered. Every inch below my neck is hidden behind this strange black outfit, but somehow, I've never felt more exposed.

When I had walked out of the bathroom with it on, Soren began to bark something at me and stopped. One quick look at me, and he swiftly turned away, just waving a hand to follow him.

Darius is here as well. When I had asked Soren why Sebastian isn't joining us also, all he muttered was something about someone having to stay back and keep an eye on the city. I wish he was able to come with us. I would feel safer if he was with me, mediating between me and his brother.

But it was just the three of us. Darius, Soren, and me. I'm sure this trip is going to be especially fun.

I'm about to ask them how I'm supposed to survive the swim with them when the sight of the two males stripping stops me. My mouth gapes. "What are you two doing?" I demand and turn around.

"Do you really think we want to swim in full royal attire? Come on, human, use your head."

I scoff a laugh and slowly turn to face them again. Soren pulls off his shoes and socks.

"Well, no I suppose not." I twirl a loose curl from my up-do. Half asleep in the wee hours of the morning, I opted to pull it into a low bun, but without the help of Addeah, it is sorely lacking in security.

He gives an annoyed look, like he would if I was his younger sister, then rolls his eyes before proceeding with the rest of his clothing. He pulls off his jacket and shirt to reveal the muscular canvas beneath. Next, he replaces his shirt with a sling that creates an 'x' across his back and puts two long swords inside. The front of the sling has multiple pockets and small straps, most likely for holding smaller weapons like knives or throwing stars. He grabs at his jacket and pulls out one knife no bigger than a letter opener and tucks it in. Even with the tiny arsenal hanging off his chest, I still notice the gills on his rib cage.

Darius does the same, taking off all loose articles of clothing until they're in nothing but shorts that seem to be made of the same material I currently wear. It's black and tight, ending just above the knees. His sling is heavier, thicker, with more pockets and places to store things. It also contains a sword, but the front of his chest has multiple colored glass vials and who knows what else is stored in the little pockets.

Darius is stoic as he finishes undressing. He also is very muscular. There are many scars that taint his pectoral muscles, almost like claw marks from a cat that went too deep.

I look at the water. Yep. Still scary and dark. Did I mention how much I didn't want to go down there? "So, why is it that I have to go too?" I question.

Darius refuses to answer. He looks to Soren who is still apparently mad at me for, well everything, really. Arguing with him. Stealing a creature that may be dangerous. Almost having his father killed. Being a human. Not drowning in the first place. So many options to choose from.

Soren double and triple checks his sling before finally giving me a moment of his time. "I don't trust you to be in the kingdom without me."

Right. Of course, because humans are a major threat to merfolk. How dare I even exist, I think.

I cross my arms in annoyance. I wish Sebastian could at least be the one I travel with and not Mr. Grumpy Pants.

I glance between the two half naked mermen and the black water. "Well, are either of you willing to explain how exactly, I am going to survive this plunge then?" I turn and look at the mermen for an answer.

"The suit you wear will keep you from freezing to death. It's created specifically to keep body heat in, not allowing any to escape in the frigid waters, apart from what heat comes out of the top of your head, but that will be necessary to keep bare, so you don't overheat from the swim either. And don't worry, Miss Constance. We have something else for you too." He pulls out four small vials of purple liquid. "I went to the healers' quarters last night and gathered a few of these vials." The liquid left little bubbles sticking to the side of the glass before fizzing up and popping when it reached the tiny sliver of air at the top. At my silence, he continues, "It's a potion that will allow you to breath underwater for a certain amount of time. It's meant for younger merfolk still growing into their gills but should do the trick for you as well."

I take the vial from his hand and roll it around in my fingers. "A potion? Like magic?"

"Yes. Take this orally and you will be able to breathe as if you were born a mermaid."

"How long does it last? Will it hurt?"

Darius puts a large brown hand on my shoulder reassuringly. "It depends on the potency. Most likely a few hours, but no more than five. I brought three more in case you need it. One for each of us to carry. And in a sense, yes, the transformation will feel… not necessarily painful, but probably uncomfortable."

Lucky me.

Soren crosses his arms and gives me a look as if to say *time is ticking, hurry up, human.*

I skeptically look at the two mermen that watch me before I uncork the vial and examine the purple liquid one more time. "Bottoms up!" I throw my head back and dump the contents down my throat in one quick swig. Like downing a spoonful of disgusting cold medicine. Except this is worse. Much worse. Like letting rotten, uncooked fish slide down my throat. I cough and hack at the horrible taste it leaves in my mouth, before a dull ache makes its way around my abdomen. I can feel it stretching and expanding, forming slits on my sides. It feels similar to period cramps, the constant tightening and expanding. The feeling is certainly uncomfortable, but luckily not painful enough I feel like curling into a ball on the ground. Some months are like that. Only a few moments pass until the ache subsides.

I run my black covered fingers over my rib cage and feel three openings on each side. Gills. I have gills. My eyes widen and I look to Darius.

He nods in approval before handing me another vial. I tuck it into a pocket on the sleeve of my arm. He walks over and gives Soren one as well who slips his in one of the small pockets of his sling. Securing it tightly before patting it with his hand. That leaves the third vial for Darius to carry.

"Can I at least know where we're going?" I inquire.

"We're going to pay a visit to the Siren's Hollow." Soren, ready to go, struts to the spot right in front of me. An edge of caution echoes in his voice as he says, "Listen to me. What we will see when we're out there…much of it isn't what it seems. There will be things you see that are not there. There will be creatures there that appear harmless. They are not. And whatever you do, don't get lost in the music. Do you understand me?"

That edge in Soren's voice— was it concern? Concern or worry for me? I try to puzzle it out, but he's already blinked away whatever look he had in his eyes, the sternness of his commands gaining strength once more. "We need to go. Captain, lead the way."

Darius dives headfirst into the water, leaving growing ripples in his absence.

"You next, human. Don't get lost."

I turn to him and stick my tongue out childishly. The black water has already stilled from Darius' entry. Another stray curl dangles in my face. My heart *thump-thumps* in my chest like the beat of a drum. I tuck that stray hair behind my ear before I take a few steps backward, pinning myself to the cave wall for a second before running toward the black abyss and jump. I inhale a huge gulp of air and close my eyes before the plunge overtakes me. Within a second, I'm completely immersed in dark waters. It chills my ears and nose, but surprisingly the rest of me is comfortable and warm.

My eyes are still closed. Will the salt of the ocean sting like it did whenever I went swimming with my parents in the summer? I prayed not before prying them open.

Darius and Soren are there with me already, looking at me expectantly. I see them as clearly as if we were on dry land on a sunny day. He and Darius look different in the water. Their hands and feet elongated and webbed. I look at my own hands and feet. Sure enough, even under the black fabric, I can feel the difference, see my fingers and toes have stretched longer. If this isn't the most magical thing I will have ever experienced in my life, then I can't even imagine what could top it. This potion magic is confounding.

"Stay close or you'll get lost," Soren says under water.

It sounds strange in my ears, almost melodic if not slightly muffled.

I can't help but smile ear to ear at the two mermen waiting for me to follow.

Darius offers a pleased smirk in return before glancing in Soren's direction. Then he turns and swims away, out of one of the dark tunnels that surrounds us.

I look to Soren. His face is amused; his mouth displays a rare upward tilt. But his words remain clipped. "Don't get lost!" that sweet melodic voice says urgently.

I obey and swim after the captain, as graceful as a sword fish, gliding through the water with little effort. I thought I was a decent swimmer before, but my definition of a great swimmer just changed drastically.

Soren follows close behind me. He was right. There was no way I would get out of here on my own. We take multiple turns down multiple tunnels in the cave before hitting open waters.

The outside of Emora looks like a volcano underwater; apart from the tiny sea creatures crawling around the rocky surface.

If humans ever do figure out how to reach this depth, they would never suspect that an entire kingdom resides on the inside of this rock.

I look up at the expanse of ocean blue, not sure how far exactly we are from the surface. I look down and the space between us and the sea floor is also incomprehensible. I always felt small whenever I went out on the boat with Papa for deep sea fishing or sailing, but in this moment, it is a whole new kind of small. Like I am one grain of sand in the entire ocean.

Soren swims next to me, urging me to stay focused. We carry on our journey through the vast depths of the ocean. Breathing underwater feels unnatural. My nostrils and mouth are useless for breathing because the gills are doing all the work. I can feel them at my sides expanding and retracting, filtering through the water. In fact, a tickling sensation covers my torso with each liquid movement, and I wonder if fish feel the same sensation. The rest of the swim is silent and long.

I was surprised when we didn't run into any schools of fish, but maybe that was because we were mermaids and that would make them our prey? I figure it was just another question in my never-ending list of questions about Emora and its citizens. Maybe I can ask Addeah when we get back before I am set free. That was the one thing that excited me most. After this trip, I am to be set free, with all the provisions I will need for my journey. I got the pearl and now we are going to get the answers Soren wants and the deal will be complete. I can finally get out of here and save my papa like I had planned. We can be a family again. My heart swells at the thought.

A couple hours into our journey, I spot a mountain of brown rock in the near distance. The scene before us is serene. It's exactly the kind of image I had growing up when my papa told me stories of mermaids. Magical. Beautiful. Peaceful.

A soft hum grows louder the closer we get. The rock is dark brown, with life surrounding it. A host of colorful fish swim leisurely around their homes on the rock. Rays of light cast spotlights on the entrance as if to say "welcome."

I look to Soren and Darius flanking me, expecting them to look how I feel. But their faces tell a completely different story. Darius has his sword out as he swims closer to the entrance, scanning every crevice of the rock. Soren's jaw is clenched, and his sword is drawn as well.

We must be closer to the surface, because sunshine beams across the mountain side.

We swim up to one of those entrances, lit up by that beautiful ray of sunlight. The melodic music grows louder. It's so pleasant, I have the faintest idea that maybe I should stay here for the rest of my life.

The tunnel here is different than those of Emora. It's a straight swim to the entrance and before I know it, Darius,

Soren, and I are popping our heads out of the water to reveal a clean, white polished floor. Two mermaids stand at the entrance and help me out of the water.

"Welcome," they say unison as I squeeze out extra water from my messy bun. How can their voices be so beautiful? Like a songbird.

"Hello," I say, but Soren and Darius step in front of me, swords at the ready. They didn't let me say anything else or even let me offer a hand to introduce myself. I felt the gesture rude since we are guests here but decided it was best not to argue with the prince in front of strangers.

"Take us to her," Soren snarls.

The two mermaids look at each other, look back at us and bow at the neck before leading us away from the cave entrance and further into the mountain.

***

"To what do I owe the pleasure of having the heir himself in my domain?" a voice dark and light, old and young, reverberates in my ears. The rich melodious voice belongs to a woman, sitting on a throne made of pure gold. She must be a siren, considering Soren had said this place was called the Siren's Hollow. Her hair is corn-silk, reaching well below her exposed belly button. Her skin is a shimmering sun kissed citrine. Her bright and young cat-like eyes, accentuate her luscious pink lips, the bottom naturally pouty.

"You know why I'm here. I've come seeking answers," Soren says. He pulls out the giant orange pearl from his sling, holding it between his thumb and forefinger.

The woman's eyes light up with greed. Her slender fingers reach out as if to snatch the pearl from Soren's hand.

Soren merely pulls it back and wags a finger at her. "Uh-uh. Information first."

Those cat-like eyes slit. Her pouty lip protrudes even further. She slumps back in her throne and crosses her mile long legs.

The room is silent, except for that other worldly song.

I wonder if Soren and Darius have ever wanted to make this place their home instead of Emora. That nagging want creeps into my mind again; I believe I should stay here forever.

"Very well, prince," the siren sings, "I will give you what you want. Unless you would prefer to stay here and rule with me forever instead? It would be the easier of the two paths."

"Pass." Soren nods to Darius who keeps his sword at the ready.

The Siren arches a brow. Straightening her back at Soren's quick dismissal of her offer. She closes her eyes and opens them with swift intensity. Darkness envelops the room, apart from the siren, now glowing translucently green. That ethereal voice begins to boom around us.

> *Save your father you may try, but don't be fooled,*
> *the king will die.*
> *Objects you will seek. Three.*
> *A chest. A book. And a key.*
> *One in the depths of the beast's lair.*
> *Another in the home of despair.*
> *Last is trapped in the betrayer's snare.*
> *But be wary, handsome prince.*
> *Change is stirring*
> *Far from sense.*

At the end of the fortune, the light grows back into the room. The siren no longer glows green but still radiates beauty. Her hand stretches out—ready to take her prize.

Soren's jaw is clenched, causing a large vein to pop out of his thick neck. "Couldn't you be more specific?" he snarls out.

"You know the laws of our kind, prince. I do not interpret your fortunes, lest it change the paths of fate. Take it and be gone." She grins, examining the prince from head to feet. "Or stay and let me snack on you." She somehow manages to make her perfect white teeth look unpleasant as she smiles at Soren, licking her lips as her eyes roam painfully slow down his body.

"Prince," Darius whispers. His face is trained to give none of his emotions away, but his hand clings to that sword with such force, I would think the handle will soon break.

Soren doesn't take his eyes off the woman but slowly opens his palm to reveal the pearl. His feet move with caution toward her.

Her eyes grow increasingly hungry the closer he gets, like a cat that has finally trapped its mouse. Just waiting for the precise moment to strike. But I don't mind her look. I get this sense she is harmless. She would never hurt us, that voice hums in my ears.

Soren plunks the pearl into her hands, back pedaling to his place between Darius and me.

She holds it preciously in her open palm, smiling at her new treasure and brings it close to her chest. "Foolish prince," the young and old voice croons. "As much as I love our bargain, there are three of you and only one pearl." Her unpleasant grin pulls at the edges of her face.

Next to me, Soren stiffens, baring his teeth at her. His back goes taut before placing his body directly in front of mine.

I'm so confused, I almost ask the question, why is Soren being so rude since we are guests here, but before I can utter a syllable, Soren wraps his hands over my ears, panic growing in his eyes. "Snap out of it, Constance!"

Foggy. My brain feels like its sailing through a dense fog unsure which way to go.

The music. It stopped. And along with it goes my entire perception of this place. What was a moment ago a spotless, shimmering throne room of gold, is now a rotten, grimy den. The throne isn't gold either, but an arrangement of bones. Mostly human bones by the looks of it.

And the beautiful siren is only in my memory. What stands in her place is utterly terrifying. A monster with stringy black hair adorned with a crown of rotten algae, barely covering her black, soulless eyes. The white perfect teeth I thought she had are replaced with obsidian, grimy razors, jutting out in all different directions. But her fingers. Recognition hits me like a bolt of lightning. I have seen fingers like this before. Deathly pale, long spindly fingers pointing at me.

The monster cackles. Throwing her head back before turning to me. That other worldly mix of voices whispers softly, "This is the part where you run before my beasties eat you alive."

Chapter 25

Soren shoves me toward the exit before the two soldiers, also monsters, lunge for us, roaring with disappointment at their miss.

My heart pounds in my chest as my feet do their best to keep upright on the sticky ground. How had I not noticed the awful, putrid smell that permeates this entire place?

Ear piercing shrieks echo all around us. The halls aren't white marble and brightly lit. They are dark and difficult to navigate.

Darius is at the front of us, sword in hand. Those monsters, sirens, start popping out of nowhere, claws and teeth slashing and snarling. Each one, falling at the edge of Darius' sword.

But when one falls, two more take its place.

I turn to look behind me as best I can while running forward. Three more come barreling toward us from where we came.

"Keep going, Constance!" Soren barks, pressing me forward as he turns, withdrawing his double swords, slicing each siren clean through before turning back and running with us.

We're almost back to the entrance. It must be close. It felt so much closer when we walked in here.

"This way!" Darius calls from ahead of us. He has made a path, leaving corpses in his wake.

I check to make sure Soren is still right behind me. Then we sprint toward Darius' voice.

The water entrance. It's here. We will get out of here.

Darius urges Soren and me to jump in first. We do so with little hesitation and dive feet first into the freezing water. My neck prickles at the sudden temperature change.

Bubbles muddy my vision until they float away. Soren grabs my hand with his free one, the other still connected to one of his swords and drags me along in the water.

He takes us quickly through the tunnel with such speed, my shoulder makes contact with the jagged walls on every turn. Open waters, where freedom awaits.

I exhale dramatically with what oxygen was left in my lungs, causing big bubbles to cloud my vision. The gills begin to take over. Then I see it.

We are not alone.

My heart sinks to my stomach when I see an army of hundreds of soulless, skeletal sirens, waiting just outside the entrance—our means of escape— to feast on our flesh.

I look to Soren, panic in my eyes. His focus is not on the small army ahead of us, but from where we came.

Darius. He should have caught up to us by now.

I squeeze Soren's hand, forcing him to look at me, just for a second.

He draws his attention away, concern plain as day on his face.

"I'll get him," I say under the water, taking that small letter opener-sized dagger from Soren's sling before he can disapprove. I'd never handled a knife for anything more than flaying a fish with Papa before a family cooked dinner, but I figure the concept of stabbing is pretty straight forward. Aim the pointy end at anything that comes for me.

Soren gawks at me, dumbfounded.

I turn and swim back into the tunnel, barely making it anywhere before a large merman crashes into me.

Luckily, I have the good sense to get the dagger out of the way, cradling Darius from his impact with me by putting my free hand against his torso.

Soren looks as relieved as I feel. Until I notice large, red puffs leaking out from multiple places on Darius' body.

My eyes widen.

He is in terrible shape, barely able hold up his weight in the water. I wrap my arm underneath him to keep him from sinking to the bottom of the ocean.

Sirens shriek around us. Growing impatient at the sight of Darius making it out of the tunnel alive instead of their sisters. They must have been hoping for a two-front ambush.

Soren eyes Darius and me. He looks to the army of claws and teeth and rot.

Then he sheaths his sword.

What's he doing?! We need our weapons to get out of here!

He pulls his arms close to his abdomen. They shake at his concentration.

Then I feel it. A sudden shift in the water, like the dense feeling in the air before a heavy rainfall.

Soren flies his hands out, palms outstretched against our awaiting foes. The water shifts and whirls into a tornado of power. It was a tornado—an underwater tornado raging through the flanks of sirens. A large pathway of water divides them. Sirens who got hit are either left unconscious, floating down to the depths of the ocean or whirling away.

"Let's go!" Soren takes up Darius' other side, who is now unconscious, head dangling in front of him. Blood leaks from his wounds continuously, leaving a steady stream of red.

We swim as fast as we can while dragging Darius' body along with us.

The sea of sirens gain back their composure, closing in on us from all sides.

With one hand, Soren calls the water to do his will, sending strike after strike at the onslaught of monsters.

A dull pain cramps at my sides.

Soren lets go of Darius, causing me to falter on my hold, but I do my best to keep the captain upright and continue swimming away with him.

Soren uses both of his hands now, sending smaller, faster waves at the sirens who get too close.

So many. There are so many of them. I don't know how much longer we can keep this up.

Darius' limp body becomes heavier by the second. I don't know what's going to give way first, my grip on him or my lungs.

My lungs. The cramping I'm feeling—it's not from fatigue. The potion is wearing off. My fingers and toes are shrinking, the webbing between them receding. The salt content in the water stings my eyes causing me to squint to see anything happening around us.

Soren is above us now, as my body, Darius' along with me, sink farther and farther down. He's fighting as hard he can to keep the sirens at bay. A blast of water sends two sirens shrieking, spinning out of range. He looks down at me and the captain.

I try to say something, but the potion has completely worn off now. I am completely, entirely human again. Soon I will drown. Fire scorches my lungs with every passing second.

I recall the spare vial pressing against my arm. I try to reach it and keep kicking, hoping Darius and I don't sink any further away from Soren and his protection. But I can't get to it. Not without letting Darius go.

Two options lay before me. I can let Darius drop, unconscious, into the open waters, where any awaiting beast could snatch him up. Or I leave the vial where it's at and pray for a different sort of miracle.

I brace myself for the long, uncomfortable death of drowning. Again. Kicking my legs to keep us as close to protection as possible. I will keep him alive for what he's done for me. For Soren. For his wife, Addeah. I will not fail him for as long as I can. Even if it kills me.

Edges of blackness circle my vision. The last thing I see through my slitted eyes is a raging billow of water blasting out in a full circle around Soren. Leaving him alone enough to look down at us, his hand outstretched.

Then nothing. Darkness embraces me like an old friend as I pass out.

Chapter 26

I wake up on gritty, solid ground. It feels like lying on sandpaper. The texture scuffs against my cheeks. Drums pound in my head. My body, legs, and arms are lead. My hair is still soaking wet, but the black suit is entirely dry.

"Ugh," I groan, rolling up on my hands and knees to find Soren's bare back facing me. He's sitting on the ground, hunched over a limp body. *Darius.* "Oh, no, Darius," I gasp and crawl over to them immediately forgetting about my tired, achy body. Darius' eyes are closed. Scratches and puncture wounds cover his torso and arms with some kind of yellow ooze dripping from them.

"Venom," Soren mutters without so much as a glance in my direction.

I search Darius' face, his chest, and notice the subtle rise and fall of his sternum, and sigh with relief, slumping onto my bottom next to the two mermen. "What can we do to help him?"

"I've been putting a salve on his wounds for hours now. Eventually it will withdraw all the toxins in his system, and he will be well enough to travel." Soren continues to stare at his captain. Hands draped over his knees, head slightly slumped. Although my hair is still dripping wet, the bun I created long gone in the chaos of our ordeal, Soren's shorter, jet-black hair is dry.

I look at our surroundings. Rough, rusty-brown rock flanks us. A tranquil pool of green-tinted sea water laps a few feet to our right. But above us, oh, I thought I may never see the sight again. Through a hole in the ceiling, a glowing, cream colored, full moon casts rays of light into the small space. It is the reason I can see anything in here at all. "Are we—are we above ground?" I whisper, in awe.

Soren keeps his attention on the body in front of him, dabbing at the yellow ooze with a torn piece of his shorts, then rinsing it in the water next to him. "In a manner of speaking. I brought us to a sea cave, but this particular hole can only be found if you swim under the water. It'll be safe enough for the night."

"Oh," was all I could manage to say. Safe from the sirens. Safe from drowning. I try to think back on what went down at Siren's Hollow.

I remember the beautiful siren, her fortune, and then siccing her kin on us. Us fighting our way out and Darius getting hurt. We were completely surrounded and the potion I took had worn off.

I definitively thought I would die right there. And yet, here I am, sitting in the moonlight.

"How did you do it?" I ask, leaning over my knees, dipping my head in his direction. Trying to get Soren to look at me, searching for those tropical blues.

He does the opposite, turning his head the other direction. Like a child in trouble, not wanting to face his consequences. "What do you mean?" Such a bland, detached response. What is his problem? If this were any other time, he would be barking orders at me by now or getting snippy. But he just sits there, defeated.

"You saved us, Soren. I know you did, even though it's a puzzle to me. We were surrounded by hundreds of sirens. And I tried so hard to keep Darius with me, but I passed out. The last thing I saw was you, using that water magic you have to keep the monsters from getting too close." Soren draws his knees to his chest and hugs them. His face downcast to the water's edge, watching the small ripples crash into the cave's lip. "You could have let me drown but you didn't." Against my better judgment, I tentatively put my hand on his, both now resting on his knee. "Thank you."

That slight physical connection awakens something within him. He draws his attention away from the water to our hands, gently resting together before he steadily raises his eyes to meet mine. "Don't thank me."

"Why not? You saved me. Saved us."

"I don't deserve your thanks. I got you into this in the first place." His voice raises with each word. "You could have died, and it would have been because of me. Both of you almost—" he stops short.

I couldn't believe what I was hearing. Was he really blaming himself for what happened? It wasn't his fault the leader of the sirens betrayed us, even after we brought something she would want in exchange for the information Soren sought. He couldn't have known what she was going to do.

"I put you, the captain, so many people in harm's way because I was too stubborn to see the inevitable. You heard what the Queen of the Sirens spoke. The king—my *father*, will die no matter what I do." Soren yanks his hand from under mine, rubbing it over his face and jaw.

I press my lips together, contemplating what to say. I tuck my dripping wet curls behind my ears as best I can and crawl in front of Soren, crossing my legs in a pretzel shape. Gently, I take hold of his wrists and bring his hands down. "That Siren Queen said a lot of things." I duck my head further down, to meet his eye-line. "Don't you remember? She also said she can't explain the fortune to you. That you can and will seek out those three objects. One or all three of them may save your father." I squeeze his wrists reassuringly. "And besides," I begin, "of course your father is going to die." Soren's eyes are piercing daggers at my comment, but I explain further, nonetheless. "Everyone dies at some point. It may be today, or tomorrow. Or... maybe, you find whatever cure he needs, and he lives another twenty, maybe thirty, years. We don't know. But isn't there worth in trying?"

The anger fades from his eyes, replaced with skepticism. He scoffs, shaking his head in disbelief. "Why are you trying to console me? Why are you doing any of this?" He glances at Darius, the cave walls, the water.

"Well, for starters, we had a deal *prince*. I get you the pearl, the answers you seek, and you set me free with a new set of provisions and a boat. Remember?"

"No." He shakes his head once more, "No, why did you go back into Siren's Hollow after Darius when you knew he wasn't right behind us? Why did you choose to keep holding him even though you knew the potion was wearing off? Why try to comfort me right now when all I've been is anything but pleasant to you since you arrived?"

Darius stirs next to us, groaning faintly before falling back asleep. The ooze is building up around his wounds. I look at the wet piece of shorts fabric near his head then release Soren's wrists gently. I proceed to pick up the damp cloth and dab at the wounds like Soren did moments ago. Mimicking his movements of swiping the toxins off in a gentle scooping pattern and rinsing it off in the water below us.

"Darius has been nothing but kind to me since I've been here. He saved me from drowning the first time. Clothed me in the dungeons when I needed it. I wanted to return the favor somehow. Besides," I look over my shoulder where Soren still sits. "Addeah would murder me if I let anything happen to him. She scares me, you know?"

Soren laughs softly, a ghost of a grin brightening his face. "Yes, she scares me too."

"But in all seriousness, I wouldn't have forgiven myself if I had lived and he hadn't."

"That still doesn't explain why you're being civil with me now." He shifts uncomfortably, until his back finds the cave wall. He crosses his arms, causing those chiseled biceps to bulge. He stares at me, expectant.

"Well," I say, turning back to Darius' wounds. "I know what it's like to want to do anything for your family—your father."

"Really? How so?" Skepticism lingers in his voice.

I raise an accusatory eyebrow. "I tried to inform you in the dungeons, remember? Or were you too busy being angry at me for not drowning in the first place to actually listen to what I had to say?"

He flinches like I had just slapped him in the face. "Well, I'm listening now."

I dip the piece of cloth in water again. It looks like Darius' wounds are clean enough at the moment, so I neatly fold the cloth and set it down next to his head. I crane my neck to face Soren.

There's genuine curiosity in his features. His neck is slightly inched forward. His brow furrows at the middle.

"I was on that boat—the one that you capsized with I presume those special royal powers—searching for my own father. He's been missing since late winter, leaving my mama and myself and our entire household practically penniless."

He uncrosses his arms and folds his legs inward. Keen to hear every word I say, so I continue.

"Mama found a suitor for me to wed before I was considered unsuitable to marry. Except this particular suitor was… the sort of man I could never love."

Soren arches a brow. "So, you ran away because of a boy?"

Heat floods my cheeks. "No! Not entirely," I fidget with my thumbs, twirling them in circles underneath the black smooth fabric. "I also desperately want to find my papa. It kills me not knowing what happened to him.

"I know Mama misses him too. They have a love that's unmatched. It must be torture on her soul to be without him. It's a burden on both of us." I look to the water, concentrating on anything but Soren's judgmental stare that is no doubt painted on his features as I admit my selfish actions. "I want to find Papa and bring him home safe and sound. If that keeps us from becoming destitute, keeps me from marrying a pompous snob, then so be it." I grab the wet ends of my hair and search for split ends.

That guilt emerges in my stomach again at the thought of my motives. Was I truly going to save my father out of the goodness of my heart? Or was it out of selfish desire to rid myself of the responsibility Mama had placed on me?

Soren asks, "So your father's been missing for months. Do you have any idea where he's at?"

"No." I yank away a split end.

He pauses for a long time before replying, "Constance, how do you know he's not already dead?"

I pluck off another dead end of hair and toss it toward the lazy water. "I know he still lives. I may not know where he is exactly, or what has happened to him, but I know he's alive. I feel it deep within my bones, as if he's calling out to me, reassuring me all will be well. If only I could find him." A loose strand of hair falls from my mane. I decide to wrap it around my black finger until I have thoroughly cut off its circulation.

"Hmm," Soren contemplates. "And your mother? What's her situation like right now?"

"I don't know much, but I know we were running out of funds fast because she doesn't have the heart to get rid of any of the staff in our household. I gave her my engagement ring in secret and told her in a note to sell it discreetly. Spread out the earnings for as long as possible until I returned, but it's already been over a week, and I'm no closer to finding Papa than I was when I ran away. In fact, I think I'm even farther behind than when I started." I unwrap the hair from my finger and watch it drift into the lapping water. "I fear she'll run out of funds before I get the chance to even go home."

"That's why you were so desperate to get out of the dungeon. You feel like time is running out for your mother."

"Yes." Tears well up in my eyes, even though I do my best to blink them away. Using the back of my hand, I catch the droplets before they have a chance to roll down my cheeks.

I look up from my watery vision, and there is Soren. His face isn't judgmental at all. In fact, his eyes have softened, his mouth relaxed. He almost looks…concerned? Empathetic? Gingerly he raises a shaking hand and wipes an escaped tear from my cheek. "I would never let that happen." His hand remains there, a simple comfort.

I search his warm tropical gaze. "Never let what happen?"

For many moments, Soren doesn't say a word.

I think he may not, but I continue to gaze into those eyes of his, urging him to continue. It's the first time I have really noticed how much lies underneath. Something within him is at war with itself, battling a dilemma I cannot know. Until one side wins out.

Then he speaks. "I can send money to your mother for as long as you need, in whatever form she'll need, until you return home." He let's go of my cheek, leaving my face suddenly chilled in its absence. "It's the least I can do for what you've done for me."

My heart inflates at the gesture. It is so out of the blue, so uncharacteristic of him that it takes me a moment to come up with a response. "You—You don't know how much that would mean to me. Thank you."

Darius' groans, shifting his head in pain or discomfort, I am not sure. We both turn our attention to the captain. I reach down to grab the cloth, but Soren beats me to it.

"You should get some sleep," he says as he gently scoops out more accumulated yellow ooze. "We'll be in this sea cave all night. At least until mid-morning. All the blood the captain spilled into the ocean is bound to have attracted creatures we don't want to mess with."

I gulp at the thought. "You mean, like sharks? The sirens?"

"Well, yes sharks and the sirens will be attracted to the blood as well. But trust me when I say there are far deadlier things we want to avoid." Soren dips the cloth into the water until its ooze-free.

The horrible shriek from the dungeons echoes in my memory. I shudder. "Okay," I tuck my hair behind my ears again because they refuse to stay put. "Are you sure you don't want to sleep first? I know I was out for a couple hours, but you've been up the whole time already—"

"No, I'm fine. I'm trained for nights like this. Get some rest, Constance." He continues dabbing at Darius' wounds, which surprisingly look better than they did ten minutes ago.

As if on cue, my body produces a long, tiring yawn. "Alright," I concede, "but if you need to switch, wake me up. I don't mind looking after Darius too."

He grunts in response, busy tending to the captain's slashes and punctures.

I turn on my heels and head for the spot where I woke up. The moon casts a spotlight on it as if it's meant for me this night. Like it knew I needed to be bathed in its glorious luminescence after so long without it.

"Constance?" Soren speaks so softly I almost believe his voice is only in my head. I turn around. His back faces me, but his head is turned slightly so I can see the profile of his face. "I'm sorry. I should've never said you should've drowned that first night." Another pause. "I'm really pleased you didn't, actually."

I tuck my hair behind my ear for the last time tonight and look down at the sandy rock beneath my feet, grinning. "Me too, Soren. Me too."

Chapter 27

I assumed sleeping on the rocky ground without a blanket would have been difficult, but surprisingly I slept hard. Probably thanks to my insulated black suit and the fact I was entirely exhausted from our confrontation with the sirens *and* almost drowned yesterday. Those kinds of things tend to wear a lady out.

I stretch my arms straight over my head, arching my back and pointing my toes as far as they'll go in a typical morning stretch.

The sea cave is dimly illuminated by the morning sun, even if it has not peaked over the hole in the ceiling yet, I still see more now than I did with the moonlight.

Darius still sleeps next to the water, but he's managed to turn onto his side, body facing inward. I walk over with the stealth of a cat, examining him without waking him up. His wounds look red and are beginning to scab over that ebony skin—no trace of yellow ooze anymore. That's a good sign.

Our little hideout is missing something. It's just Darius and me. Where is the brooding merman? *Where is Soren?*

As if on cue, a muscular, black-haired merman springs forth from the water at the lip of the cave. I throw my hand over my mouth, practically jumping out of my skin.

He is wearing the same shorts he did yesterday. One leg ripped at the hem. His sling lays flat across his broad chest. Water drips from his body, causing tiny *clink* sounds as droplets hit the ground.

"Where did you—" I begin to whisper, afraid to speak too loud and wake Darius.

"I figured you needed something to drink. Here." He hands me two unopened coconuts. His hand is large enough to carry both with ease. Or maybe it's the webbed fingers that help him hold them. I take note as those little webs of flesh gradually recede.

Coconuts. Now that he mentions it, I *am* thirsty. Not to mention starving. I notice my lips have begun to feel crusty and my skin unusually dry, deprived of hydration. We didn't eat or drink anything at all yesterday. My stomach growls angrily in response.

I reach out to take the coconuts but look at Soren dumbfounded. He has dark bags forming under his eyelids. Did he sleep at all last night? I do the math in my head. He's been awake for at least twenty-eight hours or more. He must be exhausted.

"What?" He walks away from us to shake the excess water from his hair, like a dog after a bath.

"I, um, I don't know how to open this without a knife or something." I raise the coconut in my hand, trying not to dwell on the way Soren's shoulders slump.

"Oh, right." He reaches into his sling and pulls out that little letter opener of a knife, handing it to me.

"Thanks." I make light work of poking out the eyes and dumping as much coconut water as I can down my throat. In no time, it's empty. The remaining contents either down my gullet or dribbling down the corners of my mouth.

I proceed to make quick work of the rest of the coconut and open it to reveal the sweet fruit. Using my hands to scoop out the subtle nutty goodness.

"I know it's not much, but we can get a full meal and purified water as soon as we get back to Emora." Soren sits against the wall, watching me.

I wipe at my mouth with the back of my black covered hand. "Aren't you going to eat? I will share."

"No, I can wait till we get home." He gestures to the second coconut, urging me to open it as well.

I look at the coconut, then to the sleeping captain. "I think we should give this one to Darius when he wakes up. He'll need the energy for the trip." My stomach growls again, protesting my choice to stop feeding it. I throw a hand over my belly and shush it.

A hint of a smile tugs at Soren's mouth before his entire face turns serious. "Constance," he begins. That authoritative tone creeps back into his voice.

"Yes?" After last night, I'm not sure what he's going to tell me. Is he going to tell me I need to be more lady like when we get back to the castle? Is he going to thank me for saving the second coconut for Darius, even though it was the obvious right choice? I can't tell by his facial features where he is going to lead our conversation.

He shifts awkwardly on his toes before drawing his arms over his chest. "Technically our…deal… is over."

Oh. In all that's happened in the last twenty plus hours, I completely forgot about our deal. It's over. I stole the pearl, and he traded it for his answers. The deal is done.

Soren walks toward me to say something but catches himself and instead looks at the water growing brighter and clearer with the rising sun. "But I was thinking about what you said about your mother and father. And well…" He picks up a pebble and drops it in the water, watching the ripples expand before dying out. "I was wondering if you would stay longer and help me find the three objects the Siren Queen foretold?"

My mouth falls open slightly. My hunger and thirst forgotten. I'm not sure what to tell him.

He rushes out his next words, further explaining his new offer. "It wouldn't be for your freedom though or the new supplies. You have already earned that. But I will send out a small fortune to your mother's whereabouts. And in return for your services, I will lend a hand in search for your father."

My ears feel muddled, like I didn't properly hear him. Did he really just offer my mama money and his help to track down my papa? There must be a catch. Right?

Darius stirs next to us, groaning softly.

"I um, I don't…" I begin. My mind clutters with all Soren's offer could entail. "What if it takes years to find these objects? Will you only give my mama money if I find them? I can't guarantee I can help find them."

Soren turns from the water and strides toward me, towering over me with his formidable size. He speaks with such quiet intensity, yet another one of his gestures that has caught me off-guard. "I will give your mother what she needs regardless of your decision. I owe you at least that much."

"Alright, but my papa—"

"We can tackle searching for both at the same time: your father and the objects," he proclaims. His eyes scan my face before adding, "If you wish."

My hands rake through my knotted hair. Do I stay under the sea, away from the sun, the moon, *my world* for that much longer while my family struggles?

Darius stirs again, rolling up onto his knees.

"Think about it," Soren whispers before walking over to Darius and helping him sit up. "Captain, how do you feel?"

Darius winces with each movement of his abdomen. His face scrunches up with every minute motion. "My Prince, I will not lie…" he starts, "…I've fared better." Then he looks Soren in the eyes and chuckles with some difficulty, scrunching his face at the pain it causes him, but smiling, nonetheless.

Soren chuckles in response. "That's true, but if my memory serves me correctly, you've also been worse." He helps his captain up to his feet, supporting him under his arm. They walk to the edge of the cave, and Soren lowers his captain against it. Using the wall to support him. He coughs hoarsely.

I realize then that I still need to open the other coconut for him. I jog over to my sleeping spot and grab the letter opener knife and coconut, poking a good size hole into the top before offering it to Darius. He drinks the contents in one long gulp, not a drop of the sweet liquid wasted. "Ah, thank you, Miss Constance. And thank you for your actions at Siren's Hollow—coming back for me, helping me stay afloat. You are truly a gem of valor."

I draw the coconut away from him to break open the rest of its contents before scooping it out for him, offering him the fruit. "It was the least I could do. I suppose in some ways we are even now."

He smiles between scoops.

"Are you ready to see your wife? She must be worried sick."

He takes another chunk of fruit in his mouth, practically swallowing it whole. "Yes. I believe she's been worried sick about all three of us, though. We mustn't keep her waiting much longer." Darius uses Soren as leverage while he hobbles over to his sling, pulling it over his free shoulder. Soren helps him with the other side. Then Darius, with much effort, pulls out his extra purple vial, handing it to me.

I make quick work of uncorking the potion bottle and let the putrid liquid slide down my throat. It takes no time at all for that tingly, crampy feeling to return as my body readies itself for the plunge back into the ocean. Back to Emora.

Chapter 28

The swim back to Emora is surprisingly short, which tells me Soren carried Darius' and my unconscious bodies for hours before finding a place to hunker down for the night.

I side eye him as we prepare to lift Darius out of the black pool of water and onto the path behind the waterfall at Emora's edge. Soren's facial features reveal nothing except adamant determination to get us back to the castle. His sole focus is getting Darius out of the water and into the infirmary. But I notice the slight tremor in his arms as he hoists Darius' body up and out of the water, onto the stone path. The circles under his eyes look worse as well.

Just then Soren's eyes shift to my direction, catching me examining him, and I swiftly look away, wrapping my arm around Darius' side, shifting his arm over my shoulders so he can use me as a crutch.

Soren uses his arms to propel himself out of the water. He pulls out his clothes from their hiding place and puts them on hastily. Then proceeds to help lift Darius' legs as he puts his pants on. "No need to put his shirt over his wounds, since the healers will most likely take it right off," Soren orders.

He takes his place on Darius' other side, holding up most of the captain's weight, before the three of us walk toward the castle at the heart of the city.

Most citizens are still in their homes, probably eating breakfast or getting ready for their days, but some early risers are out and about. We get a lot of bewildered looks. One citizen even stops us and offers to run to the castle to retrieve a healer.

Darius assures him he is fine, and we are almost there. The merman looks like he wants to argue but bows his head instead. Surely arguing with the captain of Emora's army and the prince would have consequences, even if he did think we should have someone else tending to the injured captain besides a prince and a fake princess.

By the time we reached the entrance to the castle, a few guards had spotted us, shouting orders to get a healer out here and prep one of the rooms in the infirmary.

Lamia finds us first. She runs toward us, toward Soren, lifting her teal blue, silk skirt up by her fingers, and falls into Soren's free arm practically knocking all three of us down. "I was so worried," she whines, digging her face into his shoulder. "Why didn't you mention that you were going to be gone for so long?"

Soren grunts, easing Lamia off him. "I'm sorry, Lamia. We had something important to do and it took longer than expected." He's so gentle with her, as though she were made of porcelain.

I think of last night. All he must have gone through to bring two unconscious bodies to safety. I think of his demeanor toward his father and his concern for his brother in the sparring ring. Perhaps there's more to Soren than meets the eye.

Lamia looks over the captain eyeing each of his wounds before locking eyes with me. It is as if she had only now realized what had happened; Soren left without telling her where he was going or who he was with. Hate fills her translucent eyes as the realization hits her.

"Once again, the little witch returns," she murmurs under her breath just loud enough for me to hear. Her hands clutch Soren's shirt tighter. "Why are you still here? Don't you have other things to do? Places to be?"

"Lamia," Soren warns, an edge in his voice. "Be respectful. Constance is the reason all three of us are still here." Lamia's rage simmers and is replaced with hurt. She judges my attire, looking me over from my matted hair to the skintight clothes I still wear and back to Soren.

"Pardon my interruption," Darius says with some difficulty, "but I would really like to head to the infirmary now."

As if on cue, another female comes running with less grace but more ferocity. Her perfectly placed curls bounce with each stride. "Oh, honey," Addeah begins, stopping forcefully in front of her husband. She takes his face in her hands and scans his eyes before planting a delicate and long kiss on his lips. She pulls back just enough to see his face and the wounds on his body, before motioning for me to let go, taking my place at his side. "Oh, my love, let's get you going. I've been worried sick." Addeah looks to Soren. "I'll take it from here, Soren. Go on and wash up now. You smell of rot and body odor." Her nose scrunches up as she speaks her last sentence. Without another word, Addeah, even though she is much smaller than Darius, carries the load of his weight into the castle and out of sight.

"Let's get you cleaned up too." Lamia runs her hand down Soren's chest and gently wraps her manicured fingers around his bicep before leading him into the castle as well. Her body language makes it obvious she knows I'm here but is choosing to act like I'm not.

Soren turns in my direction, locking eyes momentarily, opening his mouth, and then snapping his lips shut before walking into the halls of his home with his betrothed.

I inspect my own hands still covered in the black fabric of my suit, taking note at the bits of coconut wedged into the stitches before I look after the two figures growing smaller with each step they take. Now I am all alone at the entrance before walking in by myself, suddenly feeling not just alone, but lonely.

* * *

The moment I walk into my room, Squish comes wriggling over to me in excitable bounds before taking his long tongue and licking my ankle.

At least someone is happy I had made it back to the city safely.

I scoop him into my hands and scratch his chin before placing him on the bed and walking into the bathroom, ignoring the mirror attached to the vanity.

It takes me three shampoo scrubs and one hour later to feel clean before I shimmy into my sheets and drift off to sleep with Squish nuzzled against neck.

I'm not sure how long I was out after that, but a knock on the door wakes me from my slumber.

Squish scampers across the sheets and under the bed at the intrusion.

The door creaks open as a masculine hand wraps around the frame. I can see bits of black hair and a straight nose peaking past the threshold.

"Hello? Constance?" he whispers.

"Come in," I call over, straightening up in bed, running fingers through who knows what kind of bed head I have, as Sebastian comes in with a plate full of food and a tall glass of water.

"I assumed you would be hungry after the unexpected overnighter you three had." The smell of hot bread fills my nostrils as he puts the steaming plate on my nightstand.

I gleefully dig into the food, chugging the water in between each bite. "You know the way to my heart, Sebastian," I tease after finishing off a third of my plate.

He grins at that. "What can I say? Food is the window to the soul." Casually, he leans on my bed near my feet, resting on his forearm on the sheets. "So, tell me all about your adventure. It must've been some ordeal to take so long."

I swallow a large lump of bread before replying. "It was pretty standard really. The usual. We got there, the sirens tried to attack us and eat us, Darius got injured protecting us, I almost drown—again. The normalcy of a typical Tuesday." Sebastian's eyes sparkle as he rests his head against his splayed palm waiting for me to explain further. "Yes, it was—it was unlike anything I have ever experienced in my life. Remind me to never ever, *ever* go to the Siren's Hollow again."

"Ha! I probably should've warned you about their cannibalistic habits and all."

"That would have been most helpful." I shove his shoulder playfully before taking another bite of food.

"To be fair, I really thought my brother had told you what you were getting in to."

I look at Sebastian incredulously before gulping the last drops of water in my glass. "Your brother has a way with words. That way is not really saying what needs to be said and being unnecessarily cryptic."

Sebastian rolls onto his back and cackles, "Well true, he's not well known for his strong communication skills. But wow, you went into the Siren's Hollow, not knowing, well anything really, and lived to tell the tale. You might very well be the only human alive who can say that." He sits back up, legs dangling off the edge, wrinkling the edges with his fingertips. "So, what kind of answers did the queen give? Is there a cure for my father?"

Nothing remains on my plate, so I ease it on the end table before looking back at Sebastian. The Siren Queen did give answers, but would he want to hear that his father may very well die no matter what they do? "Sebastian, I um— maybe we should wait to discuss the divination until your brother is with us and then we can decipher her words together."

Abruptly he stands up. "Constance—just…" irritation darkens his face. He turns away from me, pacing toward the door. His shoulders rise and fall with deep breaths before he turns around. "He's my father, Constance."

Even though I am not properly dressed I have half a mind to go over to him and hug him from behind, wrapping my arms around his torso. But I don't. Instead, I remain in bed, clutching the sheets between my fingers as I respond, "I know." Which I do. I know how it is to worry about a father, to not know whether he lived or died. It was painful and it could make you do foolish things.

We lock eyes. The irritation in his recedes with each passing moment. Neither of us speaks. Then he lets out a low breath, tucking his hands under his armpits. "Okay. You're probably right. We should work it out together. I'm sorry for lashing out."

I give him a sympathetic smile. "It's okay. I understand." Sebastian takes the smile as an invitation to come closer, kneeling next to the sheets. He takes my hand and places the faintest kiss on top.

"I really like you, you know that?" He states matter of fact. "I wish…" Sebastian's finger traces circles on top of my hand, "…I wish that your deal wasn't over with my brother. That you would stay here in Emora longer."

Those light circles tingle, radiating up my arm. Warmth works its way up my neck. Sebastian always seems to have a way to make me blush at his affections. I look down at our connected skin. "I like you too," I say barely above a whisper. "And, well, you may just get your wish."

He stops caressing my hand to look up into my face.

"Your brother made another offer to stay and help find the objects he needs in exchange for his help to find my own Papa."

"Really?" His eyebrows raise to his hairline. "You should definitely take the offer!"

Although Soren's offer caught me off guard at first, the longer I mulled over his words, the more it made sense to accept it. The ocean is vast, and the number of places Papa could be are many. It would be beneficial to have someone with me to cover more ground. It would also be safer. And I wouldn't mind having the excuse of spending more time with Sebastian. "Yeah, I think I will."

That irritation from earlier has completely dissipated, replaced with sheer joy. "More time for us to get to know each other. But at this moment, I need to go." At my confusion, he explains further. "I would stay with you longer this morning, but Soren wasn't looking well. I convinced him to rest for the day, and I will take his duties off his hands. But after dinner tonight, the three of us should go to the library and start deciphering that prophecy." With a swift kiss to my cheek, Sebastian turns toward the door and opens it. "Don't get into too much trouble until then, Freckles." With a wink, he exits my room, leaving my stomach swimming with butterflies for the rest of the day.

* * *

Dinner is business as usual.

No king.

I avoid the weird eel gelatin.

Lamia's eyes pierce the side of my face like daggers. Soren, although he looks more rested than this morning, went back to his somber mood, avoiding all contact with me. Sebastian does whatever he can to annoy Lamia. In some ways it feels like I am eating with a bunch of siblings I never had—except for the fact that I have a crush on Sebastian which is not so sibling like.

I can't help glancing his way admiring his symmetrical features and that black wavy hair that curls slightly above his ears. He catches me looking more than once but meets each glance with a grin.

After dinner we excuse ourselves at different times— so Lamia does not get suspicious of our plan— and head to the library.

The windows display late evening upon us as we walk into the dome shaped room.

"Well, well," Sebastian rubs his hands together mischievously, "time to finally hear what this prophecy was, yeah?"

"Be patient, Sebastian," Soren orders. He walks around to all the exits, scans all the aisles to make sure no one is here with us, not that I ever imagine there would be. This place always seems to be deserted, but Soren takes no chances.

"Please, brother. Who else comes to the library at this hour?" Sebastian finds one of the chairs near the middle of the room and straddles the seat cushion, his arms resting over the back.

Soren's only response is to give a typical glare in his younger brother's direction before sweeping the rest of the area.

I look between the two brothers before deciding to sit next to Sebastian in an adjacent chair. It's quite comfortable really, designed for long afternoon reads with its extra plush sage cushions. I practically sink into a cocoon of coziness before Soren marches toward us, seriousness etched onto every feature.

He picks a seat similar to Sebastian's but chooses to sit in it like a prince at a meeting. Proper, apart from the forward angle of his back. His hands squeeze his knees. He looks to me. "Constance, did you decide on my offer yet?"

"I did." I sit up straighter. "I've decided to help you and in return you will help me in my search for my papa and help keep my mama and our household safe from destitution."

"So my charming skills of persuasion worked after all," Sebastian croons winking at me as he wags his eyebrows.

I blush at the gesture. Soren doesn't seem to appreciate his brother's comment. Irritation flickers in his eyes. "What do you m—" he begins before thinking better of his question and looking back to me. "Good. Then let's discuss our next steps." Soren pulls out a piece of marked up paper. His writing is clear and concise and much smaller than my own. Written on it is word for word what the Siren Queen had prophesied. I lean over the arm of my chair as Sebastian reads it through.

> *Save your father you may try, but don't be fooled,*
> *the king will die.*
> *Objects you will seek. Three.*
> *A chest. A book. And a key.*
> *One in the depths of the beast's lair.*
> *Another in the home of despair.*
> *Last is trapped in the betrayer's snare.*
> *But be wary handsome prince.*
> *Change is stirring*
> *Far from sense.*

I read it again over his shoulder as Sebastian mulls over the words. Soren sits in silence, his hands clasped together under his chin looking at his brother expectantly.

Sebastian must read the words more than once because it feels like ages before he speaks. "Well, this is rather interesting." He folds the parchment and hands it back to Soren. "It sounds like a wild goose chase."

"It's all we have."

"Are you sure the Siren Queen was telling the truth?" Sebastian inquires.

"She may be a greedy, cannibalistic, sadist, but she's true to her word when she makes a bargain. She speaks the truth," Soren replies.

"So, no matter what we try our father will die? Then what's the point of trying?"

"I don't know as much about sirens as the two of you, but the Siren Queen's prophecy sounds more like a riddle. Riddles are meant to be tricky. Meant to be misleading. Just because she said your father will die doesn't mean he can't be saved first giving him years to live. It's worth the try." I look to each brother, doing my best to reassure them of my theory, even though in my head I don't know if I'm right or not.

Sebastian smiles sadly at me. "True, Freckles. True." That moment of sadness slips away, replaced with determination.

"Well, there's three objects. One of them is a book. Could the book be in this library?" I ask, looking around the mass of leather-bound sources of knowledge that consume us.

"Not likely," Soren replies. "The library's neither a place of despair, nor a home to a beast. And I highly doubt a library is capable of betrayal."

That's a good point, but I push onward. "Well, what about the third object being trapped by a betrayer? What if you have someone in the castle that's keeping this book hidden from you in plain sight? Someone that may not want your father to get healthy perhaps?"

Sebastian scoffs. "I highly doubt we have a betrayer in our midst. Emora is a peaceful place. I would assume we are looking for someone who ran away from Emora back in King Cyrus' prime; someone he kicked out for that. And for the book being hidden in the library, I've personally looked at every single one of these manuscripts. None would be the book we are looking for."

My brows knit together. "How do you know that?"

"Because," Sebastian gets up from his smaller chair and finds the couch that matches my seat, jumping on it. He interlaces his fingers and cradles the back of his head. Lounging. "I'm fairly certain the book we are looking for is the Book of Dominion. Wouldn't you agree, brother?"

Soren stiffens slightly but nods in agreement. "Yes. It's what I feared."

I observe their nonverbal exchange. "I'm sorry, the Book of what? Will it not help?"

Soren stands up, pacing back and forth in front of Sebastian and me. "The Book of Dominion. It's a book of legend. Tales of its inscriptions claim to bring forth unimaginable things: power beyond all measure. Some which are described to defy the laws of nature. I had thought it merely myth until the Siren Queen's prophecy."

"Okay, so this Book of Dominion, why is it to be feared? What's so dangerous about a book?" I watch Soren pace back and forth. His pattern leaves marks on the library carpet.

Soren stops in his tracks to listen to Sebastian as he answers. "The book is said to have unequivocal magical properties. A book that may even cheat death itself. A book we are desperate to find."

I don't know what to say about Sebastian's words.

A book of magic that can cheat death? I've never heard of such a thing. Although, up until recently I hadn't thought mermaids existed either.

He continues, "This book has been hidden from those who seek it for good reason. It can give whoever wields it the power to move mountains, to change the course of fate. It is unnatural. In the wrong hands, it can do unspeakable damage."

"Whoa," I say adjusting the skirt of my dress. "I guess we have a winner. Now, where would this book most likely be?"

Soren hasn't said a word. He stares at his brother, inspecting him like he's trying to puzzle out a mystery. Then shakes his head, erasing whatever thought he had stirring in his mind before pacing again.

"At least we have three ideas, even if they are vague. Either a beast's lair, a home of despair, or a betrayer's snare. Do prophecies always rhyme?" I ask.

"Ha! If the sirens can help it, they do. That is oh so helpful, is it not?" Sebastian teases.

"Let's start researching. Sebastian, if you know all of the books in here, pull down any that have to do with beasts of the sea. We can narrow down our search there," Soren orders.

Sebastian gets up from the couch and bows dramatically before turning on his heel, disappearing in the stacks.

Soren looks after his brother as he says without even looking in my direction. "I'll do the same for home of despair. Maybe it's related to Emora's history. Any history related event that has left a mark of hopelessness or something of the like."

He stomps off without so much as a glance in my direction.

So, what am I suppose to look for?

I ponder over the words. A chest, a book, and a key. They tumble in my mind, rolling over and over like a lapping wave. The brothers seem certain of what book to find, but what about the chest and the key? Will the key go into the chest? What could be inside the chest that is so valuable to the king's health or is the chest itself somehow magical?

Then I recall that night in the castle when I ran into the creature who remained in the shadows. A key she had called me. At the time, I didn't know what she was, but after our trip to the Siren's Hollow, I am certain she's a siren. Questions pile up in my mind. If she is a siren, why is she here in the castle? Why didn't she try to eat me like the other sirens did? Why didn't she use her siren song to lure me into the shadows to devour me that night? But most importantly, what did she mean when she said I was a key to three? Am I the same key in the Siren Queen's prophecy? A shiver raises goosebumps up my arms.

I don't have much time to think further on the matter because Sebastian comes back to our original spot, tossing a pile of ten books onto the floor in front of me. "Let the research begin," he says as he wriggles his eyebrows at me and pops a squat on the floor near my feet. He uses the side of my cushioned chair to lean against before pulling the first book from his pile and reading.

So, I follow his lead and pull the book closest to me into my lap. It's titled *Creatures of the Southern Hemisphere*. Let the research begin, indeed.

Chapter 29

Hours pass by of Sebastian, Soren, and me pulling information from books. So far, I've read about everything from sea dragons to selkies, kelpies, grindylows, sea serpents, hippocamps, bunyips, and many other creatures I can't pronounce.

Next thing I know someone is gently trying to wake me up— a strong hand tentatively rocks my shoulder.

"Constance," Sebastian softly speaks, tickling my cheek with his breath. "Constance, wake up."

I pry my eyes open. My tongue is sandpaper against the roof of my mouth. Drool has escaped and must have dribbled down my chin while I slept. Consciously, I wipe it away and sit up. "Sorry. I'm awake. Did you find anything yet?"

"No, not yet," Sebastian responds. He keeps his hand rested on my shoulder.

"It's late," Soren chimes in from his seated position on the floor. Books are sprawled all around him in a messy circle. He pauses momentarily from the book currently in his lap to look up at me. "You should go to sleep. We can work on this again tomorrow night."

"Are you positive? I know I dozed off, but I'm feeling more energized after my cat nap. I can stay longer," I say just as a yawn overcomes me.

"Yeah, real energized there, Freckles. Come on, I'll escort you back to your room." Sebastian motions to help me off the cushions.

"But what about all the books?" I ask. Even with Sebastian's help, it takes more effort than it should to haul myself out of the seat. I push harder than I need to, overestimating how much force it takes to stand, landing clumsily against Sebastian's awaiting arms. He steadies me easily before turning me to face the door.

"I'll put them all away when I leave," Soren states, not deeming to look up as he responds this time.

Sebastian keeps his hands on my shoulders but turns momentarily to look at Soren. "Are you sure, brother?"

"Yes. Go."

Sebastian furrows his brow, analyzing his older brother briefly, something unreadable flickering in his eyes before turning back to me. "Come, milady. There's a very comfortable bed calling your name." Sebastian steps to my side and allows me to lean against him as we wobble toward the exit.

I can't help but smile as I loop my arm through his. "Take me to my destination, Prince Sebastian," I joke then turn back to Soren. "Goodnight, Soren. We'll see you tomorrow."

He mumbles a goodnight, engrossed with the literature in his hands.

Sebastian walks me to my room where Squish waits patiently for me to crawl into bed. Thanks to the research overload, my dreams are plagued with sea creatures lurking in the shadows, ready to devour me whole.

* * *

Addeah walks in early in the morning. I don't even have time to properly stretch or express a verbal greeting before she walks up to me and embraces me in a bone crushing hug. It isn't until this moment I realize how desperately I missed this motherly affection. Someone who is glad to see me and embrace me. It makes me miss Mama.

"Oh, child," she exclaims, "I'm so sorry I haven't been down here yet for you." Her grip tightens even further before she releases me from her death grip, staring at me— gratitude reflecting in her eyes. "I need to express my deepest thanks to you. You sweet child. After Darius had been properly treated for his wounds, he told me what you did."

"Oh, it wasn't—" I begin, but Addeah brings her hand up to stop me.

"No, Constance. It was. You risked your life—twice, from how I see it— to save him and bring him home to me."

"Well, you know, I was just returning the favor." I say sheepishly. It didn't feel right to accept the praise from Addeah. In fact, I would say it was Soren who saved us with his magical princely water powers, but the look on Addeah's face keeps me from saying this thought out loud.

Addeah grips my arms and leans her forehead against my own, her eyes never drifting from my face. "Something tells me you would have done it under any circumstance. Thank you." She proceeds to grab the sides of my head and gently brings my face down just enough to place a kiss on my brow.

"How's Darius faring?" I ask, drawing my hand up to take one of Addeah's. A comforting gesture for her.

"He's on the mend." She nods in assurance, more so for her benefit than my own.

Then she takes strands of my hair, noticing curls tangled within each other. "Let's get you ready for the day. Go get in the tub, and I'll pick something out for you to wear." She smiles, and I oblige.

Chapter 30

A week. A full week has gone by with nightly researching and nothing to show for it.

It's midday, and I decide to walk to the library on my own and get some more research done when a peculiar sight catches the corner of my eye. Down the same hallway I was first confronted by a siren is a hooded figure lurking in the shadows.

It creeps away from me, padding further into the darkness.

At first, I believe it's the creature, but it can't be. Peeking out of the cloak is a silky strand of teal-blue hair.

"Princess Constance!" a male voice echoes down the hall. I turn to see Soren walking briskly in my direction. He halts an arm's length away from me.

I dare a quick glance down the dark hall. Nothing. But surely it wasn't all in my head.

Soren must notice my confusion because he looks down the hall as well. "This section never stays lit for long. No matter how many times the guards light the candles, they always go out." He inspects my face, brows furrowed. "Did you see something?"

I shake my head. "No, nothing. I just…" Just what? Do I tell him I saw what could be his fiancée lurking in the dark hall? "…I was on my way to the library to—"

He interrupts with a dismissive wave of his hand and motions for me to follow him. "We'll go later. First, come with me."

He doesn't wait for a response before striding back toward the direction he came. I must pump my arms dramatically just to keep up without actually running.

He leads us through the halls and into the inky, musty smelling strategy room.

But we are not alone in here. Awaiting our arrival are five mermen.

One I recognize as the one-legged, peg-legged soldier helping Darius with inventory. "I'm delighted to see you again, Jed," I say in way of greeting.

Jed's eyes light up, and his white scruffy covered jaw drops open. "Princess Constance, it's an honor. Thank you for remembering a lowly soldier like myself."

Soren clears his throat next to me before introducing the other four strangers. "Constance, this here is Dox, captain of our finest ship in Emora." He points to a man the epitome of a what a pirate should look like. Dox has salt and pepper hair tied back at the nape of his neck with a piece of red ribbon. His clothes are different shades of black. Black boots, black weathered jacket, and a black pirate hat.

He hobbles a bit closer to Soren and me before bowing over his large belly. I notice a compass dangling from his belt loop, before he stands up straight again. "It's an honor to serve ye, Princess," he says. Even his voice belongs to a pirate.

"I'm sorry," I begin. "I don't understand what you mean." I try to look apologetic at my naivety.

Dox looks to Soren. "My boy, ye haven't told her yet?"

Soren has the audacity to look a little embarrassed. "That's what I am getting to," he says before turning to me. "Constance, this is the crew I've put together to help in your search for the human merchant."

I stiffen. Do these mermen know I'm human and I shouldn't be here?

Soren continues, "Their orders are to send the sum of earnings to your desired location for the human patron you work closely with, and then they'll be off to search for the merchant who does important routine trades with you."

He's not mentioning that the "patron" is Mama and the "human merchant" is Papa. So maybe they only have a variation of the truth. Even with this realization, my body can't seem to relax. We're walking on the edge of a cliff with the information Soren is telling them. If they found out the whole truth, would they rebel? Would they stop their mission? It could be disastrous for me and my parents. I try to swallow down my nerves.

"Oh, don't worry, darlin', Soren told us all about your line of work. We ourselves have dealt with plenty of humans before. They're not much different than us, after all," Dox chimes in, clearly sensing my unease.

"Anyways," Soren interjects, "This here is Fleck and Cam. They rank directly beneath Captain Darius." He points to two beautiful mermen, who may be even more handsome than the princes. Both have sun kissed golden hair, but one's cropped short while the other flows freely over his ears. Most of their features are completely identical apart from the different hairstyles and their eyes. The one with the flowing hair has rich, deep brown eyes. The short haired one has a set of orbs like nothing I've ever seen before. They're a deep violet with flecks of various colors, shimmering with each movement he makes like a diamond in the sunlight.

"Pleasure to make your acquaintance, Princess Constance," the long-haired merman says, voice dripping with honey. Oh my, even his voice is attractive. He takes my hand and places a warm kiss on top, those deep brown eyes never shying away from my face. "If Soren had told me you were this attractive, I would have come with a bouquet of roses."

Soren lets out a low growl at the twin, but I can't help but smirk. The way he speaks gives me a similar sensation I had when we were in the Siren's Hollow; like I wouldn't mind staying with him forever.

"Fleck, enough," Soren orders. The beautiful merman, Fleck, only barks a laugh and falls back in with the others.

The other twin just nods his head in my direction.

Annoyance laces Soren's next words, pointing to the last of the crew members standing behind the rest of them. He's a tall, young merman with broad shoulders that hunch slightly forward. "Last is Griffin, a soldier in training."

Griffin doesn't need to move around to look at me because he's a head taller than everyone else. "Princess." He waves. Even though his skin is warm like a cacao plant, I can see heat rise against his cheeks.

I smile and wave in response.

Soren clears his throat while Dox shuffles to the table and pulls out multiple pieces of rolled up parchment, unraveling each one with his fingers for all of us to see. Then Dox licks his pointer finger and peels the layers of parchment apart until he finds what he needs and places it on top of all the others.

It's a map. A map of all the islands in the area.

"This is the one we need, aye? Where 'er we off to first?" Dox asks, looking to me for answers.

I run my fingers over each one, the pieces of land slightly raised above the parchment's landscape. I find Ohani Island: my home. It's labeled with fine script, and I trace the letters with my finger. A lump gets caught in my throat, and it takes great effort to swallow it before speaking. "This is the island you'll need to go to first. You'll need to ask around for Helena. She lives in one of the houses off the coast. She's my…" what word did Soren use again? "…patron. The funds go to her."

The crew all crowd in to see which island I am talking about. Dox shoos them away and turns back to me. He nods in understanding. "We'll get it there. And what about the merchant?"

"Truth be told," I begin, making eye contact with each of the mermen in front of me, "I'm not sure. He's been missing for a while now. But uh," I look back down at the map and trace a path with my finger, trailing over the islands that are on his typical route. "This is his usual trade route. He starts at Ohaku."

"What's the name of your merchant?" the quiet twin asks. It's the first thing he's said since I've been in here.

At first, I want to say Papa, but I stop myself. I had never called him by his first name. "Atlas," I say. The name feels weird on my tongue. Atlas. Not Papa. Not father. Just a human merchant's name. "He's about six foot and has blond and grey curly hair and tan skin from being in the sun often. His eyes are brown. The locals should know him by his name alone. If you ask around, maybe they can determine the last time they saw him."

The mermen look at me and all nod. Dox makes a grunting noise as he leans over the table to roll up the maps again. "Well, that's enough to go on for now. We'll report back in three days' time."

"Wait," I interject, "I'm not coming with you?"

"Aw, she already wants to spend more time with us," Fleck muses, winking at me. He gets a swift elbow to the gut from his brother, Cam.

"Don't worry, Princess Constance. We know you're busy at the moment with other matters of trade. Prince Soren told us all about it," Jed chimes in. "When you have more free time, we can take you with us."

"I hope you get your work done quickly," Griffin offers softly.

"Alright, lads, let's get a move on," Dox commands before shooing the motley crew out the door. But before he can exit himself, Soren halts him in his tracks. "What is it, my boy?" He gruffs, scratching his rounded belly with one hand, clutching his rolled-up maps in the other.

"There's one more thing we need to give you," Soren says secretively. "Constance," he looks to me and gestures me to sit down in one of the chairs around the table, offering me a quill, ink, and some parchment. "Write what you need to for your... patron."

Mama. He's giving me a chance to write to my mother. To send word I am alive and okay. Liquid starts to pool in my eyes before I blink it away. I give Soren the smallest smile before nodding and turning my attention to the parchment in front of me.

At first, I want to write down everything that has happened here. The merpeople, the magic, the monsters. But I can't. I know I can't tell her everything, because it would make me sound as though I had lost my mind. Plus, Soren would have a fit if I mentioned anything about Emora to another human. So, I choose to write the truth with a few omissions instead.

I tell her I am alive and well. I tell her a storm did some damage to my boat but that I had found a way to continue my search for Papa. I tell her I had found friends in the most unlikely places and the funds being sent to her is from a new acquaintance I met during my travels who is paying me for helping him with his troubles. I explain to her that depending on how long it takes to find Papa, money will come every month until my search has ended.

I sign my name at the bottom and tell Mama how much I miss her and love her and that I pray she can find it in her heart to forgive me for the way I left.

Before passing it into Soren's awaiting hand, I do a double check of all the things I said. I didn't mention anyone's name or the fact I am currently residing hundreds of feet below the surface in a city filled with merfolk. Confident it will pass Soren's inspection, I hand it over to him.

To make sure I didn't write anything incriminating, Soren reads the letter himself. His face twitches toward the end. But he doesn't say anything about it before rolling it up and placing it in a clear bottle, sealing it tightly with a cork, and passing it to Dox who waits patiently in a seat across from me. "Give this to patron Helena discreetly. No one else needs to know of it."

"Yes, prince," Dox replies. He takes the bottle. Bows at the waist before dismissing himself from the strategy room and out to open waters to help my family.

"Thank you," I say to Soren once we're alone.

He looks at me, an expression I can't quite read etched on his face. But he doesn't say anything. Instead, he walks out of the room without so much as a syllable uttered in response. By now, his silence doesn't surprise me.

* * *

Two nights later, we're in the library researching. Still.

"What about a water nymph?" I suggest. "Do they have any need for special books or a chest? Maybe they have this Book of Dominion, and that's where they draw their special powers?"

"Nymphs are gentle creatures. They typically stick to their own kind. Live a simple life. I wouldn't really call them beasts," Sebastian offers, flipping through *Mystical Creatures and Where to Hunt Them*.

"Okay, well, what about grindylows? This passage here says they store up treasures found on their victims. Maybe a group of them are harboring the chest we need." I point to the passage I'm reading.

Soren sits cross legged on the floor. His beard has grown slightly. I can tell it's bugging him because his tongue every so often licks the facial hair below his nose. He catches me staring and quickly retracts his tongue. "Grindylows aren't sea creatures. They mostly reside in freshwater lakes burrowed in pockets of lake weed and algae. Beasties yes, but I highly doubt they harbor what we seek."

I stand up and pace. It's been frustrating. Night after night we go in circles. Sebastian and I look at all the different creatures of the sea. Soren reads up on wars and famines in the Mer-history dating back to the early hundreds.

"This whole prophecy seems pointless. Couldn't the Siren Queen give us a little more to go on?" My foot kicks a pile of books next to me sending the stack toppling to the ground in a scattered mess. I rub my eyes and sigh before bending down, reforming the tiny tower.

That's when I see it. On the cover of one of the books. The binding is worn brown leather with an imprint of an enormous creature using its numerous tentacles to bring down a ship. "This," I breath, picking up the aged book. "What if it's this?"

Both mermen look up from what they're reading and peer at the book in my hand. My eyes dart between them.

They stare at each other as if talking in a silent sibling language before Sebastian responds. "That's a picture of the kraken. It's just a legend." He dismisses me, going back to his own research. But I can't shake the feeling this is exactly the beast we are meant to encounter.

I step closer to them. Sebastian lounges on the couch. Soren is crisscrossed on the floor near his brother's feet. "Less than a month ago, I believed mermaids were just that. Legends. Myths. Nothing more than fantasy. Why can't this creature—this beast—also be real?"

Soren picks his head up, brows furrowed. Contemplative.

"Well maybe, Freckles," Sebastian says, licking his thumb before using it to turn to his next page. "But our father told us the story of the kraken when we were kids. He used it to scare us away from dangerous parts of the ocean. Even he has admitted to us it's just a story."

I huff.

Soren remains silent. His eyes go distant as if he's solving a riddle. "Brother," he speaks, "she may have a point."

Abruptly, Sebastian perks up, closing the book in his hand with a *clap*. "Wait. Really?"

"There are many wonders in the oceans even we don't know about. It wouldn't surprise me if the kraken is more fact than fiction. Especially considering in the story father told us, the kraken easily disguised itself from its prey."

My heart jumps a little, pride swells up inside my chest at my discovery. Who'd have thought that Soren would actually be on my side for once?

I shake the old book in my hand. "I have this feeling, this gut feeling, that the kraken is the beast. What else is said in the story?"

Sebastian sits up straighter, resting one foot over his thigh. "The kraken is said to be larger than any beast in the oceans. It has ten tentacles full of suckers and hooks designed to trap and catch its prey—rendering escape impossible. The mouth of the beast is lined with rows of razor-sharp teeth and breath so putrid it smells worse than a thousand rotting corpses." I swallow the growing lump in my throat. "Stories say the kraken hunts anything in its path, from unsuspecting ships to sharks to merfolk, anything will do to quench its never-ending hunger."

I breathe deeply. "It surely fits the criteria of beast-worthy."

"Oh, yes, our father said that its l—" Understanding dawns on Sebastian's face before he grins widely. "Constance, you're a genius! I could kiss you right now!" My stomach does a little flip at his admission, but Soren looks annoyed at his brother's declaration. Sebastian doesn't seem to notice. "Father always said the kraken resides in its lair, awaiting unsuspecting curious mer-boys like ourselves to come swim by its *lair* before devouring us."

Soren whispers a fraction of the prophecy, "One in the depths of the beasts lair." He runs his hands over his face. "I think I know where we can find its lair as well."

"Where is that?" I ask. From Sebastian's description I am not sure I want to know the answer.

"My best guess is Shipwreck Grave. It's where father warned us not to venture when we were little. I always figured it was because it was too close to human lands, but maybe not. And if the stories are true, it's also a likely place for the kraken to hide. There's an abyss nearby: an ideal place for hiding."

Sebastian leans forward. I opt to sit back down in my comfy chair. One hand still clings to the book with the picture of the kraken on the front. The other rests idly on my bobbing knee. "Okay, so, what object do we think could be there?"

"Definitely the chest, right?" Sebastian questions. "I mean, if we're talking shipwrecks, there could be all kinds of chests from pirate ships or merchant ships that met their untimely fate."

"That makes sense to me," I say.

Soren counters. "But we can't go searching and expect to find just the chest. It may be the book, and we don't know it. We must keep an open mind."

"That's true," I begin, my knee bouncing rapidly. "Does that mean we also look for the key there as well?"

In a swift but fleeting moment, Sebastian and Soren exchange glances. "I doubt we find some key in the kraken's lair," Sebastian says.

"Sebastian," Soren barks.

Sebastian raises his hands defensively. "Actually, yeah, you know maybe you're right. Best to keep an eye out for all three."

Their exchange feels weird, like they are keeping something from me and don't want me to know. I don't have much time to ponder over it before the conversation shifts.

"I think it's time to go to bed. Get some rest tonight. I'll make arrangements to go within the next twenty-four hours and search. In the meantime, try to get some shut eye." The princes begin to put the books away in neat piles.

I want to say something, but a feeling in my gut stops me and instead I find myself putting the books in neat piles right along with them.

Rest. I need to get rest. That's the order given to me, so that's what I will do tonight. I mutter my goodnight to Sebastian and Soren as they continue to put books away then quickly turn away and leave the library without giving either of them a chance to catch up.

Chapter 31

I had thought Soren would come barging in during the early hours of the morning like he did before. But he doesn't. Gleams of morning light trickle into my room.

Squish and all his pink squishiness rests peacefully on one of the pillows. Careful not to wake him, I quietly wedge myself out of the sheets and go to the vanity to braid my hair. If we are to go swimming into the kraken's lair today, I need to make sure my hair stays in place this time.

Halfway through my poor attempt at a French braid, Addeah walks in, black clothes and belt in hand. The clothes look like the same ones I wore when we went to Siren's Hollow.

"Good morning, Miss Constance." She drapes the fabric over the edge of the bed and turns to me, noticing my hair. "Honey, I think you need some help."

My lips quirk up. "Guilty."

Addeah works her fingers through my hair, separating sections before weaving them together in a secure braid starting at the nape of my neck. She quietly hums while she works.

"How's Darius today?" I ask.

Her fingers never falter as she responds, "He's doing much better. Almost healed entirely. Starts back on his duties about the castle today."

"So soon?" I give her a worried expression through the vanity mirror.

"Yes," she says, " our healers can work wonders and from my understanding, I think we heal a bit faster than humans. He should be good to go so don't fret." The last bit of my hair is added to the braid before Addeah ties it off in a simple but secure knot.

"I'm surprised Soren hasn't taken us out for the day yet," I say. I drape the braid over my shoulder playing with the little tail at the end. "Last time we left so early and abruptly."

Addeah sighs. "Yes, you did. And if you were to do that again on me now, I'd have butchered you all and served you to little Squish here."

My pink pet wakes up at the sound of his name, those black beady eyes looking at us briefly before he circles his spot on the pillow and falls back asleep. "Which is exactly what I told Soren the other day when he came to check on my husband."

I chuckle. "It appears he listened. He told me you scare him a bit."

Addeah straightens up, a sense of pride shows in her posture. "Of course I do. He may be the heir and future King of Emora…but to me he is like the son I never had."

It never occurred to me that Darius and Addeah may have children. They both look slightly older than me, but they could also be much older and just blessed with youthful looks. I take a moment to really observe her face, noticing the faintest wrinkles on the corner of her eyes.

"Do you?" I ask.

"Do I what, child?"

"Do you and Darius have any children of your own?"

She looks away, focused on something beyond the room. "No," she says softly, "I reckon we don't." I swear her eyes become moist before she rapidly blinks away her thoughts and plants her gaze toward me. "Not yet anyway. It was…difficult to try when Darius was going through his training. There were many factors that delayed our efforts. But now that we can try again, I fear—we may have waited too long." Unconsciously her hand slides to her abdomen. The vacant space within.

"Hopefully not." I reach over and take her hand in mine. "Because you two would be excellent parents." I smile warmly at her, giving that hand a reassuring squeeze.

Her features are thoughtful as she flashes her pearly white teeth at me in full bloom. "Thank you, Constance." Tears start to well up in her eyes again, but she regains her composure with a few quick blinks and a deep sigh. "Well then, let's get you ready for breakfast first. Then you can come back, and I'll help you into that black thermal wear before your departure. Will that suffice?"

I nod assuredly. The rest of our morning together is quiet as she wraps me in a simple pink morning gown and shoos me off to the dining hall for breakfast.

The doors to the dining hall are slightly ajar. Through the crack, I can see the elongated table, but no one sits in their typical seats yet. I think I may be the first one here as my arm reaches to swing the door wide open, until I hear hushed voices on the other side.

"I just don't understand why she's still here," a female voice hisses just behind the door, presumably against the wall. "It's been almost a month. There is something seriously wrong with her."

I pull my hand away from the doorknob and tiptoe against the wall. My ears strain to catch every word.

"Lamia," a deep male voice speaks just as softly. Soren. "She's our guest. And she's helping me with trade matters. I need her here for the time being."

The female voice, Lamia, laughs mirthlessly. "You need her? Soren, there's something you aren't telling me. Why did you leave the other day without telling anyone? Without telling me? You're always sneaking off doing who knows what? And you haven't made any time to help with the wedding planning." Although I can't see her face, I imagine her lower lip slightly protruding outward in her typical pout. "What's really been going on with you? You've always been distant with me, but lately we've grown even further apart. I can feel it in my bones, Soren. Why won't you just let me in?"

I hear an exasperated sigh. "I spent a whole day helping you find the right ribbons for the chandelier. And we looked at the menu together and—"

Lamia interrupts, "That was one day, Soren. One day."

I imagine Soren crossing his arms as he speaks. "I'm just—it's not that simple." The sound of boots scuff against the floor as if one of them is drawing closer to the other. Or creating more distance. I'm not sure. "There are things I've been dealing with lately that are my burdens to bear."

"I am your betrothed. Will they not soon be my burdens as well?"

A long pause. Soren doesn't have anything to say to that.

"It's her, isn't it? It must be," Lamia says breathlessly.

"No, this isn't—"

"Of course it is! I have eyes. I see the way you act when she is near. And you try so hard to not look at her, not pay attention to her, as if she means nothing to you…" Lamia's voice trails off.

I press my ear even closer to the wall when a hand appears on my shoulder.

"I'm not sure princesses were taught to eavesdrop."

My feet are practically taken out from under me as if someone had yanked the rug that I stand on. I jump, letting a squeaky yelp escape my lungs. It's Sebastian, plastering on a toothy grin from ear to ear at his triumphant scare.

He's wearing his fancier, royal clothes this morning, with a deep purple jacket and matching vest.

"I didn't mean to eavesdrop." I cross my arms over my chest defensively. Sebastian gives me an incredulous look. "Well…maybe a little." I shrug a shoulder up while I admit the reality of my situation. But what else was I to do? Walk in and make it even more awkward?

"Well, at least you're an honest eavesdropper and that's what counts." He pokes at my uplifted shoulder. "Shall I escort you in? You can pretend to laugh at something witty I said. It'll drive Lamia out of her mind…which will make it all the more fun and announce our arrival so those two can stop quarreling."

I chuckle at Sebastian who proceeds to wriggle his eyebrows at me before looping my arm around his and noisily walking into the dining room so Soren and Lamia will know they are no longer alone.

The moment we step in, Lamia is already walking toward her spot. Her hair is up in a low but regal bun today as she dons a ruby red low back gown showing off the straightness of her spine. The combination is a mix of fire and ice. If she found out I was eavesdropping, she doesn't make it known.

Sebastian and I look to Soren who's still standing against the wall. His face is placid even though moments ago, he was in the middle of a heated discussion with his betrothed. He nods once to his brother, letting us pass him before stalking to his chair.

Breakfast this morning is, oh goody, more fish. Luckily there's also a delicious fruit bowl placed in front of us. I opt to eat it first, savoring the familiar sweet juices before I try to choke down grilled pieces of meat.

The sound of silverware hitting plates is the only noise in the room. Tension rolls off Soren and Lamia. The latter refusing to look up from her plate.

In some ways I feel sorry for her. She's here to marry the heir to the throne, away from her own home. As far as I know, Soren leaves her in the dark on everything. Does she have any idea the king is dying? Does she know we are looking for a cure? Does she understand that all the time I spend with the princes is merely to help them with their cause and receive help in return?

I imagine what it must be like in her shoes. The weight of leading a kingdom with a future king who, in many ways, doesn't seem to care. The loneliness she must feel. Add in the extra stress of knowing something is being kept from her—something important— must eat away at her.

Maybe it's the awkward silence that rings in my ears or maybe it's the defeated posture of the mermaid sitting next to me that makes me say something I may regret later but… "Soren." He looks up. "How's the king doing this morning? I haven't seen him in a couple of days."

Soren pauses eating his breakfast mid chew before setting down his silverware and leaning back in his chair. His throat bobs, sending his bite of food down his esophagus before responding. "The king is fine," he says dismissively.

But I do not let it go. "He hasn't had any meals with us lately. Why is that?"

"Constance," he warns, his silverware clanging on the table.

Sebastian eyes the two of us, his back tensing.

Lamia finally looks up as well, to observe the conversation.

"If he was well, I know he would be with us." A long pause. "Just tell her." I side eye Lamia, even though Soren knows full well who I'm talking about.

Lamia's ears perk up at that, attention now fully on the two of us. "Tell me what?"

Soren's nostrils flare. His eyes lock on mine like a shark targeting its prey. "Nothing," he grunts.

"She deserves to know, Soren. She is your betrothed and the future queen of Emora," I urge.

The breakfast table becomes silent again. I continue to stare down Soren who stares right back.

Sebastian sits awkwardly at his brother's side, quietly stuffing in bites of food between glances.

Lamia merely observes, her food forgotten completely.

I break the silence. "Lamia," I start and look at her, "the king is sick, and he has been for quite some time." Her eyes widen before she looks to Soren for confirmation. He nods gravely. "We've been looking for a cure. That's why we're leaving again today in search of something that may help."

"Is that so?" She hisses. Anger directed toward me or Soren or both, I'm not sure.

"Yes," I continue, "It's why I'm still here. To lend a hand." Even though I am spilling Soren's secrets out to Lamia, I think it best not to tell her I am human. That may not go over very well.

"Well," Sebastian stands from his chair, tossing his napkin onto the table. "I think that's our cue to leave. Constance?" He offers a head nod toward the doors before backing away.

Lamia also stands, all her attention blazing into Soren. I take that as my cue to mutter my leave before stalking after Sebastian.

The doors to the dining room door seal shut on my way out.

* * *

Back in my dressing room, Addeah helps me put on my black suit. I ask her to make sure Squish is fed while I am away in case we are out longer than an evening like last time. She surveys my braid, making sure it's all secured. Addeah also mentions Darius will not be joining us. Although he's up and walking, he's in no condition to go into a battle with a mythical creature- if there is one.

In my mind, I mention that I am in no condition to go into battle either, having never trained a day in my life, but I don't admit this to her before she walks out of the room.

Moments later, an angry knock pounds on the door three times before an even angrier Soren storms in. "Let's go," he commands, turning on his heel not caring enough to look back and see whether I follow him or not.

I pat Squish's head quickly before chasing after him.

He walks so fast I can barely keep up, leading me through the city and the crowds to the entrance behind the waterfall. Merfolk veer out of the way and gawk, but none dare say anything as we pass.

Sebastian leans against the wall, one leg propped against the rock: waiting. The moment he sees us, he pushes off the cave wall and walks toward us, gathering my hands into his. "Are you ready?" he asks.

"As ready as I'll ever be," I mutter, glancing at Soren still quietly seething.

"Listen to me, Constance. You are very important." His thumbs caress my palm sending shivers down my spine. "If something feels wrong, you flee. Don't try and be a hero, okay?"

I look up at him. Worry sketched on his face. In all honesty, I'm not sure how I will do when faced with the kraken- if it even does exist. Perhaps the riddle was just enough information to say that one of the objects was in the shipwreck graveyard, but the beast's lair is still based on fiction. Or perhaps our guess is entirely wrong, and we find nothing at all. I have no idea what I am getting myself into today, and in some ways, I think that is best. To appease his worry, I offer a single nod.

Sebastian gives a soft smile back. "And if you need to, just use Soren as a merman shield." That comment earns him a glare from his older brother.

"Are you not coming with us this time either?" I ask.

"No. Unfortunately our father isn't doing well enough for both of us to leave at the same time. And between Soren and I, he is the stronger of the two. He has a better chance of getting you both out of there than I do, in case something goes wrong." He looks to his brother. "I have everything under control here. Please bring her back safe?" Sebastian asks.

Soren grunts. The only response he seems capable of at the moment. His hands work quickly at sifting through a black sack—the contents inside a mystery to me. Whatever is in there must be all accounted for as he slings it over his shoulders, above the cross sling he wore to Siren's Hollow which has two blades nestled securely across his back. He doesn't even look in my direction before diving into the black water.

"You better hurry, Freckles. He's in a mood." Sebastian proceeds to pull out a vial filled with purple liquid. I gulp it down and take the second vial he hands me, tucking it securely into the pocket on my arm. His hands cradle the sides of my head as his lips brush my brow. "Come back to me."

I can't help the blush creeping up my cheeks. "Aye, aye, matey." I tease before backing away and jumping into the black depths.

The potion has already begun to work in my body. My hands and feet expand and web. My vision improves drastically.

Soren is treading underwater, waiting impatiently. We make eye contact and without a word, swim into the maze of tunnels.

* * *

It's been a couple hours of swimming in utter silence. It doesn't matter that words haven't been verbalized. Soren's body language tells me all I need to know. He's irate. With me. With what I had revealed to Lamia at breakfast.

When my potion induced fins have had enough, I beg Soren to find us a spot to rest for a bit.

We find an underwater cave with a few small air pockets to rest in. We eat in silence. The sound of chewing the only thing to fill the cold air between us.

Soren has always been distant, sometimes even harsh, but this is a new kind of bitterness. He won't even look at me as he wordlessly dives back into the water and out of sight, not waiting or caring if I am behind his fins or not.

After what must be another excruciatingly silent hour, I decide to say something. "I had to tell her something."

Soren's eyes slide in my direction, but he continues to leave me in silence.

"She's your betrothed. She will help you rule one day." My attempt to talk has led Soren to swim even faster, breaking up a school of fish, trying to create some distance between us. But he can't shake me. His actions only egg me on. I swim faster too. "It's not like I gave her all the details. She doesn't know I am human. She doesn't know about our dealings. But if I were in her shoes and my fiancé was sneaking around with someone else, I would worry that the worst would be happening behind my back."

His pace slows. His face crumples in disgust. "I would never dishonor her like that."

"Finally, he speaks," I muse. "I haven't known you very long, but I don't believe you would dishonor her either. Nevertheless," I swim ahead of him and plant my magic induced mermaid body in his path, forcing him to stop and listen, "the mind travels to the worst possible scenarios when left with no boundaries. She was completely in the dark about all of this. I couldn't see her like that."

Soren's hands ball into fists at his side. His legs tread the water keeping him stable against the ocean's push and pull. "It wasn't your place."

"I know," I say solemnly. "It should've been *yours*."

Moments go by. Soren glares at me, contemplatively. Thoughts must be waging war in his mind because his body slowly relaxes. He blinks away the glare, replacing it with something I can't quite comprehend. "You're right," he divulges before adding, "Are all humans as presumptuous as you?"

I can't help the subtle smirk creeping up my lips. "No," I admit. "But true friends do what they think is right over what they think is proper." I shrug a shoulder.

He tilts his head to the side. "Is that what we are? Friends?" The question sounds unsure.

"Is that what you want to call us?"

Soren looks as if he is going to go back to giving me the silent treatment. He swims around me before looking over his shoulder and responding, "I haven't decided yet what I want to call you. But friend seems like a good place to start. Keep up human," he commands. There's a hint of amusement in his words.

I can't help but smile at his admission. Friends. It seems impossible really, considering our first encounter. Going from complete loathing to friendship is a big first step, one I will gladly take.

I swim after him, coming up to his side. Grateful for some much-needed conversation, I ask, "What's in the bag?"

"It's provisions," he starts, swimming at an idle pace now in comparison to the first few hours of our trip. "I figured since the last one was longer than we had anticipated, I would bring some back up supplies. Some food, water, extra vials for you, bandages…things we may need. Oh, and old fish guts."

My nose crinkles. "Fish guts?"

"Yes, I did some research on the tales of the kraken. Most of the versions I read mentioned it tracks its prey by scent. I figure we should mask our own scents as best we can in case that part of the myth is true."

I contemplate his words. Maybe I should have done more research as well. "Okay, fish guts. Check. Anything else I should know before we swim into an impending abyss of death?"

He tries to hide it, but I can tell a smirk threatens to creep up his lips. "Actually, yes. A few of the books I read said it can also camouflage. We'll have to keep our eyes peeled for not just one of the objects, but our surroundings as well. It could be right there, watching us, and we may not even know it."

"Lovely," I say. A shiver runs up my arms even though the thermal suit has kept me plenty warm on our journey.

"Constance?"

"Yeah?"

"I won't let anything happen to you. Not while I still breathe." Soren looks forward when he admits this to me. "That's what friends are for."

I survey him. His black hair, too short to wave in the water. His beard full, accentuating the chiseled jaw beneath. Soren's body is strong. Formidable even. And I knew the moment he uttered those words to me that he means it with his whole being.

"Yes," I repeat, "that's what we're for."

Chapter 32

In the see-able distance, broken sails and jagged piles of planks poke above the sea floor. Our destination: Shipwreck Grave. Soren hands me another purple vial which I take wordlessly before he pulls out a sack of very rotten, very old fish guts strung together on woven thread. I cover my nose in disgust as Soren wraps the guts around my neck like jewelry. Breakfast threatens to come up my esophagus.

"You'll get used to the smell," he whispers as he wraps one around his neck as well. He closes the sack and pulls it over his back, but not before unsheathing one of his twin swords.

The heat of the water and the distance to the ocean floor means we're much closer to the surface than we were earlier. Even the weight of the water feels lighter. But none of this quells my rapidly pacing heart. On the journey here, wildlife thrived around us. Now, only the stench of death permeates the waters. There are no fish. No sharks. Not even critters that crawl on the sea floor dare to inhabit this grave.

Broken ships pile on top of one another. Many half-sunk in the sand.

I pray we don't have to dig to find the object we are looking for.

Soren places a tentative hand on my shoulder. He draws it back and nails his arm to his side. "Stay within earshot. And stay quiet. If a beast really does live here, we don't want to give it any clue we are in its midst," he whispers before motioning to follow him down into the wreckage.

Without question, I swim right at his heels.

The ship closest to us is broken in half. Soren motions for me to check the left side while he swims right. I nod before turning fin and searching for our three objects. A chest, a book, or a key.

This ship doesn't have much to offer in the way of stuff. I use my hands to pick away algae and settled sand from possible objects only to find broken pieces of wood.

We go from shipwreck to shipwreck. Other items lay scattered on the sea floor. Cannons, crates, and old weapons. Each shipwreck sweep leads us further into the grave in search for a chest, a key, or a book. I pray it's not the key we have to find in this wreckage. The smallest of the objects.

Soren leads us to the next ship. This one intact more so than the surrounding ones. It's a massive ship, I'll bet one that contained many treasures before its demise. The sails are washed out black and holey, waving in the water like the ship remembers what it's like to be taken by a sea breeze. A pirate ship no doubt.

We float above deck, looking at all the unopened crates that lay dormant. Soren uses one hand to easily pry open the long forgotten crates, pulling out anything from sodden cloth to ruined china.

I struggle with both hands to pry open my first crate. The wood is sealed shut with far too many nails. On the third attempt I finally get my fingers in between the lid and the box and yank it apart.

A dress of once-fine cloth is nestled securely. Lace trims the neckline, while tiny beads decorate the front. I can't tell if the salt in the ocean washed out the color or if it was always meant to be this off-white sheen. My fingers pinch the shoulders of the dress before I take it out of the crate. What lies beneath it? Nothing. Just one dress that was most likely made for a very special occasion. Although it will never be worn, I decide to fold it as best I can against the waters' protests and place in back in the crate; as if it had never been disturbed.

I move the crate aside to discover a smaller one behind it. The wood warps in a way that makes it easy to pry my fingers under the lid and lift it off.

My heart leaps! There it is. A book.

"Soren!" I shout, then clasp my hand over my mouth. I forgot about the myth of the kraken for a split second in my excitement of my discovery.

Soren comes swimming straight at me, sword in hand. "What's wrong?" he hisses, scanning our surroundings. Ready to fight a threat that isn't here.

"Nothing's wrong," I whisper. "Look what I found!" I pull out the book from the crate.

Soren stares at it before drooping his shoulders, lowering his weapon. "Constance," he says with a touch of irritation, "the Book of Dominion will actually have words in it."

I furrow my brows, confused by his words. Then I get a closer look at the book in my hands. Every page is ruined by the water. There's no way this book would be of any use to us. It couldn't be what we are searching for.

"Sorry," I admit sheepishly, "I just got a little too excited."

He gives the smallest smirk and shakes his head. "Next time try to be quieter when you think you've found something," he whispers, scanning our surroundings.

I nod and pretend to lock my lips together and throw away the key.

Soren nods and points to where he's going to search next. I dive lower.

Below deck is just as cluttered. Piles of crates strewn across every nook and cranny. Using my elongated hands and feet I wade through the water, picking up a small crate, unlatching its rusty handle to reveal a set of what once must have been immaculate silverware. I pick up one of the forks nestled still in place. Pieces flake off the handle, floating in the water before I place it back down and continue my search.

I pry open crate after crate to reveal contents that may have once been of value, but no more.

Perhaps this isn't the boat either. I make my way to the farthest corner below deck. One pile of crates left to open. Sitting atop the warped, wooden crates is a trunk. The placement of it is odd. While all the other things in this graveyard are warped or rusted, or battered, this trunk is in pristine shape. The cherry wood and leather are perfectly intact, as if it had sunk to the bottom of the ocean just this morning. It doesn't belong.

I trace my fingers over engravings on the top. They're a mix of swirls and zigzags— a language unlike anything I have ever seen before. There's a latch attached to the front of the trunk. No key required to open it. My fingers clasp the one piece of metal keeping the trunk sealed shut before I twist it to the right, out of place. A faint *click* reaches my ears before I use the palms of my hands to lift the massive top.

In doing so, water around me collapses and splashes into the trunk, leaving bubbles and suds flooding my vision.

I scream.

Floating in front of me is a one-eyed, partially decomposed head, with a top row of teeth covered in gold.

My heart pounds in my ears. This is not what I expected. I shift away from the head, but the pale-blue eye follows me as if it has a mind of its own.

Soren comes racing in, swords in hand. His guts necklace lags behind him from the sheer swiftness of his movement. Pure rage fills his eyes as he scans the room, teeth bared until he notices it's only me. Rage replaced by confusion. "Where's the danger?" He sees nothing. Again. A look of irritation covers his features as he puts his swords in his sling.

I move my hands just enough to whisper. "I'm sorry." One finger points down to the decayed head. "I was startled by…that."

He notices the head, the eye lolling toward the ceiling. With an exasperated sigh, he sheaths his swords before swimming toward me, still frozen in place near the head.

The head rolls slightly away as Soren approaches. I swear it has a mind of its own.

"Are you alright, Constance?" Soren eyes the head warily.

"Yes, I'm sorry. It… I was just looking through the crates and opened up that trunk…there goes this head floating in my face looking like it's going to attack and… I couldn't help but scream."

Recognition sparks in his eyes. "Wait, you opened a trunk? Not a crate? A trunk that could also be called a chest?"

"Oh…oh! Yes," I grab hold of Soren's hand and yank him toward the trunk, which could also be called a chest, and peer inside the now water-filled middle.

The half-decayed skull wasn't the only thing secured in here. At the bottom nestled in the corner, is an ancient looking, locked, large jewelry box-sized chest.

"What do you think is in that?" I reach down to pick up the chest. Even under water it feels heavy, like whatever is inside of it is solid. The edges are lined with sapphires. The framing is solid gold. And in the center of the front is a small hole where a key could fit. "Is it a treasure chest?"

Soren reaches out and places a hand on the domed top. "Whatever it is, it is what we are looking for. I'm sure of it. It's almost like…" He studies the chest, tracing his hand over the carvings on it. "…never mind."

I wonder what he was about to say but get distracted by his face. It's full of something I haven't seen cross his features once in all the weeks I've been around him. Hope. Hope is written on his face—his eyes are shining with it. His full mouth curves upward. Then he looks at me, a real smile creeping up his lips to reveal a set of beautiful teeth. I never noticed how nice his smile is until now—when they're paired with his glowing blue eyes.

Before I can register to smile back, a shadow overcomes the ship. The little light we had from the sun has been snuffed away, leaving me, Soren, and the chest covered in darkness. Were it not for our heightened mermaid eyesight, we would not be able to see anything.

I look to Soren who's gone completely still as he sees just what has caused this darkness: the kraken.

Chapter 33

Giant suction cups, larger than my entire body squirm up the windows of the boat.

I clutch the chest tight against my breast causing bitty pieces of chum to fly off my necklace.

Without taking his eyes off the moving tentacles encapsulating the ship, Soren reaches to his back and pulls out both blades.

Instinctively, I cower behind him, watching the pink flesh surround us on all sides.

"It knows we're in here," I whisper in Soren's ear.

"Shh…we don't know that." He raises his swords above his chest in a defensive stance, putting his body between me and the tentacles.

The tentacles stop like the world around us has frozen in time.

I dare not move a muscle except my eyes; watching the legendary beast's body.

I count the seconds in my head. *Tick. Tick…tick.* Those intimidating tentacles retract from view, giving back light below deck.

I let out an extensive puff of air, leaving bubbles to fizz in front of me. "Let's get out of here," I say just audible enough for Soren to hear.

His swords remain raised, but he turns to me and nods before looking down at the chest still clutched against me. "Agreed." One sword goes back in its sheath, but Soren keeps the other out, lowered to his side. He swims against the window and peers sideways out of it, checking for the kraken's whereabouts. He looks to the left. Right. Above and below before he places one finger to the tip of his lips. The signal is clear; stay silent. He motions for me to follow him up the steps, but he doesn't go all the way up. Before hitting the deck, Soren stops again and surveys our surroundings. Without looking at me, he motions to follow again.

Despite my internal commands to stay calm, my heart still pounds in my chest. If our smell won't give us away, my own nerves surely will. Does the kraken have good hearing too? *Stay calm.*

Shipwreck Grave is silent, like being in a vast well of nothing. No movement. No sound. No life. Despite my thermal wear, a shiver runs down my neck.

Like thieves in the dead of night, we swim from wreck to wreck toward the way we entered this forbidden place; swimming swift and silent to our next hiding spot, praying we don't get spotted by the beast.

Soren finds two barrels huddled against one of the ships and darts for them. I follow wordlessly ducking behind them as Soren peeks around the edges looking at our path to safety. Only about a hundred yards left before we are out of the kraken's territory and into open waters.

I know it seems silly to believe the kraken can't go beyond the grave, but I hope for some magical reason it can't and open water is our safe haven.

Soren is about to make our next move when I get the sensation; something is watching us.

I crane my body to look behind us, but nothing's there. With a long, painfully slow scan of the wreckage, I see nothing out of place. No movement, no giant beast barreling toward us, but that sense that something is staring right at me won't go away.

I want to tell Soren to look as well. My gut is telling me something's very wrong. But before I can say anything something strong and sticky wraps around my ankle and yanks me back. Loose sand floats up my nose and into my eyes. My hands let go of the chest. I see it falling in a blanket of sand as I struggle to grasp anything that will stop me from being dragged to my death.

I hear Soren yell, but I can't figure out what he's saying. The strong, sticky tentacle raises me up to meet one giant, incandescent green eye. Then the entire creature comes into view. One moment it was practically clear as the water, then its true colors spread across its skin like ripples from a cannonball breaking the surface of the water. The kraken.

"Soren!" I scream.

The kraken drowns out any response with an ear deafening screech. The sound is so shrill I have to cover my ears.

It's breath smells of rotting corpses and my food threatens to come up again. I've never smelled anything so foul.

I struggle to get free, digging my nails into the thick hide of the beast, pushing at its rough, bumpy tentacle. But it's no use.

I scream in frustration.

Just then, like a cannonball, a whirlpool of water hits the beast. It screeches in disapproval. One after another, cannonball after cannonball pelts the kraken's hold on me until it's forced to let go.

I use the momentum of the next water cannonball to swim away as fast as possible.

Soren is mere yards away, throwing everything he has at the beast. "Constance, get out of here!"

The kraken isn't deterred by Soren's water cannons. It screams, tentacles flailing before disappearing into the background.

Camouflage. Sebastian and Soren had mentioned the creature can camouflage.

It was hunting us the entire time, and we didn't even know it because we could not see it.

I race to our last hiding spot, searching for the fallen chest. Luckily it didn't sink too far into the sand. I scoop it up with both hands, holding it tight to my chest. I spot Soren in the near distance.

Whirlpools of water swirl in each hand. His back is tense, and his eyes remain vigilant, scanning the terrain, using his legs to swim backwards toward me.

The kraken has disappeared from sight.

"Where is it?" he quakes.

Without warning, a tentacle comes rushing at Soren, colliding with his chest, sending him flying against the side of a ship.

"Soren!" I choke out, rushing to him with the chest still tucked against my body. He does his best to stand up on the seafloor, legs wobbling with the effort.

It's quiet again, as if the kraken is merely toying with us, mice caught in its trap. I can't see it, but I know it's watching us. Can sense it. That beady otherworldly eye---

"Look for the eye," I whisper to Soren.

"What?" His brows furrow like he doesn't understand.

"It can camouflage its body, but I saw its eye earlier. I don't think its eye can blend in."

Understanding dawns on him as he pulls out a sword. We both tremble, myself with adrenaline and anticipation, Soren with something I can't quite place.

There. I take one hand away from our object just long enough to point at an eye peaking around the mast of a ship fifty yards to our right.

Without even blinking Soren shoots a blast of water at the creature. Soren's aim hits true. It screeches again, the facade of water fading to reveal the beast's true colors.

No more playing. It launches itself at us, all ten tentacles outreached like sticky hands ready to capture and devour us. Soren shoves me away with both hands right before those claws wrap around his body rendering his arms and hands useless.

Think. I must think. I look frantically at my surroundings.

Soren's face begins to turn purple. The kraken wraps his tentacle around his body tighter, crushing his gills.

Think, Constance! There must be something here that can harm it! All that surrounds me is broken, warped wood and sand. But then I remember. One of the first ships had old weapons around it. Spear-like weapons.

I take one more look at Soren and drop the chest back into the sand without a second thought, swimming faster than I've ever swam before toward the old weapons. They lay half covered in the sand. There's a spear with a head that's old and rusted but it remains intact with the wooden shaft. I grasp it with both hands and circle back toward the beast.

I hide behind one of the ship's helms, analyzing the best way to approach the beast. I know what I must do, but getting close enough will be the tricky part. Only one tentacle easily grips Soren leaving nine others free to grab me if I am not quick enough.

Regardless of the kraken's hold, Soren still struggles, writhing as much as possible to get free, but I can tell he's going to lose consciousness soon. His eyes lose focus, and head begins to lull.

There's a large hole in the ship where the kraken remains. An idea hits me. I grab the mainsail from one of the ships nearby, the rope still connected. It may not be large enough to cover the beast, but it is large enough to cover me.

In one hand, I angle my spear forward. I make sure I'm just out of reach before grabbing the fabric in the other hand. I drag the giant piece of fabric in circles around the kraken.

It launches its tentacles at me to no avail.

Faster and faster I swim, the fabric slowly expands to its full height, like a strong wind has opened the sails again.

The kraken can't take its eye off of it. When I'm just above the wrecked ship I let go and let the water take the sails drifting of their own accord now and dive into the wreckage, out of sight.

The kraken continues to prey upon the mainsail, one tentacle coiling around the fabric only to find that I am no longer there. It screeches in frustration.

Now is the time.

Swimming through the hole in the ship, I push up, taking as much sand with me as possible in my free hand. I throw it in front of me where the kraken's eye is. Sand sprays everywhere creating murky water all around us.

My only chance is now. With speed of a swordfish, I race straight at the beast, spear leading the way. The kraken has no time to react before it sees me, sees the spear plunging into its eye.

A high-pitched bellow escapes the beast. Its tentacle loosens around Soren long enough for him to wriggle free, gasping for air to filter through his gills.

"The spear! Get the spear!" I shout to him.

It's all I need to say because he knows exactly what I mean. Between huffs, Soren raises both of his hands and takes hold of the spear as if it's attached to an invisible piece of rope and yanks it out of the kraken's eye only to plunge it back in with his mystical water powers.

The kraken shrieks and moans, its tentacles shriveling in on itself before it retreats further into the grave.

I grab Soren's arm, veering him toward the opposite direction. "Let's go before it changes its mind."

On our way out, I relocate the chest and point it out to Soren.

He snatches it up with both hands.

We swim as fast as possible, each looking in turn toward the kraken's last known whereabouts before meeting open waters.

Only then do I allow myself to relax a little, but I have a feeling today's events will haunt me in my dreams later.

Chapter 34

"I can't believe you went head-to-head with the kraken and lived to tell the tale. You're a superhuman or something." Sebastian chomps down on a purple-colored fruit while he surveys the chest sitting on the war strategy table in the strategy room. "So how do we open it? What do you think is inside?"

"It clearly needs a key," Soren states. He's sitting in the armchair opposite of Sebastian and myself, hands folded under his chin, staring at the chest. Contemplative.

Sebastian stands up and strolls to the far side of the room where a small stash of weaponry is stationed and picks up one of the long swords. Twirling it around like it's some kind of toy, he meanders back to the chest and raises the sword with both hands over his head—ready to strike. "Well how about we just—"

"No! Don't—" Soren tries to warn.

Too late. Sebastian brings the sword down in one swoop, ready to strike the top of the jewelry sized chest with the sword only to be met with a powerful, invisible force field, knocking him back with a loud thud against the bookshelf full of war strategy manuscripts.

"Okay…ow!" He rubs the back of his head.

Soren places a hand on the chest. "It has some kind of protective magic around it. I already tried that and now have a giant bump on my head to prove that destroying the box to retrieve its contents won't work."

"Not to mention whatever's in that box may be fragile. Destroying the box could potentially ruin what's inside of it," I add.

Soren nods before he explains how he first tried to pry the box open when we got back only to be met with the same mystical energy Sebastian just witnessed firsthand. "It needs a key."

"Couldn't our blacksmiths just forge a key to fit the hole?" Sebastian offers. He crosses his arms over his chest before bending over the object, inspecting it.

Soren responds, "Highly unlikely. My guess is we'll need to find the original key, which will also most likely have some sort of magic connecting the two objects. The Siren Queen did say we would be looking for a key."

I take a mental breath of relief. Ever since coming across that siren in the castle, I couldn't help but wonder if somehow I was the key they were looking for. But no, it's an actual key made of some kind of stone—not a person.

"Well," I begin. My hands trace the edges of the jewel studded box. "At least we can check off the beast's lair and the chest from our list of places and objects."

"True," Sebastian begins, "now we have a home of despair, a betrayer's snare, and a key, and a book. One third of the way and no one has died yet, so I'd say that's a positive." He raises his thumb in the air and gives me a wink.

I smirk at him. But the word died has struck curiosity in me. "How is your father doing anyhow?" I look to Soren.

His tropical eyes turn stormy. "Not great." His throat bobs once before continuing, "He's finding it increasingly difficult to get out of bed… but we'll find a cure for him. I know we will."

Sebastian gives his brother a sympathetic look. "We will. It's only a matter of time before he's free of this illness."

Soren eyes the chest, still sitting in that commanding chair. "I'll be in the library again tonight, researching. There must be something I've missed."

"I'll be there too," I say, trying to catch Soren's eyes, but he just stares at the chest. His body is here, but I can tell his mind is far off.

"No. Take tonight off. You need to rest."

"He's right, Constance. You've almost drowned twice and fought a kraken since you've been here. You're only human after all. Take the whole day off. Roam the castle grounds. Take a stroll through the kingdom. I'll be sure to help my brother." Sebastian takes my hands and places a soft kiss on them.

I look to Soren for approval. "Well, that would be refreshing. If I was actually allowed out of the castle."

He returns my gaze. "You are no longer a prisoner, Constance. You're a friend. Go wherever pleases you," he says but quickly breaks eye contact with me, "just as long as you don't make a big spectacle of yourself." His neck grows red under the scruff of his beard.

"Then perhaps we can have dinner later. My treat," Sebastian offers a warm, hopeful smile at the mention of dinner together.

I squeeze his hands, still holding onto mine. "That sounds perfect."

* * *

I listen to the princes' advice and take the day off, roaming about the castle grounds on my own after a light lunch. It feels so freeing to be able to go wherever I want today.

I walk through every hall and room open to the public.

Apparently, there is a room entirely dedicated to Emora's citizens' artwork.

As I walk in, common merfolk gawk at me. I do my best to ignore them, but if they don't stop looking at me, I turn my attention to them and give a close-fingered wave.

Acknowledging their gawking is the surest way to make them stop.

After the initial shock of a freckled *princess* joining the company, I am able to roam about the room in peace.

Each painting tells its own story. One is of a ship caught in a storm. Many are of royalty including King Cyrus. There is a painting of him in full armor, standing on a boulder above the sea, raising a sword in the air in triumph. There is also one of him and the queen, dancing in the middle of a ballroom.

Other paintings cover entire walls. One is of a landscape covered in waterfalls cascading down into clear pools of water. Greenery surrounds the water, so lush and full of life. Mermaids with tails, like the ones Papa used to tell me about, sit on rocks, basking in the warm sun breaking through the trees. It is by far my favorite one in the entire gallery. The brush strokes are so detailed, I feel as though I am standing right there.

I look down at the corner of the painting; the initials SE scripted in big swooping letters.

An hour flies by in the blink of an eye. I have now looked at every painting in the gallery and meander toward the castle garden.

I never did get a good look at everything the night of the ball.

I'm almost to the ballroom doors when, in the distance, teal blue hair blurs in my peripheral vision. I back pedal behind the nearest pillar as my eyes dart in the direction where Lamia walks past; or creeps past is a more accurate description.

It's an odd sight. Her usual gait and swish of her hips and high chin are nowhere to be found. Instead, she creeps along the wall, holding her heels in her hand, glancing behind her back before she makes a right turn into another hallway.

My gut tells me she does not want to be followed. So, I follow.

My heels clack against the white marble, but I do my best to stifle their echo as I make my way toward Lamia.

My head pokes around the corner of the hall. She's already at the end and makes another right turn, out of my line of vision. I speed up my pace, pumping my arms and peer around the next corner. The hallway is entirely empty. That's odd. I was certain she'd gone down this way.

There aren't many doors in this area, so I check each one by putting my ear against the brown wooden panels, listening for occupants on the other side.

By the third try, I find my mark. Just on the other side of the door, Lamia talks in hushed tones, to whom- I am not sure.

"Did anyone see you walk in with this?" she questions.

A gravelly voice responds, "No, princess. I did as you ordered."

A pause. "Good. Let me see it, then."

A popping sound hits my ears, like that of a box being opened.

Neither one speaks for a long time.

"All matters seem to be in order. You have your payment, already. Now go," Lamia orders before taking a pause. "Oh, and if you speak a word of this to anyone, I will hunt you down and gut you like the cowardice fish you are."

"Yes, princess," the gravelly voice cowers in fear.

Then the door handle turns.

All I can think now is *hide, hide, hide.*

I locate the nearest pillar against the wall and stand with my back as flat against it as possible before the door creaks open.

Please don't walk this way, I pray.

My prayer is answered.

The steps grow softer the longer I wait. Whoever it was pads in the opposite direction of me. I take a deep, silent, breath before peering around the curve of the pillar. Down the hall, is a masked, hooded figure hunched over. It walks with a limp before disappearing from my sight.

But where is Lamia?

The door opens again. Out comes Lamia, holding a small box in her hand. She must've waited to exit in case someone was lurking in the hall.

She turns to walk in the same direction as the hooded figure. Her sharp stilettos clack against the marble but then they stop. She stares at the box in her open palm and lifts the lid to reveal the contents.

I dare lean farther out to catch a glimpse of what she wants to keep secret.

This is either the best or the worst luck I've had all day. Sitting in the box is a key. It has two different colored gemstones embedded into the bow. The golden blade shimmers against the light. It's the most radiant, most mystical looking key I have ever seen.

Lamia cranes her head in my direction.

I quickly draw back against the wall- but too fast. My head thumps against the stone which causes me to groan out loud. One hand clasps over my mouth. The other rubs the back of my head where there will surely be a bump later. But I don't hear anything. I don't hear stilettos against the marble. Maybe she didn't hear me.

I dare to take another peek.

"Nosy little trout, aren't we?" Lamia stands directly in front of me. Her pale blue heels hanging from two of her fingers. The box nowhere in sight.

"I was uh—"

"Eavesdropping? Spying?"

I stand up straighter. I can't let her intimidate me. "No. I happened to be on a stroll this afternoon and noticed you were in this hall." I do my best to turn my nose up at her, even though she is a good foot taller than me. "Truth be told, I was trying to avoid conversation with you, hence my hiding spot."

She shakes her head slowly from side to side. "You don't fool me. Whatever it is you think you saw—"

"—I saw nothing."

"Don't lie to me!" she yells before checking herself, looking both ways down the hall to make sure no one else is around. "If you tell anyone, especially Soren, what you saw here, I will personally see to it you will end up chained, on the bottom of the ocean, where no one will be able to find you and the creatures of the deep can feast on you."

Little does she know, her threat is even worse than it sounds for me, a human. But I do my best to not look affected by her words.

"You know, Lamia… It would be very difficult to tell someone what you were up to, especially considering I saw nothing. But good luck with whatever it is you're keeping from Soren. Hopefully he doesn't find out what it is from the wrong person," I retort.

"You little—"

Just then, two sets of boots come stomping down the hall: guards.

Lamia and I turn at the same time to look at them.

I take the opportunity to walk away.

"Good day, Lamia." Without another word, I stride down the hall away from her.

Fresh air. I need some fresh air immediately.

I make a beeline to the front gates and out of the castle entirely into the flower paved paths of Emora's residences.

Chapter 35

It really is a gorgeous landscape. Some residence homes are carved into the outer walls of the city, decorated with front doors of every color imaginable. Other stone homes rest in packs along the paths that weave through the trees and shrubs. Much of the landscape is lathered in greenery and exotic flowers I have never seen before.

Streams of water seem to accompany every walking path in the city. Some are tiny trickles like when it rains and the excess drips off the side of overflowing gutters, while others are more like rivers that ebb and flow. Many lead into ponds every ten houses or so, but where the rest go, I do not know.

I find a stone bench resting underneath a tree with long dangly limbs covered in light pink blossoms. Sitting on it gives me a clear view of one of the ponds, so I stay and watch the fish in the water. They swim back and forth and round in circles.

I get lost in thought watching the shimmering scales beneath the water.

Lamia has a key. A magical key from the looks of it. And she doesn't want me to say anything to anyone, especially Soren. She can't be a room of despair; it just doesn't make sense… which leads me to believe she is the betrayer. But how do I tell Soren without hurting him? It can't be easy to go against your betrothed.

Something small tugs on my skirt. A little hand clutches the fabric. That tiny little hand is attached to a tiny little girl no more than five years old. Her hair is in two long braids that rest on her shoulders. Her eyes are shiny and bright with wonder as she looks up at me.

"Are you a princess?" she asks and reveals a set of baby teeth with one front tooth missing.

I can't help but smile. "In fact, I am," I reply. "What gave it away?" I scoot over on the bench, giving it a little pat.

The girl lets go of me to use both hands as she pushes herself up to sit on the bench in the vacant spot.

"You're very pretty," she says. "All princesses have to be pretty."

"Well, thank you. Does that mean you're a princess too?"

She giggles, revealing a deep dimple on her cheek. "No, silly. I'm just Lilly. What are those on your face?" she asks, using one of her tiny fingers to point.

At first, I can't think of what she means. My fingertips touch my face searching for loose crumbs or dirt and then it hits me. My freckles. "Oh, you mean these dots all over my cheeks and nose? They're called freckles."

Her head tilts to the side causing one of her braids to sway in the open air. "Why do you have them?"

"You see," I begin, "I'm a special princess with a special job. I go on land sometimes and bring back stuff under water. The sun up there gives me these."

"Oh," Lilly says. Her feet dangle back and forth.

I notice she's barefoot.

"I see you lost a tooth," I say, "Did you put it under your pillow after you lost it?"

Lilly's face scrunches up in laughter. "No, silly, why would I do that?"

It only now occurs to me that maybe the traditions of merfolk and their children wouldn't be the same as human ones.

"Oh," I say. "Then what do you do with it once it's lost?"

Her little hands raise, like the answer is the most obvious thing in the world. "I threw it in the pond and made a wish."

"Princess Constance!" a voice hollers from a distance. I look over to see Fleck and Cam striding over to us.

Lilly ducks her head into my side. "Mommy said not to talk to them," she whispers.

I furrow my brows. "Why is that? They're very nice," I encourage her. I'm not entirely convinced if they're nice. Considering I've only met them once, it's a bit of a premature opinion, but I want Lilly to feel more comfortable.

"Mommy says they're…different."

Before I can ask anything further, Cam and Fleck stop right in front of me. Lilly digs her head deeper into my side.

"Cons— uh, Princess Constance," Fleck says eyeing the little girl next to me, "We have updates of the lost merchant."

I sit up straighter. News. The first news I have had in months about my father. I gulp down a growing lump in my throat. "And?" I inquire.

Fleck side eyes Lilly clinging to me before he continues, "He stopped at Ohaku with his crew three weeks before their annual spring celebration. One of the locals remembers him specifically because he always buys something from her tent every season, like clockwork. Only this one was more memorable because there were uh…" he looks back to Lilly who peeks under my arm to look at him. He lowers his voice a notch. "…He ran into some slave traders." He says the words like it's taboo. Probably to keep Lilly from being even more scared than she already is.

Slave traders are the nastiest sort of men to run into. They don't care about anything except how they can obtain the highest profit from others' expenses. Growing up, Papa had always warned me to steer clear of them at all costs.

I stroke Lilly's braided head with my hand before speaking. "Was he taken?" I ask. A new wave of nerves crashes in my stomach.

"No," Fleck responds. "They left quite a mess at the market. Apparently your merchant stood up to them and helped chase them off."

I slouch with relief.

"However," Fleck begins as Cam shifts his weight. "It could be a new lead on the whereabouts of the merchant. We have cause to believe that wasn't the last time he encountered the slave traders.

"Captain Dox ordered us to come find you and share our intel with you. He and the rest of the crew are working on repairing some damages our boat took on the way back." Fleck bends down close to my ear. "Sea serpent. Nasty piece of work during mating season." He stands back up. "The damages have delayed our departure. However, once the ship is good as new and we've gathered supplies for the longer trip, we'll follow the trail of the miss— the merchant."

"Thank you," I say.

Fleck nods.

Wordlessly, his twin Cam pulls something from his belt buckle and hands it to me. "From the patron," is all he says.

Mama. She wrote back to me. I have half a mind to yank away the rolled-up parchment from his hands and run to my room to read it. But I don't. Instead, I reach out with trembling fingers to take hold of it. It's the most precious piece of paper I have ever held.

"Thank you, Cam," I say. He nods. "And Fleck," I add.

"Anything for a pretty thing like you," Fleck says and winks at me. His voice has put on a lighter air. It's intoxicating really.

He glances at Lilly. She has become bolder, showing a whole half of her face as she stares at Fleck with one eye. His eyes turn a little mischievous before he turns to the path and crouches down, plucking a purple flower and offering it to her. "A beautiful flower for a beautiful little princess," he says.

Lilly giggles into my side and reaches out a hand to grab the flower, snatching it away as quickly as she can.

"We'll come find you before our departure," Fleck says to me before he and his brother stride off.

With the absence of the two mermen, Lilly comes completely out of her hiding place at my side and puts the flower behind her ear. "What did they give you?" she asks, pointing to my rolled-up parchment.

I squeeze it in my hand. "It's a letter from someone I deeply cherish."

"Is it a love letter from the prince? Does it say he loves you in there? Mommy says princes and princesses get married when they're in love." She reaches out for Mama's note, but I safely pull it out of her arm's length.

I laugh. "No, it's not from a prince."

"Will you marry a prince?"

I think of Sebastian. If tonight goes well, and we fall in love, will I marry him? I do dote on him and his light-hearted nature. He makes me feel special. Will he court me like a human would? Is it even possible for a human to marry a merman?

So many questions lay before me that remain unanswered. My thoughts are interrupted by a woman yelling. "Lilly! It's time to come in and get washed up for dinner!"

"Coming, Mom!" she calls as she hops off the bench, her braids swing back and forth. She waves to me. "I hope to see you again," she says showing off her deep dimple.

"I hope so, too. It was nice meeting you, Lilly." I wave in response and watch her weave around the path to a merwoman waiting for her.

My stomach grumbles. Lilly's mom was right. It was time to get ready for dinner. I keep one hand clutched to Mama's note and practically race back up to the castle.

* * *

The first thing I do when I get into my room is plop belly first onto the bed and break the seal on the rolled-up parchment.

The words are like rain in a drought to my soul as I treasure reading every single curvy letter. She must have been crying when she wrote back to me because there are some words that are smudgy and difficult to decipher. But it's all there.

She tells me how scared she has been. How much she has prayed for my safe return. How she couldn't bring herself to sell a ring that wasn't hers so instead sold some of her own jewelry to keep the household afloat.

Most importantly she tells me she loves me and is counting down the days until she sees my face again.

I cry for a while after finishing her letter. The feeling of being homesick strikes me like lightning hitting the sand. Squish curls up into my collar bone, licking tears off my cheek. He makes the ache a little better. Then I remember I am having dinner and need to pull myself together. I scratch Squish's chin before wiping away the rest of my tears and hop into the bath. Now isn't the time for pity tears.

Dinner with Sebastian. Just the two of us. The idea sends butterflies flitting about in my stomach causing all sorts of flutters.

Squish is curled up on his pillow, looking out the window. The light is beginning to fade. I stand in front of the vanity mirror on my dressing stool, watching Addeah do her work on me. She came by to help me into an outfit and to do my hair for the evening. She's chosen a sea green chiffon fabric that cinches at the waist, the skirt grazes ever so slightly on the floor. The sleeves are sheer with embroidered flowers gathering at my wrists. It's quite the dress. A proper one made for courting. Something more elegant than an everyday dress, but modest and easy to move around in. It really brings out the color of my eyes, so I like it.

Addeah is quieter than usual, and her face is ten shades paler than normal. Her fingers work slower.

"Addeah?" I turn to face her. "Are you alright?"

She stops fiddling with the layers of my dress to look up at me and smile. It doesn't meet her eyes. "Oh yes, child. I've just felt a little under the weather the last day or so is all. I'll be fine by morning."

"Are you sure? You look…well you look like you might be sick at any moment." I observe her face. She looks like she might vomit.

"It's alright, Constance. I'll get you ready and then rest for the night."

I don't like the way she looks. If I were to guess by her paleness, I'd say she has already been sick today. Her eyes are red-rimmed. Her hair doesn't have its usual sheen.

"No," I begin, stepping down from the stool I had been standing on. "Go back now. Get some rest."

"But your hair—"

"—will be fine just the way it is," I finish for her. It still looks clean and curly from this morning. "It's been a long while since I've wore my hair completely down. Besides, I think it complements the dress quite nicely this way, don't you think?"

Addeah struggles to stand up from her knees but gives me a true smile. "I suppose that's true."

I nod in satisfaction. "Good. Glad we can agree. Now go."

Addeah chuckles weakly. "Now that sounds like the authority of a true princess. Either that or I've been a bad influence on you."

"If being a bossy princess will get you to take the rest you need then that's what I'll be," I retort. I take one of her hands in my own, my other guides the small of her back toward the door.

When we reach the door, she places a hand on the handle before turning back to me. "Goodnight, Miss Constance. Enjoy your dinner." Then she walks past the threshold and slowly makes her way to her quarters. One hand on the wall, the other clutching her stomach.

I am worried about her, but the worry couldn't possibly smother the excitement fluttering in my belly in anticipation for tonight. It is going to be just me and Sebastian tonight.

The way he jokes with me, touches me… the way his eyes linger on my face—his every gesture makes me like him more. If only Mama could see me now about to have dinner with a prince. Not a human prince of course but a prince, nonetheless. She wouldn't believe it until she saw it.

I stride back to my vanity and use my fingers to re-curl a few strands that have intertwined.

What if Sebastian tries to kiss me again tonight? What if he tries to kiss me after we eat and my breath stinks? Suddenly I'm looking around for anything in the room that can keep my breath from smelling putrid. Mints perhaps.

A knock on the door stops me in my search.

"Coming!" I call over my shoulder before giving myself one last check in the mirror. My dress is flowy and elegant. My hair cascades down my back. I pull a couple of spirals over my shoulder to frame my face which is clean and tinted slightly on the cheeks. I raise my chin to the ceiling. Boogers? None to be found.

Another knock sounds at the door.

"Coming! Coming!" I turn my heels and glide back to the door. My fingers grab the handle and open it wide to see my date.

Only it's not Sebastian.

Chapter 36

My mouth hangs open. "What are you doing here?" I ask.

Soren stands in front of me, still dressed in his royal clothes, holding the chest under his arm. His other hand taps it nervously. He begins to say something until his eyes bounce between my dress, my hair. "You um… I had a… why are you dressed like that?"

I raise an eyebrow. "Do you not recall? Your brother and I are having dinner tonight. Didn't you hear him ask me to dine with him earlier this morning?" I lean against the door, looking at him, annoyed.

Soren takes another glance at my dress. "Right," he shakes his head, "I must've forgotten. This will be quick though, I promise." Soren looks past me and into my room. "May I, uh—"

"Come in?"

He nods.

I lean out the door to take a quick view of the halls. No Sebastian yet. I let out an exaggerated breath before replying, "By all means. Come in." Turning my back to the door to create a walkway for Soren to step through.

It takes him two quick strides before he's in the middle of the room, looking around at everything from my bed to the shoes lined on the floor in color coded sequence.

"Are you judging the condition of my room right now?"

He turns to face me, his free hand raised in the air. "No, it's just…it's so clean."

"Is that why you're here? To make sure I'm being a good castle guest? Picking up my dirty bloomers and making my bed?"

An uncharacteristic chuckle escapes him. His lips quirk up as heat peeks under his beard. "Even if I were, I know enough about you to know that this room will stay exactly as you wish, no matter what I said."

His eyes soften at the corners, gazing into mine with a soft smile still painted on his face. He looks…well he looks handsome.

Friends. I remind myself we've become friends. And he is betrothed to Lamia. And I'm being courted by his brother. I should be elated that I can consider myself friends with the brother of the merman I'm falling in love with. The circumstances feel like they're from a fairytale apart from a slight tugging at my navel, nagging at me. I shake off the feeling before I pull a strand of hair and mess with it consciously. "Okay, then why are you here?" I jut my thumb toward the door. "Sebastian's going to be here any minute."

Squish lifts his head and chirps at Soren and me, clearly annoyed we woke him up from one of his many naps. Then his pink body plops onto his bottom, belly sticking out to face Soren. His beady black eyes blink at the chest, and he chirps again.

"He's what I'm here for," Soren says placing the chest down on my bed. "I was in the library doing research and discovered the true nature of the creature you stole."

"I prefer the phrase freed from bondage," I contend, walking to Squish and stroking his leathery back.

"Constance," Soren begins solemnly. "This creature is a tiny, pink locksmith. It has the ability to open any lock: magical or standard. It's the ultimate thief."

Squish gurgles at Soren and harrumphs, stomping one of his sticky paws in objection.

"I don't think he enjoys being called a thief, but that would make sense as to why Count Pesilfer was so angry he was missing." I think back to the count's anger, the rage that radiated off him when he tried to assault me in this very room.

"Exactly," Soren offers, "your new pet is special."

At that comment, Squish shows a sense of pride, chirping happily at Soren before he crawls his way over the sheets and into one of Soren's hands. Soren scratches under Squish's chin causing the creature to purr with delight.

Realization hits me. "Wait, are you saying… do you mean that Squish can open this chest?"

Chirp.

"That's my theory," Soren says, gently letting Squish back down on the bed. "What do you say, creature? Care to show us your skills?"

Squish chirps at Soren and looks to me, as if he's waiting for my approval.

"Go ahead," I encourage.

That's all the encouragement Squish needs before he sets his sticky fingers on the chest, sniffing the keyhole with his slitted nostrils.

Soren begins to chew on his thumbnail, which I notice now that all his nails are chewed to the quick. He glances in my direction before swiftly bringing his hand down only to rigorously tap them on his leg while we wait.

Squish proceeds to lick around the chest, like a cat giving a bath to its kitten, before taking two of his bulbous fingers and thrusting them into the keyhole.

I watch in anticipation, noting how concentrated Squish has become.

A flash of light shatters around the chest like broken glass.

I raise my forearm to shield my eyes from the swift flash of radiance.

Click. Just like that, the seemingly impenetrable lock, has been set free of its confines. The seam of the chest cracks open.

I throw my hands out to let my new favorite pet hop into my palms. My puckered lips place a peck on the top of his head. "Great work, Squish!"

He smiles wide revealing the tiniest chompers and gives a chirp of glee.

I continue to stroke his head and chin, thanking him for what he's done.

"One step closer to our answers," Soren breathes. His voice is awestruck. He stretches out his hand, fingers trembling as they wedge their way into the small crack at the seam, before he flicks the chest open to reveal its contents.

The room itself seems to halt in time. Soren stares at what lays inside, brows furrowed deep.

Without moving my feet, I lean over the footboard of the bed. Squish does the same.

Soren lowers his hands into the chest and pulls out what appears to be a giant fork head. An expensive one no doubt by the golden gleam of each curved prong. The tips are sharp and hooked as if it was meant to catch a fish the size of a great white shark.

"We battled a deadly mythological creature for... a fork," I say, putting Squish down on the bed. I rub my neck and let out a loose sigh. "Well, at least now we can eat whatever ponderous creature comes our way without having to cut it into little pieces. Although I foresee chewing to be problematic."

Soren doesn't take his eyes off the object. His fingers trace every curve inching their way toward the top. One pointer finger taps the tip of a single prong. Immediately he retracts his finger, drawing in a sharp breath. A trickle of blood runs down the length of his hand.

"I barely touched it," he mutters to himself.

"Excuse me?" I say, waving my hands in the vicinity of his gaze, "are you going to fill me in on what "it" is?"

Without taking his hands off the object, Soren examines it further but replies, "I can't be sure, but it appears as though it's missing pieces." He points to the bottom piece of metal showcasing a hollowed-out section, like something should be screwed into it. Then he points to the front where a small valley is indented at the nape of the five prongs. It does appear that something is meant to be there, like a wedding ring missing its jewel.

Just then a chipper knock sounds at the door.

"Oh!" I exclaim. "That must be Sebastian. I'm sure he'll be delighted we opened the chest!" I rush to the door and open it wide.

Sebastian stands there surveying the scene, a bouquet of yellow and red flowers in his hands. He's dressed well in a dark green suit and bow tie. Wavy tendrils are slicked away from his face revealing those stormy blue eyes of is. Shock registers there, quickly replaced by confusion. "Brother, what's the occasion? I thought you were going to be in the library all night?"

"I was… I am… it's just—"

"We've opened the chest!" I interrupt, bouncing at the knees. "Isn't it wonderful? Come look." I take the bouquet from Sebastian's hands and interlock my fingers with his before dragging him to the chest still laying on my bed.

Soren glances at our hands, a look of disapproval crossing his face before he blinks it away and describes what we found. "It's some piece of weaponry, I believe. But it's missing parts."

"A weapon?" With his free hand he gestures between Soren and the object. "May I just mention that figuring out how to open this was done suspiciously fast. Not that I'm complaining." Sebastian surveys the giant prongs. "What does a weapon have to do with the king getting better? And how did you manage to open it? Did you find the key since this morning's talk? That's record time."

I think about telling them what I saw with Lamia, the key she possesses, but I don't. I want to be sure before I accuse her in front of her future family. Besides, this moment feels too good to ruin right now. I can always mention it tomorrow.

"Actually," I state matter of fact, "we didn't even need the key. We have a magical key right here."

Sebastian tilts his head to the side, eyes narrowing. "You mean that…you—"

"—The creature did it for us," Soren answers, nodding his head toward Squish. Then he pulls out the artifact from the chest to show his brother. "I'm not sure yet if it's even a weapon, although the sharpness of its point leads in that direction. It's strange. I feel as though I should…" Soren shakes his head and changes his mind on what he was going to say. "Obviously it's important somehow or it wouldn't have been in the siren's prophecy."

Sebastian observes the golden, five-pronged object, wonder showing in his eyes. "Very intriguing indeed. Well, if you'd like, I can take it and do some research on it while you continue looking into Emora's history," Sebastian offers. "Divide and conquer, if you will."

It warms my heart knowing he cares so much about his father, doing anything he can to help Soren find a cure. I look up at him and reach out to squeeze his hand just a little bit tighter.

He draws his attention to me for a split second, acknowledging what I'm trying to tell him; I'm proud of him.

"No, don't worry about it." Soren puts the object back in the chest, closing the top and tucking it under his arm. He shifts his gaze between the two of us briefly then clears his throat. "You two have fun at your…" he waves his free hand in the air, "…dinner." Then he briskly moves past us and out the door. It shuts firmly in his wake.

"Well, isn't my brother the life of the party?" Sebastian chuckles. He brings up our interlocked hands to his mouth and caresses the faintest kiss on my wrist. "Are you hungry for the most amazing dinner you've ever had?"

I grin from ear to ear, leaning into Sebastian's side. "Famished," I reply.

* * *

Sebastian led us through the ballroom, across the window paned glass walls, and into the castle gardens. Apart from the night of the ball, when I had to steal from the count and was brought here to get yelled at by Soren, I had not had the chance to explore this area of the castle.

I observe our surroundings. Bushes of varying colors are in full bloom, signifying the different entry points into the open center. A canopy of trees occupies the space above, covering up most of the castle I know surrounds us. Yet, if I didn't know where we were, I wouldn't believe we were in the middle of the castle walls at all. The pathways are lined in vines and flowers of varying shapes and sizes.

I look straight up at what little of the sky I can make out, if you can even call it that considering we're hundreds of feet below the surface. That strange, illuminated ball remains in its same spot: right above the castle, never moving, but always changing the intensity of its light. It grows dim now, spewing out a cascade of blues, greens, and oranges, inking the air above us like a water painting.

We sit on a blanket next to the fountain with the scaly, winged serpent spraying water out its mouth. I notice that each scale on its body is decorated with some kind of shiny greenish-blue stone. It leaves a rainbow of mist bouncing off the water below, like a fog you wouldn't mind getting turned around in.

If I were still with humans, I would be the scandal of the season having a private dinner with a prince where no one else could chaperon us. Realistically, if I were with humans, I wouldn't be looked at twice by a prince because of my sun kissed skin and splatter of freckles. I am not considered the ideal beauty in the human world, but down here—Sebastian doesn't care at all. In fact, he's called me beautiful on numerous occasions. In this moment, I don't care what other humans would think. I only know that I feel giddy and warm, if not a little nervous, at the idea of being alone with Sebastian in this magical garden.

I sit with my ankles tucked beneath me and use my arms to lean backwards, looking up at the sky. "How is that even possible?" I ask Sebastian who's pulling out dishes and plates, spreading them out in front of us.

"How is what possible, Freckles?"

"The sky? The sunset? We're hundreds of feet below the surface, so I know it's not really the sky or the sun, yet somehow it feels very similar. How is that possible?"

Sebastian pauses his prep work for a moment, lounging on the blanket, relaxing his hand over a knee and looking at me. "That's an easy one, it's because of the Heart of Emora." His arm shoots up and points at the sphere above us, emanating light and warmth. "The heart of our city is magic based, tied to the ruler's heart in fact. In this case my father, King Cyrus. What you see and feel from that heart is the love and compassion my father feels for the city. It's the city's power source. Whatever kind of heart the ruler has, is whatever kind of power that sphere emits."

"So, what about the sky? Why isn't it all rock up there?"

"Technically it is, but you don't see it that way because father wishes his people to see something different, something brighter."

I look up at the sphere, it's color dimming to a soft cream. "From what I see, your father has a beautiful heart," I say, choosing to recline flat on my back, hair splaying around my shoulders, hands folded over my belly.

Sebastian scoots closer, propping his head onto his hand, unabashedly staring at me.

My cheeks do what they always do, give away my emotions.

"I like when you blush," Sebastian softly states. His free hand finds a tendril of my hair and twirls it. "I also like your hair."

"Really? You should see it first thing in the morning. That may leave an entirely different impression on you." I smile up at him.

His fingers busy themselves as they rake through my curls like a comb. It sends tingles on my scalp. "I doubt that. Although, seeing you first thing in the morning seems like a good plan to me."

I bite the bottom of my lip at the thought of seeing Sebastian as soon as I wake up. What would it be like? Would his waves also be sticking out every direction? Or would he wake up just the way he looks now?

He gazes into my eyes. I return the sentiment, biting down on my lower lip. "Have I told you, you look ravishing tonight? That dress really brings out your eyes." He leans a little closer, closing the amount of open space between us. That free hand cups my chin, his face getting closer to mine. His lips closing the distance between us.

Then my stomach grumbles like a whale call. Sebastian halts in his tracks. I burst out laughing. "I'm sorry," I cackle, "When I said I was famished I wasn't lying!"

Sebastian chuckles. "Well then," he begins. His eyes linger on my lips before he decides to sit up and dig into the basket of food. "It would be rude of me to keep a lady from her dinner."

I also opt to sit up, legs tucked underneath me.

"So, milady, I'll have you know I prepared this dinner all by myself. Prepare to send your taste buds on an unforgettable journey of flavor," Sebastian says. He pulls out four tins, each a different size.

"Oh, so *you* cooked this lovely meal we're about to have?"

He starts to pull off the lid from the first tin to reveal steaming hot salmon. "Well, no. But I did put the tins in the basket. I'm a very good picnic packer, you see? I don't mean to brag but I'm probably the best picnic packer of this century."

"Is that so?" I grin.

The second and third tin contain a salad and fruit. "Absolutely," he says, pulling out the final tin, "and to top off this amazing dinner…" his voice trails off as he opens the lid to reveal—

Yuck. Why couldn't it have been chocolate cake or something? I stare at the green, goopy contents: eel gelatin.

"…my favorite side dish to be sure! Let's dig in." Sebastian scoops out contents from each tin, setting up our plates before handing mine to me and picking up his own fork to eat, starting with the eel goop.

I give a silent thanks before I pick up my own fork. I eat as well but first try to shove the eel goop out of the way as inconspicuously as possible to keep it from touching the rest of my food and ruining it. Once the green goop is safely tucked away on the edge of my plate, I dig into the rest.

We eat in silence, admiring our surroundings until Sebastian speaks. "Constance," he says between bites, "not that this is any of my business, but what was my brother doing in your room before I arrived?" He doesn't look at me as he asks. Is he…well he couldn't be *jealous*—could he?

"To tell you the truth, I'm not entirely sure why he came at the time he did, but I do know he wasn't there for me. He was there for Squish."

"Oh? So he was only there for the creature?"

"Yes, I believe so. Said he'd been doing some research and thought it was worth a shot with the chest. Luckily it was. Now we're one step closer to a cure for your father. How is he doing by the way? I never see him."

Sebastian stops eating. He puts down his fork on the side of the plate, inhaling a deep breath before slowly turning to me. "He's not doing well, Constance." His shoulder's slump, his eyes fill with sorrow as he looks at me. "I fear his days are limited. If Soren doesn't swear his oath to Emora soon, to claim he is the rightful heir to Emora's heart…" He stalls, putting his hands over his face, before pinpointing me with his eyes. They look half-mad as he continues to speak. "War is on the edge of a cliff. It stirs in the waves, Constance. I feel it growing closer with every passing moment. New rumors of a rebellion whisper through the city streets every day."

I stop eating and push my leftovers aside. I sit up on my knees in order to be eye level with Sebastian. "Why won't Soren just take the oath? Wouldn't that solve everything?"

Sebastian busies his hands with a nearby flower, uprooting it and plucking its petals off one by one. "You remember how I said the heart of Emora is tied to the king? That it has magical properties?"

I nod, encouraging him to continue.

"Soren believes if he takes the oath, it would be as though he's sentencing our father to death. When Soren takes the oath, he not only claims he will be king, but he takes whatever powers our father has left."

"Will it?" I ask. "Will it kill your father?"

He runs his hands through hair. "I don't know. He's weak enough as it is with the magic of the king's birthright. I don't know the answers or what to do. But I do know if Soren doesn't do something soon, he puts our entire kingdom in jeopardy." Sebastian stares into the distance, not even blinking before he plucks the last petal from the flower leaving it bare before us.

Without another thought, I reach over and hold his hand, giving it a gentle squeeze. "Then we'll work more persistently to find the cure. I promise, Sebastian." I reach my other hand over to cup his, like a child cradling an egg, making sure I don't let it fall and crack. "I'll do whatever I can to help."

He looks at our hands for a long moment before lifting his head to meet my gaze. A smile etched on his face. "Thank you."

We stay like that for many moments, staring into each other's eyes, until a flash of an idea crosses Sebastian's face. "Enough of the doom and gloom, Freckles. We are on a date are we not?" He jumps to his feet, hand openly stretched toward me to help me onto my feet as well. "I believe I am owed a dance."

"A dance?" I question. Using his hand as a lever, I pull myself up. "I don't believe a dance was promised…" I raise my eyebrows, teasing.

"We didn't get to at the ball, and I was so looking forward to it. But you must agree, a private dance in the gardens is much more romantic." He wiggles his eyebrows at me, causing me to laugh before his free hand slides around my waist, drawing me closer to him.

I draw my free hand up onto his shoulder and grin. "I guess I cannot argue with that logic."

He leads us in lazy circles near the fountain, the only rhythm to sway to.

By the end of the night, I fear my cheeks will ache from all their use, but I can't help it. Sebastian makes me happy. I'm hundreds of feet below the surface in a world where my kind doesn't exist. In fact, I'm not sure what they would do if they ever found out I wasn't a mermaid princess. I also should be worrying more about Mama and Papa. I know Soren has given her a large sum, but those funds won't last forever. And I know Soren gathered a crew of mermen to help search for Papa. In fact, they're repairing the ship before their next departure which could happen any day. But I still feel as though I'm not doing enough. Soren is the one taking care of my family while I... what? Dance in Sebastian's arms without a care in the world? I shouldn't be this happy to be so content where I'm at…should I?

"What's on your mind?" he asks into my hair.

"Soren."

He leans back, giving me a quizzical look. "Well, it's not traditionally what I would want to hear on a date…"

Oh, no. He believes I was thinking about his brother. Romantically. My entire face grows red hot as the realization hits me. I lean into his chest and shake my head vigorously.

"Oh mercy! That came out all wrong! I wasn't thinking of... well I was... but not in a romantic way!" He doesn't respond so I look up into his face. Amusement grows in those storm cloud eyes. "I was just thinking of all he's done for my parents this far and how little I've achieved in their interests," I admit.

Sebastian halts our dancing for a moment. He rubs his hands up and down my arms in a soothing motion. "We'll find your father. It may not seem like much progress yet but trust me when I say you've done more than anyone else could've achieved in this amount of time."

I scoff. How could he proclaim such a notion?

"I mean it. The fact you've convinced my brother to help you, and on top of it persuaded him to put his most trusted crew together in search for your father is beyond comprehension. Soren would've never agreed to helping a human... apart from you. You have a proclivity for swimming into people's hearts."

Hearing his words fades my worries. All these obstacles in my life and yet, with Sebastian they all melt away, leaving a glowing warmth within me.

"I do hope I'm *swimming* into other merpeople's hearts as well," I confess, hoping he understands my meaning. It's his heart I want to be a part of.

He grins and continues to dance with me once more. "Absolutely."

The rest of the evening is peaceful. We talk and dance for hours until I'm yawning profusely on Sebastian's shoulder while we soak our feet in the cool fountain water. The mist of the serpent's spout sprays our faces like a splash of ocean water picked up by a sea breeze.

Without disturbing my resting head on his shoulder, Sebastian whispers to me fondly. "Constance?"

"Hmm?" My eyes are closed, savoring this moment of bliss.

"Can I ask you a fourth question?"

"I suppose you can. If it's asking what my favorite food is, I can tell you it's certainly not eel mucilage."

"Ha!" He chuckles. "No, of course not. I have something much more serious to ask you."

The atmosphere shifts from blissfully peaceful to warmly expectant.

He moves enough that I lift my head and stare into his storm cloud eyes. They're full of want as he shifts his gaze from my eyes to my lips. "Miss Constance... if I try to kiss you right now, what will you do?"

"Well, considering that was your third question also, I think it's only fair to give you the same answer." My breath catches. My throat bobs. "I guess you'll have to try and find out," I whisper, leaning just a bit closer, inviting Sebastian to press his lips against mine.

He takes the invitation slowly, closing the gap before parting his lips and planting a solid, confident kiss onto my mouth. It's warm and soft like a summer's day and makes me want to melt into myself as I kiss him back.

Chapter 37

"Maybe we should focus on something else," I say, rolling a kink out of my neck.

As I turn my head I notice Sebastian gazing at me longingly above the pages of his current book. It's been a week of stolen kisses and nightly strolls after dinner since our date in the gardens.

Pink warms my cheeks. I offer a coy smile in return.

"Like what?" Soren asks dryly. He doesn't even bother looking up from his book.

His hopeful mood has turned sour these last few days.

I can only imagine the culprit is our never-ending circle of research. We come up short each night.

His eyes have begun to form dark circles again. His beard, although still neatly trimmed, has grown longer.

Sebastian snaps his book shut and sits up straighter in the cushy library chair. "Maybe home of despair is something else, brother. Maybe it's not related to history at all."

Soren pins his tropical eyes on his brother, irritated. "I'm open to suggestions."

At that, Sebastian is at a loss for words. He looks to me for support, but I can only shrug as an answer. I have no idea what home of despair means. Soren could still be right, and we just haven't been looking at the right books. Or he could be wrong.

We won't know until we know and that's the most frustrating part about this whole siren riddle.

I think of Lamia. Of what I saw the other day. No matter the threat she threw at me, now seems like a good time to tell them. "We could focus our attention on the betrayer's snare," I offer, glancing between the two mermen.

"That's true," Sebastian nods in agreement. "We haven't paid much attention to that part of the riddle yet. How about the merman that tried to kill father the night of the ball? Have interrogations gone any better with him?"

Soren sighs and closes the book in his hand. He runs a hand through his straight black hair, putting the pieces out of place. "He has been…difficult. The captain has been trying to coax information with little success."

"How nice would it be? To already have the betrayer behind bars," Sebastian says. His back arches forward as he laces his fingers together, thinking.

Apparently, the captain has been down in the dungeon a lot lately.

I wish Addeah could update me, but she has been out with her illness. A different maid, Uberta, comes in each morning and night to help me get ready, but it is not the same.

"Do we even know which kingdom he is from? His name? Anything?" Sebastian asks.

"No. He wasn't on the guest list or else I would have recognized him. Time will wear him down."

I had asked Soren if I could join in on the interrogations, just out of mere curiosity, but he adamantly refused. Evidently princesses aren't to go near the dungeons. So yes, I am allowed to fight sirens and mythical beasts with him, but interrogating prisoners is a big no. I believe it's all annoyingly contradictory.

"Have you tried torture, yet?" Sebastian inquires.

Soren side eyes me, his jaw clenching. "Not yet," he grits out between his teeth. "I highly doubt he is our betrayer, anyway. I've thought maybe Count Pesilfer…" his voice trails off, lost in thought.

"He is one nasty little rat now, isn't he?" Sebastian says. "He's never liked us before, but after stealing his precious pearl, he utterly loathes us now. It's not a bad theory."

Soren tucks his knuckles under his chin. "Not to mention he has an entire trove of rare, mystical artifacts. More and more I am persuaded we'll have to pay him a visit to check."

I want to tell them my suspicions about Lamia, but words won't come out of my mouth. I don't know why it's so hard to speak up right now, but it is.

Maybe it's the fact that if I'm right, Soren will be betrayed by the one person who is supposed to stand by his side through thick and thin. Through sickness and health. Through everything. If he can't trust her, who can he trust?

It makes me sick to my stomach to even think that someone could abuse someone's heart like that. And if I'm wrong…what then?

"Lamia." Her name unintentionally comes out a whisper.

The princes turn to face me.

Soren leans closer. "What?"

"If I'm not mistaken," Sebastian starts, "you just said Lamia."

"It's not her," Soren defends. He crosses his arms over his chest, the muscles rippling in contained anger.

I feel a heavy lump growing in my throat. "But you don't know what I saw."

"Listen Freckles, Lamia's so… well, Lamia. I know she's tough to swallow but I highly doubt she's capable of trapping us in anything… apart from marriage to Soren." He gestures to his brother.

"Did you know she's been keeping secrets from you?" I retort. "Did you know that the afternoon before our dinner in the garden, I saw her conversing in hushed tones with a hooded figure?"

This new information has piqued their intrigue.

"Wait, did you confront her? Did you hear what they were talking about?" Sebastian questions.

Soren's eyes bore into mine. Interrogating me without a single word spoken.

"I didn't hear everything," I admit, "but she was handed a box and when she opened it, the object inside was small and shiny, like a key." I look out the library windows, recalling the encounter. "She discovered me eavesdropping and…"

"And what?" Sebastian encourages me to continue.

"…and she threatened me. Told me if I said anything to anyone, especially Soren, that I would be shackled to the bottom of the ocean where no one would be able to find me."

Sebastian scoffs. "Well, that's not very kind, is it?"

Soren remains motionless in his chair. "She wouldn't," he grumbles.

I try to speak, "Soren—"

"—She wouldn't!" he growls. Intensity grows heavy in the air around us.

"Brother, I believe you. But Constance does lead me to believe we need to start interrogating those within the castle walls: the soldiers, the maids, the kitchen staff. We need to be proactive, so we are not blind-sided by the possibility the betrayer is living with us."

Soren's nostrils flare. I half-expect him to send a wave of water crashing down on me, but instead he takes a deep, meditative breath. "Fine. Start with the guards." He commands with a dismissive wave of his hands, digging back into his book.

"You mean, right now?" Sebastian quirks up his eyebrows. "Well, okay then."

"Constance, go too," Soren says without even looking up from his book. He says my name like it's sour on his tongue.

"Soren, I—"

"Please. Go." He looks up from his book to lock eyes with me. Rage rolls off them.

I can understand why. He is angry about my suspicions. Angry with me for even suggesting his betrothed would betray him.

I don't want to anger him further, so without another word, I grab Sebastian's awaiting arm and let him lead me out of the library.

Once we are out of ear shot, Sebastian speaks. "Isn't he just a ray of sunshine?"

"He's cross with me. Again."

"Freckles, it's okay. He won't be mad at you forever. It's difficult to stay mad at someone with as pretty a face as yours.

"Besides, you had every right to tell us about what you saw. Although, I still don't believe Lamia's our betrayer."

"But I do. I was right about the kraken, was I not? Why won't either of you believe me on this?"

He rubs the side of my arms and looks at me, a sympathetic smirk pulling at the side of his lips. "We've known Lamia for years. She's not the nicest mermaid in the sea, but she is loyal to Soren. Always has been."

I want to tell him that betrayal can come from anyone. That betrayal cuts deeper when it's someone close to you.

But I get the sense that I will not win this argument. So instead, I nod and let him plant a firm kiss on my lips in the middle of the hallway.

"Why not take the rest of the night off? I'll start interrogating the off-duty guards. You go get some cuddles with Squish and have a nice warm bath. I'll have a maid bring you something warm to drink before bed."

It did sound nice to relax a little bit before falling asleep. The idea causes a yawn to escape me.

Sebastian grabs my hand. "And then maybe in the morning you can come watch me spar with Soren?" He smirks mischievously. "If you think you can get up that early."

I respond with a swift kiss. "I wouldn't miss it."

He leads me the rest of the way back to my room and bids me a goodnight.

He and Soren may have crossed Lamia off their suspects list, but I won't. I just need to find proof.

Chapter 38

Emora's heart has barely begun to brighten as I amble through the halls toward the sparring ring.

A voice calls out my name from behind. "Miss Constance!"

I turn to see a full armored guard walking briskly at me. His ebony face flawless apart from the scar that carves its way through his right eyebrow…Darius.

"Darius!" I exclaim, turning on my heels to meet him halfway through the hall. My shoes clack against the white marble. "It's been so long since I've seen you. How is your recovery going?" I gesture toward his torso, where the wounds were from our first venture to Siren's Hollow.

Darius places a hand on his side. "Much improved, almost as if the wounds were never there in the first place. Another week or two, and I will be cleared for all of my normal duties, including combat."

"That's wonderful to hear." I smile, offering my arm so we may walk together. He bows at the neck before standing by my side, the two of us stepping in stride with each other. "How is Addeah doing this morning? I have missed her terribly this last week."

We pass a pair of soldiers standing guard against one of the largest pairs of doubles doors I've ever seen. The soldiers give Darius and me a salute in greeting as we pass them.

"She is resting in bed as we speak. Can't keep anything down unfortunately. I apologize that she was not able to help you this morning," Darius states.

We take the next left. "That's the least of my concerns. I wonder if we should bring her some ginger tea to calm her stomach, that is if there is any ginger in the castle." Darius looks at me confused, so I elaborate. "Whenever I was little and had a stomach flu, my papa would always make me ginger tea or ginger water. It helps with the nausea and because it's liquid and easier to keep down."

The captain nods in understanding. "I shall look in the kitchen later and see if the cook keeps any on hand. Thank you for your suggestion, Miss Constance."

"My pleasure. Anything to get Addeah feeling better. There is so much I wish to tell her." After the adrenaline high I had from my date with Sebastian dampened, the first person I thought of was Addeah. I desperately wanted to share the events of my night with her. She is perhaps the closest friend I have here and would be excited to hear everything.

We reach the arena, sparse of an audience this early in the morning, except for three people: Sebastian, Soren, and my least favorite person in the castle, Lamia.

"This is where I leave you, Miss Constance," Darius lets go of my arm before bowing low at his waist.

"Will you not stay to watch the sparring match, Captain?" The thought of having to sit in the stands with Lamia by myself is nauseating. It would be better to have a buffer with us to ease the tension she no doubt will have toward my presence here.

"I have some duties to attend to this morning as well as check on my wife. My first duty going to the kitchen and trying out your suggestion." He gives a slight grin before gesturing to the three others in the room. "Do enjoy your morning. I will send another to aid you for dinner tonight if Addeah cannot make it."

"Yes, of course, thank you. Do tell her I hope she takes all the rest she needs," I say before he turns his heels walking away, leaving me alone with the princes and the royal pain.

Sebastian eyes me first as I approach the group of mer, giving a toothy smile and exaggerated wave. "There she is! I was wondering if you'd be able to get up this early."

I make eye contact with Soren next. He has dark circles shadowing his eyes. I wonder if he was up all night in the library by himself researching. "Princess Constance," he greets.

Lamia is the last to say anything. Her face tight as she says, "Constance." She eyes my hairstyle which I opted to put into a simple braid this morning, letting it rest over my shoulder. Without Addeah's help, there wasn't much else I knew how to do. "Your hair is so… quaint this morning. In fact, I think my maidservant chose that exact same style for herself."

In contrast to my plain braid and makeup-free face, Lamia is covered from head to toe in regality. Her aquamarine hair is pulled back in an intricately defined low bun apart from a five pleated strand that swings across her brow. Her lips are painted with their typical red crimson, coordinated with a flowing golden dress with red leaves splattering the hem.

I cross my arms, staring directly at her. "Yes, well, some of the most beautiful things in nature require the least amount of grooming. Would you not agree, Lamia?" I wouldn't necessarily consider myself nature's beauty, but I say this to emphasize the amount of effort Lamia puts in her everyday routine.

She sneers at my comment, running a conscious hand over her hair.

"Ladies, ladies," Sebastian interrupts, "are you going to watch Soren and me spar or do you two want to get into the arena instead?" He gets between us, grazing my stomach with his hand as he puts distance between Lamia and me, creating goosebumps on my skin.

"Lamia," Soren says, his attention focused all on her, "let me walk you to a seat." His voice is low. Gentle. Reassuring.

For the first time since our bickering began, Lamia draws her attention away from me, staring at Soren as though she were in a trance. She nods, taking hold of his extended arm before he walks her to a seat, well away from us.

"May I walk you to a seat as well, Princess Constance?" Sebastian grins, running his hands up and down my arms. He leans in close, whispering, "I can't stop thinking about you."

A new set of goosebumps rises all over my body. "Me either," I admit. "And, yes, I would be delighted to have an escort to my seat."

He points his elbow outward, giving my arm room to loop with his. Then he walks me to a spot far away from where Lamia is seated.

"Be careful while you're in there, Sebastian," I say, resting my hands in my lap, gesturing with my head at the giant pool of gridded water, set apart by large flat rafts.

He winks. "You know me, Freckles. I'm never careful." Sebastian cups one of my hands, drawing it up to his mouth, and giving it the swiftest peck before sauntering off to the ring.

I watch his back side in admiration up until the moment he pulls off his shirt and shoes, jumping into the water and swimming to the center platform.

Soren is already there, also shirtless and bare footed. The two brothers possess many similarities. The jet-black hair, the broad shoulders, sea blue eyes of varying shades, but I'm reminded that Soren is noticeably stronger as they face off. Sebastian, however, has about an inch of height on his brother, even if his muscles are not as defined, that could give him an edge.

The last time I watched them spar, I tried my best not to gawk at the half nakedness battling in front of me, but this time, I have been given permission to watch, so I observe and note all the subtleties of their physiques with each maneuver they execute.

Five minutes in and both males are already panting from the exertion of the fight. Neither has chosen to use his magical water powers yet, only hand to hand—each taking turns trying to lock the other into a position of submission or land a blow to the body that will knock the other off the raft.

Then Sebastian changes tactics. He does his best to hit Soren. He throws everything he has at him, both physical and mystical jabs. Not a single blow lands. I don't know how Soren does it, but he ducks and dodges every single attack his younger brother throws at him.

Soren barely sends an attack Sebastian's way. For some reason, he remains in a defensive position.

It goes on for many more minutes, and I wonder how either has the stamina to continue.

I peer sidelong at Lamia. Her usual demeanor of princess poise has softened. Instead, her palms cover her mouth, her body leans forward over her knees as she watches the sparring match of the two princes. Was it concern that made her gasp each time Soren almost got hit by his brother? Whatever emotion she has shown for her betrothed, she shows none for Sebastian.

Perhaps it's all a facade. A show to put on for the public eye. Sebastian and Soren don't think she's the betrayer, but they didn't see what I saw.

I turn my attention back to the princes.

The two are sweating profusely now.

"Come now, brother," Sebastian pants, "Do not go easy on me for the sake of our company."

Soren is also breathing with effort, but not to the same extent as he says, "Is it not my right to give you a fighting chance?" He smirks at his brother.

"Fine," Sebastian retorts, "if that's how you want to pl—" Sebastian doesn't finish his sentence before he scoops his arm to the side drawing up water, knocking Soren to the ground.

Soren wipes his face of the newfound water dripping off of it. "Are you sure you wish to continue?" Soren warns.

Sebastian answers with another thrust of water, but this time Soren is ready, rolling out of the way and landing in a lunge before he throws his arm out, a whirlpool of water flying through the air directly at Sebastian. It is too fast and too large to dodge. Next thing I know, Sebastian soars through the air and lands fifty feet into the water.

I stand up, searching the arena for him.

Lamia stands too, cheering for Soren.

But Soren is not celebrating. He gapes at the hand he used to move the water.

I hike up my dress and rush to the side of the arena, looking for any sign of Sebastian. Moments tick by before a head of waves breaches the surface. Relief washes over me.

He coughs like he hasn't been able to catch his breath. "Well, that was new," he sputters, slowly swimming to the middle raft.

Soren stands there frozen, still looking at his hand before he realizes Sebastian is struggling to get back on to the raft. When he notices, he rushes to the aid of his brother, hopping from platform to platform. "I don't know what to say," he says apologetically, hauling his brother up with ease.

"Well, I guess now I know for certain you've been taking it easy on me for all these years," Sebastian jokes, clutching his rib cage. A bruise already forming.

"I... I didn't mean to hit you so hard. I would never—"

Sebastian looks at his brother quizzically. "Do you mean to say that...this power is new?"

Soren nods.

Sebastian's eyes cloud with understanding. "Father," he mumbles.

"I must check on him at once," Soren states before diving into the water and hauling himself out with swift grace, grabbing his shirt and shoes hastily before rushing by me.

Without thought, I catch hold of his bicep. He halts in his tracks and looks at me, eyes filled with remorse.

"Soren, I can go with you," I offer. I think of what Sebastian had told me about the heart of Emora and the king's power. How it transfers to the heir gradually until the death of the king. If the king is dead—if Soren and Sebastian's father is dead, they should not face that sorrow alone.

Soren stares at me, longing in his face to accept my offer or to get out of my hold, I cannot tell which. "Thank you, Constance. But it is not your burden to bear."

Lamia walks up quickly, her high heels clacking against the wet stone. "Soren, my love, this is a good thing. You are becoming stronger, the way a king should be."

Soren's mouth tightens, his bicep flexing underneath my grip.

I let go.

Sebastian reaches us finally, hand clutched to his rib cage. "Come, brother," Sebastian urges Soren to keep moving. Once Soren has begun to walk away from us, Sebastian turns to me. "Thank you for the offer, but he and I will go together. I'll see you at dinner tonight," he states then brushes my hand with a gentle kiss, following in his brother's footsteps.

I watch the exit doors long after they disappear out of the arena.

"You can drop the innocent friend act anytime now," Lamia sneers.

I whirl to face her. "How dare you?"

"How dare I? How dare I?!" Her voice raises. "Don't think I don't know what's been going on ever since you arrived here." She steps closer, an accusatory finger pointed at me. "You want my crown. You want Soren all for yourself.

And don't think I'm falling for that whole 'honesty' thing with me at dinner the other night—where you forced Soren to tell me all about his father's illness. It was a poor attempt to get me off your back."

I scoff. I can't believe the words I'm hearing spill out of her. "A poor attempt? The only reason I said anything was because I felt sorry for you. Now I see my sympathies were misplaced. And Earth to Lamia…have you not noticed my affections for Sebastian and his for me? I have no interest in Soren."

She steps close enough to be nose to nose with me. In her heels, she easily towers over me like the princes do. But I'm not deterred.

I glare up into her searing eyes.

"Don't lie to me. I see the way he is with you. And just now, you with him." She sniffs like something foul is in the air. "You both reek of longing."

"His father is dying!" I yell. "How shallow can you be? His father is dying and all you are worried about is how strong he'll be as king? That's the best comfort you can give your betrothed? And let's not forget your little secret you've been hiding from him." I force a humorless laugh, taking a step back to take in all of Lamia before landing my final blow at this ridiculous excuse for a future queen. "Soren deserves so much better than you."

For the first time today, Lamia's face darkens in shades of pink. Her perfectly manicured hands ball into fists. "Careful, Constance, you're treading in dangerous waters."

"I guess lucky for me I'm a pretty decent swimmer then," I retort.

This whole conversation is nonsense. I knew Lamia did not like me, but to accuse me of trying to steal Soren away from her, and even more ridiculous that he shares these make-believe feelings is laughable.

Maybe if she had paid more attention to his wants and needs instead of her own, she would see that he needs her support through this difficult time with his father. Then again, why would she do anything for Soren that didn't also suit herself?

I begin to turn away when I see a flash of shimmering gold lurch toward me.

Lamia has her hands pushed out, veering me toward the arena water.

I try to get out of the way, but in my heels I can't catch my footing. Instead, I slip on a wet spot on the ground, tumbling into the water, but not before I reach out and grab one of Lamia's still outstretched arms, taking her down with me.

We hit the water with a splash. My dress and shoes quickly soak up with the weight of the water, trying their best to drag me down.

I kick my heels off, letting them sink to the bottom of the arena before pushing my head above the surface to take in desperately needed air.

Lamia is also there. Her makeup runs down her face. Her perfect hairdo now sticks to her forehead and neck in dripping blue wads. Her eyes have taken their true form-two balls of icy blue, iridescence. She's breathing fine, as mermaids can breathe above or below water. That is until she pins her stare on me. A sharp gasp makes me all too aware of what she sees.

My lack of mermaid eyes, no elongated hands or feet. My need to keep my head above water.

Her hands effortlessly clasp over her mouth. "I knew there was something off about you from the start. I should've guessed based on those hideous flecks of brown all over your face." She shakes her head in disbelief. "You're not even a mermaid, let alone a princess, are you? You're just a despicable human."

I don't know what to say. Even if I try to come up with a lie, there's no way she'll believe me now. I'm too busy trying to keep my head above the water, the extra weight of my dress threatening to pull me down. *Note to self: where dresses with less layers.*

A spark of an idea crosses Lamia's mind. She leers at me. "What was that thing you said again? You're a pretty decent swimmer? Let's test that theory, shall we?"

Chapter 39

I paddle as fast as I can, aiming to reach one of the floating mats, but it's useless. Trying to outswim a mermaid is like a dog trying to outpaddle a shark.

My fingertips graze the edge of the nearest mat when slimy webbed hands seize my ankle, pulling me under. I have just enough time to inhale a breath of air before my body is fully immersed.

The force of the pull leaves my dress floating in all directions around me.

I can't see my attacker, but I can feel her hand clenched to my ankle. Underwater is her territory.

No doubt she is stronger here in so many ways. Her body is built for it and mine is not.

I won't be able to claw my way up to the surface with her holding on. So, I do the only thing I can think. I dive down to where her hand holds me and dig my nails into her skin as hard as possible.

She screams and lets go, giving me just enough time to put my head above water for another gulp of air before being dragged back beneath.

This time Lamia's staring right at me as she pushes my shoulders down, directing my body to the bottom.

I struggle in vain, my lungs burn, pleading for another gulp of air. Is this truly how I die? One final drowning attempt in a world where I don't belong to send me to my watery grave?

I do my best to take one last look at my killer's eyes. Blue and predatory, blazing at me. The last thing I will see in this lifetime. Lamia grins wickedly as I struggle, until a force so wild and angry throws her off me and out of the water completely.

With the absence of her pushing me down, I do my best to swim upward, but I've already used too much energy fighting to keep off the floor of the sparring ring. My lungs won't make it until I reach the surface.

It doesn't matter though. Within a matter of seconds of being freed from my captor, I too am jolted through the water and land hard on one of the floating mats.

I gasp and cough up some of the water that had weaseled its way into my lungs. A strong and reassuring hand at my back, patting me.

"What have you done?" the angry voice yells. At first, I think he's cross with me, but when I look up there's Soren, facing a dog-soaked, slumping Lamia.

Lamia's eyes and limbs go back to normal as she rubs her head like she hit it on the ground when she landed. Her wrist is dotted with five puncture marks, bits of blood trickling from each one, courtesy of me. "What I did? You know what she is, and yet you—"

"Guards!" Soren yells. Two guards come running into the arena, each assessing the situation. Confusion marks their features. "Take Princess Lamia to her chambers. Do not let her out for any reason whatsoever. Send her meals to her room until I say she can get out."

The guards obey, aiming for Lamia, helping her off the wet floor before she jerks out of their grip.

For the first time ever, raw hurt crosses her face. Her eyes fill with tears. Once again, he has chosen something that was not her. To help me and blame her.

To be fair, it was her fault we got into an argument at all. I would feel sorrier for her predicament with Soren had she not just tried to murder me.

Soren stays knelt beside me, hand protectively on my back. "You came back," I choke out, my voice hoarse.

He draws his attention away from Lamia, long enough to look at me. "Sebastian forgot his shoes. I ran back to get them." He assesses my body, roaming each spot like a doctor. "Luckily, I did."

I offer a small smile in response to show my appreciation of his heroics. Yet again, he saved me. I ponder over Lamia's words about Soren's feelings toward me, but quickly write them off. He wouldn't have to save me so much if I would just stay out of trouble. That's my problem.

I look over to Lamia. Real tears stream down her damp skin. She notices me looking at her, so she turns about, holding her head high and letting the guards take her away. No more arguments from her for now.

"I should walk you to your room," Soren offers, helping me onto my feet.

"No," I state. "No, I'm fine, truly. Go see your father."

Using his power over the water, Soren shifts the mat to the edge of the arena, helping me onto the walkway. His face is riddled with concern. "I'm sorry," he says, regret mixed with anger in his voice. "I should've never left you alone with her. She would've killed you."

I gulp at his statement. Not speculation, just a fact. If Soren hadn't come back for his brother's shoes, I would be a body only, floating in the water.

The look on his face makes me put on the bravest mask I can to ease the burdens he has put on himself. "That's just the common hazard of being a human here, I suppose. How about next week I tell you when I'm about to drown so you can plan accordingly?"

My joke doesn't land though. Soren is solemn when he says, "Your death is no laughing matter, Constance." He scans my face warily, deep emotion lingering in his eyes.

"I know," I manage to speak.

"Let me take you back to your room," he offers again.

I refuse. "Your father and brother need you now. Lamia is guarded and stuck in her room until further notice. I'm in no danger now thanks to you. Go," I urge. "Be with your family."

He stares at me, discerning. "Only on the condition that Captain Darius will be on guard for you. Outside your door or in your room, that is up to you."

I plaster a smile for his sake. "I can agree to that."

* * *

Hours later, I have bathed and thrown on my nightgown; not feeling the need to leave my room for the rest of the day.

Darius kept me company in the room for a little while until I asked if I could nap before lunch. Which was a fruitless effort on my part. After all of the events that have come to pass while I've been here, napping during the afternoon seems so out place.

I toss and turn under the sheets while Squish quietly snores on the windowsill in the beams of light coming through. I have half a thought to close my curtains and darken the room up, but then his nap would be interrupted, and I didn't have the heart to disturb him.

A knock interrupts my attempt at sleep before Darius pokes his head in with a warm smile on his face. "Miss Constance, lunch is here, and you have a visitor as well."

I don't have time to ask who as Addeah walks in with a tray full of goodies, her perfectly toothed smile broad and welcoming. "Hello, child!" she greets. "My husband tells me you had quite the ordeal this morning. Tell me all about it."

"Addeah," I exclaim, throwing the covers off my legs not caring that Darius sees me in my nightwear and throwing my arms around her, careful not to knock the tray from her hands. "How are you feeling? Are you well?"

She puts the tray next to my bed and gives me a proper hug, warm and firm, like Mama used to give me after Papa and I would come home from a fishing trip. "I am well at the moment. Better than I've been the rest of the week. Healers think it was a stomach bug.

"Your ginger water remedy has done wonders. I was finally able to keep some bread down this morning."

"Did the healers have anything else to say?" I retract from her embrace to look at her face. I can tell she's lost some of the plump in her cheeks, her skin still paler than normal. But other than that, she looks markedly improved.

"Not much. Just that I need to keep sipping on my tea throughout the day, eat bland food until my stomach completely settles, and go easy until I regain my strength."

I grab her hand and give it a firm squeeze. "I cannot express how relieved I am to see you again."

"Yes," she says, "but let us move on to other matters of the heart and eat up this lunch before it gets too cold." Addeah grabs the tray from the nightstand and sets it between us. She motions for me to start eating but doesn't lift a finger to grab anything for herself.

I take one of the pieces of bread and nibble off the end. "Will you not eat with me?" I ask.

"It is by-law that maids do not eat with royalty," Addeah says. "Plus, I am still sensitive to many foods."

"Well, I suppose it's a good thing I'm not royalty then, isn't it?" I grab the other piece of bread, extending it to her. "Maybe just something light?"

"You have a point there." Addeah takes the other piece of bread, breaking off bits before popping them in her mouth. "Now, tell me all about your night with Prince Sebastian."

"That's my cue to wait outside," Darius interrupts. He walks over to his wife, placing the most tender kiss on her forehead before bowing at the waist and walking out of the room to stand guard.

When I hear the door click shut, I turn back to Addeah. "Oh, Addeah, it was magical. Simply perfect in every way!" I exclaim. My cheeks burn at the thought of Sebastian's lips on mine.

"Tell me," Addeah says between bites, "where did he take you for dinner?"

"The castle gardens," I beam, "near the serpent fountain. He's everything I hoped love would be, Addeah." Even though I'm in my nightgown, I manage to jump enough to get my legs tucked under me to sit on my knees. "He was charming and funny and…" I pause for dramatic effect. Addeah leans in closer to hear my next words. "…he kissed me. A kiss unlike anything I've ever experienced," I squeal, throwing my fists over my mouth as though I have spilled a secret.

Addeah giggles with delight. "That's wonderful, child. I'm glad you enjoyed yourself. I had hoped—" she begins but stops her thoughts short.

"Hoped what?" I grin.

"Never mind. Sebastian is a fine prince, and he makes you happy," Addeah says running her hand over my cheek like a mother to a child. "So, if things work out, does this mean you plan to stay in Emora with us?"

Truth be told, I had not thought that far ahead. What if Sebastian is my one true love? What if he and I are to be married? A merman prince to a common human? So far all I've worried about is getting out of here to reunite my family. It never occurred to me that there are alternatives after I have found Papa. But now that she mentions it, my mind imagines the possibility.

"I um, I'm not sure," I admit. "The thought is tempting to say the least."

"Well, we would love to keep you," she says, nibbling on the last few pieces of her bread.

"Not all of you," I say, shaking my head. "Did Darius inform you on what happened this morning?"

Addeah takes her time chewing before replying. "Yes, I did hear of Lamia's outburst this morning and her attempt to rid of you." Addeah shifts uncomfortably on the bed. "It was divine intervention that Soren came back and saw you two," she says.

My fingers idly mess with the tips of my curls. "Yes, I believe that's part of the problem."

Her brows furrow in confusion.

"Not a problem that Soren saved me…again, but that in doing so Lamia sees me as a threat. And she now knows I am human. Who's to say she won't blabber to the entire kingdom about me and form a riot."

"Don't worry, child," Addeah assures, before moving onto the fresh fruit. "Soren would never let that happen to you. And neither would Sebastian."

I shrug. "I suppose. But can you believe Lamia accused me of having feelings for Soren and that he returns those sentiments? Has she not seen the disdain he has shown for me? It's taken the entirety of my time here to go from loathe and disdain to tolerable.

"She's a standard case of paranoia to be sure." I say, fiddling with a loose thread on my bed sheet. "Besides, Sebastian is courting me. It would seem obvious to the outsider that my affections were elsewhere."

I look up to find Addeah has stopped eating all together. She looks at me, clearly struggling on what to say next. Moments tick by before she chooses her response. "Yes, sometimes Lamia sees things with a distorted reflection of the truth."

Her comment feels a bit odd to me, but I brush it off and move on to a different topic of discussion. I eat the rest of lunch as we laugh and gossip about everything we wanted to tell each other for the past week.

After a few hours, Addeah tries to stifle a yawn to no avail.

"How about you get some rest?" I suggest.

"But what about you?" she questions before another yawn hits her.

"Me? I'll be fine. Look, I'm already in my nightgown. My hair is…well, frizzy but it can wait till morning, and I don't plan on going anywhere or seeing anyone except Squish." At that comment, Squish lets out a happy chirp and hops onto my shoulder. "See?" I say, "All is well here. Now go. Rest." I stand up from the bed, causing my pet to jump off my shoulder and back onto his favorite pillow. Then I help Addeah stand and usher her out the door where Darius remains on guard.

He looks to his wife and says the same things I have been telling her. Rest. She obliges and walks off to wherever their chambers may be.

* * *

That night I lie awake staring at the ceiling, puzzling out all that is left to understand. The siren's prophecy runs through my mind like a dog chasing its own tail.

Save your father you may try, but don't be fooled
the king will die.
Objects you will seek. Three.
A chest. A book. And a key.
One in the depths of the beast's lair.
Another in the home of despair.
Last is trapped in the betrayer's snare.
But be wary handsome prince.
Change is stirring
Far from sense.

We have the chest from the kraken's lair and a strange weapon held inside it. We didn't need a key to open it because of Squish. That leaves the key, which is in Lamia's possession. But now that she is on lockdown can we focus on the book for now? The book, most likely the Book of Dominion, an all-powerful source of knowledge and magic must be held in the home of despair—whatever that means.

The riddle isn't the only thing on my mind. I also think of Lamia's accusations, Soren and Sebastian's father, Soren's growing power and how he so easily knocked his brother off the sparring mat without even trying.

The king of Emora. How must he be doing now? I'd have thought Sebastian would come by at least once to check on me after this morning, but maybe he's still with the king at his bedside.

Hours drag by until I can't take it anymore. Curiosity drags at my navel, pulling me out of bed. I throw my covers off and head to my closet for some slippers and a robe to cover up with. I grab my compact of blush and tuck it away into my robe. I also take the lantern from my nightstand.

I open my door.

Even at this hour, Darius stands guard.

"Darius?" I question.

He looks back with a start.

"Miss Constance, what are you doing up at this hour?" He yawns. His eyes are bloodshot.

"I can't sleep," I admit. "Do you think you could walk me to the library? Sometimes a good book is all I need to wind down for sleep." I shrug my shoulders apologetically.

Darius lets another yawn out, rubbing his eyes. "I suppose we can go there but let us do it with haste. Your room is safest for you at the present time."

"Not to worry, I don't plan to be long."

* * *

Darius leads me to the library. He struggles to stay awake, which provides the perfect opportunity for me to sneak away. "Darius, please do sit while I look around. No one ever comes in here, anyways. I'll be safe looking through the stacks for a moment by myself," I veer him toward my favorite green couch and guide him to sit down.

"Miss Constance, it's my duty—"

"—to protect me. I know. But I promise I won't be long. You need to sit. I'm sure your feet are hurting from standing guard today."

He looks at me warily. Does he know what I plan to do?

He puts his hands on his knees and leans back on the couch. "Very well, but please be quick," he states. Already his eyes begin to drift shut before he rapidly pries them open.

"I promise," I say as I walk away into the book stacks. I pretend to look around for a book to take back to my room, glancing every so often at Darius. His eyes become heavier and heavier the longer he sits until they don't open again. Soft snores echo in the empty space of the library.

I smile and begin working on my real purpose for coming here. I walk through the stacks until I find the entrance to the secret passages.

Chapter 40

Times prior when I wandered these dark, dirty passages, I stumbled backwards into them without warning and walked aimlessly. The other I was fleeing from the count's bedroom with Squish in tow.

This time, I am prepared. In one hand, I have a lantern to light my way and in the other I have my blush powder compact Addeah uses to brighten my cheeks before dinner. As soon as the secret passage door closes, I pull out the blush and with a finger trace an arrow on the wall pointing to the direction I just came from. It's faint, but different enough so that when I need to I can find my way back. When I have the light next to the arrow a faint shimmer tells me it can be found. Losing my way in here isn't an option.

I take a moment at every turn to pull out the compact and draw an arrow showing the direction I just came from. It takes longer this way to search for what I am looking for, but it's safer.

"Does the pretty thing need some help finding her way?" A cruel and crackly voice breathes to my left, sending chills down my spine.

As swiftly as I can, without blowing the candle out, I spin my lantern in the direction of the voice.

There she is. Concealed in the same black raggedy cloak that covers everything but her soulless, black eyes and ghostly pale fingers. She shies away from the kindling flame, sticking as close to the wall as possible.

"I know what you are," I say, attempting to sound brave and menacing.

The siren tries to creep closer, but I thrust my light in her direction, causing her to retreat further into darkness, but still close enough to touch me if she outstretched her hand to its fullest length.

Another chill courses through my veins. How close had she come to me before she spoke? I had no idea she was even there until she made herself known.

Her voice is raspy, like it's been used far too many times without proper lubrication. "Not an are, but a was. Nothing is as nothing does. Creeping, crawling, all useless in its name. No not a name. Not a name no more than an are." She continues to jabber nonsense, making this entire encounter all the more unsettling.

"You're a siren. I've seen your kind before, and I'm not afraid. I won't let you eat me," I say with enough bite that she backs away again, recoiling in on herself.

"A siren…" she begins, her eyes widening with recognition. "Not a siren, no more will be. The blessed man but cursed me." She turns to leave, muttering similar things to herself over and over again, like she forgot I even existed.

Part of me wants to let her leave- the larger part of me does, but then I see her bare feet, scuffling against the dirty path. What was the rule of sirens again? A question for an object of worth?

"Wait!" I call out after her. I stride in her direction but stop a few feet away, far enough that she cannot touch me. "Do you want to make a deal?"

She turns back to me, those black eyes peeking through the raggedy curtain. "Does the key have anything to trade with?" She rasps while her black eyes rove over me.

She said it again. She called me a key. One of the two things I wish to know more about. I look at her cloak, her bare, bony feet.

"Yes," I say. "You asked if I was lost in here. I'm not lost per say, but a little direction might do me some good." I point to her exposed toes. "If you can point me where I want to go, I'll give you my slippers. They're not black but they'll protect your feet better than going barefoot."

The siren slides toward me, a snake assessing its prey. Her eyes move down to inspect my slippers. They're cream colored with lace trim. A stark contrast to the siren's attire. "The key needs direction. Direction to the hole. It is that way you must go." She points behind me. How she knew what I was looking for in here is beyond me. Perhaps part of her mystical siren power. She continues, "Look for the chip in the wall, ten steps right, your destination will be in sight."

I murmur her words to myself repeatedly as I bend down and remove my shoes. The ground is cold and dusty, no doubt already leaving a grey imprint on my bare feet. I toss the shoes at her feet and back away cautiously while she slouches over, struggling to put them on. In her jostling, the cloak falls from her face revealing the creature underneath. Black beady eyes, razor sharp teeth half rotted away, and stringy black hair longer than my own clumped together with oil.

She notices my stare and pulls her cloak up hastily, leaving nothing but her eyes showing under the fabric. But it's too late, I've already seen the demon beneath, its image doomed to haunt me forever.

I swallow back my fear. "Thank you," I manage to whisper. "Would you like my robe as well? Yours could use some mending or even an upgrade— with all those holes. You can either scrap it up to fix yours or use it as it is."

The siren peers at the silky robe I have draped over myself. It's not cream like the shoes. It's more of a deep blue, that in dark light could easily be mistaken for black. She outstretches her hand as if to touch the fabric, but I step away in response. Her hand retracts, but she nods. "Pretty key wants to know what she opens. I will take the robe for this."

"Okay," I say, slowly pulling my arms out of the sleeves. "I do want to know." I fold the robe over my arm. I won't give her what she wants until I have my answer. *One object for one question, that's how it works,* I remind myself. "You called me a key of three. Can you explain further to me what that means or what I'm supposed to open?" I really ask two questions in one sentence, but perhaps she'll answer both because of the way I worded it. I hope that she does.

"The key of three. Power. Treasure. Freedom. Keys unlock things. One will soon be open," she begins turning away from me mid-explanation.

"Wait," I say, "I still don't under—"

She turns back rapidly, startling me. "—a key of three." She ticks her spindly fingers off with each word. "Power. Treasure. Freedom. Open the lock, and it will reveal itself as not what it was to be. Pretty thing is the key even though she won't want to be."

I sigh, exasperated. "Can't you be a little less cryptic?"

"We cannot say more than we see. It's against the rules and rules offer punishment. Punishment like me," she begins laughing between sentences. "Not an are but a was. Nothing at all and nothing has no name…"

She rambles on again. It's an odd feeling, fearing something and feeling sorry for it at the same time. Clearly this particular siren is broken and mad beyond reason. Maybe I can't trust her words after all.

"Hey! Don't forget this!" I interrupt before tossing my robe to her.

She catches it in midair, tracing her fingers along the silky hem. "Luck to you, pretty key. Our paths will cross again, as I foresee." Without another word, she turns away from me, walking into the shadows of the secret passage, pulling her new robe over the old one.

I'm left by myself again, but now without shoes or a robe, only my nightgown to cover me. It's a bit drafty in here, but I assure myself the more I move the warmer I'll be.

What did the siren say again? Look for a chip in the wall first. *Well, if she's wrong at least I have a way back. Here goes nothing.* I turn around and begin searching the wall for a chip. Each turn, I continue to pull out my compact and draw the faint arrow marking the direction I came from.

I take another left and see it. A chunk of stone is missing from the wall on the vertex of the turn. It's jagged, and I wonder what could have made this big of a dent in the solid stone.

Okay, I've found the chip, next is…ten steps to the right. I count each step deliberately before it puts me at a crossroads. Left or right. The right side has nothing that I can see, but the left side shows a long, slender outline, turned away from me.

I hide my light around the corner before tip toeing barefooted to my destination.

"You're not supposed to be here!" I whisper shout at the figure eavesdropping in front of me.

Sebastian yelps, clutching his heart in shock and closing the peephole that gives vision to the king's chambers. "You could have given me a heart attack, Freckles! Not to mention given away my position!" he whispers hastily.

I chuckle under my breath before scurrying back to my lantern and lifting it up to his eye level. "Not so fun being on the receiving end, is it?" I joke. "What are you doing here anyways? Wouldn't it be easier to check up on your father by actually being in the room?"

He smiles against the warm light of the candle. "Not my style, really. Besides," he lowers his eye to the peephole looking in again, "I checked on him with Soren earlier, but Soren sort of dismissed me for the night. This is more…a discreet kind of checking up."

"Uh-huh. I see," I say. My hand lowers the lantern to the ground.

Sebastian leans away from the small hole in the wall to look at me skeptically. "Why are you here?" Then he acknowledges my lack of shoes and robe with a gesture of his hand. "And why are you in nothing but your nightgown?"

I sigh. "I suppose curiosity got the best of me, and I wanted to see if you three were alright; you, Soren… your father."

"You know you could have just come to the king's chambers and knocked." He offers before peering back in the hole.

"Perhaps that's not my style, either," I tease. "Besides, I doubt Soren would let me in now. I'm supposed to be locked in my room after the incident I had with Lamia."

Sebastian halts his eavesdropping to look at me, jaw dropped to the floor. "What do you mean *incident with Lamia?*"

I huff. "She found out I'm human by shoving me into the arena and trying to drown me. But it's no great matter," I lie. "Hazard of being human in a city immersed in water." My shoulders shrug in an upward motion.

Sebastian stares at me dumbfounded. "I… are you sure you're alright? Lamia should be severely punished for this." His voice grows in anger with each word.

"Soren has her locked up and guarded in her own room. As long as she isn't aware of these secret tunnels—"

"She isn't."

"—good. Then that's one less thing we need to worry about for the time being." I stand a little straighter, not just to assure Sebastian that I am alright, but perhaps myself a little too.

He looks at me intensely before wrapping me in a tight bear hug. I welcome it openly, hugging him back in the dimly lit secret passage.

We stand there holding each other for one prolonged moment. Sebastian lets go and rakes his eyes over my nightgown, a question behind his eyes.

"Right." I look down a little embarrassed by our physical proximity and my lack of proper attire. "Did you know there's a siren that lives in the castle?"

He lets go, looking even more puzzled.

"I've run into her twice now. Once in the halls after our meeting about information on the count. The other time was tonight. I didn't know what she was the first time, just that she scared me and kept calling me a—"

"—Wait. You saw her weeks ago and didn't tell me?" Hurt radiates in Sebastian's eyes and suddenly I feel bad I didn't say anything to him.

"I'm sorry," I apologize. "With all of the scheming and trying to fit in as a princess and all the other life-threatening situations, it slipped my mind."

Sebastian looks at me, shifting his gaze between my eyes and lips before he lets out a long breath. "It's fine. It's just that she's dangerous and…" He puts his back against the wall, crossing his arms. "…Her name is Bashiri, by the way. Kicked out of her own home because of some law she broke. She tells fortunes for us sometimes when we can find her. That's part of the deal my father made with her when she asked to seek refuge here. Well, that and to not eat any of the citizens or guests." Sebastian uncrosses his arms and rubs his eyelids with his fingertips. From being tired? Stressed? Both? Both is the most likely answer.

"Bashiri," I repeat. "It's funny. She was talking about not having a name or at least I think that was what she was talking about. It was hard to tell with all the rambling." I think her words over in my head.

"Running into her still doesn't explain your choice of attire, Miss Constance." He folds his hands behind his back and leans against the wall, looking at my nightgown, mischief lingering in his expression.

I chuckle. "Right, yes. I walked into the passages with a robe and shoes as well, looking for the peephole to check on you guys. Then I ran into the siren, Bashiri. It was a complete shock. But then I remembered her prophecy about me being a key—"

"—A key?" he interrupts.

"Strange, isn't it? Well, I figure I would try to get more out of her than the nonsense she spewed the first time by making a deal. Plus, my supply of blush was nearly exhausted," I toss up my compact for emphasis. "I traded my shoes for the way here and my robe for more information on her first riddle. But truth be told after hearing her speak for a second time, I can't be sure I trust everything she says. She's rattles on like a madwoman."

Sebastian peeps in the hole again, this time like he's making sure no one is listening to our conversation. "Constance, what did Bashiri tell you about being a key?" He leans in, ready for an answer.

"I don't know really," I admit. My fingers rub my arms for warmth. When I stopped walking, my muscles became cold again. Wordlessly, Sebastian takes off his own jacket and throws it over my shoulders. It smells of dirt and sea salt. "Just that I was a key… a key of three."

Sebastian mulls over my words in his head before responding. "Yes, it does sound rather insane, doesn't it? If I were you, I'd forget her blabbering." He leans one shoulder against the wall. "But if it's something, we'll figure it out together."

A crashing sound comes from the other side of the wall halting our conversation, Sebastian investigates first.

"Just a broken glass," he whispers over his shoulder.

I nudge him, so I can take a look at the king's chambers as well. There in the middle of the room, is the king hunched over a broken mug. A dark stain splotches his pristine rug. Soren is on the floor, cleaning up every little piece of glass with his bare hands before walking them over and out of my sight. Then he walks back into view, guiding the king by the elbows to stand up straighter and letting him use his body as support to walk back to bed.

The king moves at a snail's pace. His fingers shake in a way that's out of his control. Soren eases him into his covers, tucking him in like a sick child. The king's eyes are already closed shut before his head hits the pillow, and I wonder for the first time since being here if our efforts to save him really will be futile.

Soren's face is more vulnerable than I've ever seen it. He sits on the edge of the bed, cradling one of his father's hands in his own. He rests his forehead onto their set of interlaced hands. A single silver stream runs down his cheek and into his beard.

"We should continue searching for the cure tonight," I turn to Sebastian who's taken a seat against the wall, knees propped up.

His eyebrows scrunch together. "What, you mean right now? At this hour?"

I move away from the peephole and glide my body down the wall, joining him on the floor. "Yes. Who knows how much longer your father has. I can't…" I struggle to find the right words, "…I just hate seeing the pain your family is in right now."

Sebastian gazes at me before reaching for my hand. He strokes my skin with his thumb methodically. "I'm just thankful we're handling this better than when our mother passed away," he admits.

I look at him but stay silent—a way to show him I will listen if he wants to talk about it. Up until this point, no one besides the king has really talked about the queen so openly. Other than the fact she died and was loved.

He continues, "Soren was sorely grieved by her passing. We were only children, he and I. Couldn't have been more than twelve and nine, I think." He pauses momentarily, leaning his head against the wall to look up. "Mom died of a sickness as well. Something the healers couldn't identify and couldn't cure. It was devastating watching her wither into nothing but a hollow shell.

Soren did his best to shield me from the worst of her symptoms. Always made sure I saw her during her best moments. When she still had the strength to plaster a smile on for me. But not Soren. Soren saw the worst of it rarely ever leaving her side during her final weeks." Sebastian looks back down at our entwined hands, and I realize it's because he can't make himself look me in the eyes at his admission. "I think her death is why he's dead set on finding a cure for father—a chance to do something he never could for mom."

I squeeze his hand in comfort. "I'm so sorry. No child should lose a parent at such a young age."

He squeezes back, offering a lopsided grin that doesn't meet his eyes. "Like I said, I suffered the least from her passing. My father fell into such a deep despondency, he wouldn't let anyone in mom's quarters to clean it or move anything. He went in there every single day for years just to smell her perfumes or hold her favorite pair of slippers. Soren on the other hand has flat out refused to go in there," he says. A humorless chuckle escapes his mouth. "I guess we all deal with grief in different ways, huh?"

Something Sebastian says resonates with me. The wheels in my mind spin until a revelation clicks into place. I sit upright. "Sebastian. Siren prophecies…" My mouth hangs open slightly as I put the pieces together. "…are they general truths or are they based on the receiver's life?"

He tilts his head to the side. "What do you mean?"

"I mean… what if the prophecy is directly tied to Soren's life? I mean, you said so yourself that your father told you stories of the kraken all your life. And it just happens to be where the chest is found?"

Sebastian sits up a little straighter. "I guess that's a possibility. But what about what's in the chest? The broken weapon?"

"Hmm. I'm not sure but I'd bet it must be important to Soren somehow."

He looks at me, a quizzical expression etched on his face. The flickering of the candle casts an even darker shadow between the crease on his forehead.

"Think about it. Why else would the siren have him go searching for it if he wasn't meant to use it somehow? And just a moment ago, you said despondency."

"Yes, so?"

"So, isn't despondency another way of saying losing all hope? Or for that matter, being in a state of *despair*?"

At the mention of the word, Sebastian blinks in recognition, his mind seeming to catch up with my own. "A home of despair," he whispers more to himself than to me.

I smile, triumphant. "What could possibly be more despairing than losing a mother? All this time, we've been looking at Emora's history when we should have been looking at Soren's history! That room—your mother's room— is where his despair resides."

A giant grin stretches over Sebastian's face. "Constance, I believe you to be the smartest human I've ever come across." He beams, hastily drawing me in and landing a kiss onto my lips. "Let's go there now and look."

I stand up, wiping dust off my nightgown. Then I jerk my thumb toward the peephole. "I agree. Let's go get Soren."

"No," Sebastian says putting his two hands out in front of him.

"Why not? We have a greater chance of finding something if the three of us are looking for the book together," I offer.

Sebastian slowly puts his hands down. He shakes his head. "I know…it's just—if you are right then Soren won't want to go into mother's room and disturb it. It wouldn't be called a room of despair for nothing. I think it'd be better if we went together and looked." He checks the peephole again before turning back to me, his voice lower this time, "Then, if we do find something we can tell him. But if we're wrong, and we don't find anything then no harm is done. Right?" He shrugs his shoulders for emphasis.

I think on it, turning his solution in my head, looking for any logical flaw in his reasoning. When I can't think of any, I nod. "Very well, lead the way."

Chapter 41

When Sebastian said no one was allowed to come into the queen's quarters besides the king himself, he wasn't joking. Even the hall in the secret passageway seems riddled with extra dust and spiderwebs. Or at least whatever little creepy crawlies hundreds of feet below the surface make sticky webby things in dark places.

We walk through the threshold of the secret door connecting the passages to the former queen's room. The smell of sweet plumeria and coconut hangs in the air.

I close my eyes for a moment, picturing that painting of the beautiful woman with the long brown hair holding her child. The smell makes me feel like I know her just a little bit better. I imagine her walking outdoors in the garden, young Sebastian cradled on her hip and young Soren holding her free hand pointing to all the different plants.

As if thinking the same things as me, Sebastian says, "I can't believe it still smells like her after all these years." He closes his eyes, inhaling the sweet aroma.

The room itself is from a dream, a beautiful haunting dream. Every piece positioned perfectly right where it's supposed to be yet covered in layers of dust.

I'd have thought the queen's bedchambers would be larger, but the room isn't much bigger than my own, apart from an extensive walk-in closet next to the bathroom.

The furnishings are all in pristine condition apart from the two-inch dirt coated over everything. A couch and matching chair set sits idly to the right of the door. Green and gold fabric covers them. Beneath the furniture is an ornamental rug full of swirling flowers accented by the same gold found on the couch and chairs.

Sebastian wanders over to the couch, swiping at the dirt, creating a tornado of dust in the air before he plops down, sending another wave of particles swirling in the air.

A very un-ladylike sneeze escapes me as the dust begins to settle again.

"Bless you," Sebastian calls over his shoulder. He doesn't look at me though because he's entranced by the dirt-covered couch, tracing swirls in the dust on the unoccupied cushion next to him.

What must he be thinking to be back in this room? What importance is that couch to him? Did his mother hold him before bed on that couch? Read to him when he was sick?

I get lost in thought about what could have been Sebastian's childhood before prying my eyes away to look at the rest of the room.

Her bed rests against the wall farthest from the secret passage door. Made to perfection, the seafoam green sheets are tightly tucked in on the sides, pillows upon pillows placed in a pleasing way against the head rest.

On the opposite side of the room rests her vanity. She has a set of emerald jewels and a crown splayed out on the top as if she planned to wear them the day she passed.

However, the most peculiar, or rather impressive, thing in her room is the wall next to the window. There lies a shelf unit packed with books from floor to ceiling. Seems like a good place to start looking for the Book of Dominion.

"I'm going to start here," I call over my shoulder to Sebastian who hasn't moved off the couch.

Standing right in front of the rows upon rows of books, I realize I will need a ladder to reach the ones at the top.

As if on cue, Sebastian carries up a ladder. He makes an *oofing* sound as he angles it against the shelf. A hand gingerly presses against his sides.

"Are you alright?" I ask, concerned.

"Mhmm, just some bruised ribs from earlier. I'll heal."

Right. Soren blasted him in the arena just this morning.

He pats the wooden steps. "This might be helpful," he says with a wink. "You check the bottom shelves. I'll check the top."

I decide searching them methodically and reach for the book farthest left on the bottom shelf. It reads *Emora's First Love: A History of the First King of Emora*. The front cover has a note written in big swooping letters:

"My Dearest Soren,
May this be enlightening to you in the darkest of times.
Love, Mom"

"Sebastian?" I ask, flipping through the book, "What exactly does the Book of Dominion look like? I mean does it even say "Book of Dominion" on the front cover or…" my question trails off as I clap the book closed and place it back where it belongs before looking at the next one.

He too skims through a book as he replies, "Honestly, I'm not sure. I've never seen it with my own eyes. But I imagine it to be a black bound one… old and weathered from its age. Legend states it's the oldest book in our world's history." He flips through another one.

I watch him. I can't help it. The way his wavy curls dangle off his forehead and the slight parting of his lips as he concentrates on our task—it makes me think of our kisses in the garden.

Lamia's wrong. How can she accuse me of having feelings for Soren when Sebastian is so endearing and so charming? I would think it was obvious he's the one for whom I have affections.

My insides warm and then he looks down at me, catching me red handed.

His mouth tilts upward. "Am I the only one working here, Freckles?" he teases.

Pink blooms across my cheeks. "No, sorry," I stammer, "I was just uh—"

"—ogling the most handsome merman in Emora? It's all right, you can admit it." He winks.

I grin back. "Okay, maybe a little." I break my gaze with him and pull out the third book on the bottom row. "So, not sure what it looks like, but it's probably old," I repeat more to myself than back at Sebastian. "Make sure you shake the books too in case a key is stuck in one of the pages," I add.

Sebastian looks at me, brows furrowed.

"Well, it's better to be thorough than possibly miss one of the objects, is it not?" I counter before adding, "even though I still think Lamia has the key we want."

He shakes his head and chuckles under his breath. "If you say so."

It takes us almost an hour to skim through the entirety of books on the queen's shelves. Not a single one is the Book of Dominion. The only thing we have to show for our efforts is the gray dust covering our clothes; like dirt on a potato.

We split up and look around the rest of the room. I check her vanity and bathroom. Sebastian looks all around her furniture and bed, even going as far as taking off all the sheets and pillows, checking for hidden compartments, but nothing.

"That book has to be in here," Sebastian grunts, carrying the ladder back into his mom's old closet. He walks out with a pair of sea foam green slippers. "My lady," he bows down to put them on my feet, but I take a step back.

"Sebastian, I can't use those," I say. "They were your mother's."

He looks up from his bent position, "Yes, they were. However," he scoots closer to me, gesturing for one of my feet. "I know for a fact if there was someone in need of shoes, my mother would happily have lent hers to said lady. Now, if you will lend me your adorable, dainty, dirt-covered foot."

I hesitate for a moment, but then reluctantly give in to his request. The shoes are the most comfortable slippers I have ever had the pleasure of wearing. They're silky and plush on the balls of my feet, not to mention I fit in them as if they were made just for me.

"A perfect fit," Sebastian replies pushing his hand against his knee to stand back up and look at me. "For a perfect princess." His eyes linger on my lips before placing a gentle peck on them.

I grin at the sweet sensation it brings me. "You know I'm not really a princess," I raise a single eyebrow. "But thanks for saying so. Now," I look around the room again, wanting to refocus on our mission, trying to figure out where to look next. "If I were the queen and was in possession of this powerful, mystical book or hiding a special key…where would I hide it for safe keeping? Have any ideas?" I ask Sebastian. She was his mother after all. Maybe he has some insight into her psyche.

"I wish I knew," Sebastian says. He strokes his chin thoughtfully.

"Did she have a jewelry box with a lock or someplace she kept her really expensive necklaces and tiaras?" I question.

"No, my father saw to that. He kept most of her jewelry in the castle trove and would personally fetch what she wanted. She didn't keep much jewelry in here." He paces back and forth, staring at the ground.

I walk toward her closet. "Maybe she has some secret compartment in here. Let's check."

Her closet is considerably large. A small crystal chandelier hangs dead center, illuminating the vast array of color-coded fabrics. The left and right sides are lined with more dresses than any one female could ever need in a lifetime, but I suppose that's just one perk to being a queen: you can afford to have as much clothing as your heart desires.

The back wall is just like the bookcase, except with shoes. A floor to ceiling rack covered in shoes. Two lanterns occupy the sides. They give more light deeper into the closet. This area is certainly big enough to hide something.

Sebastian follows after. "It can't hurt to check, but the closet is pretty standard. I have one just like it and there's nothing unusual about it."

"I don't know, Sebastian. Maybe she sewed the book inside one of her gowns for safe keeping or something. We're running out of places to look." I do the same with the dresses that I did with the books, starting from the one farthest left and working my way over. I check each one to see if it's heavier than it should be, or if there's a bulge in an odd spot. "Start on that side," I say to Sebastian.

He takes a moment to note how I am checking the dresses and does the same on the opposite side.

The fabrics feel expensive. All of them are extravagant, each weighing at least ten pounds with jewels meticulously sewed in intricate patterns on the sleeves and bust line.

"There's something quite peculiar about this," Sebastian begins. "All these dresses are beautiful and regal, but that wasn't my mom."

I make it to the final section of dresses. "What do you mean?"

"I mean, they're all extravagant, but my mom's everyday clothes were far simpler. Yeah, she wore a couple of these dresses when we would host a ball or she would have a special date night with Father, but I don't see any of the outfits she wore on a daily basis."

We reach the end of the clothes. I pull out the last dress on my side and rummage through the sparkly lavender fabric. "Maybe your father took those for safe keeping?" I suggest.

Sebastian thinks on it for a moment before nodding. "It's possible."

"Well, there's nothing in these dresses as far as I can tell." I notice her entire back wall and the hundreds of shoes that line it." Do you think the book could be small enough to fit inside a shoe?"

Sebastian walks to the wall and picks one up, weighing the queen's flat in his hand. "Perhaps." He grabs the ladder again with some difficulty, pulling it up to the shoe rack. "Same thing. I'll go high, you go low."

"Very well," I say and look through each shoe. They come in every shape and size, many of them don't look nearly as comfortable as the slippers that hug my feet.

There are silk shoes, stilettos, leather, and wooden. There are even some shoes with odd spikes jutting out. I go to pick one up and immediately regret it, dropping the heel to the ground.

"Ouch!" I yelp drawing my thumb up to my lips and sucking on the wound. The tiniest bubble of blood swells where the spikes pricked me.

"Are you okay?" Sebastian calls from atop the ladder.

"Yes, I just… this shoe is a walking hazard."

He looks down at me, at the fallen shoe. "Pick it up by the heel only when you put it back on the rack."

I bend down and do as he says aiming to touch only the heel. Luckily the shoe didn't land on my foot. Somehow, I feel if it did hit my slippers, those spikes would go straight through the silk and stab my flesh.

The rest of the shoes are as empty as the first ones we checked.

Sebastian climbs down the ladder and lets out a deep sigh. I can see the disappointment in his eyes.

"I'm sorry," I say, "I really thought this was the room of despair." I slump down, sitting cross-legged, resting my head in my palm.

Sebastian looks down at me and leans against the shoe rack. "Not to worry," he says. "There's nothing to be sorry about. It was a hunch that turned out to be wrong." He shrugs one shoulder. "At least now we know."

"I suppose," I say as I draw invisible circles on the carpet with my free hand.

We searched high and low in this whole place and have nothing to show for it. No book. No key. No way to save the king.

Disappointment bubbles in my insides. I guess it was a good thing we didn't invite Soren here just to bring up the pain of his past *and* be wrong.

"I guess we should head back to the secret passages and call it a night," I say, hoisting myself off the floor and dusting the dirt off my hands the best I can.

A flicker dances in Sebastian's eyes. His eyebrows raise. Then he looks to the two lanterns on each side of the shoe rack, walking up to one searching it scrupulously before looking back at me with the biggest toothy grin. "Freckles," he says, "I give you a secret room."

Chapter 42

Without another word Sebastian pushes down on a piece of the lantern which sets the wall trembling—a hidden door opening the way to another room. A secret one.

I smirk. "Nice work, Detective Sebastian," I tease as I step through the threshold and into another part of the queen's chambers.

Sebastian follows after me.

This room's nothing like what we saw in the other parts of her quarters. It's a smaller room, about the size of my own back home. And it's much cozier. A fresh new wave of coconut and plumeria waft up my nose.

There's a single, worn couch in the corner and a coffee table stacked with books and an old jewelry box. One empty cup stained with some drink sits by the stack of books. In another corner is a different rack of clothes, all much simpler than the ones we recently rummaged through.

Sebastian immediately goes over to the clothing rack and inhales the scent of them, closing his eyes. "It's like she never left," he says to me. "This, this right here is my mother."

The room is warm, cozy, simple. I feel I would have liked her very much.

"I'll check over here," I say as I walk to the couch and sit down, flipping through the books on the table. There are a few romance novels, a history textbook, and an instruction manual on how to sew, but no mystical ones.

I move onto the jewelry box, but inside there is no jewelry. All that lies in it are small paintings of two boys and the king, her family, and some dried flowers strung together with twine.

I slouch back into the couch, a yawn escaping me. If everything wasn't so dusty, I imagine I could fall asleep right now.

Sebastian slumps down next to me. "Anything?" he asks.

"Nothing. Not what we're looking for anyways," I reply. "However, I did find some very cute paintings of a chubby, handsome baby." I point down to the jewelry box.

Sebastian picks it up and opens the lid. "Ah yes, that handsome chubby faced baby is in fact, Soren," he says taking out the first painting.

My jaw drops. "No, that's Soren? I could have sworn it was you!" I nudge his shoulder playfully.

He proceeds to rummage through the pictures, pulling one out at a time before he finds his own. "This," he hands me the painting, "is me as a baby."

The baby has dark wavy hair and stormy blue eyes. It's far thinner than the first baby, but still very cute. "Ah, yes, now I see the resemblance," I say. "Show me the rest," I gesture to the jewelry box.

His eyebrows furrow in the middle. "Right now?"

"Uh-huh," I nod resting my head on his shoulder.

He reaches out and picks up each painting, explaining who they are and what they do. Each one has its own story.

One is of his brother and him all muddied up and grinning. "This one was horrible to sit through. Soren and I had an argument while playing heroes, and we tussled into the mud. Mother made us sit through her painting for hours just to capture the moment in oils. It was quite unpleasant. All the mud caked on… it made every part of me itchy."

I laugh, nuzzling my nose into his arm.

"Oh, and this one was the first time I could use my powers. I was only five here and my family was so proud. I had accidentally splashed father in the face. He was so angry at first and then laughed it off like it was the funniest thing in the world to him. So of course, mother had this moment painted as well." Sebastian looks at the painting of him and his father soaking wet with a forlorn expression.

In no time, all that is left are the flowers. "Do those have any significance?" I ask.

"Yeah, I think so," Sebastian says picking them up, leaving the box completely empty. "She used to tell me of the time when father courted her, before she was queen. The first thing he ever did for her was pick flowers from the garden." He touches the delicate petals in his hand, recalling the story. "She told me, if there's one thing I really need to do to gain a ladies' attention and show her I care, it's to pick her flowers myself. Do the work myself and make it special."

I think back to the yellow and red flowers Sebastian gave me for our dinner date. Did he pick those himself like his mom advised?

"That's sweet," I say placing my hand on his arm. He looks down and smiles before turning to put the flowers and paintings back in their rightful place.

"Hang on," he says putting his mom's items on the table instead. He stares at the jewelry box. "Look here." His finger points to one of the corners.

At first, I don't see anything, so I lean in closer.

The bottom of the jewelry box isn't connected to the corner. Which means it isn't the real bottom of the box at all. It's a fake bottom to trick thieves into thinking they found the treasure they were looking for, when in reality, the real prize is hidden underneath, on the true bottom.

I recall my own mother having a hidden drawer in her jewelry box as well, where she kept her wedding ring at night.

I wedge my nail into the tiny gap at the corner and lift.

Our breaths catch at the same time, because laying there at the bottom of the secret compartment in the secret room is a dark brown, leather bound book with three intertwining swirls. No title.

We look at each other, and I reach in to grab the mysterious book. As soon as my skin touches it, the book hums with energy.

Sebastian observes as I flip open to the cover page. The first piece of parchment, in bold script reads *Book of Dominion* with a note underneath that reads *Sacrifice is the ultimate power.*

I flip through the first few pages. Each one is a spell of some sort, listing ingredients and steps. There are all kinds of incantations. Storm summoning, power transfers, gaining strength of a thousand lives, power of persuasion, siren renewal, but I don't see anything on healing the sick.

"May I look?" Sebastian asks.

I hand it over to him. He flips through a couple of pages, landing on one and reading it thoroughly, but I can't see which one he's reading up on.

"Did you find anything to help your father?" I try to peer at the book, but he shuts it and stands up, offering me his free hand.

I take it and stand up as well.

"I haven't found it yet, but I'll keep looking through it tonight," he places the book inside his pants pocket and begins to walk out of the room, grabbing my hand and taking me with him.

I follow close behind, my hand interlocked with his. One more thing to find. The key. I just know Lamia has it. Maybe now that I helped uncover the second item, the princes will believe my gut instinct. That's all we need that's left in the riddle.

"Sebastian, I can't believe this! We are one step closer to finding a cure. We should inform Soren right away, don't you think? He's going to be elated! And then I really believe we should search Lamia's belongings for the key."

Sebastian gives my hand a reassuring squeeze. "Absolutely we can, Freckles."

We walk through the closet, into the bedroom, and in front of the secret passage.

Sebastian pushes in one of the stones, revealing our way out of the queen's quarters. "Let me do it in the morning though, okay? By the looks of it," he points to the window, showing the heart of Emora twinkling above the city, "it's about three in the morning. Let him get some sleep, and I'll tell him at breakfast. Besides, you should get some rest as well. I need you energized to help find the final object later today," he says, pressing a gentle kiss on my temple.

I think on it. He does have a point. I'm sure Soren has been up most of the night helping the king. If he's asleep right now, we should let him rest.

Another yawn escapes me when I realize I would really enjoy some sleep right about now too. A late morning in bed might not be such a bad idea. "Very well," I say, "I believe that's an agreeable idea." I push up on my tiptoes to give Sebastian a swift kiss.

His eyes lock with mine, sadness growing in his pupils and then they become alert, staring in the direction past my head. "What's that?" he asks pointing at something behind me.

I turn to investigate the darkness.

Next thing I know, something solid and heavy hits me in my temple. My body doesn't even make contact with the floor before I completely black out.

Chapter 43

I'm cold and nauseous. My head throbs. My body aches. At first, I think I'm back in my room, suffering from a migraine, but there are many things that don't add up. I'm not covered in blankets with Squish curled up by my head. I'm not even lying down. Before I even open my eyes, I know this is not my bedroom. This is my nightmare.

My hands are chained to something cold and steely above my body, propping me up, causing an ache in my shoulders and neck. Or maybe that's from the massive head shot I vaguely remember taking. Something wet and sticky cakes my hair to the side of my face and neck.

It takes a great deal of effort to open my eyes, which confirm I am not in a bedroom at all. Everything is a bit of a blur, but I am in some sort of cave. Rocky walls surround me. The ceiling is low. Two sets of chains dangle from the center of it. I'm attached to one of them.

The only light in the room comes from a couple of lanterns casting long shadows on the wall. One of those shadows moves.

A figure in dark clothing is turned away from me, messing with something on the only table in the room. He's tall with wavy black hair. I would know that head of curls anywhere.

"Se-S-Sebastian?" I croak. My tongue feels like lead in my mouth.

The figure turns confirming my suspicion. It's Sebastian, holding an ancient looking dagger, long and thin. In his other hand is a rock. He strikes metal against the stone, sharpening the blade.

"Hey, Freckles," he says too casually, methodically grinding metal against stone. "How are you feeling? I pray, not too unwell."

"I—Where are we? What's going on?" I ask. If he's there, and I'm here, why am I still chained up, and he is free? Shouldn't he be helping me out of these binds?

"Your head was hit with quite the blow, Constance. Best to take things slow," he replies, not quite meeting my gaze.

He puts the rock and dagger back down on the table so he can pick something else up; the Book of Dominion. He draws his hand up to his mouth and lightly licks his thumb before turning a page. I notice his palm is wrapped in cloth. "It's quite the interesting read, really. The power of persuasion spell has already been quite useful. And there are spells in here I wouldn't ever have thought of but will come in handy in the near future. There's a spell to give yourself herculean strength, a spell to find what was lost, a spell of transformation. A spell to mend a siren's song. There's even a spell to transfer power—or in my case, a birthright." Sebastian steps closer to me but stops an arm's length away before finally looking me straight in the eyes.

My head continues to throb. I struggle to focus on him. Even with just a couple feet between us, he doesn't look quite right. But I try to understand despite the pounding in my head. "The book, Sebastian. What does the book have to do with me? Did you—were you the one who tied me up?"

"You are the key, Constance." He cradles the book under his arm and with the other pulls a strand of hair plastered to my cheek, tucking it behind my ear. "The key to my power."

My mind shuffles through those familiar words. The words Bashiri, spoke to me. *A key of three. One for power. One for treasure. One to be free.*

"Why?" I choke out the question.

"Humans are fascinating. For merfolk that never see the surface, they're practically mythical. Rumor is that human blood is a key ingredient for a fair amount of mer-magic. Particularly," he raises the book in his hand, "forbidden magic."

My *blood* is the key. The key to Sebastian's power. But it can't be. It must be something else.

"You don't have to do this. There must be another way," I plead.

He scoffs, his mask of casual mannerisms slipping. "Come now. You're smarter than this." He brings his free hand to his temple, tapping the side of his head. "Did you really believe that finding the objects in the siren's prophecy was going to do anything for my father? It even says in the prophecy he is going to die! And do you know what that means?" He turns away from me to pace back and forth.

I say nothing, waiting for him to continue.

"It means Emora will be placed in the middle of a territorial war! Soren has failed as heir to the throne. He hasn't the guts to do what needs to be done here and ensure Emora's prosperity. Its peace. He doesn't *deserve* the birthright."

"And you do?"

This whole time he was so lighthearted, so easy-going, so romantic and warm. But the Sebastian in front of me now is none of those things. All I see is a delusional, power-hungry merman.

He stops mid-stride, choosing to come closer to me. So close his breath lingers with my own. "Absolutely. I know what needs to be done. What sacrifices need to be made."

"And what sacrifices need to be made, huh?"

For one prolonged moment, I see something like guilt in his eyes. They droop at the corners, the smallest shimmer wells up on his bottom lid. He darts his eyes away, clearing his throat, before coming back to meet my gaze and the look has vanished. "You," he whispers.

My heart drops. All this time, all our shared moments, meant nothing to him. What I thought was growing affection, dare I thought even love, was a ruse to keep me here until he got what he wanted.

My stomach pitches. I might very well vomit.

Sebastian reaches out to push back my bloodied strands of hair, but I yank my face to the side at his touch, sickened by the thought of this merman touching me.

Sebastian retracts his hand momentarily and sighs, drawing his hand back up to pull the sticky hair from my cheek despite my protest. "My dear, Constance…you must think me a monster, but it's still me." His hand splays over his chest. "My heart beats stronger than ever. I feel deeply for you… Unfortunately, there's a reason it's called sacrifice."

I muster up as much saliva as I can and spit toward his face, which he easily dodges.

"Soren will never let you go through with this. He's stronger than you are." I do my best to test the chains around my wrists to see if there's any room to slip through them. But there's not enough space. The metal snags at my skin leaving raw angry marks on my wrists.

Sebastian smiles sadly, putting his hand up to wrap his finger around one of my curls. "Soren will play right into my hand, because I know his weakness."

I put as much venom as I can summon in my words. "Whatever you have planned, he will never fall for it."

"Well," he says, drawing his hands behind his back, book still clutched in one. He takes a giant step backward. "One of us must be right. And fortunately for us, we get to see who's right very, very soon. Because you see, when I leave you in here, all I have to do is mention that you're in danger and my noble brother will come running without a second thought. He's already in a frenzy searching for you.

Ever since the captain lost your whereabouts this morning. Come to think of it, this is all unraveling perfectly."

I let out a feral growl and struggle against my chains.

Sebastian pulls out a handkerchief from his jacket pocket and shoves it in my mouth.

I use my tongue to spit out as much as possible causing him to let out a long, exasperated breath.

"I'm sorry, Constance, but you're going to have to keep quiet when we come back in to rescue you. Otherwise, my plan could fail." Before attempting to gag me again, he walks back to the table to retrieve some rope. This time he shoves the piece of cloth deep into my mouth and finishes it off with the rope wedged between my teeth, securing it at the back of my head.

I writhe in protest, offering curses to his name that are too muffled to make out.

Sebastian looks at his handiwork and nods with approval before grabbing my head with his hands and placing a kiss on the top of my brow. "There are guards outside this dungeon room. If you manage to free yourself, which I highly doubt, they'll be waiting for you." His voice takes on a somber tone. "There's no escape. Not anymore."

Without another word, Sebastian sets the book down and grabs the dagger from the table, hiding it in his jacket sleeve before he turns on his heels and walks out of this wretched cell, closing the door with a loud thud.

My rage was keeping me pieced together, but now, as I hang in the middle of a cold, damp dungeon awaiting my death, I can feel the pieces of my heart chip and shatter.

Tears well in my eyes until they are full and heavy, dropping down to the rocky floor like a leaky rooftop.

How could I have been so naive? So trusting? I'd known him for little more than a month and thought what we shared was love. It was tragic. It was pitiful, and I was ashamed that I could be fooled so easily.

Long minutes pass. I let the tears silently fall until my body can't produce anymore.

Think, Constance, think. You will not let this scumbag prince best you. Think of a way out. I calm my breathing with deep, purposeful breaths and look around the room again.

I take a closer look at the table Sebastian used. The rock still sits there, as well as the Book of Dominion. I'm not sure what I can do with either—maybe hide the rock in my hands if I could get it up to them and thrash it down on Sebastian's unsuspecting head. Or tear at the book with my feet so the spells become unreadable.

Neither are great plans, but they are better than nothing.

I test my chains once more, except this time, I measure how far I can stretch while still being tethered to them. My shoulders bark at the extension they're forced to be in as I lean an outstretched foot toward the table. It remains mere inches away. If I could just reach a little farther… ugh.

Muffled shouting disrupts me from my scheme. I look to the door as it's opening and in comes Soren, twin swords in hand. His tropical blue eyes ablaze as they reach mine.

I scream at him with all my might. *Turn around! Run! This is a trap!* But he can't hear any of it. He just scans the room for other possible threats.

Then I see Sebastian sauntering in behind him. I scream against my gag harder, writhing and struggling against my restraints to help him. To do anything to avoid what I know will happen next.

It doesn't make a difference.

Soren has no time to react as his conniving brother thrusts the dagger into his gut, yanking it out forcefully, only to drive it back in.

Soren barely has time to turn around and look at his backstabbing brother before Sebastian uses the hilt of the dagger to strike him on the head, rendering him unconscious.

"No!" I scream through the gag.

Sebastian tucks his dagger away and hauls Soren's limp body toward the second set of chains. With a few grunts and mishaps, he gets his brother chained to the ceiling just as I am. He rubs his ribs from the exertion.

I turn my head to Soren. Our bodies are close enough to touch.

With the gag still in place, I find it increasingly difficult to breathe. As though I am suffocating.

Sebastian notices and loosens the rope, pulling out his cloth. "There we go. No more need for that," he states as if he has done me a favor.

I ignore him, choosing to turn my attention back to Soren.

Blood soaks his shirt, his face becoming increasingly pale in the dim light.

"Soren?" I whimper, "Soren, please wake up. You have to wake up." I plead with him even though he cannot hear me.

He makes no sound, no movement. His head lolls to his chest.

Sebastian wordlessly takes the rope he used to gag me and ties one of my chains to Soren's, intertwining our hands. The stretch of it pulls at my shoulder.

He checks the strength of his knot and looks up. Thoughtful. "You know what's interesting about this whole thing?" He turns to me, pulling the dagger back out, pointing the bloody tip at my chest. "None of this would've been possible if Soren had just let you go in the first place. But he couldn't. He heard Bashiri rambling on and on about a human key and knew he needed to free you for his own selfish agenda." He steps toward his brother, fisting Soren's hair to pull his face up to his own. "See how well that worked out for you, brother?" He lets Soren's head drop and turns his attention back to me. "Ironic really, because the only one that's benefiting from this is me." He laughs mirthlessly. "Funny how things work out, is it not?"

I can't believe what I'm hearing. It's just one blow after another.

All this time, they knew Bashiri's prophecy about me. And used it for their own gain. My heart breaks just a little bit more.

"Will it be worth it?" I ask.

Sebastian chooses not to answer. Instead, he grabs the book and flips to a page, mumbling something to himself.

"Will the power be worth the guilt of murder?"

He stops his mumbling and looks at me. "For Emora, I will do what is necessary."

Sebastian continues mumbling whatever incantation is in that book. He raises the dagger and points it at our intertwined hands.

"Sebastian, please, there's got to be another way," I plead as he makes a deep cut from my palm down to my wrist. I let out a scream. The pain is sharp, stinging like a hundred bee stings. Immediately, blood oozes down my arm.

Then Sebastian makes the same cut on Soren, pressing our hands and arms together, mixing the two rivers of blood. The contact sends new waves of pain into my hand. I gasp.

Sebastian chants louder in a language I am unfamiliar with.

Particles of black mist come out of thin air. It swirls around us like a typhoon, sending my hair flying in all directions. It grows thicker and thicker, until Soren and I are swallowed up in darkness.

Chapter 44

I would take drowning over the pain I feel right now. Black smoke swirls around Soren and me.

It feels like my energy, my life, my very soul is being sucked right out of my skin.

Through the dense smoke, I struggle to see Soren. "So—Soren?" It comes quieter than a whisper.

I feel so weak.

I am going to die.

Clanging of metal on metal interrupts everything.

Sebastian stops chanting. The mist pauses its swirling, remaining suspended in the air, frozen in time.

There are shouts just outside the door.

Now that Sebastian has stopped chanting, the black smoke starts to recede like mist disappearing in the air.

I can make out someone near the entrance, one of the guards. He comes barreling in back first, hitting his head on the hard floor.

His foe comes in after. It's Darius, poised and ready to fight like the captain he is. Along with Fleck, Cam, and Griffin trailing close behind.

"Stop this now, prince," Darius orders in that calm voice of reason.

Sebastian responds by grabbing Soren's fallen blade and charging at the men. Darius is not deterred. He goes head-to-head with the prince. They fight like it's a dance, each stuck to their partner move for move.

That gives Fleck, Cam, and Griffin a chance to run over to me and the still unconscious Soren.

"That's a lot of blood," Griffin says, untying the rope that keeps our hands together. His face turns sickly green.

"It's fine," Fleck states, "just get them out of these chains."

"Sorry m'lady," Cam apologizes as he pulls out a thin piece of metal, wedging it into the lock until he hears a click.

My wrists fall at the release.

I'm so drained that the moment I'm free of the chains my legs give out. Luckily Griffin catches me in his arms, using his body as a wall of unrelenting steel to keep me upright. He rips his sleeve with his teeth and tightly wraps my injured hand with some cloth before pulling my arm over his shoulders.

Cam busies himself with Soren's restraints, setting the unconscious heir free. He nearly falls to the floor before Fleck catches him with a grunt.

"I think he needs to lay off the workouts before we save him again," Fleck groans under the weight of Soren's dead weight.

Cam tucks his tool away and takes to Soren's other side, hoisting the heir's free arm over his shoulders.

I look down at Soren's torso. Blood has soaked through it completely and is now seeping into Cam's side.

"We need to get them out of here!" Griffin barks as he lifts me into his arms. I'm too weak to protest, so I do my best to hang on as tight as I can.

All five of us trek toward the entrance. Griffin carrying me. Fleck and Cam supporting Soren's limp body.

We reach the doorway.

Right outside the threshold lies two more unconscious soldiers.

Griffin turns around, giving me a good look of the view behind us.

Sebastian and Darius continue to duel. Both panting from the exertion.

With one hand, Sebastian clutches his side.

Out of the corner of his eye, he notices us escaping, locking eyes with me, longing for something no longer there. Which leaves an opening for Darius to swipe Sebastian off his feet with the stroke of his sword.

It doesn't knock Sebastian unconscious, but he falls on his bruised ribs, giving Darius enough time to run through the doorway, close it, and lock Sebastian inside.

"Quickly," Darius orders, "to the ship."

We make it up the long winding stairs and out into the open air. Emora's heart glows faintly, like that of a pink sunrise.

Griffin's breaths are quick and ragged from the labor of carrying me.

I motion for him to put me down to catch his breath, and he obeys, grateful for the break.

From below, I see soldiers scurrying about, shouting orders at each other. My shoulder leans against the edge of the mountain for support. "How on Earth are we going to get Soren all the way across the city?"

"We don't need to," Darius says matter of fact. "We just need to get him to the ship. Don't trust anyone but our company right here. Who knows how many soldiers have aligned themselves with Prince Sebastian?" He twists his sword in his hand as he surveys the frenzy of confusion going on below.

The motley crew all nod in understanding before we make our way down the stairs carved into the mountain's side. Darius leads the way. Griffin wraps his arm around my side, keeping me steady as I descend the steps.

At the bottom, I think we'll veer toward the waterfall, but Darius has other plans. He walks through a wall of vines at the base of the mountain to reveal a dock full of ships.

My mind shifts back to the ball. I wondered how all those merpeople got into the city. This must be the main entrance. A fact no one bothered sharing with me.

"Hurry up!" an older merman calls from the deck of one of the ships. Jed. He's waving his arms and pointing past us.

Next to him, Addeah and Dox run up the side of the boat, waving us down. Urging us to move faster.

Four soldiers come running after us, shouting to halt.

We race to the ship, sprinting across the gangway. Darius kicks it into the waters just as the first soldier reaches the edge of the dock. He stops just in the nick of time, the tips of his boots peaking over the edge.

I lean over my knees, gasping for air.

Cam and Fleck place Soren gently down on the deck.

More and more soldiers pile onto the dock, staring after us with malice, until Sebastian comes running up from the rear, eyes blazing with anger. He orders the soldiers to move to the side, inhaling a long breath of air before his hands rush in front of him.

The ship halts in its tracks.

No.

It doesn't stop.

We're being pulled back to shore.

Soren's powers. Sebastian used that spell to not only take Soren's birthright to the throne, but to steal his powers as well.

I lean against the railing, and my heart drops. This is it. We were so close to escaping only to be caught again.

A tall figure hobbles up next to me. He smells of blood and sweat. It's Soren, with his arms outstretched in the same stance as his brother. I can't believe he's conscious let alone standing and fighting. His shirt is drenched in his own blood. Sweat drips down his temple as he struggles to out-muscle Sebastian.

If anyone had suggested Soren could lose against Sebastian in a head-to-head match, I would have said that person was delusional. But it's happening.

Even as Soren uses all his might to halt our progress, Sebastian's power now outranks his, and he knows it too. He lets out a blood curdling war cry before his hands drop.

At first, I think he has given up, but Soren shifts his weight angling his body to the side and drawing his arm back as if he is about to throw a punch. The effort is difficult for him, but he thrusts his arm through the air and with that gesture a tidal wave of unsuspecting water lifts from the ocean depths plummeting straight into Sebastian.

The wave hurdles him into the mountain side, knocking him unconscious.

The ship no longer pulls toward the dock. Dox gains control of the wheel again, sailing us away from Emora, toward the open ocean. "We're gettin' outta here!" Dox hollers, pumping his fist in the air.

Soren looks upon his beloved city one more time before falling flat onto his back with a hard thud.

"Soren!" Addeah gasps. "Get over here and help me get him below deck to the sick bay," she orders, pointing to Griffin and Cam. Griffin takes Soren under the arms. Cam grabs his ankles. They carry his limp, unconscious body below deck.

"I'd better follow," Jed says, grabbing what appears to be a medical bag on his way down to help.

I watch them, utterly speechless at what to say or feel. Should I be relieved we escaped death? Should I be grieving for the love I thought I had with Sebastian?

I slump down against the side of the boat, the adrenaline of our escape has worn off, and a new wave of exhaustion pulls at me.

Darius walks over. "Miss Constance, we better get that hand checked out." He notices the blood crusted to my hair. "As well as that nasty bump on your head. But for the moment," he pulls out a purple vial, "take this. Just in case."

I look at the purple liquid and back up to Darius' dark face.

"We'll have to head down before we can travel up," he says handing me the vial. I take it without a word. "Now, let's get you cleaned up so you can rest." His voice is so gentle, so lulling—or maybe I'm just so exhausted that anything will call me to rest right now.

Darius offers me a hand, hauling me up from my seated position and proceeding to lift me up into his strong embrace.

We don't even get below deck before I fall asleep in his arms.

Chapter 45

I wake up with a jolt. A pounding in my head. Urgently I struggle against chains, but there are none.

I'm on a simple cot surrounded by wooden planked walls. No chains chafe my wrists.

I look down at my body. My filthy nightgown has been replaced with a fresh linen shirt and pants—both of which are a bit roomy but comfortable.

I feel my hair, which has been neatly plated into a braid. No blood, but when I stick my hand against my pounding head, my palm stings at the contact.

I look down at the tight wrappings weaving around my hand and wrist.

Instantly my mind goes to Sebastian and my heart breaks again. *How could I have been so blind?* A tear escapes my eye, trickling down my cheek.

"That needs to be kept clean, you know? Had to use ten stitches to stop the bleeding. You're lucky you didn't bleed out," a female voice calls from across the room, interrupting my indulgence of self-pity. It's Addeah. She's sitting on the only other piece of furniture in the cabin of the ship: a simple wooden chair.

I try to stand up but wobble against the rocking of the ship, falling back down into the cot.

"Careful, child," Addeah says, standing up to help me steady myself. "You've been through a whole lot these last twenty-four hours. Best to take it easy." With her hands wrapped around my shoulders she ushers me to lay back down.

She guides me on my back. I stare up at the ceiling. There's a small hole I stay focused on. "What happened?" I croak, my throat parched for water. When was the last time I ate or drank anything? I turn my gaze upon Addeah. "What happened after I fell asleep?"

She looks at me in that motherly way of hers. Her fingers stroke my forehead in a calming manner. "Darius and I watched the soldiers. Some thought of following us, but most didn't know what to do after Soren knocked Sebastian unconscious." She looks away, trying to puzzle something out. "I'm not even sure why they would go after us in the first place," she admits.

"It was—" I cough from the dryness of my throat.

Addeah notices and fetches some water with a ladle from a basin in the corner. Gratefully I gulp it all down.

"It must have been some spell Sebastian cast. He has the book," I say.

Addeah's brows furrow.

"The Book of Dominion," I clarify, wordlessly asking to get me another scoop of water. She takes it from my hands to fetch more. "It holds all kinds of spells. He must've used it on the soldiers somehow." I look up at the ceiling.

Talk of Sebastian makes me want to cry or vomit or scream. Maybe all three at the same time. "I was a fool," I murmur. Another tear escapes the corner of my eye.

Addeah notices my angst. She wipes my tear away and strokes my forehead again. "Child, he fooled us all. None of us knew what he was up to, or what he was capable of."

We were caught unawares, and he *did* fool us. Me. Addeah. Darius. Soren.

"Soren!" I jolt up, panic rising in my chest. He could be dead right now. All the blood. His fall to the ground. "Where is he, Addeah?" I ask with alarm, making my way to stand up and find him.

Addeah heaves a sigh, and without another word nods for me to follow her out of the room.

We're below deck, walking past several doors before we reach one at the end of the narrow hall. Its door is shut, but a circular window lets me see in.

There's Soren, lying on a cot no bigger than the one I woke up on. His head and torso are entirely bandaged. Red seeps through the white cloth like spilled wine on a carpet.

It feels as though someone has taken my heart and squeezed it, suffocating it.

He appears dead, until I see the steady rise and fall of his chest.

A wave of relief washes over me and that squeezing sensation subsides.

"He's stable for now," Addeah whispers as if not to wake him. "But his wounds are severe. It's going to take time to fully recover."

"We'll all need time," I say studying Soren's resting body.

Silence fills the air as Addeah and I watch the rise and fall of his chest, caught up in our own thoughts.

Addeah breaks the silence first. "We can come back and check on him again soon," she says. "What would you like to do now?"

I knew she meant what did I want to do on the ship while we waited. She's probably looking for an answer like rest or eat, but my mind travels to so many other avenues. What *did* I want to do now?

I wanted to run away from one monster only to be caught by another. I wanted to save my family from destitution by rescuing my father, but he is still lost. I wanted to be enraptured by the love I thought Sebastian could provide, but he betrayed me.

There are all these things I want, yet I received none of them, even with all the work I had put into this entire ordeal. I think of how Sebastian had played me, guiding me into his trap as though I were a horse with blinders. He manipulated me with stolen kisses and false flattery. And I was all too eager to be led straight into his whirlwind of flirtatious banter that I lost sight of my own objectives. I dishonored my family, my papa, by not trying harder to find him, misdirected by my own selfish desires. But not anymore. I won't let anyone or anything lead me astray from my path again.

The real question is not what I would like to do, but where do I go from here? I'm still betrothed to a man I don't love. My family's still counting on me for survival. Papa's still missing. I have an entire list of things I need to change, to fix, before I can go home. But one item has jumped to the top of the list...

Revenge.

Acknowledgements

There are many people I need to thank for the publication of this book.

To my husband, thank you for staying up with me all those nights listening to me rant and type away while you watched sports. You were the one that pushed me to finish this book and have supported me during all the ups and downs. I love you so much, honey!

Evan, Heather, and Mom, thank you for being my beta readers in this book's early drafts. You really made a difference in how the story has begun to unfold. I love my family members!

Susan and Richard, thank you for watching my sweet baby and giving me the time I needed to write this book. You two are the best in-laws I could have ever prayed for.

Mom and Dad, thank you for the endless support and talks about this book on our long drives and after Wednesday night dinners. I could not have asked for better parents.

Brandon and Jordan, thank you for helping me with all the technical stuff and formatting. We all know I'm technologically challenged and need my brothers' help!

Stephanie Taylor, thank you for your expertise in copyediting and proofreading! I said it once, and I'll say it again, if you had a nickel for every comma I missed or misplaced, you would be one rich lady!

Kelly Carter, thank you for creating my beautiful book cover!

I also want to thank God for all the blessings and support He has given me. This book would not have come to life without His helping hand in it all.

And last but certainly not least, thank you, dear reader. It brings me such joy to share pieces of my heart with you in this story. If you loved the story, please find the time to give an honest review. Be prepared for more to come.

About the Author

Victoria Nance grew up, and remains tied to her roots, in Indiana. She's married to her favorite person and best friend. She and her husband have a toddler and a baby on the way. She's grown to love reading mainly from her mother's influence. Her favorite genres include fantasy, romance, and thrillers. There are few greater simple pleasures in life than sitting down, reading a book, and falling in love with a story that unfolds within your mind.